LOR

Robin Lloyd-Jones was born in London in 1934. His father was an officer in the Indian Army and he spent some of his childhood years in India. He took a degree in Social Anthropology at Cambridge in 1957, worked as a teacher and in 1971 became Director of the Curriculum Development Centre in Clydebank. Since 1980 he has been Adviser in Social Subjects with Strathclyde Region. A keen mountaineer and sea-canoeist, he has lived in Scotland since 1960.

He began writing regularly in 1975 when he joined a local writer's workshop and his first published work was an article in *The Scots Magazine* in 1979. Since then he has published a number of articles, contributed to an anthology of writing about mountaineering, and has had published a children's book, *Where the Forest and the Garden Meet* (1980). In 1980 he won the Scottish Association of Writers' Constable Trophy (for the first 20,000 words of an unpublished novel). In 1981 he became President of the Scottish Association of Writers.

He lives in Helensburgh with his wife Sallie, their three children and four cats.

Robin Lloyd-Jones

LORD OF THE DANCE

An Arena Book
Published by Arrow Books Limited
17-21 Conway Street, London W1P 6JD

An imprint of the Hutchinson Publishing Group

London Melbourne Sydney Auckland
Johannesburg and agencies throughout
the world

First published 1983

© Robin Lloyd-Jones 1983

Lines from 'Lord of the Dance' by Sydney Carter are
reproduced by kind permission of Stainer & Bell Ltd.,
82 High Road, London N2.

Set in Linotron Sabon by
Rowland Phototypesetting Ltd
Bury St Edmunds, Suffolk

Made and printed in Great Britain
by Hazell, Watson & Viney Ltd
Aylesbury, Bucks

ISBN 0 09 931010 4

To my wife Sallie,
my true prize

I danced in the morning
When the world was begun
And I danced in the moon
And the stars and the sun
And I came down from heaven
And I danced on the earth –
At Bethlehem I had my birth.

Dance then wherever you may be,
I am the Lord of the Dance, said he,
And I'll lead you all, wherever you may be,
And I'll lead you all in the dance, said he.

SYDNEY CARTER

One

In all Christendom I have seen no highway to compare with this, the great highway in the heart of Akbar's Mogul Empire – four hundred miles of broad tree-lined avenue running from Lahore to Agra. In the shade of one of these trees I stretched out and rested my sore feet. The midday sun had reduced the flow of humanity along the great highway to a trickle. Buffalo rested in the fields, unyoked from their ploughs. The only sounds were a fly buzzing, a yearning flute, and Brother Peter farting in his sleep. I had taken the usual precaution of sitting upwind of him, for Frog, as I have called him since our childhood days in Devon, always did sweat profusely.

The sun was in the sign of Libra, when all nature seems poised between the seasons, when day and night hang equally in the scales. It was the month named Kartika, the month of the Hindu New Year. It was what we foreigners, we white barbarians, call October. The monsoon rains were over, the rice harvest nearly in. At this time Lakshmi, the goddess of plenty, is prayed to above all others. And at this time, as the floods subside and bullock carts no longer sink axle-deep in mud, the season for military campaigns begins. For, although the Mogul Empire embraces the whole of northern India and exceeds the domain of our own gracious sovereign Queen Elizabeth by some twelvefold or more, Akbar seeks to push his boundaries wider still.

Three days ago Frog and I had heard the distant rumble of cannon-fire. It had lasted from dawn till dusk. A peasant surveying the broken mud walls of his fields had only shrugged when I asked who was slaughtering whom. Yes, an army had passed this way. Whence they came or whither they went he could not say. He only knew that, like the locusts, they had made passage through his countryside.

7

'All armies are alike,' he said. 'Our granaries emptied, our carts commandeered, no women safe.'

But he did not complain. It was the karma of those of low caste to suffer such calamities. Wars, like floods, like the locusts, were to be expected and endured.

Frog twitched and moaned, his knees drawn up in the foetal position. I studied his bare feet. Scaled and horny, fissured, cracked and ingrained with dirt, they had conveyed him many a mile in the last eighteen months. His toenails were several hues of purple, brown and black; grey fungus and other mucilaginous substances grew between his toes. I marvelled at the fecundity of nature. Even Frog's bottle of holy water had turned green and was thriving with aquatic life. Beside him were his shoes, his staff, his Bible, his framed picture of the Virgin Mary with her golden halo, and a copy of the Koran, translated from Arabic into Latin. Inside the cover I had written: 'Presented by your friend Thomas Coryat on the occasion of our departure from the shores of England for the land of the Great Mogul, May 1575.'

I had hoped that my gift might help Frog to a better understanding of the Muslims among whom we would be moving. But no; he used it to fuel his scorn, his hatred of the Antichrist, learning by heart such passages as might confound the enemy through the words of their own prophet. It is the same with us physicians and chirurgeons. We fit the evidence to whatever theory it suits us to believe.

A flat oval insect emerged from the region of Frog's groin. Fleas, bugs, the burrowing fly – Frog is a generous and impartial host. The bug clambered on to his hand, which was tattooed with the Crusaders' fitched cross, the proud badge of those who have visited the Holy City of Jerusalem. The ship which took us to the Holy Land had been packed with pilgrims, most of them, like Frog, indulging in orgies of credulity. At Venice, then at Rhodes and again at Jerusalem, Frog parted with good money to gawp at three different versions of 'The One, True, Unique and Miraculously Preserved Holy Crown of Thorns'.

The bug now tackled the vast desert of Frog's stomach and the mountainous folds of his grey cassock, which were not unlike the dry, brigand-infested wastes we had crossed before descending into the plains of northern India. By which time I could not help noticing that, as Frog's ability to speak Hindustani improved, so did his capacity for annoying all and sundry by preaching what they had no wish to hear. Descending from rough cloth to smooth skin on Frog's neck, the bug encountered another of its kind. Their mating habits, I discovered, were most interesting. The male takes up a position diagonally across the body of the female, instead of at the rear as is customary in animals. Be watchful, little bugs, or you shall burn. For Aristotle says that flies and other insects spontaneously generate from putrefying fluids. And what Aristotle says cannot be wrong – according to the Church.

Perhaps the female would lay her eggs upon Frog's person. Perhaps whole generations of bugs had lived and died upon his body. Whereas I scratch and curse when visited thus, Frog never seems to notice – a fact that he attributes to the power of prayer and I to the thickness of his skin. But supposing these bugs could hold philosophical discourse with one another, what matters might they not debate? Is Frog the centre of the universe? Is there life beyond Frog? And the orthodox would declare that Frog fell from space and persecute those who claimed that there never was a time when he did not exist.

The male bug ran across Frog's lips, which shuddered fleshily with each expulsion of air. Frog averages 22,636 breaths a day, by my calculation. I have often pondered as to why we breathe at all. At the University of Padua they taught us that we take in air to ventilate the body, for there is some source of heat, probably the liver or the heart, which makes constant cooling necessary. The bug reached Frog's left nostril and began to explore. A hand came up and squashed it into a brownish smear. What mess would you make, Brother Peter, should some unseen hand descend on you? Bone, skin, flesh, fat, marrow, blood, semen, mucus, tears, bile and excreta. A snore rolled out of Frog. Beneath his robe swelled and rose a column of desire. Who was with him in his dream? Supposing it was Mary – yes, he'd always lusted after Mary, my wife! – I rose and kicked him.

Frog's snore changed to a moan of despair. 'Sweet Jesus, by thy Holy Wounds, I sin even in my sleep!' He looked at me, and knew that I knew. 'Kick me, Coryat, kick me like a dog, low, wretched creature that I am!'

The locket round my neck swung against my arm. They say that time heals what reason cannot. It is not true. To look at Mary's unblemished face is to break upon the rack. The seasons pass, the wheel revolves, the rack tightens.

'God have mercy on us!' Frog groaned. 'We are punished by our sins as well as for them.'

I picked up my hat, avoiding his eye. Agra was our destination. But, wherever you go, guilt and memories pursue. Mary, Agra, the centre of the Mogul court, where the great libraries amassed by Babur, Humayun and Akbar himself are to be found. It was at the University of Padua, a seat of learning far in advance of anything in England, that it dawned on me that Christendom and the ancient Greeks and Romans did not have a monopoly of wisdom where the art of healing was concerned. And it was while at Padua that I talked with Venetian merchants who had heard something of the wonders of Indian surgery. At Agra lay the medical knowledge of centuries, gathered from Arab, Indian and Chinese sources. Not that untested theories in dusty manuscripts impress me overmuch. Nobody who has studied at Padua under Gerolamo Fabrizzio d'Aquapendente thinks that way any more. It was he who led me to the writings of Servetus and Vesalius. Men such as these have taught me that no statement, however long-held, or however revered the authority, should be taken on trust unless tested by direct observation. But Agra was still a hundred leagues away . . . Oh Mary!

After several miles of pleasant, fertile land, the highway joined course with the river Yamuna, a slow, brown river about half a mile wide, flowing southwards towards Agra. Three days ago we had heard the sounds of battle. Now, on the third day, the dead rose again. Corpse after corpse surfaced and floated slowly down the Yamuna. Friend, foe, camp-follower, innocent villagers – they all looked much alike. A man of medicine like myself knows that putrefaction of the flesh produces certain vapours which enter the body's cavities. But Frog, of course, had jumped to some absurd theological conclusion.

'Thomas, it is the Second Coming!' He fell heavily to his knees in the dust. Throwing back his head, he cried out: 'The sea gave up the dead that were in it, and death and Hades gave up the dead that were in them, and each person was judged according to what he had done.'

I looked closely at Frog. His eyes bulged even more than usual; his breath was shallow; saliva ran from his open mouth. Observe, test, record was ever the exhortation of Fabrizzio. I made a mental note of his condition.

Presently flocks of pigeons settled on the risen corpses. Why the vapours of decay should be produced more abundantly in hot climes I know not. But I have observed it to be so.

'Do get up, Frog. Come and give me your opinion on this matter. The women all float face upwards and the men face down.'

I pondered on this for a while. Then came the carrion crows. As their beaks punctured the distended stomachs, the quiet countryside was filled with the sound of popping and exploding flesh.

'The unbelieving and the abominable, and murderers and whoremongers and sorcerers and idolators and all liars shall have their part in the lake which burneth with fire and brimstone, which is the second death.'

'Frog, I assure you, the dead are descending, not rising. The waters have taken them back again.'

Tears coursed down Frog's cheeks. 'A river of souls and not one did I claim for the Lord; not one embraced the true faith! Where was I, miserable sinner that I am? Where was I when there was God's work to be done?'

It was a rhetorical question, but I told him, all the same. 'Mostly you were breaking your vows of chastity with dark-eyed village maidens.'

'I have failed in the service of the Lord!'

'Now, my dear Frog, since the Day of Judgement seems to have been postponed, do you think we could try and reach the next village before nightfall? You know how it is – if we arrive after dark, they throw stones at us and turn us away.'

'*Mea culpa*! *Mea culpa*! The flesh must be mortified. I shall crawl there on my knees. Every inch of the way on my knees. Oh, *mea culpa*!'

'Couldn't I beat you with your staff instead? It would hurt just as much and it would be so much quicker.'

'Oh, all right. If you insist.'

'I'll keep hitting you till we get to that tower on the horizon, will that suffice? . . . On the other hand, a little blood-letting would do your choleric humour much more good.'

Frog glared at me and jumped to his feet. He had a peculiar fear of the leeches, as I well knew. I only said it to goad him into action, for Servetus tells us that the efficacy of blood-letting must be questioned.

Whack! Frog gave an ecstatic moan. 'Blessed are they whose offences have been forgiven.'

Not to be outdone, I quoted from *The Compleat Apothecary*. 'Mandrake root cut with the sun in Scorpio doth wonderously purge the bowels.'

Whack!

'What good is it, my brothers, if a man claims to have faith but hath not deeds?'

Whack! 'Two scruples of bezoar; inner bark of elm, one ounce; twenty drops of spirit of sal-ammoniac, makes tonic for the heart.'

Whack! 'Ah! Harder, harder!'

I remembered that Servetus had been burned as a heretic and the flames came from his own books piled around his feet. And I laid the staff to Frog's back doubly hard.

And so we came to the tower. I had supposed it to be a watch-tower, or perhaps a dovecot. But it was a victory tower built by Akbar's passing army. A tower of heads. Clouds of flies rose at our approach.

I broke the silence. 'Truly, death is our companion today, Brother Peter. Will a time ever come when death is not always at our side?'

'Doubtless, Satan would have it so.'

'I would have it so! All true men of medicine would have it so!'

'It is upon the life hereafter that our gaze should be intent.'

'But, Frog, think of the suffering that could be prevented. Why, Paré in his treatise says –'

'Coryat, cease your godless prattling!'

'I will not! I'm not one of your cowed and ignorant country flock, I don't give a fart for your Church!'

With a howl, Frog flung himself at me. We rolled and grappled in the dust, too evenly matched for either of us to triumph. We had always been evenly matched – the friendly tussels on the common; that time he had challenged me when I smiled at Mary; the mock battles in Badger Wood – I relaxed my grip.

'Pax?' I enquired.

'Pax,' he grunted.

I helped him to his feet and dusted down his cassock. 'Allow me to return your staff, Brother Peter.'

He gave a mocking bow. 'Your hat, Master Coryat.'

Letting out a roar of laughter, he clapped me on the back. Arm in arm we followed the river Yamuna till the grimacing heads were out of sight.

In the distance four men were approaching. Presently we saw a beast, possibly a small dragon, nuzzling a corpse on the river bank.

'Frog, I have been counting all the creatures we have observed, of whose existence we were innocent when we started on our travels. How many more must there be that we know not of?' And we fell to arguing about the dimensions of the Ark.

'Three hundred cubits would not be long enough!' I declared. 'Think of all the food the animals would need . . . unless, of course, they ate each other.'

Frog was incensed. 'Oh yes,' he cried. 'You have a fine way with words, but eloquence without godliness is as a ring in a swine's snout.'

Then he summoned the Bible to discomfit me. 'He who sins before his Maker, may he fall into the hands of a physician . . . Ecclesiasticus, thirty-eight, fifteen.'

That hurt. I could have argued the point. Christ was a healer, was he not? But it hurt. I cannot deny that quacks and charlatans abound with their patent remedies, and every barber, because he can draw a tooth, thinks he knows it all. Hippocrates was right: 'Life is short and the Art long; opportunity fleeting; evidence uncertain; experiment dangerous; experience deceptive and judgement difficult.'

The men were close to us now. Not four, but three, and a bear walking upright, led by a chain. They drew level. Muslims, I diagnosed. We, no doubt, were easily seen to be infidels. However, they greeted us civilly. They stepped off the highway into the shade of the tree. One of them opened a basket of fruit and held it out to me. I selected one that was long and yellow and slightly curved in shape. In Padua I had seen a woodcut of this same fruit. *Musa paradisiaca* they had called it, believing it to be the forbidden fruit of Eden. I bit into it and found it not to my liking. But the eldest of the three, a gaunt and dignified man with a large white turban and a grey beard, courteously peeled back the skin for me, and then I found the inner pulp to be like a starchy fig might be, or, perhaps, not unlike a Norwich pear.

All this time, the brown bear shuffled and swayed on its hind legs, making little keening noises and trying to lick its paws through the wire muzzle on its mouth. The iron collar round its neck had caused several ugly sores. Its front paws, I observed, had been deliberately scorched to discourage it from assuming its normal four-legged gait. Refreshed, the men sat back, passing round a hookah, bubbling smoke through a cooling water-chamber before inhaling it. The bearded elder lovingly unpacked his Koran.

'In the name of Allah the Beneficent, the Compassionate,' he intoned, and began to read aloud to his companions. 'God is the light of heaven and earth. His light may be compared to a niche which contains a lamp, the lamp within glass, and the glass as it were a star of pearl . . .'

Frog's nostrils were turning white.

' . . . it is lit from a blessed olive tree neither eastern nor western. Its oil would almost shine forth if no fire touched it. Light upon light . . .'

When Frog's nostrils go white, he's about to breath hell-fire, you can depend on it.

'Please, Frog; not now, I implore you, not –'

With a snort, Frog snatched up his Bible and loudly declaimed the True Word. The Mussulman bristled and raised his voice. Frog did the same. The bear spread wide its paws and roared.

There was a silence.

'*Alcoranus*,' Frog yelled, using the Latin name, '*Alcoranus* is nothing but fable and extreme frivolity. *Alcoranus* wickedly and lyingly equates heavenly bliss with feasting and impure delights!'

The elderly Mussulman was shaking with anger. There was a muttered consultation, with many a hard stare in our direction. I recalled all those accounts of unbelievers being forcibly circumcized. I would rather be killed on the spot than suffer a lingering death through blood-poisoning in that particular part of my anatomy. They drew their daggers. My hand flew to the hilt of my sword. But they were only gathering and cutting wood.

14

The Mussulman pointed to the growing heap of branches and addressed Frog. 'Holding the most blessed Koran, I shall walk through the blazing pyre. And you, likewise, shall carry your Bible. Whoever comes safely through the flames shall be judged the bearer of the truth.'

The pile grew bigger. A line of women in saris, balancing water jars on their heads, stopped to see what was happening. A bullock cart loaded with melons creaked to a halt. Men carrying hoes joined the circle round the pyre. The owner of the bear prodded it with a stick and it began to dance. Someone lit the pyre.

Frog was on his knees, gripping his Bible hard. He was pale, and sweat was gathering in the shallow lakes of his pockmarked face. His fear reminded me of the time that Mary had stood on the far side of the ravine in Badger Wood and dared us to jump across and join her. We had both funked it, and Mary had refused to speak to either of us for a week.

'Thomas . . . I . . . I don't think it would be right for me to continue with this folly. It is a presumption born of vanity . . . I mean, what right have I to expect, sinner that I am, that I will not be consumed?'

He waited for me to agree. I didn't feel like making it easy for him. He tried again. 'You see, Thomas, when the Evil One said, "If thou art the son of God cast thyself down from the cross," Jesus replied, "Thou shalt not make trial of the Lord thy God."'

Frog looked appealingly at me with bulbous eyes. I shrugged. 'Tell that to them.'

We passed close to the flames. Involuntarily Frog lifted his Bible to shield his face from the heat. I approached the bearded Mussulman.

'Although Brother Peter thirsts for this ordeal, I am trying to dissuade him from it. It seems to me that proof by fire is not conclusive. Many churches and many mosques have burned in the past, thus showing that things sacred are not immune from fire.'

Relief, hope . . . something flickered in his eyes. Then a cheer went up from the crowd and his jaw set in a stubborn line. Raising his Koran, he stepped towards the pyre. Frog was the colour of wax. My nose informed me that he had lost control of his bowels. He didn't move.

Suddenly the crowd was breaking up, running away. A quarter of a mile across the paddy fields, columns of smoke were rising from a village. Horsemen galloped from hut to hut with blazing torches; muskets were firing, women screaming. The bear let out a startled 'Wuff!' and crashed to the ground, a musket-ball lodged in its skull. More stray shots slashed through the foliage and thudded among the branches overhead.

I found myself crawling along an irrigation ditch. Some way behind followed a blubbering and wheezing Frog. The worms of remorse and self-disgust, I knew, would be eating at him. What would it be this time? Flagellation, stones in the shoes, a bed of thorns? I stood up.

'I think we're safe enough now.'

Round Frog's neck was the bear's iron collar. Without a word he handed me the other end of the chain.

'The cramp, the stitch, the squirt, the itch, the gout, the stone, the pox. The mulligaws, the bonny scrub and all Pandora's box.' So ran the rhythm in my head as I tramped along the highway. Behind me, on the end of the chain, shambled a big grey lump of misery called Frog.

'The bloody-flux, the griping-guts, the plague, the phlegm, the –'

Yelling horribly, a figure burst through the undergrowth, whirling a curved sword above his head. 'Death! Death!' he roared, and slashed at the undergrowth. 'Death! Dea . . . aagh!'

His piercing yell changed to an agonized gargle as, whirling, he caught sight of us. He stood open-mouthed, while slowly his sword sank to the ground. His legs, I saw, were as thick as my waist, and Frog and I together would not have tipped the scales against him. Then this veritable giant let out a mighty guffaw. 'Tremble not, good sirs! Your heads are safe! I was merely remembering how we defeated the Afghan at Panipat.' He held out a severed clump of wild guava. 'See, I have the head of Hemu himself!'

He removed his domed leather helmet, wiped his brow with the sleeve of his tunic and looked us up and down. Frog he dismissed at a glance. Despite my doublet and breeches of plain fustian, I think my leather boots made by old Ned Copley of Honiton and my sword of good English steel impressed him. At any rate, he bowed and said, 'I am Dadu, foot-soldier in the service of General Ghulam Khan.'

I said, 'The army is several days' march to the south, I believe. Are you wounded that you have fallen behind?'

He winked expansively. 'We had what you might call pressing business at the last village, didn't we, Ali?'

I looked around, but could see nobody with him. He squatted on his hunkers, making his thighs swell like fatted sucking-pigs.

'Yes, very pressing business. Women are like beds. Give me the big soft ones every time, for they are best to lie on.' He grinned. 'Well, us soldiers have a duty, you might say, to bring into the world at least as many as we dispatch.'

He turned to Frog. 'Do you like them fat?'

Frog snorted angrily. Dadu eyed the chain round Frog's neck. He wagged a finger at me.

'In this country we are more enlightened. We do not keep our slaves in chains. Treat them well and they do not want to run away.'

Frog went purple, but held his tongue. Doubtless this was some new exercise in humility.

Dadu stared at my broad-brimmed hat. 'Would you be Tartars, perhaps?'

'We are Christians,' Frog announced.

'Where's that?'

'We are from the lands beyond Turkey, where the white races have their habitation.'

Dadu addressed his invisible companion. 'What do you think of that, Ali? He says he's white, but he's the colour of a brick.'

I laughed. 'Unexposed to sun or wind our skins are of lighter hue.'

Dadu leant forward and jerked up the hem of Frog's cassock, receiving a rap on the knuckles for his effort.

'Three days ago we heard the cannon roar,' Frog said.

'My commander, General Ghulam Khan, did lose his nose that day.' Dadu told us that the general had ridden out in person to offer terms of surrender to the rebels. He had returned with his nose cut off. 'It is a punishment reserved for adulterers and thieves!' Dadu fumed. 'It was a slight upon us all! Yes, the cannons pounded them that day, and many died who would have lived but for that insult.'

'Against whom do you fight?' Frog asked.

Dadu fumbled under his tunic and produced a gold mohur. 'Now, what's written on this coin?'

Frog shook his head. Dadu gave him a friendly thump on the back which sent him sprawling.

'Never mind, I can't read either. But I have it on good authority that it says "Allahu Akbar". Now, I ask you, the words being the same, does that mean "God is great" or "Akbar is God"?' He returned the coin to its abode somewhere in the folds of his cotton trousers. 'For myself, as long as it buys a skin of wine and a woman for the night, what care I?' He rocked gently to and fro on the backs of his heels. 'The fat ones are best. Ah! When I think of Gulbehar, a full moon among women! And the deep, engulfing embraces of Ajmillah . . .'

Ox carts, double-yoked and loaded with grain, were rumbling by.

'Oh yes, as I was saying, Shershan – you know, the general who led the campaigns in Kabul and Gujarat – Shershan sees the second meaning in these words. Many Muslims rally to his banner, fearing that their emperor has strayed from the path of orthodoxy.' Dadu shrugged. 'One thing is certain, anyway. If it weren't for religion, us common soldiers would soon be out of work, wouldn't we, Ali?'

I handed Dadu my goatskin water-bottle. He took a drink. 'If you ask me – and Ali is of the same opinion – the ills which beset us will not be cured until the last king has been strangled in the entrails of the last priest.' He took another swig. 'Which is to say, those that seek power cause far more harm than the likes of me, who merely seek pleasure.'

Frog's nostrils were going white again. Hastily, I asked, 'Who is this invisible personage that you address?'

'Ali is with me wherever I go. When I'm lonely he is there; when I'm troubled he is there. And if I doubt his presence he sends me a sign.'

Frog stirred with interest. 'Is it God that you mean?'

'Eh! What? . . . No, it is Ali, my tapeworm. We are old friends. Inseparable, you might say.'

A plumpish woman, carrying a large basket of lentils on her head, walked towards us on the highway. Clapping his helmet on to his head, Dadu cried: 'Come, Ali, it is a soldier's duty to protect the weak!' He brought his hands together and bowed to me. 'May our paths cross again. And I do entreat you, good stranger, be kind to your slave. If I may give a foreigner a word of advice . . . you should dress him in brighter clothes. In this country we set great store by that kind of thing.'

With a cheerful wave and a shout of '*Shabash*!' he fell into step beside the woman. 'That is a heavy load for such a lovely creature,' he cooed. 'I have a camel with a long neck, a very long neck, and two hairy humps, that would willingly give you a ride. It would like nothing better than to serve you. Yes indeed, it is rearing to go!'

I did not hear her reply.

'Take not thought for the morrow' was always Frog's text for the road. It was today that worried me. We had set off not knowing where our next sleeping-place would be. How far to the next village? How far?

'*Kitna-dur*?' I called to the passers-by.

'*Kitna-dur*?' I shouted across fields newly sown with millet, wheat and grain.

'Just another bend to go, may your weary feet find rest.'

But we walked all day. For so wondrously refined are the manners of this country that they gave only the news which would be most pleasing to our ears.

'Ah, Frog, what wouldn't I give for a slice of game pie and a quart of Devon cider!'

'Or hog's pudding, stuffed with oatmeal, tripe and spices!'

Our purses were almost empty. Our only fare for the day had been the fruit offered by the Muslim travellers at the roadside.

'Do you smell roasting meat, Coryat?'

When you've covered thirty miles on foot since dawn, there's nothing arouses the appetite so much as the smell of roasting meat – the appetites of penitent monks not excluded.

'Sucking-pig!' Frog exclaimed.

'It's veal, I'll wager!'

'No, no! Sucking-pig, I'm certain!'

'Veal!'

'Perhaps we should go and . . . I mean, maybe they can tell us how far to the next village.'

We rounded a bend. Amidst some trees a straggle of people stood on the steps of a small Hindu temple.

Not pig, not veal, but human flesh. Here, on the broad steps which ran down to the river, the bodies of devout Hindus were cremated. A Shivite priest conducted the proceedings. His naked body was smeared with the ashes of the dead, and a yellow mark, the trident of the Lord Shiva, was daubed upon his forehead. I walked down the steps to a boatman who was standing beside his narrow craft. Yes, he had brought the body. Yes, they were from the village that had been destroyed. Today the son of a local raja had been born. But the planets were not in favourable conjunction. To divert the bad omen from the boy, the raja's men had burned the village.

'What's the next village downriver?' I shouted, as he poled away from the steps. He shrugged. He had never been there. He did not even know its name. The temple steps must suffice us for the night.

The sun was a vast red ball on the horizon. Frog was praying, holding his crucifix before him. From a minaret on the far bank of the river came the high-pitched Muslim call, '*La-ilaha – illah – ah, Muham-madur-Rasulh-ilali* . . . No God but one God and Muhammad the Ambassador of God.'

On the age-worn steps, the Shivite priest tended the burning corpse. The abdomen, I noted, had burned more quickly than the rest. He lifted the half-charred chest with a stick and bedded it down where the flames were brightest.

I watched the sun drop from sight and pondered on things. Evidence uncertain, Hippocrates had said. My eyes told me that the sun rose, moved across the sky and set, yet Copernicus had shown that it was not so. But here was Frog, thirty-three years after Copernicus had published his great work, still stubbornly refusing to accept that the earth was not the centre of the universe, still comforting himself that the earth was placed in the heavens like a yolk in its shell. And for how long would fashionable London society continue to flock to astrologers and magicians with their ills? But was it surprising if the new learning struggled and sometimes drowned in a sea of ignorance, superstition and bigotry? How often had Mary chided me for being unable to distinguish her seedlings from the weeds and for rooting out the wrong ones? And judgement difficult.

Two

Dawn on the river Yamuna is a time of mist. A spider's web was decked with moisture. The leaves of the temple's *nim* tree were dew-tipped. Upstream, a group of women were slapping and thwacking wet garments against the flat stones on the bank.

The highway was astir already, for people prefer to move in the cool of the early morning, when the ground is damp and there is less dust in the air. Past the temple flowed the merchandise of northern India – carpets from Lahore, Patna cloth, Ajmer grain, Multan hides, carried by camels, ox carts, overloaded donkeys and men staggering under weights almost as great.

I pulled a silver ear-trumpet from my back-sack and held it to the heart of the sleeping Frog. Mary's shocked white face floated before me. I concentrated hard on the heart beats: counter-rhythms to the pounding of cloth on stone.

It is more than twenty years since Servetus challenged Galen's theory that blood passes directly between the ventricles of the heart. Servetus suggested that it finds its way from the right side of the heart to the left by traversing through the lungs via the pulmonary artery. But Servetus they burned at the stake, and the question is still unresolved. In London they ... Mary was forcing entry to my thoughts again ... In London they teach that the blood moves through the body by the sucking action of the heart which draws it up much as a drink is sucked through a straw, causing the blood to rise and fall like the tides of the sea. I have my doubts about the ... about the veracity of these teachings, but the truth, so far, has escaped us all ... Honiton, a church, a service in progress, Mary beside me at the altar. Those whom God hath joined let no man put asunder. But this was the burial service I was seeing. Mary's burial service. Yet she was alive, standing there, white-faced, staring at me. She was being pronounced as one who is dead. She was a leper.

There is a passage in the *Lilium Mediconae* which I know by heart. I had read it and reread it, hoping I was mistaken, hoping for some different interpretation. 'The occult premonitory signs of leprosy are a reddish colour of the face, verging to duskiness; the expiration begins to be changed; the voice grows raucous, the hairs become thinned and weaker and the perspiration and breath incline to foetidity; the mind is melancholic with frightful dreams and nightmares; in some cases scabs, pustules and eruptions break out over the whole body; the disposition of the body begins to become loathsome.'

I had run in terror and revulsion to Frog. And Frog? He had been sweet on Mary and, if the truth be known, still was, despite his vows. Yet his conscience had demanded that the Church and officialdom be told. After that, things developed their own momentum. She had been called before a jury of doctors and pronounced to be a child of Lazarus and, as such, to be *judicati, apopulo sequestrandi et Malentaria ducendi* – adjudged, separated from the people and consigned to the lazar house. Mary, my Mary, was an object of disgust, a doomed and despised leper. And, by the law of England, lepers are classed with idiots, madmen and outlaws. From this moment on she would be forbidden to eat with any person other than a leper, to touch a child, to speak to a healthy person except in a whisper. Weeping as he celebrated over her the words for the dead was Brother Peter. She was sprinkled with holy water and led from the little church at Honiton to the lazaretto at Exeter.

I visited her just once. Oh, the hurt, the accusation in her eyes! Those eyes which had been like crystals, now bloodshot; that voice so musical, now hoarse; her skin, once soft, spread with black spots and livid lumps. She had clung to me, pleaded with me not to leave her there. Three months later Frog and I left for India. I loved her; but I loved my own flesh more. The thought of my limbs rotting, of . . . I rushed down the temple steps and plunged into the river. I cried out and kicked and thrashed at the water. I held myself under till my lungs were bursting. Then I shouted and cursed and cried out some more.

I walked up the steps feeling calmer and suddenly very hungry. I tickled Frog's face with a leaf. He slapped hard and swore.

'Do you think, Brother Peter, that if you prayed for manna from heaven it might be granted?'

'You're not meant to pray for things like that.'

'It seems to me, Brother Peter, that the Christian Church is no different from other religions in keeping a good stock of excuses in readiness for when prayers, offerings, or what you will, fail to have the desired effect.'

Frog glared, then shut both eyes. His lips began to move. He opened one eye and looked at me suspiciously. 'You're wet.'

'Yes.'

'You've been crying.'

'I have not.'

'Yes, you have.'

Faintly at first, growing louder, came the earth-shivering heartbeat of an army on the march. A hundred thousand feet stamping in time to drums; hooves thudding, ten thousand wheels groaning and trundling. Around us, the foliage exploded, birds rose in startled clouds.

Through the mist swayed elephants bedecked in dazzling finery. This was my first sight of these magnificent beasts. From travellers' descriptions I had imagined them to be something like giant pigs with elongated snouts. Not so long ago I had thought our shire horses to be among the strongest of God's creatures. In the Holy Land I saw camels and had been impressed. Now I was overawed. It was not just their mountainous bulk and strength, or the knowing look in their eyes. Their whole slow-moving presence was overpowering. I trembled as a mouse does when cornered by a cat. Leading them was the biggest elephant of all, tusks silver-capped, flanks hung with pearl-encrusted cloth-of-gold. On its back with a box draped with green velvet.

'I think that is the Koran it carries,' Frog shouted in my ear. I shivered.

Then column after column of foot soldiers swing by, twelve abreast, shields slung on their backs, swords dancing at their sides. Each battalion was different, marking the extent and variety of the Mogul Empire. We saw pointed helmets of beaten brass, long Tartar gowns and curved swords, shields of transparent rhinocerous hide; we caught glimpses of dark, fierce eyes through face-guards of polished steel. One group of warriors wore grey quilted coats and quilted headdresses for protection; another had armour made from some kind of tough, knotted string. There were rocketmen and matchlockmen and a detachment carrying sharp-edged circles of steel. I wondered if Dadu had caught up with his comrades and might be somewhere among the tramping columns.

With the mist blushing pink, a hundred horsemen jingled past, lances raised, pennants flying, then another hundred and another. The mist became suffused with gold, and still the army unwound before us. Camels and more camels; a mile of camels laden with baggage. The ground reverberated; dust tingled in the backs of our nostrils. For close on an hour, huge war elephants passed by, dragging heavy siege-guns, or bearing wooden forts on their backs, manned by archers and harquebusiers. A castle, mounted across the backs of four elephants, bristled with cannon. Again panic gripped me. Only the thought that Frog would laugh at me made me stand my ground.

'Surely no one could resist such might,' I said.

'You heard the talk along the road, Thomas. They say the rebel general has gathered almost as many men to his banner.'

'And they say that, so far, Akbar's army has but snapped at the heels of the rebel. What carnage there will be if they ever meet head-on!'

The mist dissipated. Clouds of dust hung in the air, through which straggled another army more numerous, even, than the one whose passing we had witnessed – a vast horde of camp-followers, water-carriers, cooks, grooms, labourers, menials, and many with their families. There were traders and vendors of every description, mobile stalls, entertainers, prostitutes. The girls made lewd gestures at us.

'Lascivious and wicked jezebels!' Frog bellowed, cracking the mask of sweat-soaked dust on his face. 'I cry out against the painted face of whoredom that enticeth man to fulfil the lusts of the flesh, provoking the Lord to wrath and indignation!'

The men accompanying the girls were as ugly looking a bunch of cut-throats as ever I saw. I jerked Frog's chain to keep him quiet.

In the current of humanity that flowed by, there now appeared the floating wreckage, beggars by the thousand. They shuffled, hopped, crawled or dragged themselves along, displaying their withered limbs, their amputations and deformities. In all, I would estimate that this rabble, which stretched to the horizon, outnumbered the soldiers who had gone before by ten to one. They had been filling the highway for nearly three hours when an ox cart approached the temple.

Inside the covered cart a woman was screaming. Although we doctors are expected to leave matters of childbirth to the womenfolk, there is no mistaking the sound of a woman in labour. Beside the cart, a man ran in circles, beating frantically on a drum as if to drown the noise. A small, fat figure, whom I took to be a child, seized the rope that ran through the nose-ring of the two oxen and began to lead them off the road. A gaunt, hollow-chested man, driving the cart, cursed him and lashed at him with a whip, but the small figure hung on, and the cart jolted to a halt beside the temple.

It has always seemed to me ironical that the greatest danger most of us ever face in this world is the moment of our entry into it. Certainly it is not a matter that should be left to the care of old crones whose ways are steeped in superstition, magic and other erroneous suppositions.

More screams emanated from the cart. The men fidgeted and avoided each other's eye. Between fits of coughing, the driver hurled abuse into the cart. 'Hurry up, you stupid girl! Can't you be quicker about it? Already we're being left behind!'

I stood up. 'Is anyone with the woman?' They ignored me. 'I am a physician,' I announced.

The news was received with indifference. The driver, a man older than the others, eyed me coldly.

'These things are best left to the gods and the stars. She will be all right. Only last week she consulted an astrologer who foretold a healthy boy. And it was only this morning she made *puja* to the goddess Parvati . . . So, you see, there is nothing to be done. . .' He broke into a fit of coughing, before adding: 'Except, of course, that the army marches into the distance and we shall be left at the roadside here without the safety of numbers to protect us, or an audience to pay for our performance . . . Hurry up, girl!'

A cry of pain answered him.

'I think I had better take a look at her,' I said, edging towards the cart.

He flicked his whip in front of my face. 'We have no money to waste on doctors and their useless nostrums.'

'I make no charge!' I retorted sharply.

He gave me a hard, suspicious stare, then lowered his whip.

The girl lay on a pile of old rags. I guessed that she was no more than fourteen or fifteen. She had a thin face with large, expressive eyes. Her left nostril held a jewelled nose-ring. Rivers of sweat had caused the red *talik* mark on her brow to smear and run. The atmosphere was oppressive. Incense smouldered in a dish. A lamp with three wicks smoked near the curtain, which I had pulled aside on entering. One of the wicks blew out. She whined in a shrill, frightened voice: 'Quick! Light it again. Don't you know anything? An even number brings bad luck!'

I crouched beside her. She would not let me touch her. She screamed at me to go away. But, when the pain started again, she clutched my hand and made no objection when I wiped her brow.

I talked to the girl, Mohini, trying to gain her confidence, trying to keep her thoughts from her pain and fear. I told her my name and a little about myself.

'How many wives do you have?' she asked.

'None.' Perhaps it was true in the eyes of the Church, but it felt like a lie.

'Are there no women with you?' There was anxiety in her voice. I shook my head, and she started a nervous monologue. Which sari should she put on when it was over? Should it be the blue one with the silver border, or the green and yellow one? Yes, the blue one, she thought. Did I like her bracelets? They had been given to her by an admirer when they had danced at Jaipur. No, perhaps the green and yellow one would be better. She gabbled faster and faster.

'Is this your first baby?' I interrupted.

She nodded. 'I shall call him Prajapathi,' she said. 'For it was by the god Prajapathi that he was conceived.'

She related how the troupe – they were itinerant dancers – had encamped near the cave temple of Revari. In the darkness of the inmost cave, beside the altar, an echoing voice had spoken to her saying that, because of her devotion, he, Prajapathi, would assume the mortal form of a Brahmin priest and lie with her. She, naturally, had consented to this most holy act. Somewhere in the course of this pathetically naïve tale, I discovered that the troupe was from Rajasthan and that the ill-tempered driver, who kept shouting through the cart's bamboo screens, was Gampopa, their *nayaka* or dancing-master, the leader of the troupe.

Mohini's hand tightened on mine. Her back was arched, her knees drawn up. A gush of greenish fluid soaked the rags beneath her. Many a midwife have I questioned concerning all that happens behind the closed doors. Occasionally, when things have gone badly wrong, I have been summoned to fumble under the sheets and drag forth a dead infant, or to ease the last hours of an exhausted and dying mother. But here, in the stuffy, dirty little cart, I, a doctor of some experience, was about to be initiated into the mysteries of the human female giving birth to her young. Mohini gave a sharp cry. I cursed myself for a pompous ass. Here was no specimen to be studied unfeelingly, but a girl fighting her loneliness and fear and smiling bravely at me.

'Khorat,' she said, attempting my name, 'when the time comes, be sure to note the exact position of the sun in the sky. Upon this depends the accuracy of his horoscope.'

I gave her a sip of water. It must have been close on midday, judging by the heat inside the cart. I became aware of the silence on the highway. Gampopa was coughing again. Frog was making the most of the occasion by recounting the Nativity of Christ. Mohini lay back, listening, a pleased smile on her face. Suddenly she sat up.

'They didn't draw a circle round the cart!'

I stared at her.

'A circle!' she shouted. 'To avert the evil eye!' She fell back with a groan. 'I wish there was another woman here.'

'Surely there's more than one female in a dancing troupe.'

'The others were in the front cart. They won't have stopped. If we don't dance, we don't eat – that's a saying of ours.'

Her face screwed up in pain. 'A circle!' she panted.

I stuck my head outside and suggested that somebody might draw a circle in the dust.

'We men cannot go near the cart without defiling ourselves,' said Gampopa, who had dismounted and was standing apart with the others. 'And think of the expense!' he exclaimed. 'Think what it would cost in offerings at the temple to atone for such uncleanness.'

The intervals between Mohini's pains were becoming shorter, I observed. It was important that my patient be in a calm state of mind. I climbed out of the cart and scratched a circle on the ground round the vehicle. Frog watched this performance with glee, making some foolish pretence that I subscribed to such superstitious nonsense.

Mohini began to hum in a nervous high-pitched way. It was a popular song of love which we had heard up and down the highway for the last month or more. Her song suddenly lurched into a long, agonized note.

'It's coming!' she gasped. She was breathing hard, in great sobbing gulps.

I pulled her sari up to her waist. Perhaps I was aware of her slender legs, the smoothness of her thighs, but only fleetingly before the marvel of new life emerging absorbed me totally. Beyond the orifice of her organ of generation, an oval shape was visible. She rested, panting, soaked in sweat, clinging hard to my hand, still jerkily humming shreds of her ridiculous song. The blood-smeared oval shape moved forward, parting the lips of the vulva, stretching them till surely they must split. At first I was not sure what I was seeing. Then I realized it was the top of the baby's head. It slipped back and the lips closed again.

'I'm tired, Khorat! I'm so tired!'

'Not long now.'

It was coming again. This time the whole head appeared, face downwards. The baby let out an indignant yell.

'Well, Mohini, he's going to have a lot to say for himself! He's only just got his head out and he's telling us what he thinks of the world!'

There was a pause. I could hear the oxen snuffing and stamping. With a miraculous spiral movement, the shoulders emerged. I was shouting with excitement:

'Come on! Come on!'

Ignorant, superstitious, courageous, wonderful Mohini gathered her strength and pushed, gave a loud cry and was delivered of a child.

I held up the baby by the heels. An ugly little creature, covered in blood and white grease, for all the world like a freshly skinned rabbit.

'How is my son? Tell me how he is, Khoratji!'

'Yes, you have a son, Mohini; a beautiful boy.'

I tied off the umbilical cord with thread from my bag and severed mother from child. I cleaned the baby as best I could with a rag and tepid water, wondering at the strength of the grip on my finger. He mewed like a kitten.

'Prajapathi!' Mohini called softly. 'Prajapathi,' she murmured, holding out her hands. As she took the infant into her arms, her face softened. Fresh tears ran down her wet cheeks. Did ever pain and joy so sweetly mingle?

Tenderly she annointed her son's head with clarified butter and smeared his little body with castor oil and saffron powder. To me, the young Prajapathi looked in a worse mess than before I had cleaned him, but Mohini was happy and began to sing again.

Outside, in the blinding glare, I handed a bloodstained bundle to Gampopa.

'This needs to be buried deep, where the jackals cannot devour it.'

'Oh, so it died then. Just as well. Dancers are better without these encumbrances.'

'No, Gampopa, the baby Prajapathi lives. This is the . . .' – I didn't know the word for afterbirth – ' . . . just the rags she lay on, Gampopa. But Mohini says it would be an evil omen were the wild animals to dig them up.'

For the first time I became fully aware of the other dancers. There was Chaitan, a boy of about nine. A man, slightly younger than myself, with a goitrous swelling on his neck and throat, gave me a formal bow, made *namaste* with his hands and beat a roll on the drum slung at his side. Another man, who was obviously his twin, did the same.

'We call them Yin and Yan,' Gampopa said. 'Yin is dumb and Yan is deaf.'

Chaitan pulled at my sleeve. 'Meet Rani and Rati, the two most important members of the troupe.'

He led me to the two white, hump-backed oxen. They regarded me with sad brown eyes, their fly-ringed ears and nostrils twitching incessantly. From the other side of the cart, in a series of backsprings, bowled the small fat figure I had previously observed. A twist of the body, a double somersault, and he landed lightly on his feet in front of me. The grotesque features were not his own, but a mask.

29

'A welcome to you, Khoratji!' I had not expected a voice so deep from one so small. 'Bamian the dwarf, at your service!' Barrels rumbling in a cellar would have been more restful to the ear. 'How is Mohini?' he boomed. He was the only one to ask.

Raising one of his fat little arms, he pulled off the mask. I stared. Bamian was laughing. At least, his chest heaved, and the noise rolled out, but the expression remained one of twisted rage. I was looking at a second mask. With a flourish he removed the unmasked mask. I saw the joke . . . if it was a joke. The two masks parodied the real face. With a cruelly sharp observation, they drew attention to the slobbering lips, the lopsided mouth, the bulbous eyes, the protruding forehead.

'What are you all standing there for?' Gampopa demanded angrily. 'Get the cart back on the highway! If we don't dance, we don't eat!' He wiped the spittle from his lips with the back of his hand and said to me: 'An army always needs entertaining, and with the Dasshera festival coming soon there should be no lack of . . .' He ended with another coughing fit.

The cart was ready to go. The four men were gathered in a circle, holding a muttered council, punctuated by rolls and drum-taps, quick hand-signals from Yin and Yan and frequent glances in our direction.

Gampopa beckoned to me. He proposed that Frog and I join forces with them. 'These are dangerous times. Bandits and deserters and men driven to desperate deeds are rife everywhere.' We agreed.

The ox cart trundled through the afternoon with Mohini and her baby asleep inside. Above the plodding Rani and Rati squatted Gampopa. He smoked a pipe with a curving stem of beaten silver. The sickly smell of opium hung in the air. With each inhalation, his gaunt cheeks hollowed, stretching the skin across his cheekbones even tighter. Absent-mindedly he stroked Chaitan, who sat beside him. The boy wriggled coquettishly under those long, knowing fingers and burst into song. His voice soared and dipped, sighed, broke and soared again.

Yin and Yan lagged behind, arguing with each other after their own fashion. Bamian trotted on his short legs beside Frog and me.

'And what led you to take up dancing?' Frog enquired in a kindly tone, stooping as he spoke. Bamian gave a furious grunt, seized

Frog's chain, which was trailing on the ground, and whacked the monk's bare foot. Frog howled and hopped up and down.

'I'm not a child!' the dwarf fumed. 'Don't speak to me as if I was!' He fixed Frog with an angry stare. 'You find me repulsive, don't you?'

Frog denied it.

'You're thinking I'm only in the troupe because people will always pay to see a freak!'

'No, I'm not thinking that!'

'You are!'

'I'm not!'

'What are you thinking, then?'

'I'm thinking that my foot hurts.'

Bamian swung on the end of the chain, using Frog like a maypole.

'Ow! Let go, you repulsive little wart!'

'Aha! I thought so!' Bamian came to earth, looking positively triumphant.

Contritely, humbly, Frog advanced his other foot. 'Please, good dwarf, smite this foot now.' He screwed up his face in readiness, eyes tight shut. Ignoring the proffered foot, Bamian whacked the injured one for a second time.

'Ah! That's not fair!'

Bamian caught my smile and grinned hugely, displaying strong yellow teeth. 'I have always been a dancer,' he said. 'And that's because I was born into the caste from which dancers come.'

Not that Frog was listening. He was limping along, muttering to himself that Our Lord, in the Sermon on the Mount, had been quite specific that it was the other cheek which was to be offered.

Bamian sprang on to the moving wheel and, by a superb piece of footwork, retained his balance on the narrow rim. 'My mother gave me to a dancing troupe when I was four. It was a famine year.'

Gampopa bubbled on his pipe. 'The younger the better,' he grunted. 'The suppleness of even the very young is not enough. The body must be trained, the muscles educated.'

Mohini's voice drifted sleepily from the cart. 'I think Prajapathi started to dance when he was still inside me. One day he shall dance before princes.'

'Yes, we of Rajasthan are entertainers, not temple dancers,' Bamian said, jumping down from the wheel.

Gampopa scowled. 'Entertainers we may be, but we draw on the same traditions as the temple dancers. The precepts of the *Natyashastra* are our precepts.' He stood up in the cart and glared around him, daring anyone to contradict him. 'Our dancing, all dancing, is first and foremost an offering to the deity; and only secondly is it an entertainment.' He started coughing and sat down.

There was blood in his phlegm. Possibly it was the chine-cough. There are quacks in England who swear that a bag filled with earthworms and hung around the neck is the only sure remedy. As the worms die and dry up, so will the cough disappear. Paracelsus, on the other hand, says that an infusion made from the lungwort is the best cure, because he mistakenly thinks their leaves resemble the human lung. Obviously he has never looked for himself but, like many others, goes only to the pages of the ancients such as Galen and Aristotle. As for myself, I say: observe, test, record. And, in the meantime, I hide my doubts from my patients, for it seems to me that confidence in the cure is the most essential ingredient of any medication.

In the distance, Akbar's army was a mere cloud of dust. 'Like a pillar of smoke by day,' I said, nudging Frog. This seemed to rouse him from his reverie, for, gathering up the loose end of his chain, he mounted the moving cart and began to preach.

The storyteller is a well-known and popular figure in India, and Frog's stories were ones that had fascinated people down the centuries. The dancers listened, Yin's darting hands and tapping drum retelling the tale for Yan.

'And God said, let us make man in our image, after our likeness: and let them –'

Bamian gave a harsh laugh. 'Take a good look at me, my friend. Are you telling us that your god made me in his own image?'

'Be quiet and don't spoil the story!' Mohini shouted.

But Bamian was incensed and would not be silenced. 'I think this Creator was indulging in a cruel joke. Why else would he incarcerate us in bodies whose natural tendency is towards disability and disease?' The dwarf was panting with rage. 'Either that, or this whole world is just a fart from God's arsehole; a clumsy, wasteful, blundering piece of work!'

'Such words are sucked from the teats of the Devil's breast! Hold your heathenish, blaspheming tongue!'

I must say, as a man of medicine, I have thought on numerous occasions that, if the Almighty made the human body, his son might have said a great deal more than he did about how it worked and why things keep going wrong with it.

We passed by fields newly irrigated and rows of bending women, knee-deep in mud, planting out the seedlings for the second rice crop. Notwithstanding our argument of yesterday, Frog launched, so to speak, into the Flood.

'That's not how it goes!' Chaitan shouted. 'You've got it all wrong! Everyone knows that Vishnu, in his first three incarnations, saved the world from the Flood. In the form of gigantic fish, tortoise and boar, he saved the world. Everyone knows that!'

A man overtook us at a run. 'Beware the Chota Chua!'

Gampopa jerked out of his opium dream and lashed the oxen into a faster, lumbering pace. A pony galloped by.

'The Chota Chua are coming!' called the rider. 'About an hour behind!'

'What are they?' I asked.

Yan answered with an incomprehensible gush of half-formed, eliding words; Yin's drum beat a tattoo.

'A plague, like the locusts or the rats,' said Bamian.

A bluish ring of smoke rose from Gampopa's pipe. 'Worse, much worse.'

'Children,' said Chaitan.

As we hurried along, I learnt something of the Chota Chua. In lean years, these lawless bands of children multiplied like mould in the rainy season, their ranks swelled by the orphaned, the abandoned, the hungry and the desperate. Even the children of the wealthy, it was said, sometimes succumbed to the strange lure of the Chota Chua.

The sinking sun filtered through a golden gauze of dust. The *mohur* trees glowed scarlet like dying embers. Prajapathi was sucking contentedly, and Mohini, child-woman that she was, sang in a girlish voice of the bitter-sweetness of maternity. The flat landscape stretched away endlessly, broken only by thin, motionless columns of smoke, which told of a village, an island amidst the fields. Gampopa swore and spat over the side of the cart. He swore again and turned the cart down the narrow, rutted lane which led to the village. The vast host, beneath its moving cloud of dust, was too distant, he said, for us to draw up with it before dark, and the Chota Chua were coming up behind. All agreed that, what with robbers lurking in the woods and the demons and ghosts that prowled by night, there was no question of pushing on once the sun had set.

We were still some way off when what seemed like the entire population of the village poured out to greet us.

'It's usually just the dogs rush out to bite you,' observed Frog.

'The dancers! The dancers!' They shouted.

'The dancers are here!'

'They've come at last!'

We advanced down an avenue of cheering people. Gampopa glared at his troupe. 'Have your wits deserted you? Perform!'

Yin and Yan struck up on drum and sitar, Chaitan joined them on his flute, and Bamian somersaulted and tumbled beside the cart. Villagers thronged excitedly around us.

'We seem to be expected,' I said.

'Somebody is,' answered Gampopa out of the side of his mouth, 'and it might as well be us.'

Garlands of flowers were hung around our necks. Willing hands led the cart through the village to the gates of a large house. This, we were told, was where the zemindar, the landowner, lived. The walls enclosing its courtyards had been newly whitewashed and patterned with coloured rice, as people are wont to do in these parts when wedding festivities are afoot. The solid wooden gates opened and a tall, silver-haired man stepped out. He wore a surcoat of grey silk, close-fitting trousers and embroidered shoes. A bony hand clutched an ivory walking-stick. He waved it impatiently, encompassing the sun, low in the sky, the stage that had been erected in one corner of the yard, the crowd who were now silent behind us.

'You were expected sooner. Sunset is the appointed hour for the dancing to commence.'

'*Huzoor*, the Chota Chua are abroad. We had to make a long detour to avoid them,' Gampopa lied.

'Ah yes, the Chota Chua. We are protected. Our Brahmins have

been chanting mantras since midday and goats have been sacrificed.'
He looked hard at Gampopa. 'Where are you from?'

'*Huzoor?*'

'I ask where you and your troupe are from.'

Frog strode forward. 'I will not be party to this deception. These
are not the dancers you expected.'

The crowd stirred and buzzed behind us. Gampopa shot Frog a
look of pure hate. The zemindar smiled. 'I know that they are not the
dancers from Delhi. But you are wrong – they are expected. When
the troupe from Delhi sent word they could not come, I prayed at our
household shrine to Ganesha. As we all know, the Elephant-Headed
One takes special care of those undertaking ceremonies of religious
import.'

Gampopa made a good recovery. 'Then, *huzoor*, Ganesha has
indeed favoured you today. We are from Rajasthan, whence hail
dancers far superior to those of Delhi. We may be small in number,
but we are good.'

The news rippled through the crowd like wind through a field of
corn. The zemindar smiled again and inclined his head. 'So be it.'

In a corner of the yard, behind the stage, Gampopa gave his orders.
'The first half of the performance will be something seasonal. Since
Dasshera is nearly upon us, we will perform "The Host of Hanuman".' There were nods of approval. Gampopa added for my
benefit: 'It is from our great epic the *Ramayana*. We tell the story in
our dance and song of how Hanuman, the Monkey King, came to the
aid of Rama in the forests of Sri Lanka.'

Bamian's dark eyes glittered. His body was tense. 'And the second
part of the performance?'

Gampopa turned on him with a snarl. 'For a wedding feast, what
else can it be but "The Love of Krishna and Radha"?'

A stifled whimper came from the cart.

'It has to be!' Gampopa shouted angrily. 'Mohini, make ready to
dance!'

'No!' I protested. 'That's monstrous! She must rest!'

Gampopa regarded me much as a python regards a rat before
devouring it. His tongue flickered over his lips, taking in a gobbet of
blood and mucus at the corner of his mouth.

35

'She is young,' he said. 'Young bodies recover fast enough. Get up, girl! Either you earn your keep, or out you go! Remember, all of you, if we don't dance, we don't eat!'

Mohini emerged from the cart, Prajapathi in her arms. She cast a swift, shy glance in my direction. Slowly and stiffly she walked up to Gampopa. She crouched at his feet.

'To Ganga the great Mother Goddess and to you my *nayaka*, my guru, I dedicate my dance this evening.'

She held up her son to him. Gampopa dipped a finger into a small pot containing a yellowish paste, a mixture of sandalwood and the ashes of burnt cow-dung. On the baby's forehead he drew the shape of a trident, the mark of Shiva.

'Shiva, Lord of the Cosmic Dance, recognize this member of our caste.'

Then the others gathered round the mother and her child. Bamian the dwarf, the dumb, goitrous Yin, deaf Yan, the pockmarked Brother Peter, Gampopa coughing in the background. They exclaimed over the smoothness of Prajapathi's skin, the perfection of his tiny limbs. What diseases will invade and despoil that body? For come they will. And how little we are able to combat them!

Mohini looked past them, seeking my eye. There was an expression there which filled me with unease. Certainly there was a bond between us. How could there not be after so intimate, so stupendous an event? But dog-like devotion from a barefoot girl whose head was stuffed with superstitious nonsense was an embarrassment I preferred to avoid. She came up to me and stood close.

'Look, Khoratji, his eyes are blue.'

'They'll soon change to brown, Mohini.'

'I know, Khoratji, but for a short time, at least, my son will be like you.'

'How do you feel?'

She shrugged and hung her head, drawing patterns in the dust with her toe.

I said, 'I see you chose the blue and silver one.'

She giggled, whirled around, and gave a yelp of pain.

'You must be careful, Mohini. You must rest as much as possible.' Even as I said it, I knew the advice was unrealistic, futile.

Yan had been laying out in a circle pots of oxides, coconut oil, small hand-mirrors and rows of paintbrushes such as artists use. Gampopa tinkled a brass handbell.

'I must leave you,' Mohini said. 'For us dancers, the performance starts now, with the ritual of the make-up . . . not on the stage, but here, the moment the first brush touches the face.' She explained with a seriousness I had not thought to see in her. 'Brushstroke by brushstroke, layer by layer, line by line, we must vacate our minds and bodies and let a new being enter.'

'It is meditation,' Gampopa said, ringing the bell again. 'Now go and leave us to it.'

A puff of coloured smoke and a twelve-foot demon towered above us. Cries of wonder rose from the audience – men of the soil squatting, bare-legged, under the stars in the rich man's courtyard. To the double-headed drums, clashing cymbals and the wild strings of *vina* and *tampura*, the huge masked figure stamped and gyrated round the stage. Torches flared and guttered on the walls. In their flickering light the whirling, tilting head seemed to change expression, to weep, to laugh, to glare and grimace.

In the balcony above the yard sat the bridegroom and his veiled bride. Her dress and mantle were encrusted with bells, mirrors, cowrie shells and coins, her head and arms heavy with silver ornaments. Fireflies glowed in the trees. Coloured lanterns hung from every branch.

A handsome youth in princely costume, with flashing sword in hand, engaged the demon in acrobatic combat, keeping, all the while, in perfect time to the pounding drums – the drums played by Yin and Yan. Deaf Yan, who squatted opposite his twin, following his every nod, blink and movement. I nudged Frog, who nodded and whispered:

'He seems pleased enough to be part of the performance.'

'But, Frog, what meaning can it have for him? And if he cannot hear the music, how strange must seem those antics on the stage.'

'And you, doubting Thomas, you who are deaf to the music of the heavens, is there not a lesson to be drawn from this?' Frog was always one to labour a point.

'Sh!' said a voice behind us.

A fatal thrust, a flash of light, and the demon disappeared before our eyes. In its place a jackal fawned at the prince's feet. I have never seen a trick so cleverly done. Frog was gripping my arm with excitement. Another cloud of smoke and an even bigger demon appeared. Then Hanuman the Monkey King made entrance, coming to the aid of Prince Rama. My scalp prickled. What I was seeing was not Gampopa playing the part of Hanuman, it *was* Hanuman. Of Gampopa there was no trace. Every posture, movement, grunt, angle of the head was pure monkey. And, throughout the prancing, leaping, physically demanding action, not once did I hear the faintest cough.

The first half of the performance ended. Gampopa remained on stage. The villagers surged forward, laid offerings at his feet, bowed down before him and worshipped him, for it was no mortal that stood there, but the god himself. I began to understand why the troupe looked up to this disagreeable man as their guru. Then the painted, costumed figure coughed and hurled abuse at someone backstage.

Behind me a little boy let out a deep sigh. 'Father, if I practise on my flute, can I join a troupe like that?'

'And who will help me in the fields? Who will take the water-buffalo to pasture, or keep the birds from our *champaka* tree?'

'Where are they from, father?'

'From Rajasthan, my son, which is famous for its dancers, so I've heard.'

'Is that the place just beyond the next village, where the wild mangoes grow?'

'No, sapling, it is many days in the direction of the setting sun.'

'There should have been fireworks!' grumbled the man's neigh-bour. 'All the grandest weddings have fireworks. Don't they know how to do things properly any more?'

'True, true. But the dancers are good. I wonder what he is paying them.'

'Whatever it is, he can afford it, the prices he charges for his grain.'

'Father?'

'Yes, my sapling, my son?'

'That demon . . . it . . . it wasn't real, was it?'

'No. Though I could have believed it was.'

'Father, if I practise on my flute very hard –'

'Sh! They begin again.'

The audience bubbled with pleasure, recognizing an old favourite from the *Gita Govinda* – 'The Love of Krishna and Radha'. On to the stage floated Mohini, skirts swinging, ankles jingling with silver bells, palms eloquent and henna-dyed. Her song throbbed and quavered in rhythms exotic to my ear. I pictured her stretched and tortured flesh. Then I was seeing only the sheer beauty of her movements, the suppleness of her body, the mobility and expression of her eyes . . .

'They flame with gems,' sang Chaitan, a youthful Lord Krishna. 'O grant me a draught of honey from the lotus of thy mouth; make thy arms my chains. Thou art my ornament; thou art the pearl in the ocean of my mortal birth!'

Mary, you were my ornament. You were the pearl in the ocean of my life. Mohini, it is your lotus mouth I crave.

Three

I lay wrapped in my cloak. Another morning; another river mist. I had lost count. It must have been nine or ten days since the troupe danced at the wedding feast. I had been troubled by fevers, pains in the joints, bad dreams. I had been out of sorts for at least a week. Mohini, as much as anything, troubled me. She followed me constantly. The more she tried to please me, the more irritating she was.

And Bamian was in a foul mood. The bag of silver, his reward for a fine performance, seemed to weigh heavily on his spirits. He tried to gamble it away but was, unluckily, in luck. Prajapathi fretted dismally through the night; Mohini was tired, although, if anything, her incessant and inane chatter increased. Rani went lame, the left wheel fell off, the troupe dropped further and further behind Akbar's army. Though we had seen no sign of the Chota Chua, rumours of their presence abounded. With each new report of their proximity, Gampopa's bad temper grew, and was vented on Mohini in a hundred spiteful ways.

In fact, everyone seemed out of sorts. Part of my annoyance was with myself. It offended me that I should be attracted to a girl of such woeful ignorance. Until I put her right on the matter, she actually believed that people of the white races hatched from eggs which grew on trees. How could such grace and silliness coexist? But the flesh has a will of its own. Perhaps a purgative might help.

Beside me, Frog was on his knees, galloping through his prayers at a speed incomprehensible to mortal ear. The dancers were already up and at their exercises. Gampopa beat time with an ebony stick. Crack! Chaitan yelped.

'Knees!' barked Gampopa. 'Knees! Knees! Feet turned out!' Crack! 'Further! Stretch those muscles! Stretch!'

Turning to Mohini he croaked between coughing fits: 'Hands! Remember . . . hands that swim like a fish! Back like a horse about to spring! Bearing like a peacock!'

Swish, swish went the cane, beating out the time. Crack! against a knee. I watched her. Undulating, bending, stretching. I imagined her supple young body lying next to mine. It was a long time since I'd had a woman. My hand crept down the front of my breeches . . . the stretching, splitting vulva, the afterbirth slipping to the floor like offal in a butcher's shop . . . My hand never reached its destination.

Bamian the dwarf walked by on his hands. 'Not up yet?' said the upside-down head.

'No,' I replied, removing my hand.

'We dancers are early risers. We have been at our exercises these past two hours.'

'You say that every morning, Bamian.'

'Knees turned out! Bend! Bend!' came Gampopa's voice.

'I'm glad I'm not one of his pupils,' I said.

The fat lips overhanging the hairy cavern of his nostrils moved. 'Dancing requires a discipline more rigid than anything you'll find in Akbar's army.' He shifted his weight on to one hand and scratched his belly. 'It takes at least eight years to make a good dancer.'

Those dark eyes, nine inches from the ground, must have been watching me closer than I thought. 'She would never look at me, of course.' The dwarf's voice was bitter. 'I visit brothels for my pleasures.'

'I hope you don't have to pay full price,' I said.

Bamian flipped into an upright position, cast me a swift look from coal-black depths, then let out a laugh reminiscent of an organ's base notes.

Frog leapt to his feet and began prancing about, slapping his legs and thighs.

'A national dance, perhaps?' Bamian enquired.

'No!' snapped Frog. 'Ants up my cassock!'

We examined the ants' nest on which Frog had been kneeling. The little creatures scurried and darted in all directions, seemingly with no pattern to their movements. Bamian built obstacles in their path, watching them struggle to surmount them, even climbing on each other's backs to do so. He caught two in his hand and, drawing a circle on the ground, put them inside it.

'A golden mohur if yours leaves the circle first. Which one do you bet on?'

'No, thank you, Bamian.'

'How about cards, then?'

'No.'

'Dice?'

'I have too little money to chance losing any.'

'Ah, but you might win all this!' He chinked his bag of coins.

'If you're so anxious to be rid of it, why don't you give it away?'

'It's not the same. I have to stake it and lose it.' His face contorted with some intense emotion. 'Hope is the cruellest trick the gods play on us. The cards, the dice . . . they remind you that you must lose in the end, that hope is an illusion. When I'm purged of hope, then I know a certain kind of calm.'

'But, Bamian, surely it is foolish to throw away money like that. At least you could put it to some good purpose.'

'No, not foolishness, Khoratji. Man can do nothing against fate and its capricious dealings. True wisdom is to mould one's life in agreement with the decrees of chance.'

Frog, who had been hovering on the fringe, could contain himself no longer. 'To believe in the dominion of blind chance is to deny man's free will. Gambling is wickedness. Gambling is precipitation into the frightful and horrible darkness of irreligion.'

Bamian's thick lips parted in a sneer. 'I have heard you speak of the need for faith. Faith is nothing but a kind of gambling. If everything you preach was absolute certainty, where would be the need of faith? And where would be the merit in believing?' He rattled his dice to emphasize his point. 'You prostrate yourself before your god; I prostrate myself before providence. Your salvation, so you say, is in Jesus Christ; the dice are my salvation. On to their square shoulders I shift my problems and my worries.' He took a step towards Frog, who flinched and backed away. 'Tell me this,' Bamian demanded. 'Does your god reward the good, the intelligent, the honest, the hardworking? No. Wealth and happiness in this world are a matter of chance. It is to chance that I give my money as an offering.'

Frog's fists were clenched. 'Eternal torment awaits such as you!'

Bamian tilted his head back to stare up at Frog, his eyes like two loaded muskets. 'Then your god is infinitely more wicked than the most wicked of men. Even the worst of tyrants has some motive for tormenting his victims – to prove his power, to instil fear, for revenge – but an omnipotent god can have no aim other than to amuse himself.'

Bamian was jumping up and down on the ant heap in his anger. Frog turned his back on him and walked towards the trees.

'Frog, you're not trying to obstruct the path of science again, I trust.' To determine the amount of fuel the human body burns, I was conducting an experiment. Every day I would weigh Frog's intake of food and compare it with his output of waste matter. Observe, test, record. The trouble was that Frog did not share my enthusiasm for this line of inquiry. He had to be watched to ensure that nothing escaped being put to the scales. Sometimes he was even so devious as to bury the vital evidence.

Frog drew himself up with dignity. 'Would that you paid as much heed to that which issues from my upper orifice; I mean the words I let drop; and in particular I mean the Word of God.'

'Why, Frog, I do assure you, there's as much truth to be found in your excreta as in the Scriptures.'

I ducked as his staff whistled past my head. Then Gampopa was standing on the cart letting loose broadsides of instructions, interspersed with the grapeshot of abuse. Oxen were yoked to the cart, baggage stowed, fires damped. The mist slipped away and once more there lay before us the wide horizons and vast skies of the Indian plains.

Ahead of me walked Mohini, the baby Prajapathi slung in a fold of cloth on her back. I had been sufficiently brusque with her to gain a small respite from her attentions. She was talking to Yin, an arrangement which suited her admirably since he couldn't interrupt her flow. I carried Frog's chain over my shoulder, giving it a hefty tug whenever he lagged behind, which was frequently, since he was studying the Koran again and not paying much attention to what his feet were doing.

'What news of the army?' Gampopa called as we came abreast of a wagon loaded with firewood.

'Last night they camped outside Muttra . . . This morning, so I hear, they moved south again.'

Gampopa cursed.

'And what of the Chota Chua?' Chaitan asked.

'Their numbers grow all the time.'

'But where are they?'

His laugh lingered in the air long after his wagon had lumbered by.

Mohini still blithely chirped away like a brightly coloured bird. I asked Bamian about the forthcoming Dasshera festival. But it was Mohini who seized the opportunity to be my informant.

'We celebrate the victory of Rama over the demon Ravana,' she said, hopping and skipping round me in circles, or walking backwards in front of me. She recounted in a series of breathless rushes how Prince Rama was banished for fourteen years to the forests, accompanied by his wife Sita; how Sita was abducted by Ravana and how Hanuman led his army of apes to assist Rama in the final battle. 'Evil were the omens for the Rakshases of the Demon King. Jackals howled and birds screamed at dawn; the sky was blood-red, and Rahu endeavoured to swallow the sun, causing an awesome eclipse; a headless horror appeared in mid-air and . . .'

Prajapathi woke and began to cry. She swung him to her breast. It is a wondrous thing to see a baby, seemingly helpless, unable to focus with its eyes, so easily find the nipple and so powerfully suck on it. Her breasts were the exact colour of the honey from the gorse-gorged bees of our Blackdown Hills.

' . . . and Sita said, "Chaste and innocent have I remained. O Rama, do not doubt me. Better death than thy dark suspicion."'

Mohini's delicate hand made the *kartari-mukha*, forefinger and little finger joined, the rest of the hand outspread – a gesture which I now knew showed separation and death. The eloquence of her undulating wrist, the exquisite movements of her neck . . . I was bewitched once more.

A country market had been set up in open ground near the well. Carts tilted on their shafts. Villagers squatted barefoot in the dust next to hillocks of purple onions, mounds of big white radishes, pyramids of grain. A hand heavy with rings and bangles brushed aside a hair. A

44

dark hand, a tiny movement, but memories, like the stalking tiger, pounce when we are off our guard: Mary.

To one side sat a group of about twenty men in white cotton robes. Most were performing their ritual ablutions before prayer, washing hands, arms, face and feet, doing each of these three times, as is the way with Muslims. Mohini shifted her baby on to her back and began hauling water from the well. Prajapathi wailed and hiccuped in protest at being torn from the main interest in his life, then fell asleep. Mohini tipped the water from the leather bucket into a brass pot she had fetched from the cart. She lifted the vessel to her head in one beautiful, flowing movement and walked away with a carriage proud and straight, such as one sees only in the nobility of our own land.

Frog and I seemed to draw hostile stares from the Muslim group. One of their number, a young man, approached the well. I gave him the customary civility.

'*Salaam alocum!*'

'*Alocum salaam!*'

'Where is your party making for?' I asked.

He shrugged. 'To the north, to the east and to the west.' He hauled at the bucket.

'By which reply I gather you have come together for company and protection and will soon disperse?'

A nod, slow in coming.

'And where did your journey start?'

'Hereabouts.'

'Well, has it been a long journey from hereabouts to thereabouts? Or, to draw the sword of quiddity from the scabbard of prevarication and come to the point, from whence do you return?'

He concentrated on the rope. 'From Mecca . . . Mecca . . . Mecca.' The proud word echoed down the well.

'Ah, you and your companions have been on a pilgrimage!'

'Yes.'

'A long way indeed. What route took you to Arabia?'

'Sea.'

'God's teeth, Frog! I've had patients part with limbs more cheerfully than this fellow parts with words!'

45

The bucket came to the surface. 'I think they're Nazarenes,' called out the young Muslim.

Angry men encircled me. The cause of their hostility was not that we were misguided, pig-eating, unclean infidels, but the indignities that had been heaped upon them at the port of Goa by the Christian authorities. Both on the outward and the homeward journey, the Portuguese authorities had not allowed them to proceed until their passes, allowing tax-free passage to pilgrims, had been stamped with the image of the Virgin Mary.

'They say their prophet is the son of God, but we all know that God had no wife!'

Dear Heaven! Frog's nostrils were going white again! I hacked him on the shin to take his mind off things.

'There is only one true faith!' proclaimed a strident voice amongst them.

'Yes, and that's followed by the Shiah sect!' someone shouted.

'Who said that? None other than the Sunnis are enlightened!'

'Wrong! Wrong! The Twelvers have the true interpretation!'

Suddenly we were forgotten. Furious arguments broke out, each sect claiming an exclusive monopoly of revealed truth. Some quoted Averroes, some al-Ghazali, and all used the Koran to prove their points. Thankfully our little group departed from this scene, Chaitan leading Rani and Rati quietly away. We were about fifty yards up the road when their leader, their mullah, called them to afternoon prayer. The pilgrims faced Mecca and knelt with their foreheads touching the ground. The sight was too much for Frog. Wrenching his chain from my hand, he strode back down the road towards the prostrate company. I left the others to go on and followed after Frog.

Holding up his wooden cross, he called upon them to see the error of their ways and repent. 'You who have been led astray by false prophecies, cease to wallow in your vomit! All who reject the light, all who rashly and insolently refuse to worship the Cross of Christ Crucified shall know the Stygian smoke of that pit which is bottomless!'

I managed to pull the zealous fool away. Even then he struggled to return, until I gave him a bloody nose with my fist. A stone hit him in the stomach, doubling him up. One of their number dashed up to

Frog, knife in hand. There was a flash of steel. I expected to see Frog's guts hanging out, but all I saw was the cord, which bound his Bible to his waist, hanging loose. I drew my sword and stood over the gasping Frog. No attack came. The sight of his copious flow mingling with the dust probably saved our lives; it seemed to appease their anger. Only when a mangy pye-dog was beaten howling down the road did I see what had been in their minds. Tied to its tail and bumping in the dirt was Frog's Bible. Uttering a hoarse cry, Frog gave chase.

Frog is not built for running far. When the jeers were nearly out of earshot and the stones were out of range, he stopped. Further up the road, the dog stopped too. It chased its tail in tight circles, trying to remove the unwanted encumbrance. It succeeded, sniffed at the open pages and urinated over the Good Book.

On the stained and stinking page I read: 'Thou art snared with the words of thy mouth.'

'Proverbs, six, two,' said Frog automatically.

On the other page, on the piss-sodden paper, were the words: 'But her end is bitter as wormwood, sharp as a two-edged sword.' Mary. My anguish and Frog's stupidity collided and exploded.

'You loathsome unbandaged sore!' And my fist split his lip. 'You suppurating ulcer on the human race!' My feet thudded against his ribs. 'Next time you feel like becoming a martyr, do not include me in your plans!' Thud! 'Do you hear?' Thud! Thud!

Frog knelt beside his Bible, taking my blows, making no effort to defend himself. He was crying. I stopped kicking him and embraced him, my brother in guilt.

I drew my sword for a second time and laid it gently on his shoulder. I spoke to him tenderly. 'I dub thee, dear Frog, a swinking, cogging, jadish prattler; a bescabbed, fart-shotten, monastical fusti-lug; a flogging, surfeited, whore-hunting piece of carnal concupi-scence. In fact, not a bad fellow at all!' I raised my sword to place it upon his other shoulder. 'Arise Sir Cod. Arise and –'

A man burst out of the trees and seized my arm. 'Stay, sir, stay!'

It was Dadu the soldier. 'Execution of slaves is no longer permitted by Mogul law, however undisciplined and lazy they might be.'

'But this one is really quite the worst you have ever seen!'

'No, sir. I am afraid it is definitely not allowed.'

'Well, just an arm then? Or perhaps an ear or two?'

Slowly and with great dignity Frog rose. His back straightened. Chest swelling, jaw jutting, he faced Dadu. A tremor invaded his cheek, his lips began to quiver. Suddenly his face crumpled. Clutching his sides he staggered about the highway barking, roaring, braying with laughter. He rolled in the dust, kicking his legs; he howled and gasped and groaned till fresh tears ran down his face.

'He has not been bit by a dog of late, has he?' Dadu asked anxiously.

'Yes, my friend, a mad dog I fear, for see how he thrashes on the ground.'

'Your poor slave! When was this?'

'Two weeks ago. The ravening beast came rushing out of the bushes at us.'

'What was it like?'

'Very big; the kind that strays from the pack to sniff after every bitch on heat.'

Dadu drew his dagger and advanced on Frog. 'Where is the wound? Perhaps it is not too late to draw the poison.'

'Alas, he is twice bit. The first was a nasty nip to his vanity; the second went deep to the bone they call the humerus.'

Bafflement and comprehension struggled on Dadu's face. 'Bushes . . . every bitch on heat . . . Ali, there is some riddle here which I see as clearly as a wild boar in a thicket . . . in other words, I see it not.'

When all was explained to him, he helped a weak and giggling Frog to his feet, mixing apologies and guffaws in equal parts. Frog, I thought, looked younger than he had done for many a month. This seemed like a good opportunity to be rid of Frog's iron collar and chain.

'You see how your penance rebounds on me,' I said, by way of argument. 'It casts me in the role of cruel master. People think ill of me. For your humility I suffer.'

Frog was contrite. Doubtless he was making a mental note to do some further, equally irritating penance, to atone for his thoughtlessness. I held out my hand for the key.

'I threw it away,' Frog declared.

'No matter!' cried Dadu, hefting his huge double-edged sword. 'One tickle from this little toothpick will break the lock . . . Now, if you lay your head here, so that the lock is on this stone . . . just so . . .'

Frog was less than enthusiastic about the idea.

'Have faith! Have faith!' Dadu laughed.

Frog continued to be reluctant.

'Have faith!' Dadu snarled, forcing Frog to the ground. He lifted the mighty weapon in both hands. It hovered high in the air, then came whistling down. At the last moment, Frog jerked his head away. The sword clanged on the rock. Dadu wrung his hands and bellowed with rage. He seized Frog and held him down with one massive foot.

'You're going to be freed whether you like it or not!' He whirled the sword above his head. Crash! The lock fell apart. A grinning Dadu lifted an ashen-faced Frog to his feet as if he were a baby and dusted him down.

Dadu glanced from me to Frog and back again. 'We soldiers meet all sorts. I'd hazard a shrewd guess that you two are seeking your fortunes, or else you're fleeing from justice.'

'We are seekers and fugitives both at once,' I said. 'Brother Peter, here, seeks souls, and I hope to extend my knowledge of the Art.'

'Ah, you've come to the right place to learn the Art of Love!'

'It is the Art of medicine to which I refer!'

'And from what do you flee?'

Frog spoke of the persecution of the Roman Catholics under our Tudor Elizabeth. It was only six years since the Pope excommunicated our queen and absolved Catholics from their duties of allegiance to the Crown, since when, Catholics have been regarded as a danger to the State. I, in my turn, told Dadu of the follies of the College of Physicians, who still held that the study of theology, of Latin and of Aristotle better fitted a man to practise medicine than an understanding of the human body.

Unspoken was the name of Mary. Lying heavy between us, but heavier by a thousandfold than Frog's chain of penitence, was the image of a slender girl, my wife, Mary.

'A military life is the very thing for both of you!' Dadu exclaimed. And he urged us to accompany him all the way and offer our services to General Ghulam Khan.

'There's no lack of work for a man with the skills of surgeon, and the rewards are high. As for this business with the souls . . . why, on the eve of a battle, when men contemplate death, there is no finer opportunity!'

In our straitened circumstances a chance to refill my purse was not to be lightly dismissed. But Agra was where libraries of accumulated knowledge lay. Of all the places in the world, Agra was where I might learn of a cure for that most dread of all afflictions, leprosy. Oh yes, I have studied the European scholars on the subject of leprosy. I have read Theodoric, the distinguished surgeon of Bologna, the celebrated Lefranc of Milan, Valeseus de Taranta. I could quote at length from Gilbert's 'De Lepra' in the *Compendium Medicinae*; or from Guy de Chauliac in his *Inventarium Sive Collectorium Partis Chirurgicalis Medicinae*. I know all about the symptoms, the *signa univoce*, the *signa demonstratia infallibilia*, as taken respectively from the face, the extremities, the blood, the humours of the body. I am well versed in these. But what of the cures? In England men still put faith in healing wells, or in concoctions which owe more to the black arts than to science – to wit, the blood of infants two years old, diffused through a bath of heated water. Perhaps at Agra I should find more than contradictory lists of articles capable of producing leprosy – too much meat, too little meat, too many vegetables . . . *Juzam*, as the Arabs call leprosy, had long exercised the doctors of the East. Perhaps at Agra . . .

The ravine in Badger Wood, a summer long ago. Month after month that ravine had lodged in my thoughts like a beam in the eye, grating at my self-respect, taunting me with my cowardice. I had returned to it, determined to jump it. For three hours I had stood on the brink, trying to match my resolve to the act. When darkness fell, I had slunk home. And the ravine of leprosy . . . On the other side stood Mary, waiting, hoping. But I had not found the courage to make the leap.

Dadu grasped my arm in a bruisingly affectionate grip. 'I've seen gateposts look happier than you! But here are some beauties to cheer you up!'

He referred, as far as I could see, to half a dozen black tents which were gliding towards us. The women, wearing the traditional *burqah* of those in purdah, carried baskets on their heads. Dadu smacked his lips and sighed heavily as they passed by, clucking like broody hens.

'How can you tell what they look like beneath all that?' I asked.

'The eyes.'

'I am afraid I find a glimpse through a crocheted slot insufficient evidence.'

'But the eyes tell everything!'

We had not gone far when we met Bamian standing on his head in the middle of the road. He stuck out his tongue at Dadu.

'What's this!' Dadu roared. 'A headless man with a pink cock?'

Bamian flipped on to his feet. Giant and dwarf looked each other up and down.

'Piss on your head!' exclaimed Dadu.

'Bite your balls!' Bamian replied.

A further bombardment of obscenities seemed to confirm their friendship, and Bamian swarmed up Dadu to sit astride his broad shoulders.

Frog shuddered. 'Thomas, I sin in thought. I would rather have a toad down my back than that dwarf perching on me like an obscene growth.'

'Who am I to stand in judgement? A man of medicine who runs in dread from the sickness of his own wife!'

For Bamian's benefit, Dadu recounted, with great relish, the whole episode with the Muslims. The fact that he had not been there and had received only the barest account from me in no whit inhibited the gusto of his rendering of the tale, nor prevented him from taking a major and heroic role in all that came to pass. Bamian bounced up and down with delight, drumming his heels on Dadu's chest in merriment at Frog's discomfiture. Frog's good humour evaporated like a puddle in the Indian sun.

'Is the defilement of God's revealed message to man so amusing?'

Dadu gave a massive shrug, which nearly unseated Bamian and made them laugh so much that Bamian toppled backwards off Dadu's shoulders, landing with a thump in the dust. Still laughing, they moved ahead.

'You would not so mock a man's bride,' Frog said to me, more in sorrow than in anger. 'The Christian faith is my bride and I am a man in love. I sometimes wonder, Thomas, if you know what love is; if ever you truly loved her.'

The thrust went deep. We walked in silence, avoiding each other's eye.

*

Nobody rode on the cart without Gampopa's permission. It was a privilege grudgingly given and quickly withdrawn. Chaitan had the best seat, beside Gampopa. Dadu sat at the back of the cart, his long legs dangling over the edge. On acquainting himself with the rules, he had suddenly developed a bad limp. This old wound, he said, flared up on occasions. Next to him, shuffling a pack of cards, sat Bamian, who had pleaded a severe case of short legs. Mohini, carrying her baby, had been made to walk.

Gampopa stared ahead impatiently. 'Boy! You have sharper eyes than I. Does no temple break the horizon?'

'No, my guru.'

I asked Mohini why Gampopa had been repeating this question throughout the day. Grateful for any crumbs of attention, she replied, 'It is Aardra Darsanan today.'

I waited for the usual flow of irrelevancies. 'Well, what does that signify?'

'That the full moon and the star Aardra are in conjunction.'

'Damn it, woman! Why is it that, single-handed, you resemble a band of chattering monkeys until I want to know something, then you –'

'But, Khoratji, I thought . . .' She fought back her tears. 'We Hindus must do *puja* on this day. We dancers must make offerings to Shiva. As the bee depends upon the lotus, as the fish depends upon the ocean, so we depend upon the Radiant One.'

Her tears were forgotten. Her face shone with devotion. Is it possible, I wondered, to bridge such a gulf?

'The cards and the dice – all important decisions are best left to them,' said Bamian. His dark eyes glowed with excitement as he emptied his money-bag on to the head of an old drum.

'That's a considerable sum,' Dadu commented.

'That wedding – the bridegroom and I diced till dawn.'

'It was his bride's soft purse he should have poured his silver into, not yours!' Dadu grunted with a wink and a leer, and tossed a handful of rings and trinkets on to the drumhead. 'The spoils of war staked against the winnings of the dice!'

The game of *ganjifi* is played with round cards of lacquered cotton. Unlike our packs with their four suits of cups, coins, swords and batons, Bamian's pack had ten suits, each representing one of the ten avatars or incarnations of Vishnu.

Mohini drew near. I frowned at her discouragingly.

'Khoratji ... Khoratji ... if I might ask your learned opinion about –'

'Not now, Mohini! I'm watching them play at *ganjifi*.'

'Khoratji, it's about Prajapathi ...'

'For the hundredth time – yes, he's beautiful! Yes, his father must surely be a god! Yes –'

'He's ill! He's ill, Khoratji. Please help me!'

Prajapathi's mouth was circled by the flies which had gathered on his puke.

'Khoratji, every time he feeds, he vomits it up again.'

His head was hot. I said: 'There are herbs which, in a weak infusion, might help to sooth his colic and reduce his fever.'

'Things like that don't come cheap,' Bamian said, without looking up from dealing the cards.

'I ... I have only one silver piece remaining,' Mohini faltered.

'What!' I shouted. 'You were well rewarded for your dance. How could you have spent it all so quickly?'

'Yes, the zemindar was generous,' Mohini admitted. 'Though he thought he was paying for something else – something he didn't get.'

'So what did you do with all that money?'

Mohini hesitated. 'Don't be angry with me, Khoratji ... At the village I bought sweets wrapped in silver and threw them in the river to appease the local spirits in case they should be jealous of my son.'

I sighed in exasperation.

'And then, Khoratji, there was a temple in the village and I paid for candles ... three of the biggest as an offering to Parvati. She will surely send blessings on my child. Just think how much worse he might be but for her heavenly protection!'

'Oh God!'

'Then the temple Brahmin said he would write a mantra ... you know ... a holy text ... he would write a mantra especially for Prajapathi to keep about his person. Well, as you can imagine, the price of a holy text is not something to haggle about.'

'Yes, I can imagine!'

'Then, this morning, at that country market, I bought this talisman – to ward off the evil eye. Look, he has it round his neck.'

'You stupid girl!'

She looked so downcast, so pathetic and defenceless, standing there clutching her baby in her thin arms, that I relented a little. 'I may be able to help you. But, promise me, no more talismans or lucky charms. Good food for yourself and medicaments as prescribed only by me for your baby – is that understood?'

She knelt on one knee and touched the hem of my doublet. 'I shall be guided by you, Khoratji, by the one who brought my son into this world.'

Chaitan was playing his flute, Gampopa, between coughing, supplying a droning bass accompaniment. 'Ta, tai-tai-ta-ta, takita, takita, tun.'

Bamian was betting recklessly and losing.

'Your expression is that of a man relieving a full bladder,' Dadu chuckled, scooping more money towards himself. Bamian made no reply. He was wholly absorbed in the cards.

'How is the wound, Dadu?' I asked.

'Wound? What wound? . . . Oh, that one . . . I have so many, you see.' He rolled up his sleeve to display a scar on his muscular arm. 'Now, take this one . . .'

'Your turn!' Bamian said sharply. He had staked everything on this hand.

Dadu played a card almost without looking. 'Now, about this arrow wound. I got it in the Bikaner campaign, if I remember rightly, or was it in the –'

'Play! Play, blast you!' There was sweat on Bamian's brow, his eyes were dilated.

'Tat, tai, tata, ta,' went Gampopa.

'The eighth avatar, the Lord Krishna, wins all,' said Dadu, placing his card on top of Bamian's. 'Blind Fortune favours me today. But there's always another day, Bamian my friend, and there is, in the worst of luck, the best of chances for a happy change.'

Bamian let out a long sigh and leant against the baggage. He looked disappointed.

'I thought you'd be pleased to lose,' I said.

'It's not losing the money . . . it's the fact that play must stop.'

The cart gave a jolt. Coins and trinkets spilt on to the highway, rolling in the dust. Mohini scrabbled about, gathering them up.

'Keep them for the baby,' Dadu said.

Her young face lit up. She brought the palms of her hands together; a bend of the knee, an inclination of her slender neck that was sheer beauty.

'Remember your promise,' I said gruffly.

'Yes, Khoratji.' Her smile would melt any man's heart.

'Village ahead!' called Chaitan.

In a mango grove on the outskirts of the village was the sculptured tower of a Hindu temple. Every inch of the stonework writhed with voluptuous bodies in erotic postures and amorous embraces. Above the temple entrance, larger than the other figures, was Shiva. Framed in a hoop of flames, he stood with one foot raised in dance, his twelve arms a flow of movement, hands more loquacious than a dozen tongues.

'Why is he portrayed inside a circle like that?' I asked.

'The revolving of the seasons,' Bamian said.

'The perpetual motion of the heavens,' said Gampopa.

'The cycle of birth, life and death,' added Mohini, kissing her fretful baby.

Chaitan unhitched Rani and Rati and let them wander free. Frog stared at the sculptures, breathing hard.

'Such disgusting and depraved practices, such sinful perversions . . .'

Yelping joyously, every canine male in the vicinity converged on Frog, anointing the unhappy man, copulating with his Bible. The Muslim pilgrims, I realized, had cunningly selected a bitch on heat to carry off the Holy Word. Laying about them with his staff, Frog gained the cart and scrambled on top of it. The clamouring pack surrounded him.

'Why, Frog, the animals never gazed on St Francis with such rapture!'

The besieged Frog only cursed, and when he addressed the animals it was in language unbecoming to a saint.

Gampopa held up his hand. A hush fell on the group. Even the dogs were silent. Branches swayed in the breeze; leaves danced and shimmered.

'Shiva is the Lord of the Dance. Shiva is the source of all movement. His mystic dance is the manifestation of eternal energy.'

A dog whined. I could hear the river flowing.

'Nature cannot dance till Shiva wills it. Dancing, he sends through inert matter pulsing waves of awakening sound, and lo! Matter also dances! Dancing, he maintains the universe; still dancing, he destroys all forms and gives new rest.' Gampopa lowered his arms and entered the temple.

As Mohini passed beneath the carving, she raised her eyes in adoration. 'Oh thou, the moon-crested, with the fair throat of a conch, with eyebrows like Kama's bow, hear us, we pray!'

The other dancers, Yin, Yan and Chaitan, followed. Bamian, last in line, turned and gave an enigmatic shrug.

Dadu said, as he settled himself beneath a mango tree, 'Ali informs me that they will be several hours at least.'

All was quiet, save for Dadu's heavy breathing and strange intermittent cries from Frog. The latter was engaged in a wrestling bout with the Devil, the deciding fall to determine whether it be the cross in his outstretched arm or the temple carvings that his eyes should fix upon.

Suddenly Dadu began to fizzle, fart, slaver and perspire. 'Ho, ho! Ha, ha!' he roared. 'Sniffing after every bitch on heat . . . twice bit . . . ha, ha! . . . nasty nip to the vanity . . . ho, ho!' He wiped tears from his cheeks, gasping, 'Oh yes, Ali, a good joke, very good!'

Another cry came from the marooned Frog. 'The tumult of carnal suggestion knocketh at the door! Begone! Begone I say!'

I persuaded Frog to part with his Bible and throw it to me. I suspended the foul-smelling thing from a tree. The dogs, the deluded creatures, rushed madly to surround anew the object of their desire. Frog clambered down from the cart, his arm raised to ward off the ungodly sights on the temple. I wished that I could administer a diabolifuge as easily as a vermifuge for the expulsion of worms. But perhaps, like Dadu, he would refuse the proffered medicine.

'Oh flesh, thou art the Devil's knight!'

'What's he say, Khoratji?'

'That he and the dogs are of one mind.'

'Ah, so the Lord Shiva speaks to him.'

Dadu exposed his belly. Tattooed across his navel was a multi-coloured phallus. 'The lingam is Shiva himself,' Dadu said, working his abdominal muscles so that the lingam swelled and moved up and down.

'Some of those positions look impossible,' I said.

Dadu laughed. 'Not if you're a trained temple dancer, they're not. I remember during the Gujarat campaign we . . .'

'Our miserable flesh is like unto the pig which ever delighteth to lie down and wallow in the mire!'

It had never struck me before that the sheer weight of the Good Book was capable of suppressing desire. Without its bulk dangling from his waist, Frog's trouble stuck out a mile.

'I think we should explore the village,' I said, taking Frog firmly by the arm.

The village was a warren of mud and thatch, still showing the erosions of the monsoon rains. At least it would have a bazaar where we might haggle over the price of a chicken or buy chapathis and a dab of curry on a leaf. We walked past walls daubed with Vedic texts and portraits of Hindu deities – Lakshmi and Annapurna, goddesses of wealth and plenty, Ganesha, the elephant-headed god, eight-armed Durga, Mariamma, goddess of smallpox, and many others I did not recognize.

'I declare it was a draw,' I said, for Frog was still downcast at the result of his encounter with the Evil One.

'No, Thomas, he had me down.'

'Never mind, the Devil was fighting foul, for, indeed, he had you by the balls!'

A potter squatted in the open, turning a wheel with a stick, fashioning pots from the wet clay. A man sat cross-legged under a walnut tree, a crowd of villagers around him.

'Avert the evil eye with Ramananda! Let Ramananda cast your horoscope!'

Heavy ivory rings weighed down the lobes of his ears; ropes of amber beads hung from his shoulders. He was pointing at various open books filled with symbols, charts and zodiacal signs.

'Three thousand six hundred basic fates every day! One hundred and fifty rising over the horizon every hour! Which one is for you? Only Ramananda can tell!'

Around him were magic charms, talismans, packets of herbs tied in plantain leaves, and pots and jars whose contents were an accurate guide to the fears, aspirations and daily preoccupations of the Indian villager. There were astringents for constricting the vagina, such as juice of pomegranate flower; there were ointments to increase the size and potency of the virile member – asafoetida mascerated in jasmine oil, bile of black fowl and oil of cloves. There were potions for falling in love and potions for falling out of love and a great many to guard against the evils attendant upon childbirth. Among his paraphernalia were a mariner's compass and a Portuguese prayer book, which he consulted every now and then, claiming that the former indicated the European zodiacal signs and the latter was an almanac. Being a master of both systems of astrology, he was, he informed the company, entitled to charge double prices.

We watched Ramananda, the itinerant astrologer, plying his trade. He was consulted as to the why and the wherefore of calamities, the likely success or failure of undertakings, the sex of an unborn child, remedies for the sick, the propitious moment for the sowing of a crop. A ragged peasant paid for a verbal reading. The *jkarta* or horoscope written on a leaf was too expensive for him, despite Ramananda's wheedlings. The astrologer tossed a handful of rice to the ground. Chanting mantras which invoked the deity, he worked the rice into patterns. Around this he drew a circle in the dust, dividing it into twelve compartments. After an unintelligible harangue with some unseen person, he made a few predictions, taking care to be as vague as possible. I would say that successful astrologers observe the ways of this earth rather than those of the skies. It is the same in England. Astrologers never want for business, while honest doctors can barely make a living. Even our own queen favours that necromancer, that worm in the entrails of mankind, Dr Dee.

Ramananda looked up and caught my eye. He showed his teeth, red with betel-nut. 'There is an evil influence round you, which I can remove for two pieces of silver.'

'The only evil influence near me is yourself! And I can be quit of that for nothing!'

58

We moved on. In our distrust of astrologers, Frog and I were, for once, in agreement. He, following the dictates of the Church, held that denial of free will was irreligious. If man's destiny is decided by the stars, morality entails no merit and immorality no reproach. And I, following the logic of my own observations, believe that, although the firmament exerts some influence upon us, it is not as the astrologers would have it.

We came to a courtyard with an open gate. I could see a bolt of white cloth unwound upon the ground, sprinkled with petals of vermilion and orange hue. On either side of it men sat cross-legged. Each wore a thin silver cord, the sacred thread of the initiated Brahmin – the scholarly and highest of the Hindu castes who, on occasions, perform certain priestly functions. The wealthy house-holder, wishing to please the deity of the house and accumulate merit for the next life, was giving a feast for local members of the Brahmin caste. Two more Brahmins, ragged-looking fellows, hurried through the gates. The host, a well-fed man, descended from the balcony of the house and, taking Frog by the arm, led him to a place at the banquet. I followed, wondering whether it was the bottle of holy water round his neck that qualified Frog for this repast.

'Thou art woman, thou art man. Thou art the dark-blue bee and the green parrot with red eyes. Thou hast lightning as thy child. Thou art the seasons and the seas. Thou dost abide with all-pervadingness, where from all things are born.' So chanted an elderly Brahmin, whereupon servants passed down the seated line with fragrant, steaming trays of thick, round, fried parathas, wrapped in plantain leaves.

'*Benedictus, benedicat* . . .' Frog boomed, launching into one of his interminable graces. I prodded him with my foot.

'Not now, Frog! Not here!'

But the stubborn fool persisted. Rather to his annoyance, this performance attracted no attention whatsoever. Sulkily, he handed me half of what was on his leaf.

'Whoso sits down to the feast of life must end by drinking the cup of death,' said the Brahmin on my left. I nodded wisely.

*

They squatted silently on top of the walls and roofs; they gathered in the trees, branches bending under their weight: children – the bitter fruit of war and poverty.

Anxious murmurs ran through the assembled banqueters:

'The Chota Chua!'

'The Chota Chua are here!'

'It is nothing!' cried the host. 'It is only a small number. The main body are at the next village. I have it on good authority. After all, we sacrificed a goat, did we not?' He ran about the courtyard stopping those who were leaving, pushing them back to their places, entreating them not to worry, and to continue with the feast.

A circle of eyes followed my hand as it conveyed a crispy morsel to my tongue, watched it pass my lips, watched me slowly chew – till it turned to sand in my mouth and I could not swallow. A little boy, high in a branch directly overhead, stretched out his hands in supplication. His stomach was distended. Children near starvation often look like that. I don't know why, but I, who have prodded stomachs of every size and disposition, know it to be so. You see it in England too, of course, when the harvest has been poor and the winter hard.

I broke off a thick wedge of the hot spicy stuff and was about to toss it to the child, when my host caught my arm.

'I do not advise it, sir. I really do not advise it. It is not wise.' And he roared at the little boy: 'Go away! What are you begging for? Anyone can see you're fat enough!'

Frog glanced up, his cheeks bulging, and saw him too. His mouth fell open, half-masticated pulp dribbling down his chin.

A white cow, its ribs plainly visible, wandered into the courtyard. It gobbled up a freshly arrived tray of parathas. Our host beamed.

'What an act of piety is here performed! Gomatra the Cow Mother partakes of my feast!'

The wretched beast, still hungry, advanced upon the Brahmins. Panic and consternation ensued. No Hindu, least of all a Brahmin, would think of driving away this most sacred of animals. But concealment was another thing. Quoting texts at each other to justify their actions, the Brahmins stowed the food inside their robes, under their turbans, or stood on tiptoe holding it above their heads.

Amidst this confusion, Frog stood up and threw a large, well-stuffed paratha to the skeletal figure overhead. The boy clutched at it in disbelief, then, glancing wildly around, screamed in fear. Hunger makes animals of us all. The child disappeared under a kicking, biting, clawing mass. The branch broke. Bodies hurtled to the ground. Servants drove this gibbering, moaning windfall from the yard with brooms and staves. When the last of the Chota Chua had dragged himself through the gates, one small body remained. Frog was beside him, holy water in hand, making the sign of the cross upon his brow. A young Brahmin, trying to administer the last rites, was forcing Ganges water between his lips. But the boy was dead. Clasping their bottles, the two men glared at each other; and the cow licked the crumbs which still adhered to his fingers.

Four

On either side of the highway, fields of young wheat and barley shimmered.

'Mark, ten, fourteen!'

'Be quiet, Frog, unless you want a leech down your neck!'

After days of travelling in hourly expectation of the Chota Chua; after nights of seeing them in every flickering fireside shadow, of imagining every rustle in the tall elephant-grass to be their stealthy, pilfering approach, I was a bow wound tight, ready to let fly.

Amidst the fields, like storks in their nests, sat boys keeping watch on top of slender poles. In normal times they guarded against the incursions of forest elephants, buffalo, or wild pig. Today their vigilance was for the Chota Chua. They were here, yet nowhere to be seen. It was always the next village, or the next village but one which, by report, had suffered visitation from the hydra insatiate.

'It's like waiting for the monsoon to break,' Bamian grumbled.

And the Mogul army remained no more than a distant cloud of dust, a faint rumble of cannon-fire. Each day the mounds of elephant and camel droppings were harder, drier, more tunnelled by the maggots. We were falling further behind.

Much to my displeasure, Ramananda had joined us. Astrologers, such is the foolishness of men, are afforded a status almost equal to that of the Brahmin caste. While the rest of us walked, he sat beside Gampopa and the favoured Chaitan on the cart, his donkey hitched to the back.

'How many of us are there?' Chaitan quizzed Ramananda, laying some boyish trap or other.

'Nine.'

'Wrong!' Chaitain crowed gleefully. 'Twelve, counting Rani, Rati and your donkey!'

'And I say thirteen!' Dadu boomed. 'For Ali is of the company, is he not?'

'You've all forgotten Prajapathi,' said Mohini, near to tears.

'Mark, ten, fourteen!' cooed Frog, chucking Prajapathi under the chin. There was no answering gurgle of delight, only a vacant stare. In the last few days, the child had ceased responding, even to its mother. There was nothing I could do. Mohini's silent grief assailed me more loudly than her chatter ever did. It engaged me in long dialogues, posing questions for which I had no answers.

Mohini, of course, had been unable to resist asking Ramananda to cast her baby's horoscope. The astrologer, sensing her worry, had demanded an exorbitant fee, and the silly girl had paid it. I had raised several logical objections. For instance, Ramananda's calculations were based on the exact time of birth. Was that from the moment of conception? Or was it when the head appeared, or maybe the whole body? When the child uttered its first cry, perhaps? Or when the umbilical cord was cut? After all, exactness was everything, was it not? Ramananda had replied with a leer, as he pocketed the silver, that, when a finger points to the moon, only the imbecile looks at the finger. The horoscope had predicted a long and successful life. I feared otherwise.

'Mark, ten, fourteen!' Frog breathed, an ecstatic smile upon his face. '"Suffer the little children to come unto me, and forbid them not; for of such is the kingdom of God" . . . Thomas, it is to save the Chota Chua that the Lord hath led me to these heathenish lands!'

I rounded on him. 'Led? Then you would have it, would you, that the Lord intentionally laid foul leprosy on my wife?'

'No, Thomas. I only meant . . . perhaps her suffering is not in vain, if out of it comes something . . .'

'A pox on the Chota Chua!'

Then I reminded him of the Bona Confidentia. Frog covered his ears with his hands, endeavouring not to hear.

While making passage for the Holy Land on a leaky tub called the Bona Confidentia, Frog had experienced a revelation. When lightning struck the mast, he had suddenly known, beyond all doubt, that his mission was to work among ungodly seafaring souls aboard vessels such as ours. However, a counter-message arrived from on high, cancelling the revelation – Frog had been violently seasick for most of the voyage.

'And then there was Baghdad, wasn't there, Frog?'

Frog shook his head. 'I can't hear you!'

At Baghdad the earth had trembled. A crack, in the shape of a cross, had appeared in the wall of a mosque. Naturally Frog had taken it as a sign that he was to set about converting the local populace. Nothing I could say would persuade him otherwise. Fortunately a good solid argument of a different kind made a great impression upon him. A brick, shaken loose from the roof of the mosque, struck him on the head. By the time he regained his senses, I had made sure we were many miles down the river Euphrates.

Frog began jumping up and down and howling, the worse to hear my words. 'But this time I am sure, Thomas! This time I am not mistaken!'

'Enough foreign gibberish!' Bamian roared, causing a dozen pigeons to rise startled from the field. 'Yin and Yan make more sense than this!'

Chaitan stood up in the cart. 'Listen! Do you hear the cannon? Yesterday they spoke from the south; today it is from the west.'

Gampopa tugged irritably at the boy. 'Sit down, boy, sit down! Do not eat the calf in the cow's belly. It is only a trick of the wind.'

'What do you think, Dadu?' Mohini asked anxiously.

Dadu shrugged. 'Some generals I could name don't know which way they're heading, themselves . . . is that not so, Ali? Yes, Ali will bear me out when I say that they draw up their plan of campaign after the event. Only then can they make sense of the confusion.'

'There it is again!' called Chaitan. 'Did you not hear?'

We shook our heads. But uncertainty dragged at our feet.

Something gleamed amidst the rippling corn. I waded through the whispering crop. Bamian followed, cursing the barley beards which tickled his nostrils and ears. The shiny thing, the top of a smooth, bald head, belonged to a naked man, who lay fast asleep. He was an old man, thin with a wrinkled belly. We prodded him. His breathing continued long and loud. We shook him, we slapped him, we shouted in his ear. He slumbered on. I noticed that his right leg was gashed.

'If I fetch my pots and brushes,' Bamian mused, 'I could paint this eggish dome pink with yellow spots. It might be days before he discovered the secret of his attraction. And this shrivelled object here . . . bright green?'

'No time for that, Bamian. Here, help me bandage his leg.'

'You do not have the idea at all!' Bamian scolded. 'Bandage his sound leg and his wound will be quite free of pain, I guarantee it!'

I knelt beside the sleeping man. Bamian's dark eyes danced and shone close to mine. I succumbed to his mischief, telling myself that I was, in fact, engaging in medical research, that it would test a certain theory of mine. We bandaged the undamaged limb, Bamian smearing the gauze in the red soil.

The old man opened his eyes, saw Bamian, leapt to his feet with a cry of 'Chota Chua!' and raced towards the river. Halfway there he stopped, looked down and began limping heavily, favouring not his gashed right leg but the bandaged one.

'What did I tell you?' Bamian crowed, punching my kneecaps with delight.

We hurried to catch up our companions of the road. They were gathered on the edge of a tributary river which cut across the highway at this point. Stuck fast in the middle of the river was the cart. A furious argument was in progress about whose fault it was. The water being the colour and consistency of thick pea soup, the cart had strayed from the stony bottom of the ford and plunged into mud. Mohini had been ordered to feel for the hard-bottomed way with her bare feet. But the leeches in this stretch of the river were particularly bad. Mohini, shrouded in her own anxieties, had hardly noticed. It was Bamian who had called her back to the bank. She stood there, indifferent to the excitement around her. It was Bamian who protested on her behalf, lifting the hem of her sari to show the blood-sucking clusters fastened to her ankles, already bloated like fat, purple slugs. Frog clutched my arm, groaning and covering his eyes.

'Well, I have my legs to think of too!' Chaitan was shouting. 'So I'm certainly not wading in!' From the safety of the cart in midstream, he ventured: 'Send the twins – they don't play the drums with their legs . . . although it often sounds like it!'

There was no thought of blaming Gampopa, though it was he who had driven the cart into the mud. A man deep in an opium dream, a man reliving the sacred verses, is beyond earthbound squabbles. His face had changed. The deep-etched lines had softened, become more feminine. His voice was a woman's voice.

'Grief burns me as if I was on fire!'

'He is deep in the *Mahabharata*,' Bamian growled softly, referring to the great epic poem, the storehouse of Hindu mythology.

'He is Draupadi, daughter of the king of Panchala, wife of the five sons of King Pandu. He is . . . she is sorrowing for the death of her sons.' The dwarf's habitual cynical expression was gone. He looked up at me with rapt face. 'Listen to how he becomes each person, as only a great *nayaka* can.'

'Let Bamian find the way!' Chaitan shouted. 'He has the longest legs of us all! And they won't feel the leeches!'

From the rear of the cart he produced two hollow wickerwork tubes. He hurled one, then the other, across the intervening gap. I took a close look as Bamian strapped on his legs. They were ten feet long, jointed very cleverly at the knee on a ball-and-socket device. What intrigued me was the coiled spring of finely beaten steel, connecting the upper and lower parts in such a way that, once the weight of the body was removed from the leg, it snapped straight again. I remembered Bamian's performance on the stage. I had wondered how the Demon King walked without the stiff-legged gait usually associated with stilts. As one who has examined many different designs of artificial limbs, I was impressed.

'Did you make these?'

Bamian nodded. 'You are seeing one of the secrets of our profession. Not many outside our caste are so privileged.' He smiled. That is to say, the assemblage of lumps and protruberances which was his face recomposed themselves. 'It came to me at the temple, the other day, that you and I both, in our different professions, must pay homage to the Lord Shiva, for he is the creator and giver of life as well as the destroyer.'

Gampopa burst out again, this time in a deep rolling voice: 'All fatigue and pain have left me. I am strengthened by meditation. My mind is unclouded. I see all that is past, present and future as if it were a fruit placed in my hand.'

'He is the dying hero, Bishma, now,' Bamian said.

The dwarf inserted his short legs into the upper casements of the basketwork, then called upon Dadu to help him stand. With a gleeful grin he looked down on the giant.

'Piss on your head!'

'Bite your balls!' came Dadu's response.

Bamian waded into the river, showing great skill in maintaining his balance despite the slippery banks, the thick clinging mud and places of unexpected depth.

'More to the left!' Chaitan shouted, as Bamian probed with his extended limbs for the true way. Yin beat furiously on his drum, Yan gargled inarticulately, both pointing to the right.

A naked figure, with long matted hair, appeared on the far bank. His withered right arm was set in a permanently raised position. Within his cupped hand grew a sacred *champaka* plant. His uncut talons had pierced his palm and grown through to the other side of his hand.

'All is illusion! All is illusion!' he chanted. 'Your souls are stuck fast in the mud of illusion. Your cart is like the material body; your bullocks are the senses; the reins are the mind; intelligence is the driver, and the passenger is the soul. All is illusion!'

'Here is the place to cross, *sadhuji*,' Bamian said. 'See, I am a dwarf and the water only comes up to my waist.'

'Life is a bubble,' intoned the holy man. He stepped forward and disappeared with a splash. First to reappear was the *champaka* plant, followed by the hirsute face which chanted the words. 'All is illusion!' as it drifted downstream.

'In that case,' Bamian called after him, 'you've nothing to worry about. You haven't really fallen in and you're not really heading for some rapids.'

I was glad to observe that he was broadminded in his persecution of holy men, and distributed his disfavours on all of them alike.

Bamian found the crossing-place. A cheer went up. Laying a stick to their rumps, Chaitan urged the bullocks forward.

'*Hut*! *Hut*! *Hut jao*!'

The heavy wooden cart did not move.

'A broad shoulder needed at the back!' piped the boy. All eyes turned to Dadu.

'Well now, if it was anything but a shoulder, I'd be your man . . . but . . . well, it's this old wound, you see. Being at the forefront of the fray as usual, I received a severe blow and . . .'

'I'll go!' It was Frog, his face a pasty grey and twitching.

'No, Frog! For God's sake! I'd rather go myself!'

He regarded me with a sad, twisted smile. 'It is for God's sake that I do it. In all the other gifts of God we cannot glorify ourselves because they are not ours, but of God. But on the cross of tribulation and affliction can we glory, because this is ours.'

Crossing himself, he pushed me aside and strode into the river. Shamefacedly, Dadu followed. They applied their weight to the wheels.

'*Shabash*!' Dadu yelled, by way of encouragement. '*Shabash*!'

'*Sursum corda*!' panted Frog.

'*Hut jao*!' urged Chaitan.

And the old cart lurched out of the mud on to firmer ground. Wild-eyed and shuddering, Frog gained the far bank. Arms waving and flapping, letting out shrill cries, he charged down the road. When we caught up with him he was sitting at the side of the road with his legs straight out in front of him. His body was rigid, his eyes tight shut. Ramananda ejected a gobbet of betel-juice and looked down on Frog from his perch in the cart.

'Today there is a disposition of five planets in quincuncial aestivation; and today the moon rose in the mansion of Purnavasu and the sun's ingress into Pushya is come. Listen to one who studies the augural art. Punctures of the skin received at this time must be treated with the utmost care. Now, I can let you have an ointment . . . for a fee, of course . . . which will . . .'

I waved an arm in the direction of the laden donkey. 'For all your nebulous and abstruse books, you were no nearer to divining that the cart would get stuck than this animal was.'

Ramananda exposed his red teeth in what was meant to be an ingratiating smile. 'You and I practise arts which have much in common.' His tone was half wheedling, half conspiratorial. 'To observe the sky is as delicate a task as to observe the human body. To cast the horoscope of a newly born child just as perilous as to make a diagnosis; to interpet the cosmic symptom just as hard as to interpret those of our own organism. In both instances the chances of error are infinite.'

A pool of red juice, which had been accumulating in the trough of his lower lip, overflowed and ran down his chin. Angrily I denied any affinity whatever between his deceitful necromancing ways and the Art.

'It would seem to me,' said Bamian, dodging the donkey as it kicked out in fright, 'it would seem to me that you both have one thing in common. The calculator who claims to determine the moment of death and the physician who claims to avert it both receive patronage based on fear and anxiety.' He looked at Frog. 'And the same is true of religion.'

He seemed delighted to have annoyed all three of us with the one remark.

Frog opened his eyes. 'I'll trust in God, not in the stars!'

He groaned and averted his gaze from his legs. I sat down beside him. There were leeches between his toes, on the veins of his calf, behind his knees, in his groin. I told him all I knew about these parasites, with which, as a doctor, I had had a long and close acquaintance. I explained their hermaphroditic reproduction, their method of propulsion, their excretory system and mode of breathing. I talked of their sense organs. To them, I said, it was not a world of colour, shape, sound or smell, but of vibrations and subtle variations in temperature. As a student, I had kept a box of them in my room and had conducted a few experiments. I am led to think, although I have no absolute proof, that perhaps their bodies are rather like our tongues, receiving manifold taste sensations.

Presently Frog opened his eyes again and looked closely at the leeches. 'Thomas, I find I loathe them less with my eyes than I do with my imagination. See, there are twelve of them altogether. I shall name them after the Apostles.' He summoned up a wan smile. 'This one shall be Simon Peter, for he was the first.'

Two bends in the river went by. Frog was pale. The leeches, by contrast, were swelling and blushing like ripening plums. Bamian had removed the leeches from Mohini by applying to their backs red-hot embers from the brazier which was kept constantly on the smoulder in the rear of the cart. Several times Dadu offered to perform the same service for Frog. But the monk would have none of it. Whether it was a penance, or whether he was trying to conquer his revulsion, I was not sure. Anyway, I thought it best to divert his mind to other things.

'Frog, do you remember the old cider press at Farmer Turton's?'

'Ah! I'd trade all the luscious fruits of the East for one crisp Devon apple!'

I translated for the benefit of Bamian and Dadu who were beside us.

'What is "apple"?' Dadu asked.

'It's like a big pl —' I began. 'That is, it's like a peach without a stone.'

'Harder,' said Frog.

'And a different colour.'

'Tastes different, too.' Frog was smiling.

'I see,' said Dadu.

Frog raised his cassock and forced himself to take another look at the leeches. 'The twelve Apostles were commanded to go forth and spread the gospel,' he said, and launched into a sermon.

Mohini was trying in vain to coax her listless baby to suckle at her breast. Tears ran down her cheeks. By some quirk of feminine illogicality, Mohini continued, at one and the same time, both to be desperately worried and to believe the optimistic horoscope cast by Ramananda. At first Prajapathi had been like one of Frog's leeches, sucking ardently and tenaciously, letting go only when replete and overcome by sleep. Now he hardly took any nourishment at all. And the small quantity of milk that he did imbibe he immediately vomited up again. A week ago he had tipped the scales against both volumes of *De Fabrica*, Dadu's left shoe, two buttons and a leaf. Yesterday he barely outweighed Volume One.

'Prajapathi must drink something,' I said. 'The human body needs liquids. If he is rejecting milk, try a little warm water.'

She seemed not to hear. She walked past me and held up her baby to Ramananda. 'His skin is hot to the touch. He wastes away.'

Ramananda's eyes glittered avariciously. 'This amulet, worn till the moon hath waxed once more, will ward off the unpropitious influences that Saturn, long in rising, doth cast upon the boy.'

Mohini untied her last silver coin from a knot in her sari. I interposed myself between the simple girl and the red-toothed charlatan.

'You would do much better to listen to one trained in the honest Art of medicine.'

Ramananda waved the amulet enticingly.

I said: 'My advice is free.'

Mohini hesitated between the two of us, then took the amulet. Ramananda leered at me triumphantly. I longed to grind his smug features under the heel of my boot. How could Mohini turn to him rather than to me? I felt Bamian tugging at my belt. His tone was wry.

'My friend, I learnt long ago that it is the peculiarity of ignorance to prefer the unknown, the concealed, the fabulous, the wonderful, even the terrible, to that which is clear, simple and true.'

'So it seems, Bamian. The more mysterious a belief, the better it pleases the imagination.'

'The very pith and nub of it, Khoratji! And, likewise, the more incredible a belief, the more men pride themselves on their faith in believing it!'

Mohini was eagerly fitting the amulet to Prajapathi's stick-like arm. Before birth, I would have said the chances of Prajapathi reaching adulthood were about five or six to one. What were they now? I thought of my own brothers and sisters, all dead. Giles, Henry, Henrietta, Margaret. Names in the family Bible, tiny head-stones in the churchyard, deep lines on my mother's face. Can we ever eat the bread of indifference? My mother's grief was no less – perhaps even greater – for Margaret than for Giles.

Dadu turned to Mohini. 'I have often heard it said that disease is cured by cutting a rope the same length as the patient and tying a knot in it.' He seized the knotted rope round Frog's waist. 'Why, here is the cure ready made!' And he slashed at it with his knife.

Frog let out a yell of rage. 'You've cut off my vow of chastity!'

'Is that all?' laughed Dadu. 'From the fuss you're making, I thought at least I'd cut off . . .' He looked at the length of rope with a knot below it like a testicle. 'No, on second thoughts, I doubt if yours would be as big as this.'

Six women, carrying baskets of live chickens, prevented Frog's spluttering fuse from reaching the point of explosion. Dadu picked out the fattest of the six.

'*Shabash*! Here's a plump little bird ready for plucking and stuffing.' He prodded a chicken with one finger and her with another. 'Would you be requiring the services of a rooster, by any chance?'

She hurried on, head in air.

'How much further to Muttra?' I enquired of her retreating back.

'A hundred *gaukos*, or so' was the reply over a neat shoulder.

'Precisely what is a *gaukos*?' I asked. At Padua we had been taught to be very exact about measurement.

Dadu shrugged. 'It is the distance that a cow's bellow can be heard.'

I would have liked to know if the age, size and gender of the animal was stipulated, if there was an adjustment for the strength and direction of the wind, and on what acuteness of ear such a measurement was based. But Frog was telling of the Last Supper, and all attention was on him.

'Take, eat; this is my body. And He took the cup and gave thanks, and gave it to them saying, "Drink ye all of it, for this is my blood . . ."'

A leech, satisfied and swollen, detached itself from Frog's leg and was squashed beneath the wheels of the cart.

'Sounds like the Aghori!' Chaitan said with a shudder. The Aghori are fanatical holy men, who live in the cremation grounds, existing on the flesh of dead bodies.

At this point the river Yamuna and the imperial highway once more joined company. Thirty yards offshore a boat, its dark red sails empty of wind, drifted downstream. Its cargo sparkled in the sun. Yin and Yan pounded their drums in excitement.

'Diamonds!' exclaimed Chaitan.

'Salt!' said Bamian in a bellow reminiscent of cow separated from its calf.

Dadu slapped his thighs with delight. '*Baraf*!' he announced, banging their two heads together. 'It is ice for the Mogul court. Ice from the eternal snows of the Hima Alaya. I have heard tell it takes a hundred days to bring it down the sacred Mother Ganges, across the doab to the Yamuna and by boat again to Agra.'

The dancers ran to the river edge, marvelling at this phenomenon, Bamian bouncing like a rabbit, appearing and reappearing above the tall wild flowers. Gampopa, who remained seated on the cart, was coughing gently – a sign that he was emerging from his opium dreams. I watched Mohini moving through waist-high poppies, carrying Prajapathi in her arms. Blood-red poppies, dark red sails, pink sandstone cliffs, the purples in her sari, the honey of her skin – and her black despair which lent sharp poignancy to the beauty of the scene.

'Of course,' Dadu was saying, 'we shall never know the blissful coolness that ice can bring. Its use is a privilege bestowed only on members of the Mogul court.'

They stared with curiosity at what, in this incarnation at least, was so utterly unattainable as to be beyond envy.

'How far to Muttra?' Gampopa called across the water.

The boatman ignored him. Gampopa called again. The boatman puffed out his chest. 'In the name of Allah, what business have I with the likes of you? It is an important personage whom you address. Have you not heard that the empire depends upon the ice which I carry? For justice has a cool brow and wise laws were never penned by clammy hands.' Emboldened by the water between us, he added: 'I do not chose to answer you carters and labourers, you low-caste members of the Hindu subject races.'

Gampopa sprang to his feet. 'Low-caste! We are dancers! Do you know nothing, you ignorant, insolent person? Low-caste indeed!'

The boatman was saved from further abuse by the onset of another coughing fit. There was a rustling in the pile of straw at the stern of the boat. A familiar shiny bald head popped up.

'Honourable sirs,' said the stowaway, 'I am Bag Lal, a devout Hindu. I dissociate myself utterly, most utterly from this rude Muslim fellow.'

With a grunt, the boatman picked up Bag Lal and flung him overboard. Bag Lal clung with skinny arms to the side.

'I'll drown! Don't let me drown! Oh, please!'

As soon as the boatman prised away one finger, another clamped

fast to the gunwale. The boatman hammered at Bag Lal's knuckles
with the edge of an oar, shouting:

'You bodmashi, you good-for-nothing old goat. You lazy, shiftless
Hindu!'

And he hammered even harder at Bag Lal's knuckles. The old man
screamed, but hung on.

'Please! Please! I don't want to dr —'

A smile slowly spread over Bag Lal's face. He let go and stood up.
The next moment the boat ran aground.

'Well, don't just stand there, you useless bag of skin and bone! Get
to the stern and start pushing!'

With great dignity, Bag Lal adjusted the loin cloth he had some-
how acquired, turned his back on the boatman and walked over the
water towards us. The effect was spoilt by the sandbank's coming to
an end and his sudden disappearance. He came up splashing and
spluttering. The current caught him and carried him into even deeper
water. The scene was so like the one we had witnessed with the holy
man that I had a strong sensation of seeing the same play for a second
time, only it was on a different stage and with different actors.
Smaller wheels were turning within the larger wheels.

'Help! Help! Somebody save me!'

Frog had always been the best swimmer among us Honiton lads.
He plunged in, grasped the frail, struggling body and towed it ashore.
As Bag Lal's feet touched ground, his cries of alarm were renewed
with even greater vigour.

'Untouchable! Untouchable!' he screeched.

Gampopa lashed at Rani and Rati so that the cart lurched down
the road, Mohini fled screaming along the bank holding Prajapathi,
Dadu, with Bamian tucked under his arm, darted into the trees, while
Yin and Yan, trying to rush in different directions, bumped into each
other and toppled into a ditch. Frog, dripping and pleased with
himself, brought Bag Lal to dry land.

'Oh dear, oh my goodness!' wailed Bag Lal. 'It is a very impious act
I have performed!'

As an untouchable, outside the caste system, he explained, it was
his duty as a devout Hindu to keep his distance from caste members
and call out warnings of his presence.

'I am a Karaga,' he quavered, 'a most utterly untouchable person.

74

Oh dear, now I must atone by making offerings at the temple . . . and offerings cost money.'

The latter thought seemed to cause him more pain than anything that had happened to him so far. He repeated the bit about the money several times, his eyes boring into the purse around my waist.

Frog laid his hand on Bag Lal's arm. 'Why are you untouchable?'

Untouchables, I could see, were being held in reserve in case divine orders concerning the Chota Chua should be revoked for any reason.

'I am untouchable because, in this round of existence, that is the kind of person I was born.'

'I mean, what does a Karaga do that makes him unclean?'

'It is my appointed task in life to slaughter cows and remove their hides and also to eat their meat.'

I said, 'Why don't you stop doing those things and find other work?'

'Oh no, most utterly no. It is my appointed task which I must perform. It is my karma. There is merit to be gained in accepting one's karma . . . just as there is merit in giving to the poor.'

I ignored the hint and said, 'This morning we found you naked and sleeping like the dead. Then you jumped up and ran away.'

He looked at me with rheumy eyes. There was a long pause, during which his lips trembled on the brink of speech.

'They were so young!'

'The Chota Chua?'

Bag Lal nodded and shivered.

'What did they do?'

'Nothing. Nothing at first. I had a big stick. They watched and waited. For three days and nights they waited. If I closed my eyes even for a moment, a hundred pilfering fingers were on me. Then I'd start up and lash out and they would retreat – and watch and wait.'

He shivered again and I wrapped my cloak around him.

'I fell asleep in the end, of course. They took all I had.' His eyes were on my purse again.

'And was it they who hurt your leg?' Frog enquired.

'Ah! Sleep is a wonderful thing,' said Bag Lal.

'Tell us about your legs,' I said. 'How were they injured?'

'I don't remember. All I remember is yearning for sleep.'

'Do they give pain?' I asked.

75

'This one does.' He pointed to the bandaged leg.

He blew his nose with his fingers, carefully depositing the results thereof into a little brass vessel dangling from his neck, lest he defile someone with his snot. He gave a toothless cackle. 'If they hadn't seen me spitting into it, they'd have taken that too.'

Over Bag Lal's shoulder I could see the boatman shoving and sweating to no avail.

'Your companions,' said Bag Lal, 'dancers did I hear they are?'

'Yes.'

'Let me see now . . . I can pollute a Brahmin at three hundred feet, so . . . what kind of dancers are they?'

'They are Rajput dancers,' I said, not sure whether this was useful information or not.

'Ah, then they are a sub-caste of the Kshatirya or warrior caste.' He rolled his eyes and counted on his toes. 'Two hundred and seventy-five feet, I think, would be a fitting distance.' So saying, Bag Lal tottered down the highway, counting out the paces. 'One hundred and ninety-nine, two hundred . . . Do you know, I met an outcaste the other day who could only pollute a Brahmin at ninety feet. Poor fellow, I made him feel inferior, I can tell you . . . Two hundred and one, two hundred and . . .'

I reminded him that he still had my cloak. He relinquished it with a crestfallen air. I threw him a coin.

'We are all in your debt, old man. Brother Peter's polluting distance was well over three hundred feet till you induced him to take a plunge.'

Our companions – all twelve of them, not forgetting Prajapathi, Ali the tapeworm and Rani and Rati the bullocks – returned to where Frog and I stood. The Muslim boatman threw a rope ashore.

'You! In the name of the Emperor Akbar, I command you to tie the rope to your oxen and pull me clear!'

'You can stay there all day, for all we care!' Gampopa jeered.

'And all night!' added Ramananda.

'You can stay till you rot!' came Chaitan's treble, and Gampopa gave him an approving pat on the head.

The sun was higher. Dadu, now the accepted authority on anything remotely connected with ice, said, 'The ice-boats are only supposed to ferry their cargo at night, or in the cool of the early morning. There's a string of depots where the ice is stored in deep wells at the end of each stage.'

The boatman began to weep. His ice was melting before his eyes. 'In the name of Allah the Merciful, I implore you, I beg you . . .'

Rani swished her tail and released a jet of urine. Gampopa seized an earthenware jar, leapt nimbly from the cart and collected the offering. Another leech rolled off Frog. Gampopa squashed it with his bare heel, coughed violently and spilt half the contents of the jar down his leg before he could seal it.

'Chaitan, my peach,' he wheezed, 'fetch a wafer of dung from the back.'

It was one of Chaitan's duties to collect any droppings from Rani or Rati and dry them out for fuel. Gampopa made a parcel of the round cake with the waxy plantain leaves which we used as plates. He tied the parcel and the jar to the end of the rope and threw them into the water.

'Drink the wine of humility, eat the bread of repentance, and I will pull you off.'

'Never! Never!'

'Well,' said Gampopa, rubbing his hands and cackling with undisguised malice, 'this seems like a pleasant spot for our midday exercises.'

The dancers sat in a circle in the shade of a tall *nim* tree, their feet tucked in the lotus position. Gampopa sat on a Persian rug – a woven garden in the dust; blossom, fruit and flower for ever at the perfection of their beauty, like a foretaste of paradise. Dappled shadows played over their bodies and faces as they swayed to the gently tapping drums of Yin and Yan. First came the eye exercises. They had smeared a type of clarified butter on their eyeballs. With thumb and second finger holding their eyes as wide open as possible, they rolled, darted and slid their eyes with amazing mobility, minds inwardly concentrated.

Outside the circle, Rani and Rati wandered free, chewing leaves from the lower branches in preference to the dry, coarse grass. I, too, browsed, but on Versalius' *De Humanis Corporis Fabrica*, lingering on the superb drawings of the heart. Frog, weakened by his blood-letting, dozed beneath the cart. Dadu and Ramananda picked their noses, scratched themselves and bickered over a game of *nard*, using pebbles and lines drawn in the dust – a game which appeared to be a close relative of backgammon.

As for the boatman, he alternated between fits of ranting and bouts of pitiful sobbing as his blocks of ice gradually shrank. Slowly he hauled on the rope, drawing the dung and the urine to the side of his boat. He touched them, then recoiling like one stung, flung them back into the water.

'I shall be flogged, I shall be disgraced!' he wailed. Again he pulled in the jar and the packet. This time he opened the jar and sniffed before revulsion overcame him once more.

'Drink it up like a good little boy!' Bamian coaxed in a high falsetto.

'May Allah send you to eternal torment!'

'I am afraid that will not be possible. I am already in demand at a rival establishment. However, if you care to supply me with an inventory of the tortures and other horrors on offer, I might consider giving my custom to Allah instead of Jehovah.'

The boatman only groaned.

The exercises continued. The eyes, the neck and then the hands.

'Gesture is the soul of dance,' Gampopa said, as he led them in the *mudras*, the ancient and traditional hand symbols of Indian dance. First with single hand – *ardha-chandra*, the half-moon; *chandra-kala*, the crescent moon; the swan wing, the lotus bud, the peacock. Then came the gestures with combined hands – the *anjali* salutation, the dove, the eagle god, the flower basket, and *pataka* with all fingers extended, representing Indra's banner-staff.

'Again! Again!' Gampopa demanded, ever striving for perfection.

'Where the hand moves, there the eyes follow; where the eyes go the mind follows; where the mind goes the mood follows; and where the mood goes there the *rasa*, the flavour, the feelings, the emotions arise.'

Melted water was visibly running off the ice. Again the boat-man returned to the packet and the jar. As if holding an immense weight, he lifted the jar to his lips. Gampopa made a sign to Yin and Yan. The drums stopped. All eyes turned to the Muslim. He took a sip and gagged.

'All of it!' commanded Gampopa.

Shivering and sobbing, the wretched man took a deep breath and downed it in one gulp.

'*Shabash*!' cried Dadu.

Gampopa was merciless. 'Now the other!'

Moaning in his degradation, the man chewed and choked his way through the dry cow-dung. No sooner had he finished than, the weight of the ice now being considerably less, the boat floated free. Unadulterated hate and fury screamed out of the man. He snatched up a matchlock and discharged it at Gampopa. The ball whizzed harmlessly overhead. The man fell backwards in the boat and lay in a swoon, his craft drifting slowly downstream.

Bamian waddled up to me, an amused sneer on his lips. 'See how he tortures himself with his beliefs. It is not ironical that, at certain ceremonies, we Hindus joyfully drink the urine and eat the excrement of the sacred cow, thinking we earn great merit thereby.'

I regarded the dwarf with interest. 'But you don't believe that. What do you believe, Bamian?'

'Remember how we watched the ants the other day, Khoratji?'

'Yes.'

'Well, I think the gods look down on us in much the same way and amuse themselves with our frantic efforts.' He gave a short, hard laugh. 'You and I, Khoratji, we are part of an elaborate practical joke being played on humankind. All we can do is acknowledge the joke and enjoy it as best we can.'

Our motley procession straggled back to the highway. The glare from the white dust was painful to the eyes. Bag Lal followed at the regulation 275 feet behind us. A man was lifting water from a channel into his field.

'Peace be upon you!' he hailed us.

'Upon you be peace!' returned Gampopa.

'*Shabash*!' came Dadu's greeting.

'*Sursum corda*!' Frog called.

'Untouchable! Utterly untouchable!' cried Bag Lal, leaving the highway to avoid passing too close to the man and wading knee-deep through the mud of the paddy fields.

*

79

Ahead of us, in the shade of a mango grove, a garlanded group in festive mood were gathered.

'It's a wedding!' Dadu announced.

Our pace quickened. Weddings, the world over, are a free entertainment not to be missed. Only Mohini, normally the most excitable of beings, lagged behind. She carried her baby in her arms all the time now. Her eyes seldom left his face.

A jasmine bush was being transplanted beside a mango tree. A saffron-robed Brahmin was chanting invocations, solemnly joining the two in marriage. Frog snorted and proclaimed in a loud voice:

'I cannot but admire the goodness of our Creator in illuminating us with the light of His Gospel. For here you see the unruliness of the human mind, its puerile absurdities and coarse imaginings when abandoned to its own devices.'

'Hush, Frog! As a physician, I do earnestly advise you that such words are harmful to the health.'

'How so?'

'They will beat us with sticks if they hear you.'

The ceremony reached its climax, the two trees were invested with silver threads and hung with garlands. The guests and onlookers were showered with sweets covered in silver beaten to the finest leaf imaginable. Dadu crunched them in his mouth with relish, but the sharp, metallic sensation on my tongue was not to my liking. The wine of the *todi*-palm flowed generously; the musicians – hired, it would seem, more for their enthusiasm than for their skill – let forth a cacophony of clashing brass, blaring wind and thudding drums. Fireworks fizzed and exploded overhead. The noise was deafening.

I observed a man nearby. His facial muscles were in contraction, drawing his lips away from his teeth; skin flushed, pectoral muscles and diaphragm in spasm, head thrown back; the cry emitted from his mouth was inaudible in the din. Then I saw Mohini. She was on her knees. Her symptoms were exactly the same as the man's. Only it was not laughter which caused her condition. In her arms was the lifeless form of Prajapathi.

The host was annoyed. It was the height of ill manners, he declared, intruding with her grief on his celebration. She was hurried away.

What angered me was her gratitude. She was grateful that the gods had allowed her baby to die so near the sacred river. His ashes would float down the Yamuna into the Ganges and on, eventually to be united with the great soul of the ocean. And she was grateful to Gampopa. She had begged for firewood and he had grudgingly let her take some from the stock in the cart.

'Just a little, then. You shouldn't need very much.'

We gathered silently round the pyre. Behind us fireworks whizzed and banged and revellers cheered and laughed and called drunkenly to one another. Mohini seemed remote from it all. Numb. The pain would come. Mother and child are of one body. For the one to lose the other is a severe amputation.

I said: 'You are young, you can hope for another child.'

'Hope!' roared Bamian. 'Do not utter that obscenity! Hope is the bait that ensnares us.' He spat into the flames. 'And the way the gods keep hope alive, keep their bait fresh in this world, is to change its population as often as possible. Man's only hope of freedom is to be without hope.'

The smoke swirled in eddies, making our eyes water. Cry, Mohini, cry. Lance that swelling abcess in your soul. Scream, shout, rage against the gods, fight back. But don't look at me with eyes so reminiscent of Mary's.

The forest stirred with night-time noises, rustlings and sharp cries, as predator and prey fulfilled their appointed roles. We sat round a fire, a different fire, shrouded in our thoughts. Mohini was like a wooden doll, stiff-backed, staring into the flames.

'Time for a story,' Bamian said, adding another branch to the blaze. 'My story concerns a great khan, a mighty emperor. This powerful monarch was never seen by his subjects, for he lived in a palace surrounded by a deep moat and never emerged. His ministers, however, were loud in extolling the virtues of their master. The happiness of his subjects, they said, was his greatest desire. Yet everywhere his subjects groaned under oppression. His laws, they claimed, were unparalleled in their wisdom. Yet they were such a tissue of contradictions that the ministers quarrelled constantly about their meaning. His ministers boasted of his justice, yet the most deserving of his subjects were generally the least favoured. Indeed, as if ambition, avarice, cruelty and vengeance did not have enough natural impetuosity of their own, their flames were fanned by the justice and religion of the land. The foresight of the king was amazing, said the ministers; yet he prevented nothing. Finally, his subjects rebelled against him. The king, who in truth was mad, put to death the innocent heir to the throne, who had taken no part in the rebellion. His ministers, of course . . .'

Frog rose with an oath, seized the dwarf by the lapels of his jackal-skin coat and shook him. He made the mistake of lifting him too high, received a butt in the face from Bamian's bulbous head and released him with a grunt. Bamian fell sprawling in the fire, setting the hairs on his coat alight. He sprang out, rolling over and over in the dust till he had stopped smouldering. Frog clutched his eye, breathing hard, then strode into the darkness of the forest.

A jackal howled. The circle drew closer.

'And now I'll tell you a story!'

We all jumped. But the voice from the shadows was only Bag Lal.

I fingered the locket round my neck and watched the firelight flickering on Mohini's face.

' . . . and so the swan granted the raja's wish, and from thenceforth his son was blessed as one who has the moon on his forehead and the stars in the palm of his hand.' And Bag Lal led the age-old refrain:

'Thus my story endeth, thus the tree doth wither.'

'Why O tree dost thou wither?' came the response from around the fire.

'Thy cow on me browseth.'

'Why O cow dost thou browse?' chorused young and old alike.

'My child doth cry.'

'O child, why dost thou cry?'

'The ant doth me sting.'

'Why O ant dost thou sting?'

Tears were running down Mohini's face. She lay on the ground and sobbed uncontrollably. I longed to draw her to me and comfort her. But I observed the proprieties, sat where I was and did nothing. It was Bamian, crouching beside her in his singed fur, who stroked her hair and caressed her with his words.

Ramananda ejected a stream of chewed betel-nut.

'Now I'll cast your horoscopes . . . for a fee, of course.'

82

'We shall hear more fiction from you, I'll warrant, than in any story told tonight,' I said.

An angry retort froze on his lips. From the darkness of the woods something moaned, rising and falling. Exchanging fearful glances, the circle huddled closer.

Bag Lal stuttered out, 'If . . . if thou art an . . . an evil spirit, or perhaps a forest demon, we are but simple folk.'

The thing, whatever it was, moaned on: 'Hail Mary, Mother of God, full of grace . . .'

Dumb Yin stuffed the tail of his turban into his mouth. And deaf Yan, knowing there was something to be frightened of, but not what it was, covered his ears with his hands.

'*Pater noster, quies in caelis, sanctificatur nomen tuum, adveniat regnum tuum . . .*'

'It is a tortured soul,' I said. 'I know this kind. It will not harm you.'

They talked in whispers after that. The fire burned low. Jackals howled in the distance. Chaitan whimpered in his sleep. Mohini's crying was softer now. From Dadu's direction there was an explosion of laughter. 'The sort that chases every bitch on heat!'

And the tortured soul prayed and cried out in the blackness of the night.

Five

Prick Frog with a sharp-pointed argument and the miles unwind of their own accord. Questioning Galen's traditional authority on matters of anatomy is worth a good five miles in any weather.

'So you cannot fail to see, my dear Frog, how absurd it is . . .' – I raised my voice against the passing of a bullock cart – 'how absurd of the Church to support theories patched together more than a thousand years ago.'

'I see nothing of the sort! Galen's works are upheld by every respectable doctor in England.'

'They dare not say otherwise for fear of losing more than their respectability.' Servetus had dared. The smoke from his burning still clouded the vision of our profession. 'I have grave doubts, Frog, as to whether Galen ever saw a human dissection. Take, for instance, his description of the coccyx. It is accurate as far as monkeys are concerned, but . . .'

'Dr Dee, the queen's own physician, mark you, has made public his opinion that Galen cannot be faulted.'

'Him! What does he know of anatomy? He has never made a cut upon a man, or any other animal, come to that . . . except at the dinner table!'

Three horsemen overtook us at a gallop, enveloping us in their dust.

'When the medical schools do their loathsome and unnatural . . .' Frog breathed too hard in his excitement and choked on the dust. 'I repeat, when they do their loathsome and unnatural business on the corpses of criminals, how is it that Galen is always found to be correct in what he says about the human body? Answer me that, Master Coryat . . . or do Paduans have a different, no doubt superior, anatomy from the rest of us?'

I strode ahead angrily. What did he expect? In the English universities and medical schools, on the rare occasions that they did dissections, it was done solely to demonstrate and confirm Galen's texts. They saw only what they were looking for.

There was something different about the way Mohini was walking. There was no baby on her back. Stripped of the mantle of motherhood, she seemed pathetically young. Another cart trundled towards us, the driver asleep in the rear. Standing on tiptoe, Bamian reached up to the bullock's head and led it round in a circle, sending it plodding patiently back the way it had come.

'*Shabash*!' chortled Dadu, slapping his thighs in approval.

When Frog caught up with me, I reminded him of the time the stone-cutters had come to Honiton — men who claimed to cure disorders of the mind by extracting stones from the head. Quantities of blood and several black and greenish stones were produced for all to see; and there was no lack of people to cry out what a cure there had been. But I, for one, did not observe any improvement in the poor simpletons and melancholics who had been given into their hands. It was one of these stone-cutters who sold Frog an ancient bone, swearing it to be the collar-bone of Saint Anthony himself. In vain did I invite Frog to consider the likeness of his precious relic to the hind legs of various mammals. He simply averted his eyes and went on believing what he wanted. Even in those days Frog showed his potential as a good churchman.

'It was the collar-bone of St Anthony!' Frog protested.

'It is possible, I grant you, that those rogues had a dog by that name!'

A line of camels swayed up behind us laden with rock-salt. Foul-smelling, yellow-toothed, flea-ridden beasts.

'*Kidder jata*?' I called.

'From Multan, bound for Delhi, may the Lord Krishna walk beside you.'

Dadu trotted beside the leading camel. 'What news of Shershan's rebels and of the army led by Ghulam Khan?' We had heard conflicting reports all day.

'Ask the Chota Chua, they know best.'

'And where are they?'

'Not here, praise be to Ganesha, the remover of all obstacles.'

Flocks of cranes passed overhead, moving south. They had been arriving for nearly a month now, from the lands of Tartary and the mountains of Kashmir.

'Now listen, Frog. Surely you see that, if the Church hadn't banned dissections, Galen would undoubtedly have been proved wrong on many points. Why, Fabrizzio at Padua says –'

'Dissection is wicked, blasphemous and ungodly! And there's an end to it!'

A grizzled old scarecrow, bent under the weight of a wet buffalo-skin tight with water, ambushed us with cries of 'The gift of God! The gift of God! Cool, clean water!'

'Unclean! Unclean!' shrilled Bag Lal from the back of our procession.

'*Pani*! *Pani*! *Penika pani*!' croaked the scarecrow, sidling up to us. Frog elbowed him aside and quickened his pace.

'I repeat, Thomas, it is not for man to trespass on God's divine mysteries.'

The water-seller had loosened the skin's wooden stopper and was letting a few drops run enticingly down the outside. 'Four long miles to the next well, good sirs, four miles!'

'And I say, Frog, that God gave us eyes and enquiring minds to use.'

'Trust the Lord with all thine heart and lean not unto thine own understanding – Proverbs, three, five.'

'It is reason I shall trust with all my heart.'

'The truths of religion are beyond reason.'

'Those truths, then, were not made for reasonable beings.'

'Take care, Thomas! Those who set reason above faith and divine illumination stray into corruption and disaster.'

The water-seller bobbed up between us. 'The gift of God! *Pani*! *Penika pani*! Four long miles, good sirs!'

'Unclean! Unclean!'

'Then it would seem, Brother Peter, that faith is like a pill ... to be swallowed whole. And, like a pill, if chewed is cast up without effect.'

We rounded a rocky outcrop and saw, not thirty yards away, a well.

'A rod for the knave's back!' Frog roared, flailing his staff and chasing the old man down the road, causing Bag Lal to plunge up to his neck in a stagnant green pool to avoid defiling the august personage of the fleeing scarecrow.

A pair of bullocks worked a creaking windlass over the well. Their hooves, treading an endless circle, had worn a deep rut. A full goatskin squeaked to the surface and sloshed into an irrigation ditch. We drank deeply. In a nearby tree a monkey scratched itself and masturbated. Dadu flung a stone at it which struck the animal with such force that it fell from the tree.

'*Shabash*! That reminds me of a time in the Bikaner campaign when we were ambushed . . . or was it the Kashmir campaign . . . no, I tell a lie, it was the . . .'

I watched the onset of rigor mortis in the monkey. Gampopa too observed with a keen eye the way the limbs curled in death. Frog had fallen asleep, his Bible – still a fearsomely noisome object – open at the Book of Genesis. On the page, a grasshopper was devouring its mate.

' . . . and it took four whole days, from dawn till dusk, to behead all the prisoners . . .'

Dadu sighed rapturously as an enormously fat woman billowed, like a galleon in full sail, towards the well. She carried a brass pot under her arm. 'I will hold your pitcher for you, my beauty. I refer to the miraculous pitcher that holds water mouth downwards. And I could lend you a bucket, a big bucket, one to drop deep into your well.'

She ignored him. Dadu chuckled. 'We're not having much luck, are we, Ali? Anyway, as I was saying . . . about the prisoners . . . Ghulam Khan was annoyed when he heard about it, I can tell you . . . You see, some of them were Muslims . . .'

I remembered the corpses floating down the Yamuna, and the victory tower of heads. Already the beetles had discovered the eyes and open mouth of the dead monkey. Is our planet nothing more than an abattoir where life slaughters life?

The bullocks ambled round and round, round and round; and the creaking of the windlass mingled with the cries of partridge and peafowl in the fields. Chaitan sat astride Rani and drummed his heels against her ribs.

'*Hut jao!*'

And we meandered once more through the flat landscape.

*

It was a source of wonder to me that, in the land of the Mogul, two harvests could be reaped in the same year from the same piece of ground.

'You would think, Frog, that the villagers here would be better fed than in England, yet there does not seem to be much difference.'

'When the rains fail there is famine,' Dadu said. 'Do they often fail in your country?'

'No, Dadu, but the frosts sometimes come too early.'

'It is war, oppression, avarice and other human follies prompted by the Devil that causes men to want in a land of plenty.'

'I like it best when the crops are tall,' Dadu mused. 'At other times it can be difficult to find somewhere to make love, particularly with the married ones.'

Bamian, passing a mile or two on his wicker legs for practice, stooped and transferred my broad-brimmed hat to his own head. He thrust his hands behind his back and assumed a pensive expression, which set the group tittering.

'Here is Dr Bamian's diagnosis,' he announced. 'Firstly, I must warn you all of a most dangerous plague and infection sweeping the land, called lack of money – for which the surest cure is dishonesty.' He prodded Ramananda with a stick. 'The tenderest part of your anatomy, I diagnose, is your purse, and I recommend you relieve the swelling therein with a little charity . . . As for your swelling, Dadu my friend, that recurring swelling between your legs . . .'

'Ah! I have discovered a cure for that!' Dadu laughed.

Bamian turned to Frog. 'Here we have a severe case of the Sacred Disease, the symptoms of which are bigotry and intolerance.'

'What about me?' Chaitan asked.

'Poor boy, you have an uncurable condition contracted at birth.'

'Wh-what is it?'

'It is called mortality.'

'Oh,' said Chaitan, and laughed in the hope that it was a joke.

'And you, Khoratji,' Bamian said, replacing the hat on my head, 'it is the sharpness of your mind that gives an edge to your pain. This doctor prescribes a large pill of indifference, coated with laughter and washed down by the wine of absurdity.'

Dadu drew his massive sword. 'Talking of things sharp . . . here is a sharp medicine that can put an end to any suffering.' He swished it in close proximity to Bamian's elongated legs.

'And now it's high time I cut you down to size!'

'Don't you dare!'

Dadu chased Bamian about the road, contriving a series of narrow misses with his flashing blade. They stopped. Drawn by fifty oxen with red-tasselled horns, a vast wagon, a palace on wheels, lumbered clear of the trees. Its golden dome blazed in the sun. Surrounding it were richly turbaned horsemen. Immediately they spurred their mounts and, brandishing knotted whips, galloped hard at us.

'Avert your eyes, insolent dogs!' trilled a eunuch's voice.

Our group scattered, plunging into the woods beside the highway, a twelve-foot-tall dwarf leading the charge. Mohini tripped and fell. She crouched, covering her face as thongs slashed across her head and back.

'Clear the way! Clear the way!'

Leaning from his saddle, a eunuch dealt her another blow. I dragged him to the ground and smashed my knee into his face. Unsheathing my sword, I lunged at an oncoming horseman, causing him to swerve aside, gaining time for Mohini to crawl to safety. Then strong arms held me from behind. My companions had vanished or were crouching with their backs turned to the highway and their eyes covered.

'Strip the infidel! Beat him till he howls like a dog, then beat him some more!'

'The wheel might be a better lesson!'

On several of the vehicle's nine-foot-high wheels, bodies were spreadeagled.

'Wait!' A sumptuously gowned man on a bay gelding waved a ringed and scented hand in my direction. 'The pleasure of teaching this low-born scum a little respect must be deferred. The Princess Razziya commands his presence.'

I was dragged to the side of the domed wagon to where a carved ivory balcony protruded. The heavy curtains of embroidered cloth stirred slightly.

'Mount, stranger. One so far from his homeland arouses my curiosity.'

The voice was husky, yet melodious. I swept off my hat and made my best bow. A servant placed steps for me. I mounted the balcony. Two eunuchs stood guard. The curtains stirred again, releasing waves of perfume into the hot, still air.

'Tell me of Belait,' she said, by which I understood her to mean Europe.

I was angry. I replied, 'In Englestan honest travellers are not treated like rogues and vagabonds.'

A low, husky laugh floated through the curtain. 'You are as foolhardy as you are handsome. Take care. The ways of India are jealous ways. I am a high-born Mogul princess. It is not permitted for even the shadow of common man to fall across my path; and to break the privacy of the zenana is certain death. No man may look upon me except my husband.'

I told her that she was mistaken in referring to me as a common man. I was a man of learning, a man of medicine, who had studied the Art in the best school in Europe. Such men were accorded respect in my country, I said. Not true; but that is what I said.

A veiled handmaiden slipped through the curtains to offer me a drink of cool sherbert, on a silver tray. The princess was silent. I sipped my sherbert and wondered if she was looking at me, aware of the two sharp scimitars at the ready and the shabbiness of my clothes.

'I hear that the Queen of Englestan allows herself to be seen by the common people . . . Is that really true?'

'Yes, princess. She most particularly makes a point of doing so.'

'And does this queen of yours have a conveyance as magnificent as this?'

'Gracious princess, I have seen nothing to compare with it. And, from the reports I hear, only the beauty of the lady who sits within it could dazzle me more.'

A clumsy attempt – I am no gallant courtier – moreover, a complete lie, since I had never heard of her before. But it seemed to me as well to please, for I didn't like the way the eunuchs longingly fingered their swords and stared at me.

The Princess Razziya was inquisitive about the clothes, the jewellery and the looks of our good Queen Elizabeth. I did my best, inventing a little here and there.

'I wish to hear you speak in your own tongue,' she said. 'Recite something by one of the poets of your land.'

My mind went blank. The only thing which came into my head was the passage I had been reading the other day from Vesalius' *De Humanis Corporis Fabrica*. Trying to put as much rhythm and passion into my words as possible, I recited: 'After you have investigated the muscles of the neck, the nerves issuing from the dorsal marrow of the neck, and the organs of the body dealing with nutritional vital spirits, I suggest that the head be removed from the body, for one that has been removed can be handled with less difficulty. Heads of decapitated men are much more suitable for this purpose, especially if, through the co-operation of friendly judges and prefects, you can obtain them immediately after the execution, and so scarcely dead.'

Princess Razziya sighed. 'Beautiful! You have a good voice for poetry.'

We talked some more. I told her of my hopes of visiting the great libraries at Agra.

She commented: 'The halls of Akbar's courts are packed with people such as you, seeking favours. You could wait years without your request being heard, let alone granted. It is essential to have the patronage of some high-born person, who can pursue your interest and present your case.'

She sighed for a second time. Apparently my value as a temporary diversion had expired, for she raised her voice to command, 'Drive on! *Juldi*! *Juldi*!'

I was hurried from the balcony and my sword returned to me.

When the huge wagon had rumbled into the distance and its dust settled, the dancers, the astrologer, the monk and the soldier gathered round me, with Bag Lal the untouchable eavesdropping at long-range. Mohini caught my eye and smiled gratefully. Shyly, she lifted one of her lucky charms from round her neck. I do not hold with such superstititous nonsense, yet I did not want to rebuff the girl. I stooped to let her fasten it round my neck. The closeness of her lips, the fragrance of her skin, what should I care that Ramananda had an amused sneer on his face, or that Frog was chuckling gleefully?

'So, who is the Princess Razziya?' I asked.

'She is the senior wife of the great Ghulam Khan, the general of all Akbar's army,' Dadu said. There was awe in his voice.

Mohini sounded more like her usual self. 'They say she is very beautiful. They say she never wears the same dress twice and that she changes her attire three times a day. And they say that, for all that, the general prefers his youngest wife these days.'

'The wagon . . . what do you think it was like inside?' Chaitan whispered, still dazed by the fabulous sight that had passed by. Dadu, who had assumed the role of expert on anything remotely connected with the military, launched into a description of the silken couches, the fine carpets, the full-length baths. As his words took wing and soared into the realm of fantasy, I began to suspect that the closest he had been to the vehicle was this very afternoon.

Presently, Dadu's legs ceased to be the principal feature of the landscape. In the distance a red sandstone fortress rose like a galleon from a sea of linseed in blue flower.

'The town of Muttra lies at its foot,' Dadu informed us. 'I know of a place there – a caravanserai – where we can spend the night. The company is good and it's cheap, that's the main thing, even if the wine is watered and the meat too high for most people's taste.'

'Ah,' said Frog. 'A place where the flesh is strong but the spirit weak.'

We overtook a man who was propelling himself along the road in the fashion of a caterpillar. He would prostrate himself on the ground, then crawl up to the mark made by his forehead and prostrate himself again. The skin on his knees, chest and belly was hard and scaly like a serpent's. He was on a pilgrimage to Muttra, the holy city on the Yamuna, we learned. He had been two years on the way. He might arrive in the spring, he thought.

'We're hoping to get there tonight,' Chaitan said.

'A very holy act,' Gampopa said. 'Most meritorious.'

'A wealthy man has hired me to make this pilgrimage. It is he who is laying up riches for his next life.' His body measured another length in the dust. 'I've grown to like it down here. The smell of the earth, the vibrations. Sometimes, at night, I forget I am a man and think I must be a worm . . . It must be nice to be a worm. Perhaps in the next life I shall become a worm.'

'What of Akbar's army?' Dadu demanded.

'Ah yes. The worms and I, we are the first to know. They say that rumour spreads faster than fire, but news of an army travels even faster through the ground.' He brought his knees up to his head and flopped forward, reducing the distance between himself and the holy city by at least three feet.

'Speak, man, speak! The army – where is it?'

'It has changed direction, my friend. It now moves north-west towards Bijnor.'

'Of course!' cried Dadu. 'Where else would the Princess Razziya have been going except to join her husband!'

Gampopa turned on me angrily. 'Did you not think to ask her where she was going? Where her husband's army was? How many miles have we lost because of you?'

'But, Gampopa, I didn't know who she was, then.'

This answer did nothing to diminish his annoyance. He brought up a large gobbit of blood and phlegm, spitting it directly in the path of the crawling pilgrim.

'We must decide . . .' He coughed. 'We must decide. Do we go on to Muttra for the night, or do we turn back now?'

'Every mile in this direction is taking us further and further away from the rest of the troupe,' Chaitan declared, pouting sulkily. 'I miss them. Can't we turn back now? Can't we meet up with them quickly?' He rubbed his head on Gampopa's shoulder and leant against him.

Dadu shrugged. 'Who can say which is the right way? The army may change direction yet again.'

'I say, let the dice decide,' came Bamian's deep bass. 'Odd number, we turn back; even number, we go on.'

Ramananda shot a jet of betel-juice, also in the path of the human worm. 'And I say this is a matter for the augural art. The true situation may be divined from celestial signs.'

'Perhaps if we lit a candle for Shiva, or sacrificed a goat . . .' Mohini suggested.

'Phah!' exclaimed Frog.

'We don't have a goat,' said Dadu.

Yin and Yan pointed in opposite directions, the one beating out a frenzied tattoo, the other jabbering incoherently.

'Perhaps we could decide how to decide by throwing the dice,' Bamian suggested.

'I'm for Muttra!' Dadu announced, and resolved the matter by striding forward purposefully. The others followed. Frog fell into step beside him, lifting his voice in a psalm of praise. Dadu took up the challenge, plainsong and Indian *raga* making strange but pleasing harmony. An early evening mist rose from the river, setting the red fortress adrift.

It was growing dark when we reached Muttra. The steep river banks were crowded with stone kiosks and broad flights of stairs.

'As if,' commented Frog, 'the town itself was rushing, like the Gadarene swine, into the river.'

Gampopa was not slow to point out that Muttra had been a centre for pilgrims twenty centuries before anyone had even heard of Christ. It was here that Krishna, the most popular divinity in the Hindu pantheon, was born. And it was here that, after a battle which raged for a thousand years, Vishnu, in his third incarnation as a wild boar, slew the demon which had dragged the earth to the bottom of the ocean.

We passed innumerable temples, whose walls were covered with paintings representing the exploits of Krishna: Krishna, while yet a child, strangling a python; the young blue-faced deity striking down a monster; the mighty god, a manifestation of Vishnu, holding on his finger the mountain he rooted from the earth to shelter himself from the rain; Krishna the lover, making the young peasant girls dance beneath a tree to his flute. For the edification of Brother Peter and Dr Coryat, Gampopa translated a text on one of the temple walls:

> 'I am the dice-play of the gamester,
> I am the silence of what is secret,
> I am the knowledge of those who know,
> I am the seed of all that is born.'

Here, with darkness falling, Bag Lal took leave of us to make his way to the quarter of the town where the untouchables and outcastes dwelt. He had enjoyed our company, he shouted from his strictly held distance of 275 feet.

The caravanserai was not like the inns and hostelries of England. It was a large, walled courtyard, affording, not shelter, but space to unload and tether beasts of burden and providing security from bandits, beggars and thieving groups. Wood and dried cow-dung could be purchased for fuel and pitch-soaked reeds for torches. Dozens of small fires smoked, around which sat groups of pilgrims, merchants, soldiers. I wandered among tethered camels, donkeys and pack-ponies, among boxes of pottery, bales of cloth, baskets of spices, sacks of grain.

An unshaven soldier hailed Dadu. 'Why, if it isn't my old comrade! We heard you'd died of the pox!'

'Well, if it isn't Narullah! I heard you'd been captured and imprisoned – by our own side, of course.'

'Come, Dadu, and drink to the good old days in Jaipur and the campaign of sixty-nine!'

'If my memory serves me right, it was in Gujarat in seventy-two that you and I fought together.'

'Well, no matter. We'll drink to both victories, just to be sure.'

We joined a group consisting of the soldier Narullah and his two comrades-in-arms, an indigo merchant and his wife and a shikaree – a professional hunter from the forests. At first the talk was of the price of grain, of taxes, of a leopard seen in the district and of the Chota Chua. Then Bamian proposed a dicing match to the indigo merchant, saying:

'You're bound to win. It is impossible for the gods to be angry with a rich man like you, otherwise you would not be rich.'

'On the other hand,' replied the merchant, 'the gods obviously love fools, or they would not have made so many.' But he allowed himself to be persuaded.

As usual, Bamian bet recklessly, the pleasure being not in the winning but in the exquisite moment when all hung on the fall of the dice. Watching Bamian in the grip of his passion, I could see why our own King Henry, father of our present queen, made statute law against gambling to protect archery from being abandoned. Perhaps King Hal understood the passion too well, for they say that Sir Miles Partridge once played him at dice for the four largest bells in London and won them.

'Gambling is a snare set by the Infernal Calumniator to trap our souls!'

Bamian ignored Frog, rattling the bones, his body trembling with excitement.

Dadu and his fellow soldiers were drinking and arguing about the respective merits of virgins and married women.

'One longs for a mount not ridden before,' sighed Narullah.

'Not so!' cried Dadu. 'The mount that has not been bent to the bridle is certainly no pleasure to ride.'

'Ah, but think what a thing of beauty is a pearl untouched by the jeweller's drill.'

'No, I do not see it. Pearls are of no use unless they are pierced and strung.'

The shikaree offered me a drink from a copper jug which had been standing in the embers of the fire. It was a drink called *kahwa*, made from black seeds boiled in water – not unlike some bitter medicines I know. The indigo merchant declined to partake, declaring it to be 'the black enemy of sleep and copulation'. As for Bamian, I don't think he was even aware that anyone had spoken to him. The shikaree told me that he was travelling to the great Qamarghah which was to take place in the forests north of the Ganges.

'Qamarghah?' This was a new word to me.

'It is a royal hunting-party,' he explained.

The more he told me, the less it sounded like any hunting-party I had ever heard of. Thousands of men beat the forest for several hundred miles around, month by month, week by week, concentrating the wild animals into an ever-tightening circle, ready for Akbar and his nobles to ride in and slaughter the game at their pleasure.

'It is not for sport alone that this is done,' the shikaree said. 'It is a military exercise too. The foot-soldiers are deployed as beaters and his cavalry are given their share of practice at the kill.'

A Qamarghah, it seemed, gave Akbar a good excuse to display the might of his army in places where there was unrest. This year, the Qamarghah was being held in an area known to be sympathetic to Shershan.

'So while Ghulam Khan fights, Akbar hunts, but it is not so different after all,' the shikaree said.

We sipped our black and bitter *kahwa* and the shikaree spoke quietly of the animals of the forest, the different varieties of deer, of bears, wolves, tigers and leopards.

'It is a paradox,' he said. 'In order to hunt and kill an animal successfully, first you must learn to love it. You must observe it closely, be intimate with its ways, appreciate its moods.'

'What!' Narullah was shouting, still hot in defence of virgins. 'Do you mean to tell me you would prefer leftover morsels to a freshly cooked dish? Or used garments to those that have not been worn? Surely you would rather break the seal of a new and heady wine than –'

A shout of triumph burst from the indigo merchant. His money gone, Bamian sat, eyes closed, mouth open, purged of emotion. He reminded me of the gargoyle on the east buttress of Honiton church.

Frog thrust his face close to the dwarf's. 'The best throw of the dice is to throw them away! Dicing is the Devil's baited hook.'

Bamian opened one eye. 'Don't waste your preaching on me. See those pilgrims over by the wall? Preach to them. They are of a sect that questions many things about the Hindu way and seeks new light.'

A baited hook if ever I saw one, and one that Frog swallowed whole in his zeal for heathen souls. While Frog was on his knees praying that he might be given the words to penetrate their sin, Bamian went ahead, like John the Baptist, to prepare the pilgrims for Frog's coming. He spoke to them in a language I did not understand. He arranged them in a semi-circle around a cart and set blazing brands in front of it – all this done with an eagerness curiously at odds with his dislike of religion-mongers.

'Bamian, why do you address them in that strange language?'

'Because, Khoratji, they are Tamils from the south and do not understand our northern Hindi. I learnt a smattering when we toured the –'

'But Brother Peter will preach to them in Hindi, will he not?'

Bamian nodded, a wicked grin splitting his face. 'They expect a shadow-play.'

Frog mounted the cart, made the sign of the cross and hurled himself into a sermon about eternal hell-fire and damnation and the amazing love that God has for mankind. In his excitement he flung his arms in all directions, pointed heavenwards, wagged his fingers, shook his fists, rolled his head. His audience was enthralled. His wild gesticulations, cast as magnified and flickering images on the white wall behind him, had them spellbound, had them crying, laughing, cheering.

Frog descended from the cart, his face radiant. 'The Lord's message really touched their hearts tonight! I could see it, I could hear it, I could feel the Holy Spirit working all around me!'

Bamian was rocking to and fro on his heels, hugging himself in ecstasy. 'The beauty of it is,' he gasped, 'every single person here is sure he has taken the meaning of the play. That old man there tells me he liked Frog's version of the old classic about the prince who turned into a fish; this woman wept when the maiden was saved from the eagle's nest; these boys will talk for a long time about the wonderful tale of battles and heroic deeds.'

'Don't tell him,' I whispered to Bamian, as Frog crossed the yard ahead of us, a new spring in his step. 'Let him keep his illusions.'

'Illusion! All is illusion!' Bamian bellowed in a crude imitation of the sadhu we had met at the river, and he laughed.

'Never mind the virgins!' Gampopa was shouting at Dadu. 'Haven't you asked them about the movements of Ghulam Khan?'

From Narullah we heard that Shershan and his rebels had crossed the river at night and doubled back on their tracks. And Ghulam Khan had followed them. Yes, the worm-man had been correct in his information.

Bamian let out a roar of delight which made the indigo merchant's wife scream. 'Do you see, Khoratji? The trick I played on the carter – sending him in the wrong direction – the gods were playing on us all the time! I must be a very holy person, the way I follow the example of the gods!'

I turned to Gampopa. 'Then this must be the parting of our ways. Brother Peter and I must press on for Agra and the Mogul court.'

Mohini, I knew, would be hurt. She rose and left the circle, hiding her face. I did not follow her. Swift and early surgery before a cancer can grow is the wisest action and less painful in the long run. But Frog – I had not expected to see his face stiffen, or to see him, also, hurriedly depart. Perhaps it was another bout of the flux . . . No, he returned, carrying a bowl of water and a cloth. Kneeling before me, he removed my boots and began to wash my feet. Tears coursed down his cheeks.

'Thomas, this may be the last time I see you,' he gulped.

'What do you mean, Frog?'

'I must go where the Chota Chua go . . . it is what I am called to do. And . . . and you must go to Agra.'

I tried to raise him from his knees. How could I love such an absurd, blubbering, bigoted idiot? But I did.

'No point in drying my feet, till you've stopped crying,' I said, trying to laugh and finding the lump in my throat was in the way. I pulled on my boots, knocking over the bowl in my haste, and blundered out of the caravanserai, through streets of cloaca and crepitous ordure, to the river.

I descended a flight of steps to the water's edge. A woman crouched with her back to me filling a pot from the silver-flowing Yamuna. The tilt of her head . . . Mary. She turned. Her eyes were white crusts; the septum of the nose was rotted and the bones collapsed; the lobes of the ears were enormously enlarged. It was the hideous, lumpy face of a leper. She came towards me, arms outstretched, begging for money. I fled, screaming. I had seen none like this before. Is this how Mary will become? I ran blindly up flights of steps, through an archway and into an ornamental garden. A peacock fanned its feathers, a hundred eyes glinting in the moonlight, and gave a long-drawn despairing cry. I was deep into the maze before I knew it. I wandered, as in a bad dream, between the hedges, and found, by accident, the centre. There a fountain splashed and a sundial, bewitched by the moon, falsely told the hour.

It was here that Mohini found me. She soothed me and stroked me while I bitterly told the ugly rosary of my past, not sparing the slightest detail. My mouth was seeking hers, my hands discovering her body. We made love, urgently.

We lay together on the grass. Mohini wept quietly – for Prajapathi, for me, for tomorrow when we must part. Her life she had dedicated to the god Shiva; she must go where Shiva directed. We made love again. This time slowly and tenderly, her supple dancer's body entwined around me. Even as I entered her, the thought that had clamoured at the gates of my mind for the past week or more was there. It came in many guises. Dadu had said there was money to be made if I offered my services to Ghulam Khan. So why not fill my purse before going to Agra? Was I not more likely to be successful there if I could present myself finely accoutred? And surely no physician worth his salt would refuse so grand an opportunity to exercise and extend the art of surgery as would be presented by an army engaged in a running fight with the enemy. Besides, Frog obviously had need of me. Without me he'd martyr himself before the first day was done. My hot sperm was pumping forth, uniting with her sweet juices. I kissed her eyes and recognized the true reason why it was not to Agra but to join with Akbar's army that I would be setting forth on the morrow.

Six

It was the first day of Dasshera. There was a festive spirit in the army camp. Soldiers and camp-followers alike milled around the sherbert stalls, jostled for a view of the jugglers, snake-charmers and freaks, craned their necks to see the wrestling bouts. My companion was Faisl Abu al-Qashandi, physician to General Ghulam Khan. Faisl was older than I, slightly plump, with a small pointed beard and a black moustache shaped like a Turkish bow. He was dressed in the fashion of the Mogul court: a turban of yellow silk which matched his knee-length surcoat, tight-fitting trousers, and gold-embroidered slippers with pointed toes.

As we shouldered our way through the teeming life of the camp, Faisl recounted the casualties from the latest assault on the rebel positions. 'Having arrayed their bodies in the glorious jewels of sword wounds, they departed this hired mansion of the world and sped on their way to enjoy the eight gardens of paradise.'

'You mean they died?'

'I mean they were gathered to their forefathers and entered the dwellings of eternity.'

'They died,' I insisted.

'Well, yes, if you must put it that way.'

He caught my eye and laughed. I had taken a liking to the gentle Faisl, with his passion for rose growing, his love of poetry and flowery language. Moreover, I respected his knowledge and ability as a doctor.

Faisl discoursed on the marvellous properties of a herb called rhubarb, which came by the overland trade routes from somewhere east of China. While Faisl talked in scholarly fashion, I observed the soldiers around me, men from Rajgarh, Kutch, Kisngarh, Bundelah, Alwar, Jodhpur, many of them Rajputs, a large proportion of them Hindus, despite fighting a Muslim cause under a Muslim general. In and out of the jostling throng ran gangs of ragged, half-starved children. One of these urchins seized a silver clasp on a soldier's tunic and tore it free. There was a lightning exchange from one small hand to another, then they were disappearing in all directions into the maze of alleys between the tents. The incident was so commonplace that it hardly caused a commotion. Although the soldier cursed, he didn't bother to give chase; and Faisl's discourse on rhubarb lost not one word.

With the Chota Chua in the camp, nothing capable of being lifted and carried away could be left unguarded for a second. They could snatch food an inch from a person's mouth, or be in and out of a tent at a momentary turn of a back. Sometimes, like the jackals, they were hunted, when no better sport was available; sometimes, when they got too numerous, poisoned food was put down for them. But mostly, like the flies by day, the mosquitoes by night and the dust which invaded everything, they were regarded simply as a fact of life.

Frog's attempts to bring the Chota Chua to Christ had, predictably, been disastrous. The first time he preached to them he had returned stark naked. The indignity he could bear, but he mourned the loss of his crucifix and his Bible. Not that the rest of us were sorry to see the last of that piss-sodden volume. Like a good cheese, it seemed to ripen with the passing of the weeks.

'When will the general grant me an audience?' I asked Faisl. I had waited two whole weeks.

Faisl gave an elegant shrug. 'Fortune sits at his door like a slave. We wait upon his favour as we wait upon the clouds to drop their rain . . . Of course, a gift would help matters.'

'How can I afford a gift?' I demanded angrily.

Faisl did his best not to smile. 'Allah, in his wisdom, ordains things thus – until you have the favour of the wealthy, you cannot afford to buy your way into their favour.' He put a soft, manicured hand on my shoulder. 'I have spoken of you several times, and of the skill you have shown with the wounded men in his command.'

'I am indebted to you, good Faisl; for without his patronage, or that of the princes and nobles under him, I shall never make enough money to present myself at Akbar's court.'

A juggler was balancing a spinning-top on the end of a pole, which was itself balanced on his forehead. By word of command, he made the top cease spinning or reverse its direction. Another, having demonstrated how he could smash coconuts on his skull, placed the point of a lance against his head with the other end against a loaded wagon, which he pushed for several yards. We moved on, swapping herbal lore.

'Parsley is supposed to help men with weak brains to bear drink better,' said I.

'Rhubarb will do that too,' said he.

'Juice from the root of the male fern eliminates tapeworm,' I said, with a passing thought for Dadu.

'And so will rhubarb, I shouldn't wonder,' Faisl said, a twinkle in his eye.

We passed a group gathered round a sacrificial goat. The animal's throat had been cut. Blood was gushing forth in spurts as from a pump. A soldier knelt beside the goat, collecting the blood in a vessel. I counted the spurts, mentally timing them as I did so. What was it I was seeing? So much still to be explained! The Art is long, but life is short.

Faisl caught me looking at him as he held a pomander to his nose. 'I must confess', he said, with a little smile of self-mockery, 'that I prefer the smell of a deer's genital organs to the honest sweat of my fellow men.'

Mohini was the ocean upon which my thoughts floated. They had merely been in a trough. They rose on the next crest and I sighed deeply.

On arrival at the camp, she, Bamian, Chaitan and Gampopa had been reunited with the rest of the dancing troupe. Immediately Gampopa had plunged them all into rehearsals. For the ten nights of Dasshera, they would unfold in dance the story of the *Ramayana*. I was jealous. Shiva was a demanding lover. When she talked with Bamian, analysing each movement, commenting on minute details of dress, I felt excluded. So I would turn to Faisl and delve in his mind for the rich veins of wisdom from the teachings of Atraya of Taxila or Susruta of Benares, or from the texts of the *Charaka-Samhita*. Then it would be Mohini's turn to pout and sulk. We quarrelled often. And after each battle came the sweet balm of forgiveness and physical union, in which we slowly grew closer to each other. But even then, as we talked softly, lying side by side, I would become frightened by the yawning gap between us, between her superstition and my logic, her fatalism and my pragmatism, between orient and occident.

'Er . . . sorry . . . what did you say, Faisl?'

'I was merely asking which school of spermatology you support.'

I had soon discovered that Faisl was no stranger to the medical writings of the Greeks and Romans. We discussed the choices open to us. Pythagoras says that our seed is the foam of our best blood, and others agree that it is blood cooked and digested by the heat of the genitals. Plato is of the opinion that it flows from the marrow of the backbone – which he argues from the fact that this spot first feels the fatigue of the business. Epicurus, on the other hand, maintains it to be extract of the soul.

Faisl inclined his head to one side and tugged his beard thoughtfully. 'I know that oft-times you see Galen as a rider who has departed from the plain of veracity and dropped the reins of accuracy, but on this point I believe he has returned to the narrow bridle-path of truth.'

Reluctantly I agreed with him. Whereas Hippocrates believed that semen is the product of the brain and therefore subject to the will, descending the spinal column to be stored in the testicles, Galen states that semen is produced by the testicles themselves. If the latter theory is correct, then our sperm is outside moral control and nature is more concerned with the perpetuation of the species than with the moral perfection of man as an individual. Carried away by his own argument, Galen wrote in his treatise *De Spermate*: 'It is better to have no head than have no testicles.'

Still laughing about this absurdity into which the ancient doctor had trapped himself, we wandered through the sprawling city of canvas and calico. It had bazaars or market-places, pens where herds of cattle, sheep and goats were kept, whole streets of marquees the size of houses. There was the *maidan* or square, where polo matches were played; there were sections where armourers and blacksmiths worked; there were abbatoirs, brothels, stables, camel lines and the elephant quarters. Within this city of tents was an inner city surrounded by canauts – ten-foot-high calico screens – in which dwelt the high-ranking officers of the Mogul army. Above the canauts I could see pennants fluttering from the tops of pavilions and palaces that had sprung up like brightly coloured mushrooms in a field. In the centre of this enclosure was the royal pavilion – the Peshkana – with a thousand servants at the ready, should Akbar, his two brothers or any of royal descent wish to watch the progress of the campaign or fire a musket or two in the direction of the enemy.

Even before we arrived at the camp, Dadu had explained its plan. He knew, he said, because it was laid out in exactly the same way every time. Dancers, he said, used to be classed as camp-followers. Things had changed, though, when Akbar came to the throne. Being a great patron of all the arts and an enthusiastic follower of the dance, he had accorded dancers the privileges of warrior rank. Doctors, surgeons, astrologers and others of that ilk were always quartered between the elephant lines and the artillery.

And it was Dadu who had introduced me to Faisl. The latter was a *mansabdar*, or official, in the service of the Mogul Empire. There were thirty-three grades of *mansabdar*, ranging from a commander of ten men to *panch-rhazari*, or commander of five thousand. Faisl told me that it was Akbar's policy to pay his officers in money, never in land. They must have no territorial allegiances or ambitions. Moreover, most of them were foreigners, born outside India.

'Like myself,' Faisl had said. 'I came from Persia when I was a young man and have been in the service of the Mogul Empire ever since.'

His official position at court, he told me, was Second Physician to the Precious and Blessed Big Toe of the Beneficent. It was an honorary position, he explained, there being several hundred titles attached to the emperor's auspicious personage.

'Should the oyster of ambition ever open to release the pearl of promotion,' he said, the ends of his moustache twitching at the thought, 'then I shall rise to the most illustrious title of Guardian of the Elephantine Testicle of the Valiant One! . . . Now tell me more about the lithotomy I watched you do.'

A few days ago, I had performed a lithotomy, to remove a stone in the bladder, by coming at it through the rectum.

'I first saw it done in Venice,' I said. 'But there they said the method had first been tried in India.'

'Quite possibly so,' Faisl commented, twirling one side of his moustache between his fingers. 'Knowledge is like a river in the Aravali Hills. It disappears underground and pops up somewhere else, it turns and doubles back on itself. Is it not the case that you Europeans discovered the medical writings of the Greeks through Arabic translations?'

I drew a diagram in the dust and we squatted beside it, oblivious of the bustle around us, like any pair of dice players, like any camp-astrologer and his client. I, in turn, picked Faisl's brain about the skin graft, the rhinoplasty to rebuild Ghulam Khan's nose. When the general had been mutilated by the rebels, it had been Faisl who had been given the responsibility for this operation. I listened, fascinated, to Faisl's account of a technique which hitherto had been unknown to me.

Faisl took another dab, with his own nose, at the pomander, and sighed. 'But there is always more to learn; and the more we learn the more we realize how little we know.'

'Observe, test, record,' I said.

'The trouble is, Thomas, our own bodies, even, conspire to hide the reality from us. Does not wood feel rougher to fingers that are chapped? Does not wine taste different on the tongues of the young and the old?'

I nodded. 'And is it not so, Faisl, that music strikes our ears in different ways according to whether we are in love or no?'

Faisl spread wide his delicate, jewelled hands. 'So, is it mere vanity to assume that we, who cannot comprehend the thing most intimate to us – namely, our own bodies – can truly know the nature of anything?'

'*Huzoor!*' called a voice behind us, and coughed politely. We turned. The man bowed low. '*Huzoor,*' he said, using the deferential form of address. 'My master, the General Ghulam Khan, has sent me to say he desires your attendance upon his fifth wife, who is sick.'

It was me, not Faisl, to whom the messenger was speaking.

Within the calico walls of the inner citadel, all was splendour. I was led through gardens of hanging plants and orchards of fruit trees in pots. A hundred or more water-carriers constantly sprinkled the ground to allay the dust. The messenger conducted me past armed guards into a spacious marquee, which, sub-divided by screens and hanging rugs, conveyed the impression of a mansion of many rooms. The messenger coughed again, politely, and withdrew. Servants attired in tunics of vermilion carried a curtained palanquin into the room. An old, white-bearded mullah, in a long black gown, stood in attendance.

I was sufficiently familiar with the ways of the East to know that I must make my diagnosis without setting eyes on my patient. I addressed the palanquin, enquiring about the nature of the malady, feeling like a country bumpkin because I spoke in the coarse Hindi I had picked up along the highways of India, instead of in Persian, the courtly language.

The mullah informed me: 'Her ladyship's most noble person suffers from ulcers on the legs.'

I asked permission to feel the afflicted parts. He nodded his assent. I put my arm through the curtain. A hand guided mine on to raw, pulpy flesh, in which was a deep, moist cavity, slimy to the touch. I withdrew my hand.

'What do you think?' the mullah asked, his eyes intently upon me. I made no reply. The nose is an important instrument of diagnosis. The breath, the sweat, the faeces, all smell differently according to the condition of the body. Likewise, that organ is often the first to detect signs of gangrene and other putridities. At first I could not place the smell on my fingertips. Then, absurd though it seemed, I recognized the smell of peach. I asked to feel the patient's pulse. The wrist was thick, with hair on the back of it.

'We have the usual sample of urine,' said the mullah, producing a small glass phial.

I held it up to the light. Colour or opacity often provide a clue. Not that I am one of those piss-prophets who relies solely on the urine chart in a doctor's vade-mecum for the diagnosis of every ailment under the sun. I was puzzled by what I saw, until my eye focused on the rim of the phial and discerned a trace of cow-dung. I sniffed at the contents of the phial, dipped in a finger and put it to the tip of my tongue. For certain, no human bladder ever held this golden liquid.

The black-robed mullah leant forward impatiently. 'What says the foreign *hakim*? What treatment does he recommend?'

'For that part of the patient which gives forth fruit, I would recommend a severe pruning! And I suggest he feel his head in case he is growing horns. And, in the meantime, a good feed of hay!'

So saying, I thrust aside the curtains. There, in the act of draining a large goblet of wine, sat the general himself. It could be none other, for his left arm was strapped to his face, a flap of live skin growing from the palm of his hand on to the place where the lower half of his nose once had been. As Faisl would have said, he had been pursuing the flower of delight with the feet of intoxication. His face was flushed. He tilted his head back, filled his mouth with wine till his cheeks bulged, then, overtaken by laughter, sprayed it forth, drenching me. He lurched from the palanquin.

'A good prescription!' His tongue tripped on the words.

'Fetch the fool whose idea this was . . . and bring a pruning knife and some hay.'

Bamian was dragged in by two soldiers. Ghulam Khan took his goblet on the wrong route to his mouth, going over the top of his strapped arm, instead of under it. Red wine spilt down the front of his robe. He cursed and hurled the goblet at Bamian.

'You thought up the symptoms, so now you can take the cure he recommends!'

'Sire,' stammered Bamian, 'I only wanted to prove to you that the *hakim*-sahib was not easily fooled, that he would be worthy of . . . aah!'

Ghulam Khan slashed at Bamian's ear with the pruning knife, half removing it from the side of his head.

'Now eat!' commanded the general.

Bamian was forced to his knees in front of a pile of hay. Clutching his bleeding ear with one hand, he began to chew.

Even as I knelt beside the dwarf to bind his wound, my eyes turned again to Ghulam Khan's nose. I had hardly dared believe that such a thing was possible. Now, for the first time in my life, I was actually seeing this wonder. I thought of the destroyed face of the leper-woman at Muttra; I thought of my wife, Mary. And, for the first time since . . . since that dreadful day, I felt a kindling of hope. I congratulated myself on my wise decision to throw in my lot with Ghulam Khan's army and not to go to Agra.

'This is the best joke yet!' mumbled Bamian through a mouthful of hay.

'Not enough hay! Send for more!' he called loudly. 'And make it fresh this time! And, while you're about it, bring me a cow or two to serve!' He began to moo and bellow like a bull, swinging his head and pawing the ground in such a clever imitation that Ghulam Khan laughed till he vomited and fell insensible to the ground.

It was the third day of Dasshera. Yesterday there had been a major attack on the rebel flank. The objective had been some outlying hills. Dadu had explained to me that often a major battle was preceded by a period of manoeuvring and skirmishes in which both sides sought control of the vantage points and the favourable terrain. Whoever held the high ground overlooking the main field of battle, and could place their artillery thereon, had a distinct advantage. The objective had been attained, but the casualties had been high.

In a shaded wood, slung with awnings, Faisl and I, helped by a score of orderlies and apprentices, tended the wounded. Some were propped against trees, others lay groaning on string charpoys. Flies swarmed around their wounds, or fed, in black clouds, on pools of blood. The stray dogs of the camp had soon discovered where to come to steal offal and severed limbs. I kicked a mangy animal that was licking my steel-bladed bone-saw.

A soldier, sobbing with pain, was laid on the trestle table. His stomach and intestines had been badly ripped by a lance. Faisl held the clay stem of a hookah to the man's lips.

'*Quunubus*,' Faisl explained. 'Smoke inhaled from certain essences of the hemp plant relieves pain.'

I was learning all the time from Faisl. The soldier's sobs became quieter and he began to drowse. Faisl cleaned the flesh around the wound with wine, asking as he did so about Bamian's ear.

'Mending well,' I said. Bamian had wanted me to cut it right off and sew it on back-to-front. Because, he reasoned, so many things are said behind one's back, it would be a distinct advantage to have at least one ear that way round.

I watched, fascinated, as Faisl sutured the intestinal wound with live black ants, placing them so that their mandibles clamped the two edges together. So tenacious were these creatures that, when pulled away, they left their mandibles behind.

Faisl looked up from his work. 'We have found that thread rots after a while, producing infection, but this way . . .'

There was a commotion in the corner of our enclosure, where those that died were temporarily laid. Not content with stripping the dead on the field of battle, the Chota Chua constantly infested our makeshift hospital. In this instance, a young girl had evaded the old man who was employed to keep the dogs and the carrion crows away from the corpses awaiting cremation. She was trying to unclench a finger to remove a ring. Not succeeding, she bit through the finger and made off with it between her teeth.

We worked all morning, sewing, cutting, stanching, parrying the scythe of death where we could. Compared to wounds made by sharp steel, those caused by musket-fire are much the worse, particularly those delivered at close quarters, which become infected by grains of gunpowder and saltpetre. Faisl and I both agreed with the findings of Paré that the cautering-iron kills more patients than it cures. Perhaps an application of a honey poultice; but, above all, clean dressings contantly changed, and let time and nature do the rest.

Usually two attendants carried the wounded to the tables where we worked. Sometime during the afternoon, eight men, panting and struggling under the weight, lifted an enormous, blood-spattered body on to the table. It was Dadu. His left leg was badly crushed, the bone in splinters and quite beyond repair. He was conscious and cursing loudly. One of our own elephants, apparently, had panicked and, stampeding into the ranks behind, had trampled him down. His cursing grew louder.

'We're glad it's you, Khoratji.'

'What?'

'That's going to cut off our leg . . . Oh, yes. Ali and I have seen enough injuries in our time to know . . .' He began to swear, and gripped my hand so hard I thought he would crush it. 'There is not a soldier in the army who hasn't lain awake at night and imagined lying on the surgeon's table . . . here . . . like this . . . only, whenever I imagined it, there was always a plump ripe beauty beside me, soothing my brow and promising to care for me.'

'You'll be all right, Dadu. Only we must operate soon.'

Dadu sighed, emitting a shuddering gust of air. 'I shall miss that leg. I am quite attached to it, you might say. And that foot – we used to be quite close, although we seem to have grown apart as the years have gone by. And I have not seen it so often of late, owing to my belly coming between us.'

The effort cost him dear. He lay mumbling to Ali and to Faisl, whose delicate hand he mistook for that of some past lady-love. I offered him the *quunubus* pipe, or a grain or two of opium.

'We must prepare for the operation,' I said.

Dadu rallied a little. 'Is the day and the hour auspicious? What do the stars say? A good general does not enter battle unless he knows the ground is in his favour. Send for Ramananda. He shall decide the most propitious moment to use the knife.'

I looked at Faisl. Faisl shrugged. It was common practice. We would have to agree.

Ramananda came, spreading out his charts and compendia beneath the tree where Dadu had been laid. He asked me to show him exactly where I intended to make the amputation. I indicated the point, about six inches above the left knee.

'Capricorn governs the knee, Aquarius the lower leg,' he said, turning the page of a volume full of charts, angles and astrological signs. 'And then there is the moon to consider. This being the twelfth mansion of the moon . . .' He shook his head pessimistically.

Ramananda made more calculations, sucked red betel-juice through his teeth and shook his head again. 'This is a most dangerous and inauspicious moment, with Taurus in the ascendant. Seven days, at least, must elapse before the incision can be made.'

I took him behind the tree and shook him till betel-juice dribbled down his chin. 'You're condemning this man to death!' I hissed. 'Now is the propitious moment. We must operate now!'

'The stars say otherwise,' Ramananda intoned, avoiding my eye.

I appealed to Dadu to listen to reason. But he was content with Ramananda's reading. He even asked if I could lend him money to pay the man.

Faisl bent over Dadu. 'Remember Babur, before the battle of Khanua? The royal astrologer gave ill omen, but he defied their advice and defeated the flower of the Rajput clans.'

Dadu would not be swayed. His faith in Ramananda's prediction was absolute. 'Seven days, Khoratji. Let the heavens revolve, let the sun rise in Capricorn, then your skill will not be undone by evil constellations.'

I said nothing. In my opinion, Dadu would be dead by then. Faisl and I walked slowly down the lines of chained elephants. They swayed slowly from side to side, rumbling internally. I could walk between them now without breaking into a sweat. Every day I had forced myself to take this walk. Daily I struggled to conquer my fear, to replace my instinctive dread of them with knowledge and understanding, to oust the irrational with rationality. A week ago my terror would have rendered the elephants indistinguishable. Now I recognized Yak-danta, the One-Tusked; Burgh-mar, the Lion Slayer . . . I was so angry with Ramananda, with the gullibility of the world in general, that, for the first time in my daily visits, my mind was not fully on those huge, grey, wrinkled beasts.

Faisl was saying, 'If that's what the soldier Dadu believes, then we must respect it.'

'But it's for his own good!' I shouted. 'Could we not strap him down and be done with it?'

Faisl regarded me with an amused smile. 'Could this be the same Coryat who only yesterday raged against Islam for the forcible conversion of the heathen?'

We passed Zalzalah, the Earth Shaker, being scrubbed and manicured. Fully grown male elephants were alloted five servants. Apu, Zalzalah's mahout, hailed us.

'*Huzoor*, are you ready to try today?'

The time must come, I knew, when I would have to prove to myself that reason had triumphed by letting one of those writhing, serpentine snouts touch me; when I must let its moist, hairy interior snuffle my hand and lift the proffered food. Not today; tomorrow perhaps.

'Gangrene will set in for sure,' I said to Faisl.

We stopped to watch a mahout's wife breast-feeding a baby elephant, while the mahout himself, a little wiry man, stood fearlessly beneath the belly of his animal, reaching up to attack an abscess with a hammer and chisel.

'We could try bribing the astrologer,' Faisl said. 'It is a wonderful thing how gold shines more brightly than the stars.'

As we hurried to find Ramananda, we recalled how, four years ago, a new star had suddenly blazed into the heavens and stayed there.

'In England our astrologers claimed that it heralded the end of the world, that our bodies would be turned to stone and then burned up . . . Mark you, we did have a slightly colder summer than usual that year!'

'Well, here in India, there were some who took it to mean the death of all rulers in the world. Others, mainly the court astrologers, prudently saw in this sign glorious victories ahead for the Mogul emperor.'

According to Holy Writ and Aristotle, the heavens were supposed to be unchanging, yet the entire world had witnessed a new star bursting upon the constellation of Cassiopeia and altering its design. And almost the entire world went on believing exactly what it had believed before. And did not the astrologers' catalogues state quite categorically that the heavens contained precisely 1028 stars, a number that was fixed for eternity? But already the Dutch optic glass had shown there were more.

'Yes, my friend, I believe you,' Faisl said, smiling gently. 'It is the others you must convince. But when we find Ramananda, string not these pearls of wisdom upon the thread of argument – just offer him money.'

We wended our way through the artillery lines. Each cannon in the battery near my tent I knew by name. Adamkhor, the Man Eater; Burj-Shikhan, the Bastion Breaker; Babul-Fath, the Gate Conqueror; Aurunghar, the Strength of the Throne. We heard a cornet blaring, wildly out of tune, and drunken singing.

'Hugh Fletcher,' I said.

Alcohol is forbidden by the Prophet. What went on in private was a different matter, but public consumption was forbidden in the camp, with two exceptions – elephants and European gunners. The Mogul army relied heavily upon foreigners for its experienced artillery officers. The commander of the artillery was a Frenchman. Under him were Turks, Spaniards, Dutchmen and the one Englishman, Hugh Fletcher. He was nearly always drunk. Most of the time he was under the impression that he was pounding the Spaniards off Valparaiso, not Shershan's rebels. We found him reclining across Tars and R'ad – Thunder and Fire – with a bottle of arrack in one hand, his cornet in the other. He was dressed Mogul style – not unlike Faisl, except for the large lace ruff to which he stubbornly adhered, and the fact that, whereas the latter was fastidious in the extreme, Hugh was dishevelled and wine-stained.

'By the belly of a stalled ox, is that you, Captain Drake?'

'No, Hugh, it is Thomas.'

'Ah, captain, rough weather a-coming; the old ship's heaving more than a mite.'

'Have you seen Ramananda?'

'Sank her this morning; all hands lost, God rest their souls.' He blew a blaring, discordant note on his cornet, 'Ace of cups . . . a goblet of good wine gives you the courage to die well!' He produced another tuneless blast. 'Ace of batons – games will often end in blows!'

'What's he saying, Thomas?'

'He's just remembering mottoes, often written on our playing-cards.'

'Ace of money – it's not worth knowing somebody whose luck is out!'

We heard Ramananda before we saw him. 'Avert the evil eye with Ramananda! Let Ramananda cast your horoscope!'

I offered him money for the possibility of a miscalculation. He declined angrily. A reinterpretation of the signs, perhaps? He pretended to be outraged. It was a slur on his profession, he screamed.

'Oh, how the poison honey drips from the blossom of mendacity!' exclaimed Faisl.

I increased my offer. Still Ramananda refused. I walked away, thinking to show him that I intended to go no higher, fully expecting that he would make terms with me. He did not follow or call me back.

Faisl shook his head gloomily. 'A vagabond in the desert of infamy! He knows the longer he waits the higher the price he can demand.' He tugged his beard and put his head to one side, in the way he always did when about to quote poetry. '"Accursed greed for gold, to what dost thou not drive the heart of man?"'

I was surprised. 'That's Virgil, isn't it?'

'It is. And I fear you'll have to pay him more money.'

Under a striped awning which billowed in the wind lay Dadu.

Frog, Bamian, and Mohini knelt beside him. Faisl, who had met them previously, bowed politely to each in turn. Dadu was breathing unevenly and tossing in his sleep. Mohini bathed his brow.

'He has a fever, I think,' she said.

I told them about Ramananda, railing against him. Mohini said in a slightly patient tone, as if correcting a backward child:

'Thomas-jun, we cannot argue with the stars!'

'You stupid simpleton! What do you know about anything? No wonder charlatans thrive with the likes of you to feed off!'

They say the best of wine makes the sharpest vinegar. Mohini began to cry, her face a wet, crumpled, utterly defenceless thing. The drawbridge within me came rattling down. We clung to each other – the first time we had done so in public. I challenged Frog with my eye. He lowered his gaze. Had it not been Brother Peter who had pronounced Mary dead, although she was alive? What right had he to reproach me?

Faisl coughed politely. 'And how did the Chota Chua receive the Word today, Brother Peter?'

'Ah!' said Frog, rubbing his hands with pleasure. 'They are beginning to accept me at last. Do you know, instead of stones, it was only fruit they threw at me today.'

'Definitely a softening of attitude,' commented Faisl.

'I'll bet the fruit had stones inside,' growled Bamian.

Dadu groaned. Faisl lifted the sheet which protected his leg from the flies. In places the skin was tight with greenish-yellow pus.

'I could put maggots on,' he said. 'They eat the pus and clean a wound wonderfully, but even then . . .' He waved his hand, encompassing all the other wounded in the enclosure. 'Most of those who lie here look to their horoscopes and not to our skill as the arbiters of their fate. To act contrary to the omens would destroy their confidence both in their own recovery and in any future efforts of ours. And confidence is half the cure.' He looked at me sorrowfully. 'Let us not avert our face from hope, for the soft marrow abideth in the hard bone.'

Once more I watched the cursed astrologer plying his deceitful trade. There was the usual evening crowd around him. The thought of having to offer him an even larger sum of money made me sick with rage. He kept me waiting, pretending not to see me.

*

Twelve men, carrying a shrouded corpse on a bier, approached.
Heading the mourners was Bamian. Beside him, a Brahmin priest
chanted mantras and Mohini wailed lamentations. At the tail of the
procession, Frog dirged away in Latin.

'He died an hour ago,' Bamian said.

'Dadu?'

Bamian nodded. Dadu, bursting with life and suddenly no more, a
flame extinguished. The procession halted. Bamian pointed a pudgy
finger at Ramananda.

'You scabby imposter! The only thing you have ever divined has
been the weight of your victims' purses! *Luchcha*! *Budmashi*!'

A cannonade of curses, a bombardment of abuse, roared out from
the dwarf. 'Chouser! Quack! Mountebank, false prophesier,
murderer! So propitious was the moment seven days hence that he
died of waiting for it!'

Ramananda sneered a red sneer. 'Even that great astrological
treatise the *Surya-Siddhanta* allows of fallibility. The famous Vara-
hamihira himself sometimes failed to read the full portent of the
heavenly bodies.'

'Ah! So you admit you were wrong! How shall these people ever
believe in you again when on this bier they see the result of consulting
you?'

'The almanacs are sometimes open to more than one interpretation. We are dealing with a vast and complex cosmos . . . it is just
conceivable that . . . Ah, here is the relevant page . . . Hm . . . yes . . .
well . . . if one favours the Brajjakaka school of interpretation, one
could say that death was inevitable from the start.'

'It would not have made any difference then, when this unfortun-
ate soldier was put to the knife?'

'If you want a second consultation, you will have to pay a fee. Do
you think I'm a rich *thakur* that I can waste my time . . .'

The procession moved on. Ramananda had, to all intents and
purposes, conceded the point. Bamian crowed like a cock,
scratched the ground with his feet and flapped his elbows. Frog
intoned the *De Profundis* and sprinkled holy water over the body.

The shrouded figure slowly sat up. 'There is a mist before my
eyes,' it said. 'Everything is shadowy and vague. Is this the half-life
between incarnations?'

Disbelief, fear, awe, triumph flitted across Frog's face, then broke into the radiance of joy.

'But you're dead!' screamed Mohini.

'I don't feel very dead,' said the reluctant corpse.

Bamian directed the bearers to return, at a run, to the hospital. 'Quick, Khoratji! Go prepare your instruments for the operation!'

We hurried away, the crowd deserting Ramananda to follow us, for it is not every day that somebody is raised from the dead, and any miracle is a welcome diversion from the tedium of camp life.

'You should have warned me, Bamian.'

'I told nobody, Khoratji. Besides, your face would never have been so convincing had you known.' He swarmed up a pole and slid down an awning. 'There's more than one way to trap a monkey. I knew we could make that rancid lump of fat recant without having to pay him for it.'

'Do you mean to say that Frog really thought Dadu was dead; he really believes that . . .'

'Yes!' chortled Bamian, putting his head between his legs and grinning at me with inverted face framed by buttocks.

Already my mind had turned to the instruments I would need, to the different blades required for flesh, sinew and bone, to the clamps needed for the arteries, to calculations about loss of blood.

It was the evening of the tenth and last day of Dasshera. In the *maidan*, to the accompaniment of drums, trumpets and shawms, mounted archers galloped in a circle, aiming their arrows at a brazen ball fixed to a high pole. At each hit, the crowd roared approval, and the successful archer would rein in his steed so that it reared and capered on its hind legs in front of a raised dais where, surrounded by senior officers and a bodyguard, there was a covered palanquin. Ghulam Khan would not show himself to his troops until he could face them with a new nose.

Beside me was Faisl. He must have been the only person in the crowd not watching this amazing display of horsemanship and skill with the bow. His eyes were shut and he was speaking the lines from the *Mahabharata* in which the great warrior Arjuna successfully sends an arrow into the left eye of a fish mounted on a similar pole, by looking at its reflection in a cauldron of oil placed on the ground. For one so observant, so accurate in the detail of what he saw, it was strange that, at times, he preferred to view life, not directly, but through the vision of the poets and the painters.

'It is like using this new Dutch optic glass which magnifies things so that we can see them better,' Faisl said.

'I shall certainly need the biggest optic glass there is to see the sense in that argument,' I said.

I wished it was Mohini beside me. Her explanations of this spectacle would have been delivered in an excited high-speed gabble and totally inaccurate, but they would have pleased me in a way that Faisl's learned, witty and charming discourse never could. She was not beside me, though. She and the rest of the troupe were preparing themselves for the final episode in the story of the *Ramayana* – a performance that would last through the night and end with the dawn.

As the celebrations of Rama's victory over the demon Ravana reached their climax, I suddenly found myself noticed by the nobles and their ladies behind the calico walls of the inner city. As Bamian had cunningly foreseen, the story of Ghulam Khan in the curtained palanquin had spread, and with it my reputation as a doctor. Once more I congratulated myself on my judgement in coming to a place where a good doctor was needed and appreciated. It was much more sensible to make money here first, then go to Agra when I was in a position to gain the favours I sought.

And, thanks to Bamian, Frog was in great demand too. Wherever he went, crowds pressed round him, demanding to be healed, wanting a laying on of hands or merely to touch his robe. Bamian was hugely delighted with this unplanned child of his trickery. As for Frog, he spent much time in prayer. The more he prayed and gave thanks for this miracle, the harder it became to tell him the truth. And Dadu – this morning, as I inspected his stump, I could not fail to notice his piss-proud pride-of-the-morning. He was definitely re-covering.

The archers left the arena. The next spectacle was a fight between a ram and a billy-goat. There was something familiar about the noise of the crowd. It was the passionate sound of a crowd which has scented blood. If I shut my eyes I would not know the difference

LORD OF THE DANCE

between this and the gatherings in Paris Gardens, London, where the bull-baiting and the cock-fighting are held.

'The tissue now thrives of its own accord,' Faisl said.

'What?'

'The general's rhinoplasty – soon all connection with the original source of its vitality can be severed.'

There was a thud of horn on horn.

'It will be interesting to see', said Faisl, 'whether the skin, in its new location, retains the sensitivity of the palm.'

'Perhaps we ought to get Ramananda to read his fortune by his nose,' I said.

The goat had utterly routed the ram, which fled from the arena. Two rhinoceroses were now doing battle. To help distinguish them, one had been painted white. The army used these strange creatures as a weapon against the elephants of the opposing forces. For some reason, elephants fear them. When Dadu had first described them to me, I had wondered if they might be the unicorns I had read about in travellers' tales. Obviously they were not. These beasts were more like vast pigs in ill-fitting suits of armour. What was it that made two animals of the same kind so eager to kill each other?

A swarthy soldier on my left shouted, 'A month's pay the white one wins!'

'Done!' cried his companion, on my right.

Immediately, the white rhinoceros disembowelled its opponent and trampled it for good measure.

'Mind you settle up before we go into battle! In my experience, dead men make bad debtors.'

We were caught between a cross-fire of stinking breath – bad teeth and curried lamb to the left, stale wine on bile of empty stomach to the right. Faisl's eyebrows rose a fraction and he pressed his pomander to his face. We were saved from further punishment by a fanfare of trumpets. They heralded the main event of the evening, the climax of the Dasshera festival. A team of bullocks, hauling a platform on solid wooden wheels, bore into the *maidan* a seventy-foot-high effigy of the demon Ravana. Its legs, arms and body were made of a wicker-work structure stuffed with straw. The head was a gigantic mask of paper and cloth construction, painted and varnished. A young nobleman, dressed as Prince Rama, stepped from the dais and shot a

flaming arrow into the demon's breast. Then, as the ranks of archers
loosed their shafts, the sky burned with a thousand meteors and the
effigy roared into a tower of fire.

My thoughts returned to Honiton. Tomorrow was All-Hallows
Eve. They would be building the bonfire on the common. When I was
a boy, they used to hang a basket of live cats from a mast in the
middle of the fire. I shall never forget their fearful screeching as they
roasted. And I remembered Mary's tears of pity and her uncle saying,
'The Devil's representatives cannot suffer too much!' He changed his
tune when his wife was discovered to have warts on her chest. These,
said the black-cowled monks, were supernumerary nipples for the
feeding of familiars. They dragged her away and tortured her.

'You look sad.' Faisl put a kindly arm on my shoulder. 'I know
how it is. I felt the same when I first came to India. It can be very
lonely when all around there is celebration and you are not part of it.'

'And yet perhaps it is not so alien, dear Faisl. The same hopes and
fears merely appear in different guises.'

The flames reached a cache of fireworks, placed where the heart
would be. Rockets whizzed and exploded in all directions. Like a tree
being felled, the fiery demon slowly swayed, then crashed to the
ground amidst showers of sparks.

Darkness had descended. The crowd drifted from the dying
embers of the vanquished giant and, in quieter mood, re-formed near
the artillery lines. Here, on a small mound, a stage had been erected.
To one side, a tall canvas screen billowed gently and, from the tallest
pole, Indra's banner fluttered. Behind the screen, Mohini and the rest
of the troupe would be making offerings and prayers of dedication to
Shiva.

A *taba* throbbed. Between its steady pulse-beat twined and
writhed the clear notes of a flute. Chaitan, the youngest in the troupe,
stepped out from the screen. He was dressed for his role as Prince
Rama. He made *anjali* with his hands – two *pataka* hands, with
palms together in salutation.

'We salute the gods. We salute Brahma; we salute Ganesha,
Vishnu, Parvati and Shiva. All five we worship. To the gods and to
you we offer our life, our rhythm and our dance.'

Chaitan held his hands above his head to salute the deities. Then,
turning to where Ghulam Khan's palanquin had been placed, he held

his hands before his face. Finally, with his hands at his chest, he bowed to the rest of us. Faisl sighed deeply.

Rama and Sita, Chaitan and Mohini, their movements blending, keeping a constant equilibrium of weight and counter-weight. The variations in tempo, the clever use of heel and sole to stamp out rhythms and cross-rhythms, the sudden still poses, the explosive shuffle of the feet. I recognized the graceful aerial movements of Mohini, 'The Leaping Deer', 'The Flight of Garuda'; I knew what discipline went into the perfection of her *sudari*, that beautiful gliding motion of the head, horizontally from side to side, with a supple flexion of the neck. I applauded the elegance of her *manjara* peacock hands.

'Ah! Those tender cheeks!' sighed Faisl. 'As a flower in a barren waste, so are my eyes fixed upon him!' He sighed again. 'His light-revealing countenance opens my heart like a rosebud.'

Hanuman, the Monkey King, bounded on to the stage. Once again, distinctions between illusion and reality melted; the mind capitulated, banishing reason, suspending disbelief. Hanuman's head suddenly detached from his body and rolled about, spurting blood. It came to rest at the front of the stage, staring fixedly ahead, its lips still moving and grimacing. The audience stamped and cheered with delight. Here was a trick even better than the transformation of the demon into a jackal. A second cannon-ball struck the base of the stage.

'A hit on the waterline!' shouted the drunken voice of Hugh Fletcher. I could see him, not a furlong away, with Tars trained on the stage.

'Captain Drake will sink the Spanish galleon yet!'

He applied his taper to the touch-hole.

Bang! A cannon-ball crashed on to the stage, splintering the boards, ploughing through the line of dancing-girls, carrying away the pole which held up the screen.

'She's dismasted!' roared Hugh Fletcher. Then he was dragged away.

'Mohini! Mohini!' I screamed.

I struggled to pull aside the fallen screen. An injured dancer clutched my leg. I kicked her aside.

'Mohini! Where are you, Mohini?'

'Khoratji, Thomas-jun, I am here, I am safe.'

I held her close to me.

A sobbing Chaitan bent over the headless body of Hanuman the Monkey King. Even in death, Gampopa's art had not deserted him. His limbs were curled in exactly the manner of the monkey which Dadu had slain at the roadside well. Faisl had a comforting arm round Chaitan, was stroking his hair, was murmuring soothing words into his ear. The boy allowed himself to be led away by his new protector. Mohini wept in my arms. I looked at the grotesque death-mask of Gampopa, her *nayaka*. At last Mohini was all mine.

Seven

The tent breathed, expanding with the dawn breeze, then exhaling. Shadows of patterned fabric danced on Mohini's skin. She lay with one finger entwined in her hair. The small of her back was soft, like the bloom on a peach. I listened to the rumbling of the elephants' bellies, the clinking of their ankle-chains as they swung from side to side, a sentinel's horn sounding on the eastern perimeter of the camp, a cough from Dadu.

Dadu was my night-watchman, my *chowkedah*. With the Chota Chua infesting the camp, a *chowkedah* was essential to anyone wishing to remain a man of property. I could hear him clumping about outside. Creak, thump! Creak, thump! And the occasional muttered conversation with Ali, his tapeworm.

Bamian had spent hours designing and making a leg for Dadu. The finished product excelled even the superbly jointed pair the dwarf had made for his role as Demon King. Dadu had been delighted. At first his progress was akin to that of an infant learning to walk – except that the ground shook when he fell and those upon whom he advanced with outstretched arms usually fled in terror. More than once I was reminded of the felling of the great oak tree on Honiton common. I had carved Mary's name on its trunk, with loving care. So had Frog. Good timber for the queen's new fleet, they said. And they sawed it up.

'Why do you stir and sigh, Thomas-jun?'

'It's nothing, my love. Go back to sleep.'

I pulled the quilted coverlet over her nakedness, gold-dusted in the dawn. The Archer had replaced the Scorpion; the sun was in the ninth sign of the zodiac and there was frost on the ground.

'How can it be, Ali, that my feet are cold? Yes, Ali, both my feet!'

Creak, thump! Creak, thump!

'Mashed lentils and hot peas – that'd warm us up, wouldn't it, Ali? And all the more for you, now there's less of me!'

From one of the wooden watchtowers the muezzin's cry called the faithful to prayer: '*La-ilaha – illah-l-la* . . .' An elephant trumpeted in reply; Dadu hawked and spat. My previous *chowkedah*, a squeamish, peevish hoddy-doddy, without enough gumption to furnish a codpiece, had left my employ. My collection of various organs preserved in vinegar, the hand with the flesh carefully boiled away so as to maintain the tendons intact, the skeleton, these things had, most unreasonably, upset him. Hacking at the living with the sword or lance was right and proper, but, apparently, those who put dead bodies to the knife were practisers of the black arts.

Dadu, stout fellow, had no such qualms. He was convinced, though, that the skeleton was an old comrade called Hamza. He would reminisce, boast and philosophize to Hamza by the hour. Occasionally Hamza might rattle a bone or nod his skull, but mostly he didn't answer back or interrupt, a state of affairs that Dadu found eminently satisfactory.

A gabble of praying scattered my thoughts. Frog's quarters abutted on to mine, being part of the same structure of poles and ropes. He was keeping an all-night vigil to mark the occasion of the Immaculate Conception of the Blessed Virgin Mary. This sudden burst of fervour, after so long a silence, made me suspect that Brother Peter, God's self-appointed *chowkedah*, had dozed off.

The bracelets on Mohini's wrist jangled as her cool fingers found my hot fount of love. Sighing and panting, we journeyed towards the climactic act of life's creation, Frog matching our noise, praying louder and louder, faster and faster.

When I was five, I walked in upon my mother and father making love. It frightened me. I thought they were fighting and hurting each other. When I was ten, I saw one of the farm-hands in the long grass with his lass. The sight of those bare, white buttocks bobbing up and down, disappearing and reappearing, was ludicrous.

'Thomas-jun, do I not please you today?'

'Forgive me, my love, my mind wandered.'

I kissed her throat and soon we gathered speed, sweeping into the vortex of ecstasy and oblivion.

'Thomas! Behind you!' It was Frog's voice.

Mohini screamed. I jerked round, uprooting myself from her furrow. A shrouded figure, hand upraised with something big and heavy in it, was advancing upon us. I seized the nearest object, Hamza's skull, and, wrenching it from his body, dealt our assailant a blow. The figure fell to the ground. Too late I discovered the truth. There was no weapon; only a fingerless hand, the stumps and palm swollen into an unsightly lump. I bent over the huddled heap of rags. It was the leper-woman whom I had encountered at the riverside in Muttra; the same that invaded my dreams and lurked in the corners of my sight. Her cheeks and lips were bloodless. I could not bring myself to feel her pulse, or put my ear to her chest, but there was no obvious sign of breathing.

Dadu lumbered in, tripped and fell with a crash. Frog followed close behind.

'It was not your blow, but the evil in me that killed her. My lascivious peeping, my distrust.'

He wrung his hands and beat his head against the tent-pole. I turned on Dadu. I cursed him for a useless scoundrel, a lazy loafer. What good to me was a watchman who didn't keep watch? Dadu seemed unable to take his eyes off my dibble, still moist with the juice of love. I pulled on my breeches, while Dadu muttered sulkily that even the best of watchmen had bladders. He picked up the skull.

'Hamza, dear friend, you always were one to lose your head over a woman! Pull yourself together, man. Remember you're a soldier!'

'Hold your tongue, Dadu!'

Mohini's young face peered out from the quilt. 'Thomas-jun, could not Petagurusahib raise the woman from the dead, like he did with Dadu?'

I have explained to her — several times — what happened. It's no use. If she's set on believing something, there's no fact or reason will distract her from it. Frog denied such powers vehemently.

'Such self-effacement!' Mohini sighed, 'That is true holiness.'

Dadu was reluctant to have his miracle diluted by another, particularly by such a worthless one.

'A beggar-woman; no friends of any consequence. There'll be no trouble. We'll just throw her in the river.'

The leprous body stirred. Her eyelids fluttered; she groaned and sat up. Frog backed away in alarm.

'I touched her not! Nor made any sign, I swear it! Perverse woman, accept death as the better lot!' He groaned and cried out. 'Forgive me, Lord!' Bending, he raised her to her feet and embraced her quick but noisome body. 'God's love enfolds you as surely as my arms do now.' He released her and rushed, retching, from the tent.

'I'd rather hug a mountain bear than her,' Dadu said.

'What is your name?' Mohini asked.

The leper-woman made a snuffling, indistinct noise, accompanied by a deal of foul breath. I guessed that, along with her collapsed nose, her palette had been destroyed by the dreadful disease.

'I think she's saying her name is Damayanti,' Mohini said.

'Damayanti?' I said.

The hideous face nodded and gurgled assent. Then she opened her mouth and waved her swollen stump of a hand towards it. I recognized it as exactly the same gesture as the one that had caused me to strike her. Apparently it was not her hand which was troubling her but something in her mouth. I took a deep breath and a step closer and peered into her mouth. She had six teeth in all. One was surrounded by a large abscess.

Perhaps, if I used the long-handled pliers, I could extract the tooth without touching her. Assisted by Dadu, we roped her to a bench and tied her jaw open with two bandages. I wrestled with the tooth, a back molar, deeply rooted.

'This calls for strength; let me have a try,' Dadu said.

He grappled with the tooth, twisting and heaving, the pliers slipping off several times. Damayanti seemed remarkably insensitive to pain. Was I imagining it, or could the cackling sound she made be laughter?

I looked up and saw Bamian standing by the entrance to the tent. His mocking glance took in the bound leper-woman and Dadu astride the bench, heaving and grunting.

'Dadu, poor fellow, I did not realize you were so desperate for a woman. You should have told me. I would have found you something better.'

Dadu flung the pliers to the ground and stumped out of the tent. Bamian chuckled, picked up the pliers, wiped them on his sleeve and extracted the molar with an effortless turn of the wrist. I released the patient. She dribbled blood and made incoherent speech. Again she opened her mouth and gestured towards it.

'Not another one!'

'It is not toothache of which she complains,' Bamian said. 'It is hunger. She wants food.'

'Get her out of here! For pity's sake, take her from my sight!' It was my voice. I was trembling.

'Give her food . . . anything . . . But remove her from me!'

Coitus continuatus after *coitus interruptus*, like revisiting scenes of happy childhood, is usually a mistake. So it proved in this instance. Besides which, Mohini had a predilection for squatting positions – all very well for those who squat and sit cross-legged from an early age – but a touch of the cramps adds nothing to the occasion. I gave up in a temper and Mohini left, weeping, to do her morning exercises. And that was another thing that annoyed me. What was the point in all this training if the troupe had ceased to exist? It was not as if she needed to earn a living any longer. I was perfectly capable of keeping her. But the stubborn girl would not be dissuaded.

Harness jingled outside the tent, a horse stamped on the hard earth.

'You! Soldier! Stand up when I address you!' The haughty *castrato* tones sounded familiar.

'Me?' came Dadu's voice.

'I, Ali Pasha, Keeper of General Ghulam Khan's harem, demand to see the miserable infidel mountebank leech whom you call your master.'

'You must have come to the wrong place. This is the tent of Thomas Coryat, esteemed doctor and surgeon. However, I doubt if he can help the likes of you. Noses he can grow again, but what you're lacking . . .'

'So! You're needing a lesson in respect, are you? Break one of his legs!'

There was the sound of heavy blows.

'Oh, my leg! My leg!'

I ran from the tent. Two men were pounding Dadu's leg with staves, a third was smashing at it with the back of his sword. I

LORD OF THE DANCE

showered the contents of my purse at their feet. They ceased their efforts and began picking up the coins. Dadu clutched his leg and groaned. Blood seeped through the material of his pantaloons. It was his left leg; his wickerwork leg. I bent close, as if to examine the wounds, and smelt wine. Dadu gave me a wink, while continuing to moan most convincingly.

Ali Pasha dismounted and swaggered up to me. He was the same silk-robed, elaborately turbaned, bejewelled eunuch I had encountered with Princess Razziya, on the road to Muttra.

'The big males always howl the loudest,' he piped, a smirk of satisfaction on his smooth, sexless face. He looked me up and down disdainfully. 'The Princess Razziya commands your presence.'

'The last time you said that, I was dragged through the dust to meet her. I see your manners have not improved since then.' I turned my back on him and helped Dadu into the tent. 'Now, Dadu, what's going on?'

Dadu looked sheepish. I rolled up the leg of his pantaloon. The hollow wickerwork structure was packed with fat wineskins. One of them had sustained a nasty injury, its red contents oozing forth.

'It's like this, Khoratji . . . you see, there's a good profit to be made from smuggling wine into the camp and . . .'

'Hurry up in there! Hurry up, unless you want a whipping!' Ali Pasha pushed his way past Mohini into the tent. I covered the exposed limb. Ali Pasha glanced around and sniffed scornfully. He sniffed a second time, his eyes widening. 'Pickles! I distinctly smell pickles!' His eyes flickered greedily along the shelves. 'Some things simply cannot be obtained on campaign. I haven't tasted a pickle since we left Agra.' He seized a jar in which I had preserved a collection of brain tumours. 'Ah! Pickled *brinjal* – good! Good!' He grabbed another jar – an interesting selection of cankerous nodosities and other malignant growths. 'Walnuts! Excellent! Excellent! And onions too!'

I handed him my jar of testicles preserved in vinegar. He accepted them as his due, without so much as a word of thanks. There was just a fraction more civility in his tone. 'The Princess Razziya awaits you.'

I mounted the saddled horse which had been brought for me. The distance was not great. It was a matter of protocol. Those who attended the princess did not arrive on foot as if they were of no account. We proceeded at a walking pace, surrounded by our escort, who cleared the way through the teeming, tent-lined alleys by liberal use of their whips. Each time a knotted thong met human flesh, Ali Pasha would lick his lips and emit a high-pitched giggle.

We penetrated the red canauts of the royal enclosure and halted outside a vast complex of domed and interconnected tents. A city within a city within a city. I was ordered to dismount, blindfolded and led into a carpeted maze. Air heavy with perfume, whispers, a woman quietly sobbing, burning incense, a sigh, and always the feel of thick carpet underfoot. My blindfold was removed. I was standing in front of a four-poster bed, the curtains of which were drawn, concealing the occupant. At each of the four corners stood an armed eunuch, impassive but alert. Surrounding the bed was a quinquangle of mirrored screens in which I saw myself reflected many times over.

Princess Razziya's voice vibrated through the brocaded, flower-studded curtains. 'Come closer, *hakim*-sahib, and tell me how you fare.'

I stepped forward with a bow. 'Princess, it is your health which must be our concern. It is nothing serious, I hope.'

She sighed deeply. 'I am restless and cannot sleep.'

I slipped my hand inside the curtain and encountered her smooth, delicate wrist. Her pulse was fast, and her skin burned. Slender fingers stroked the back of my hand.

'Your reputation as a doctor is spreading fast, so I hear.'

'Your head eunuch isn't impressed.'

Razziya's hand encircled my forefinger and moved gently up and down it. 'Ah, Ali Pasha, he is a great defender of the faith, a staunch upholder of the traditional ways of the zenana. He does not approve of men, even doctors, entering the . . . the private parts . . . of the household.'

I tried to retrieve my finger. Her grip tightened. My thumb was in her mouth, her tongue caressing it. She let it slide out between her soft lips.

'You should be careful of Ali Pasha; his words carry weight with my husband.' She closed my hand round her naked breast. 'Do you like it here, my handsome *hakim*-sahib?'

'The camp has . . . many attractions, princess.'

'It is interesting, is it not, to see what replaces the normal urges and gratifications of man, if they are removed. Take Ali Pasha, now. He seeks his pleasures in cruelty, religious fanaticism and food. Do you think, O blue-eyed one, that we have anything to learn from that about the nature of love?'

'I . . . I don't know.'

'And what became of your urge?' Her breast squirmed beneath my captive hand.

'Urge, princess?' I glanced furtively at the nearest eunuch. He stared straight ahead.

'To visit the libraries of Agra, my fine poet and scholar.'

I explained to her the opportunities to be had as a field-surgeon to observe, test, record; to match theory against reality; to investigate the human body. She laughed softly and guided my hand to her moist quim and held it there.

'That is not what I hear. I hear that the real reason is a dancing-girl called Mohini . . . Oh, yes . . . I may not set foot outside the zenana, but my eyes and ears are everywhere.'

My virile member would not stay down. Those sharp eunuch eyes and even sharper scimitars could hardly miss so outstanding a breach of harem etiquette.

'Remember,' Razziya murmured, in a voice that sent vibrations down my spine, 'remember . . . you will achieve nothing without someone to speak for you. I am tired of the useless doctors at the court. If . . . if your skill is equal to my need . . .'

She released my hand. I stammered my thanks and backed away in a bent position which best concealed my condition and which I hoped might be taken for a bow. I picked up my hat and, using it to hide my embarrassment, was led blindfold from the harem of General Ghulam Khan.

I blinked in the sunshine. 'Is that you, Faisl?' My finger was still pungent with Razziya's sex.

'An interesting case,' said Faisl, falling into step beside me, and embarking on a description of how an inflamed wound was respond- ing well to a poultice of mouldy bread. 'You inherited the writings of the Greeks and we the *Susruta-Samhita* and the *Charaka-Samhita*.'

'The trouble is, my dear Faisl, that . . . what was that? I'm sure I saw the leper-woman, Damayanti. Look! There!'

'I see nothing. Anyway, you were about to say something concerning our two classical works on medicine.'

'Was I?'

'Yes. I think you were about to say that the trouble is, we inherit not only their wisdom, but also their misconceptions. A sentiment with which I heartily concur. You see, it is the same here as in your country.'

A like-minded companion is a great delight. How refreshing not to have to do battle over every departure from the teachings of the ancients.

'All the same, Thomas, the midnight of their ignorance is aglow with fireflies of sagacity.' And he talked earnestly of the many drugs, herbs and remedies whose usefulness was beyond question, of jalap, cinnamon bark, asafoetida, ginger and spikenard.

Our conversation returned to a subject we had discussed several times: with so many unclaimed corpses available to us, how best to preserve them from putrefaction while engaged upon dissection and other research. Salt dehydrated the tissues; slow boiling in vinegar was a tedious process.

'Ice,' I said.

'But, my inestimably wise Dr Thomas, our humble rank is not compatible with obtaining the quantities of ice we would require.'

'Agreed, my dear incomparably learned Dr Faisl, but the Princess Razziya could obtain it for us.'

He looked at me sharply. 'You have been treating her?'

I nodded.

'Take care, Thomas, that the scented blossom of her favour yields not poison honey.'

Outside the gate to the royal enclosure Chaitan, dressed in the same green silks as Faisl, was squatting in the dust with another boy. Faisl sighed.

'My heart drank water from his fountain and drowned in him and now the torrent snatches me away.'

The two boys incited their stag-beetles to fight, facing them up to each other, and stroking their backs so they hissed with rage.

'See his pearl-scattering grace!'

'Kill! Kill!' screamed Chaitan, as his hard-shelled gladiator tore a leg from its opponent.

'Ah, Thomas, are his cheeks not the envy of the rose?'

Our shadows fell across the arena just as Chaitan's beetle was knocked on to its back and lay with legs waving helplessly in the air. The other boy snatched up his own beetle and the prize money and departed.

'It's all your fault!' Chaitan stormed. 'I was winning earlier, but you took so long in coming!'

Faisl fondled the boy's ear. 'Never mind, my little pigeon. I'll buy you a present.'

'A songbird? You did say I could have a songbird.'

Faisl laid a hand on his shoulder and laughed indulgently. He caught my eye and shrugged. They walked slowly away, leaning against each other.

'In a golden cage?'

'If it pleases you, my pigeon.'

I whipped round. 'Why do you follow me, Damayanti? Come out from there! Show yourself!'

A soldier emerged from behind a tent and regarded me curiously. Still thinking of Damayanti, I entered the elephant lines, passing the stockades where the elephants in musth were kept. For three months in the year the male elephant goes mad and is extremely dangerous to handle. Scaly, leprous skin touched my bare arm. I yelped and jumped sideways. Zalzalah, the Earth Shaker, curled his trunk in greeting. Apu, sitting cross-legged behind the huge, flapping ears, laughed softly.

'Fear not, *hakim*-sahib. We are dreamers this hour. We share one dream, Zalzalah and I . . . the forest . . . tunnels of shade and dappled light, the smell of damp moss . . .'

Man and beast were both opium addicts. And it was Zalzalah who had taught the habit to Apu, his mahout. Some of the males, if more than usually violent and unpredictable when in musth, were calmed with opium. Thereafter they were addicted to it, and their mahouts were allowed to give them a daily supply. Invariably the mahouts became addicted too.

Apu spoke quietly to Zalzalah. The massive elephant arched its trunk over its head, lifted the opium pipe from Apu's hand and presented it to me. I wondered whether the wetness on the stem was human or elephant saliva. I had administered opium to relieve the suffering of the wounded. A good doctor should know as much as possible about the drugs he prescribes. I put the pipe to my lips.

I am not sure how long I stood gazing into those eyes, yellow and white, mixed with red. They were fascinating. All fear of the great beast left me. I proffered the rice-and-honey ball which I kept in my pocket, its long presence there testifying to my inability to overcome my horror of that writhing, reptilian trunk. I had imagined the palm of my hand being raised into a blister by the suction, my whole arm disappearing up that hairy, muscular proboscis. Now I laughed as I held out the titbit. I laughed because, seen from a long, long way off and in the total context of the cosmos, a man feeding an elephant is a most incredibly, side-splittingly funny thing. This scene, complete with comic actors, was arranged exclusively for the amusement of me, the distant spectator. Still laughing, I ran my hand over Zalzalah's rough, bark-like skin and pressed an ear against his underside. Twenty-five heartbeats to the minute, nearly one-third the human rate. I watched the sun flashing on a tusk and in that instant knew so much, saw so many interconnecting truths. Then I was sick, and reality and Bamian's voice were knocking on the door of my mind.

Bamian beckoned to me from a point at the start of the elephant lines. Some days ago Bamian had fulfilled a lifelong ambition by holding a lighted candle to a farting elephant. The result: a jet of blue flame, a near stampede and one dwarf soundly whipped and banned from the elephant lines on pain of death. So he stood, looking down the rows of swaying, chained pachyderms, trumpeting louder than the best of them.

'General Ghulam Khan, my new master, sends me to say you are invited to a feast this night.'

'What a noise!' exclaimed one of the mahouts. 'We could use him to accustom the new intake to the sound of cannon-fire!'

'What is the occasion of the feast?' I asked, when I was closer.

'A very special occasion; and only a very few special people are invited. You should feel honoured.'

'Yes, but what special occasion?'

'Time enough to find out when you get there.'

Outside my tent, holding a black mare, waited a high-turbaned, elegant young courtier. He led the mare forward.

'This mare is Rahdar, the Speedy One. She is for you, *Hakim-*

Nadir, Physician Unparalleled. The Princess Razziya wishes you to accept the gift. May Rahdar bear you swiftly to the princess when next she has need of you.' He handed the reins to Dadu and swung lightly on to his own mount. 'And the princess asks me to say that you have a healing touch.'

'A beautiful animal! Beautiful!' murmured Dadu, as the young gallant rode away. 'What's that you say, Ali? That I'm no judge of horseflesh? True. But I am an excellent judge of womanflesh, and I'm telling you, Ali, it's not the mare she wants my master to mount.'

Mohini ran from the tent and clutched my arm. 'Why does it have to be you? Let someone else attend her! Let Faisl go!'

I kissed her forehead where her red *talik* mark was.

'Thomas-jun, I beg you to tread warily. She is a spider who weaves webs of cunning and intrigue.'

'And I'm merely a stupid fly, I suppose!' I freed my arm and examined the garnet-studded bridle and the ruby in the pommel of the saddle. 'Prepare my bath. I attend a feast tonight.'

The chief guests, the very special people, indeed the only people at the feast, appeared to be Faisl, Frog and myself. Faisl and I wore the gowns, woven in silver thread, which had been presented to us on arrival. Frog had refused to cover his monk's garb with the robe of worldliness. I noted that he had also declined to bathe for the occasion. I had expected to meet generals, nobles and men of learning. All three of us must have entertained similar thoughts, for we sat in silence, eyeing each other balefully.

According to Dadu, the general needed a thousand camels to transport his personal baggage, his tents and all their furnishings and trappings. I cast my eyes around the pavilion of red cloth with its linings of Gujarat brocades, its five canopies, each of a different colour, its centre pole sheathed in gold leaf; I thought of the many carpeted passages through which I had been led blindfold; I remembered the sumptuous quarters of the general's first wife. Usually I halved any statistics supplied by Dadu. For once I believed him.

We knelt amidst piles of silken bolsters, around the borders of a blue-patterned Persian carpet. In the middle of the carpet was a large, covered, silver dish, surrounded by bowls of fruits and cold meats. Behind us were lines of servants with feathered fans on silver poles.

General Ghulam Khan made entrance, surrounded by his body-guard. Their duties, I noted, included preventing the ground from hitting him, for he was far from sober. His greeting to his three guests was a yell of rage. His face darkened, with the exception of his nose, which remained a delicate almond shade. This was the first time I had seen him since the rhinoplasty was completed. I gave Faisl an approving nod.

'Bamian!' roared Ghulam Khan. 'Where is Bamian, my jester? Have him brought here at once!'

The lid of the silver dish wobbled, then slowly lifted. 'You called, sire?'

'Did I not command you to find the five greatest fools in the camp and bring them here for my amusement?'

Frog snorted; Faisl's eyebrows rose into pointed arches. Bamian crawled slowly across the carpet, his head nodding like a tortoise, the silver lid his shell.

'Explain yourself, you speck of dust in my household, or I shall amuse myself watching you hang.'

'The hempen fever,' I whispered to Faisl. 'No cure for that.'

'*Huzoor*,' said Bamian, 'there is no greater fool than a learned one, so I reasoned that these . . .'

'Hmmm,' said Ghulan Khan, scratching his nose at the join. 'But I said five fools and I see only three.'

'*Huzoor*, I must correct you. Counting the two of us, there are five!'

'What!'

'Yes, *huzoor*. We are the biggest fools of the lot. You for sending me on such a mission, for all mankind is foolish at one time or another; and I for obeying you.'

There was a silence. I could hear Frog's stomach rumbling. Bamian withdrew into his shell. The quails in aspic trembled, the candles flickered, Ghulam Khan's laughter rolled around the tent. Bamian's head reappeared, eyes blinking. I could see from the expression on his face that walking on the knife-edge of Ghulam Khan's temper was another form of gambling.

The general clapped his hands. 'We five fools are hungry. Bring on the main dishes!'

Frog, thank God, thanked God silently, crossing himself and scratching his armpits in the same movement.

Bamian said, 'I saw a woman making that sign, the other day.'

Frog stopped in mid-reach for a morsel of spiced sheeps' brains. 'Here? In the camp?'

Bamian cracked a bone between his teeth and sucked at the marrow. He nodded. 'I heard tell she came from Malabar.'

Frog's eyes shone with excitement. St Thomas, we are told, visited the Malabar coast about fifty years after the death of Our Lord and established a number of Syrian churches there, before meeting a martyr's death. I said nothing. Bamian's elaborately casual mention of the matter made me suspicious. It was another of his baits – but for what trap I did not know.

We ate with our fingers, tearing pieces from a whole roast lamb, which was stuffed with a flavoured chicken, which was stuffed with a patridge, which, in turn, was stuffed with eggs filled with pistachio nuts. And with these comestibles Frog was doing his best to stuff himself.

'Do you often spy on Mohini and me when we're making love?'

Frog swallowed something the wrong way and turned several shades of puce.

'Frog, that bowl of rose-scented water is for washing your fingers in, not for drinking.'

'A shame on you, Coryat! If I had received the love of a woman like Mary, I'd want no other!'

'I suppose you watched Mary and me as well! That's how you keep your vows, is it? I do it for you, while you toss off behind a bush or a curtain or something.'

'I've never looked before! I swear it, Coryat! I was at my prayers, kneeling in front of the Blessed Virgin, but . . . but there was a hole in the canvas partition . . . just above her halo and . . . and . . . Oh, Thomas!'

Wine must have mellowed my anger, for the thought which was uppermost was that I would not have known of Frog's lapse if he hadn't shouted out, thinking to save my life.

'Celibacy is too heavy a burden for man,' I said.

'The Church is the virgin bride of Christ, served by a virgin priesthood. The Council of Trent has confirmed that it should be so.'

Bamian leered. 'There's all sorts of other things two virgins could get up to!'

'It seems', said Faisl, 'that Christians regard celibacy as the ideal and monogamy as a concession to human nature; whereas we Muhammadans see the ideal as monogamy, but concede polygamy as being nearer to natural instincts.'

'Lust!' snapped Frog. 'Lust! Lust! Lust! It is the prompting of the Devil and puts us no higher than the animals.'

Faisl laughed politely. 'I'd rather be accused of lust than of intolerance towards another man's religion. It is thanks to the enlightened example of the Adornment of the World, our Emperor Akbar, that Christian, Hindu and Muhammadan can sit here, sharing the same meal.' He trimmed his moustache with his fingers and sipped delicately at his wine. 'And what other Muslim ruler in the world would allow Hindus to hold high office? Or abolish the tax on Hindu pilgrims?' He turned to me. 'In your country, are Jews allowed to hold office?'

'Not even Roman Catholics are,' I said.

Ghulam Khan yawned and belched. 'You're here to amuse me with your foolishness, not bore me with discourses on religion!' He drained his goblet and called for more. 'I had intended to crown one of you as King of Fools, but . . .' He poured the contents of his goblet over Bamian's head. 'Since this wart on the arsehole of mankind has seen fit to include me among the heirs to that title, I have asked my new astrologer to perform that task.'

He snapped his fingers. Ramananda fawned into the presence of his master. My heart sank. Greed for revenge was written all over his face. Revenge for all the times that Frog, Bamian, Faisl or I had mocked him.

He held a wreath of thorns. Red betel-juice spilled from the lake behind his lower lip. 'A fitting crown for the King of Fools!' he crowed. 'They say that only wise men recognize their own folly. We shall see who is the most eloquent concerning his wrongheadedness, his stupidity.' He sucked back some of the overflow and smiled triumphantly. 'Each of you shall tell me, in great detail, sparing nothing, exactly why he is such a fool. The least persuasive shall wear the crown.'

'Excellent! Excellent! Capital sport!' cried Ghulam Khan.

Ramananda smirked. 'Of course, in your case, great general, Sword of the Righteous, there is no need. Your horoscope is crowded with benign and portentous planets, the moon's ascending mode and Mars all proclaiming the power of your intellect; while the glittering temples in the firmament continually reaffirm the rightness of your actions.'

Ghulam Khan nodded solemnly and hiccuped. It was a standard precaution for eminent people to conceal the true date of their birth, in order to protect themselves against the perils of malignant sorcery and the calculations of hostile astrologers. And therein lay some of Ramananda's undoubted power and influence with Akbar's general. Ramananda was one of the few people who would know the real date of Ghulam Khan's birth.

I stood up. 'You ill use your guests, sir. I did not expect that an Indian noble would –'

A guard pushed me down and drew his sword. Ghulam Khan laughed drunkenly.

'The astrologer's brain is addled!' bellowed Bamian. 'Addled from too many of his own aphrodisiacs. Not that they'd do him any good, they're as false as his divinations!' And Bamian began strutting about the pavilion, his head in the air, gazing at imaginary stars and falling over every obstacle in his path.

Ghulam Khan slapped his thighs and rocked to and fro with laughter. Ramananda hissed angrily. Frog was on his feet pointing an accusing finger.

'All this nonsensical babbling about conjunction of planets and favourable stars! Were all those drowned in the Flood born under the same star?'

Only then did I realize what was happening. Bamian and Frog were vying with each other for the crown! The dwarf craved risk. His expression was hungry, not unlike the look on the faces of the soldiers who waited outside the camp whorehouses. And Frog – perhaps it was enough that Our Lord had worn a crown of thorns; perhaps I had been wrong to remind him of his lapse from grace at the peephole.

Frog pressed on with his attack. 'When Jacob and Esau were born so close together that one held the other by the foot, how had they such different lots in life?'

Ramananda's reply was to tell Frog, in every detail, how utterly deluded he had been when preaching to the Tamil pilgrims; how they had not understood a word; how it was only his own vainglorious hopes that had let him believe otherwise; how his so-called friends had sniggered behind his back.

'That's what makes you a fool!' Ramananda snarled and rammed the cruel thorns on to Frog's head. Frog did not cry out. He stood there, shoulders sagging, head bowed, blood running down his face. At Ghulam Khan's bidding, the guards, grinning broadly, knelt before him, Abbot of Unreason, crowned King of Fools.

I was making love to Mary. I was the pestle to her mortar, the pin to her cushion, the crew to her pleasure boat. Then her organ became a long, writhing, hairy, elephantine, foul, leprous thing. Shouting, I woke. My head ached. There was a pain in my toes. I had ejaculated over Mohini's back. Her breathing was too even, too controlled; shudders ran through her body. I turned her on her back and kissed her breasts. Her milk flowed. My spunk spilt for Mary, her baby's milk, our tears shed for things that could never be; I rubbed the mixture into her nipples, her stomach, her groin, till her body trembled and cried out in a different way. The tight, hard knot inside me unravelled; the fortress into which I had retreated crumbled. And I knew, by the softening of Mohini's face, that her love unclenched and extended welcoming *anjali* hands to me. We had quarrelled again. At dusk, a messenger had brought yet another gift from the Princess Razziya, a diamond and ruby brooch. The princess grew weary of waiting for me, the messenger said. She languished for want of my healing touch. I lay with Mohini in my arms. She sang softly, one of India's haunting *ragas*, suffused with yearning. A fall of moonbeams made pools on the rush matting. Mohini slid from the bed. She stood naked in the moonlight, her black hair shining, her nose-jewel glinting.

She danced the dance of Lord Shiva in his half-male, half-female aspect. The goddess creates and the god destroys so that life might begin anew. Mohini was both god and goddess, the left side of her body gentle, graceful, feminine, the right side forceful, vigorous, masculine. She was more eloquent than any orator I had ever heard, wiser than any philosopher I had read. I saw, most lucidly, that all existence is part of the Great Dance; that there is no part of creation which does not have its own life-cycle, whether it be the ephemeral insect or the rivers, rocks and mountains.

Something was scrabbling and scratching at the base of the tent. The Chota Chua, perhaps, or hungry jackals scavenging for food. Mohini covered her nakedness. I unsheathed my sword and stood with it raised. A pair of fat little legs squirmed under the canvas wall, then a well-rounded bum, finally Bamian's bulbous head. I smacked him playfully on the buttocks with the flat of my sword.

'Was the doorway not big enough for you, Bamian?'

He laughed harshly. 'I always said that life was a cruel joke. So, what better way to die than as the victim of a trick?'

Mohini brought him a cup of wine from one of Dadu's illicit bottles. Bamian gulped it down.

'Khoratji, Ramananda has contrived a clever plan to have me burned alive.'

Mohini gave a cry of dismay. I said, 'I did not think his malignity would be content with wounding Frog. What malefice does he spawn now?'

Bamian recounted how the astrologer had told Ghulam Khan of a dream. In this dream Ghulam Khan's ancestors had come to Ramananda saying, 'We lack entertainment. Tell our worthy relative upon earth that he must arrange entertainment for us.'

'I suppose, after the first thousand years or so, being dead must become a bit monotonous,' I said.

According to Ramananda, the ancestors then requested that Ghulam Khan's jester be sent to them. The way to do it, Ramananda advised, would be to bury Bamian under a thousand bundles of hay. When set alight, they would produce a column of smoke which would carry the dwarf up to heaven, where the general's ancestors dwelt.

'Well, I pointed out to the general –'

'Sh! Not so loud, Bamian!'

'I pointed out to him that charred remains aren't very good at making jokes. But the drunken fool dismissed this as an insignificant point.'

'You mean he approved the plan?'

Bamian nodded grimly.

Mohini said, 'Bamian, if . . . if you see my baby while you're up there . . .'

'You stupid girl!' I snarled. 'How can you think the dream is true? Do you not question the general's right to burn an innocent man? And do you really expect Bamian to accept his fate?'

Mohini hung her head. I turned to Bamian. 'Why have you not sought safety in flight?'

'I consulted the dice, Khoratji. They indicated I should come to you.'

'And how did you read that in the dice?'

'A three and a five. Your tent is the third one in the fifth row, is it not?'

'That could just as well mean that you should be thirty-five miles away from here by now! You must leave immediately. Tell me what you need and I —'

Struggling bodies filled the tent. At the centre of the whirling mass, clutching four men to his chest in a bear-hug, was Dadu.

'Run, Bamian, run!' he roared, as he crashed to the ground.

Too late. In rushed more men. A pistol was held to my head. Bamian was grabbed, bundled into a sack and carried off.

Mohini begged me to go. Then she begged me not to. Dadu dropped hints that I should and Ali that I shouldn't. They watched as I mounted the black mare, Rahdar. My petition to Ghulam Khan, on Bamian's behalf, had failed; so had Faisl's. Now I sought the intercession of his senior wife, my patroness, the Princess Razziya.

I passed Frog's quarters. Frog had been acting strangely of late . . . more strangely than usual, that is. He was refusing to allow anyone into his tent and hardly communicated with his friends, devoting more and more of his time to the Chota Chua. I supposed that his resentment over the way we had deceived him about the Tamil pilgrims had come to a head and burst. From the rear of his tent arose the same awful noise that had assailed my ears for the last three days. Sometimes it was like a hundred pigs being slaughtered simultaneously, at other times it was more akin to the howling of rabid jackals. It was, in fact, the attempts of three score or more Chota Chua to sing alien Latin psalms. Still wearing his crown of thorns, Frog stood, surrounded by ragged and naked children, frantically waving his arms in time to the psalm which he hoarsely bellowed. My greeting went unacknowledged.

I rode across the open ground hard by the elephants' fodder store. Men were dumping bales of hay in readiness for Bamian's pyre. The exact spot had been marked out by a square of bales. Seven mullahs, paid by Ghulam Khan, were consecrating the allotted ground, praying in relays night and day until the appointed hour. According to Ramananda's calculations, the most propitious moment for Bamian's ascent to heaven was five days hence.

I was led into one of the public state-rooms of this amazing ephemeral edifice. As I waited, I reflected that I, who had fondled her most intimate parts, had no idea what Razziya looked like. From her voice I would guess that she was a flower not yet faded, albeit a flower desperately in need of watering.

Musicians entered, filling the chamber with sounds of flute and the stringed *sarinda*. Then Razziya's covered palanquin was carried in, surrounded by her handmaidens and her eunuchs. I bowed low and enquired after her health.

'I sent for you and you sent herbs and medicines. Why did you not come yourself?'

'Your Highness, there are many of the general's men badly wounded, many dying . . .'

She dismissed their suffering with a scornful laugh. Her voice softened and lowered by a semitone. 'And what about the ring I lent to you. Would you not like to wear that again?'

'Princess?'

'Fool! Is there no subtlety in the West? When you examined me, I put a ring, a very special ring around your finger . . . perhaps you do not remember, perhaps . . .'

'Ah! Princess, I have thought of nothing else! A jewel beyond compare!' I poured out the eulogies I had heard Faisl use to describe the boy Chaitan.

'Flattery is a form of insult,' she said. 'Who but the vain or the stupid would believe such nonsense?'

To deny that it was flattery was simply more flattery. To agree that it was flattery was to insult her. A sort of gargling noise came from my throat. She was delighted at my discomfiture. Her mood became more gracious. She asked the reason for my requesting an audience with her. Dispensing with all the lies about my burning desire for her company, I told her about Bamian.

'Yes, it will make a most interesting spectacle,' she commented.

'Interesting! Cruel, unjust, vindictive . . . these are the words to use!'

Princess Razziya and all her handmaidens burst into peals of laughter. 'I see nothing funny!'

The musicians stopped playing and rocked with laughter. Even the impassive faces of the eunuchs began to crack. Razziya breathed deeply.

'If all doctors could make their patients laugh like that every day, there would be no need for any other medicine.'

'Glad to be of service,' I said, bowing stiffly.

'You used the wrong word,' she said. 'The word you used has . . . special meanings in the harem.'

The handmaidens tittered. I scowled at them. 'The right word from you, princess, would save the dwarf's life.'

'The general, my husband, is a shrewd man. A diversion of that nature is good for the morale of his men . . . You! You with the flute! I appoint you to take the place of the jester.'

The wretched musician flung himself to the floor, begging for mercy. 'I am not good enough to play in heaven! I play false notes. I am not worthy of the honour.'

'In that case, you are not good enough to play for me either! Have his lips cut off!'

I said, 'I did not come here to trade one life for another, but to seek justice.'

'We shall see. Those who seek favours must render services. . . You are dismissed. As for this miserable flautist . . . a hundred lashes . . . false notes indeed!'

I left the chamber to the sound of swishing canes and the screams of the flute-player, who cried out in his pain how merciful, just and benevolent was the Princess Razziya.

A servant handed me Rahdar's reins. My foot was in the stirrup when one of Razziya's handmaidens, in flowing muslins, slipped from a side entrance and beckoned to me. I walked Rahdar past the girl and stopped to adjust a stirrup leather.

'The princess rides at dawn along the banks of the Yamuna . . . the grove where the banyan trees meet the water's edge . . .' She glanced around. 'Be there tomorrow.'

I bent lower over the strap.

'Have no fear, *hakim*-sahib. The eunuchs will be well chosen . . . and well paid for their silence. And we, her handmaidens, would never betray her.'

I nodded. Bamian's life probably depended on it.

I shivered as I rode the black mare. Who but a fool would commit adulterous acts with the wife of one of the most powerful men in the land? Who but a madman would spurn the advances of the capricious Razziya – a ruthless and influential woman, feared throughout the empire?

Rahdar shied as a dark shape detached itself from the shadows and hurtled straight at me. Could vengeance be so swift? It was Damayanti. She clung to my leg with her leprous hands, her feet dragging in the dust. I spurred Rahdar into a gallop. Damayanti hung on, looking into my face with her jellied, pustular eyes. Then she let go. I turned and flung a gold piece at her prostrate body. Before she could reach it, a horde of Chota Chua materialized from nowhere and were fighting each other for it.

I made no mention to Mohini of an intended assignation with Razziya. I simply said that she had agreed to mention the insignificant question of Bamian's life to her husband.

The unknown excites the imagination, not only to fear, but to lust. Over and over I had created, in my mind, the body which belonged with that vibrant voice, that eager, squirming quim. At such times I found Mohini's adoring gaze, her joy on my every return to our tent, her close attention to my needs, her disappointment when duty called me from her company . . . I found these things excessively irritating. And that injured expression of hers only increased my impatience.

'All these tears are shrinking the carpets,' Dadu grumbled. That evening, he and Hamza, the skeleton, were playing cards by candlelight. He had propped Hamza into a sitting position against some cushions. When it was Hamza's turn to play, Dadu would select a card at random from the bony hand. Although it was a game of skill rather than chance, Hamza was winning.

'I'll remove that grin from your face before the game's over!' Dadu growled.

Mohini sat cross-legged on the floor, rolling her eyes and wobbling her neck. In Frog's tent, the massacre of the psalms continued. Whoever coined the phrase 'Practice makes perfect' had never met the Chota Chua.

I was working on the corpse of a drowned soldier which had been brought to me only a few hours ago. He or it – and I am inclined to use the latter, for plainly the body is no longer inhabited – was laid on the table, surrounded by candles. I had opened up the chest and was observing the action of the lungs as I blew air into them through a reed. For ease of insertion into the trachea, I had cut a small hole in the neck. Some medical books, still in use, portray the lungs like a bladder. As any butcher could have told these authors, had they bothered to ask instead of relying upon the writings of the ancients, lungs are more like tough, squelchy honeycombs. The lungs in this corpse were saturated with water. I observed, in the flickering candlelight, that the lungs emptied themselves naturally of the air which I pumped in and that, each time this happened, quantities of water were expelled with it. Could it be that our bodies use air for purposes other than ventilation? Breathing must surely perform some more vital function. Why else do men die of strangulation and suffocation? And what would be the effect of pumping air into a body that had ceased to breathe? Observe, test, record. But the thought of bringing people back from the dead made my scalp prickle.

When there was a lull in the fighting and the flow of wounded was reduced to a trickle, I did not normally lack for clients. The nobles and their ladies paid gold for my treatment of the many ailments which had no origin in battle. Today I should have been visiting a case of gravel in the kidneys, performing a lithotomy to remove a stone from the bladder, treating agues, administering a herbal vermifuge to drive forth worms from the belly, and diacodium for diverse melancholy conditions of the stomach . . . should have been – but I was not. Messages arrived with excuses, evasions and stories of unlikely recoveries. Suddenly my services were no longer required. Coincidence? Or were there rumours circulating? Rumours about Razziya and me, rumours which would almost certainly reach the ears of Ghulam Khan.

I blew vigorously into the lungs, expanding them to their utmost, the better to display their shape. In fact, the only patients I had treated today had been two cases of smallpox. Not that there was much I could do for them. The illness runs its own course and the person either recovers or dies. Faisl tells me that the worst outbreaks are always in the hot season and that, this being the cool season, it may not spread. We shall have to wait and see. Why is there always so much blood in the lungs? And what is the relationship between them and the heart? Grasping the heart in my hands, I observed the root of the pulmonary artery. It is close to the right ventricle and whitish in colour; it ... I glanced up. Ali Pasha, the Chief Eunuch, stood at the entrance to the tent, framed against the stars, looking at me as a cat looks at a mouse. Behind him was an armed host. My hand gripped the stilled heart. Mohini was oblivious to all, her eyes rolling, her hands speaking the language of the dance. Dadu, frowning over his cards, had seen nothing. An avalanche of bodies descended on us. I was on the ground, two people astride my chest and several more sitting on my legs; Mohini was flat on her face, a heavy foot on her neck; Dadu was tied to the tent-pole.

The young captain in charge of the host had fainted at the sight of the opened-up chest. One of his subordinates was fanning him. My breeches were pulled down. Ali Pasha grabbed my testicles and pulled. I screamed.

'You should be thanking me,' he said, leering into my face. 'I am about to relieve you of the root cause of all man's problems.'

I did not know I had such strength. It took seven men to hold me down. Ali Pasha drew his sharp, curved sword. He was licking his lips and giggling.

Hamza pitched forward, an extended finger pointing to one of the spilled cards.

'The Snake of the Ravana suit!' whispered a soldier.

'An ill-omen!'

They glanced at each other uneasily. Ali Pasha gave another high-pitched giggle. 'An ill-omen for this fornicating infidel!' His grip tightened on my genitals. He raised his sharp, fearful instrument of castration. The corpse let out a loud groan; a long, continuous groan, a voice speaking from hell. Ali Pasha dropped his sword and fled. The soldiers followed, dragging their captain, who had fainted for a second time.

I pulled up my breeches. Mohini's eyes were round with fright.

'The corpse . . . how . . . how could it . . .'

I began to laugh. I couldn't stop laughing. 'The air in the lungs,' I gasped. 'The air moving over the larynx causes it to vibrate and emit sound.'

'Don't untie me just yet,' begged Dadu. 'My leg trembles so, I don't think it will hold me up.'

I drew Mohini to me. She pushed me away. 'Fornicating . . . that's what the eunuch said. You've been fornicating with Princess Razziya! I hate you!' Sobbing, she fell to the ground.

'Listen to me, Mohini!'

'I won't! I won't! You love her more than you love me! I'm not good enough for you any more!' She tore at her hair, rent her clothes.

'It's you I love, Mohini! You know I love you. But there's Bamian's life to think of.' I stroked her hair and told her all that had transpired.

'You stuck your finger in a hornets' nest and no mistake!' commented Dadu, who could hardly help overhearing, since he was still tied to the tent-pole.

Mohini clung to me. 'Bamian is doomed,' she said. 'We cannot save him now.'

Outside, there was frost on the ground. Today was the start of Advent. The stars were fading, there was a blush in the eastern sky. Vapour poured from Rahdar's nostrils as I saddled her. I mounted. My eyes met Mohini's. I scooped her into the saddle.

'Er . . . excuse me,' Dadu called out. 'Do you think you could untie me now?'

We rode, not towards the Yamuna and the waiting Princess Razziya, but towards the rising sun.

More gifts awaited me on our return. A pair of thigh-length Gilgit boots of embroidered felt, a velvet cloak sewn with pearls, a miniature painting in a gold frame. The painting showed two lovers on a terrace engaged in ecstatic sexual intercourse. The man wore a large European-style hat. The value of these gifts filled me with foreboding. I sent Dadu to return them. He was to say that I considered myself to be unworthy of such favours; that to be allowed to serve so

great a lord as her husband and, therefore, the righteous cause of the
Emperor Akbar, was reward enough. I had no doubt that Ghulam
Khan would be informed of every move in this game. Perhaps if he
realized I had taken heed of his warning . . . Rahdar I kept. To return
a gift already accepted was too gross an insult. The knife-edge I
walked was sharp.

Faisl advised handsome gifts to both parties.

'But I don't have anything to give!'

Faisl preened his moustache and stroked his beard. 'She admires
your poetry.'

'But I can't write poetry, you know that!'

'She doesn't. And I have several poems, written for Chaitan, which
only need a little bit chopped off here and there.'

'And Ghulam Khan?'

'Well, now. What he would like most is Mohini. I've seen him cast
admiring glances at her more than once.'

'Give him Mohini?'

'Yes.'

'Never!'

And more cases of smallpox awaited me too. The red flower, as
the soldiers called it, was in bloom. This day it killed more people
than did Shershan. Not that all its victims were fighting men. Many
were camp-followers. It was particularly rife among the Chota Chua.
Indeed, that is probably where it started. At least the outbreak kept
me busy, kept my mind off the fate that was to overtake Bamian
before the day was much older, perhaps made my own removal
slightly more inconvenient than my continued presence.

Frog, at any rate, would be safe, despite his unceasing contact with
the Chota Chua, for the disease seldom strikes the same person twice.
Frog says that this is because God, in his infinite mercy, does not visit
such punishment upon us more than once. Bamian says it is to do
with immutable laws of chance. I say we do not know.

Mohini brought me a bowl of goat's milk. She knelt beside me and
put her head in my lap. 'Thomas-jun . . . you will not be angry with
me if . . . if I . . .'

'What is it, my little gazelle?'

'If I make *puja* at the shrine of Mariamma and pay for an amulet to
ward off the red flower? You . . . you will wear it . . . to please me?'

148

I drank from the bowl. She was endearing, touching, infuriating.
'We shall see. Maybe it will subside soon.'

'Thomas-jun, apart from you, there is nobody dearer to me than Bamian. I could not bear to watch him burn. Must I go with you?'

'It is a terrible thing to die alone, my love. At the last, his eyes should find his friends, not those who come to watch him die out of pleasure, amusement or mere curiosity.' The lump in my throat was making it difficult to swallow. I sipped at my milk noisily.

'Khoratji! Khoratji!' Creak, thump! Creak, thump! 'Khoratji, do not drink from that bowl!'

Dadu lumbered into the tent. 'The drink!' he panted. 'It has been poisoned!' The milk had been heating on a fire outside the tent. Mohini had turned her back and Dadu, returning from an errand, had seen a woman slip a white powder into it.

'Go after her, Dadu. If we can discover what the poison is . . . Take Rahdar.'

Dadu lurched out of the tent. I felt dizzy. Pains were starting in my intestines. I mixed up an emetic and swallowed it. I vomited. How much had my body absorbed? Kettledrums beat a tattoo inside my brain. I swallowed more emetic and vomited again.

'Who is it, do you think?' I asked Mohini. 'The general, or his senior wife?'

Mohini was weeping and clinging to me. 'It's that jealous whore, Razziya! If she can't have you, she's going to make sure no one else can!'

Brow clammy, mouth dry, pulse 108, Dadu returned.

'I caught her! I beat her till she told the truth.' He looked at me quizzically. 'It's worse than I thought.' But he was grinning. 'It was a love-potion! The girl was sent by the Princess Razziya.'

I began to feel better.

Dadu continued, 'The powder contained, among other things, certain of the lady's bodily excretions – her menstrual fluid, to be exact, which, if imbibed with the rest of the magical concoction, would undoubtedly have enslaved you to her.'

Mohini hastily proffered the emetic. I waved it away. 'The potion has not had the desired effect, I assure you.'

Dadu sighed. 'Her cheeks flushed most prettily when I beat her; her bosom heaved most beguilingly, her . . .' He stopped and sniffed.

We all smelt it. In the clearing beyond the elephant lines, a thick white column of smoke rose high into the air.

'So soon! The hour has crept upon us!' cried Mohini.

Bamian was burning and my thoughts had been entirely upon myself, imagining pains that did not exist. Bamian's pain would be real enough. I seized the beaker of emetic and drained it to the last drop. Let the gut-wrenching, bile-spilling vomit drive out all other thoughts.

On the edge of the *maidan* was a small hill or mound – the same mound upon which Gampopa and many of the dancing troupe had died. As the carrion crows returned from the scenes of skirmish to roost in the woods south of the camp, a strange procession approached the hill. It was a sacrifice to Mariamma, goddess of smallpox. The men offered their own tortured bodies in propitiation.

Five men were harnessed to a heavy wooden cart by means of barbs inserted in their backs. They pulled an effigy of Mariamma, made of red wood which oozed a red sap. Behind the cart, two men carried gibbet-like structures on their shoulders. Some walked on spiked sandals, which pierced their feet at every step; others had cheeks stuck through from side to side with knives, or bristled with sharp stakes inserted under their ribs and weighted with iron bells. At the rear of the procession, surrounded by Chota Chua who plied whips to his back, was Frog. He wore a crown of thorns and dragged a heavy wooden cross.

The goddess Mariamma reached the top of the mound. The gibbets were erected and their carriers hoisted into the air by hooks inserted into the muscles of their arms and chests. Frog set down his cross between the two gibbets. I saw him lie down and spread out his arms. I saw a large iron nail driven through his feet. I heard his cry of pain. I began running towards the mound. The crowd had grown, swelled by the beggars, vendors, hawkers and tricksters, who know a good opportunity when they see one. By the time I gained the top, Frog had been crucified.

Eight

'And how is Brother Peter?' Faisl asked.

We were walking down the elephant lines. Chaitan was beside him, noisily chewing a length of sugar-cane. Both wore surcoats of bright saffron with sashes of emerald green.

'He sleeps much and says little,' I answered.

'He was in a swoon when you lifted him down, was he not?'

I nodded. Chaitan swaggered ahead. More food and less dancing had made him fat. He turned and addressed some Persian endearment to his lover. Faisl flushed with pleasure.

Bamian . . . Bamian had been right to select us three for the biggest fools he knew. A clever man enslaved by a conceited boy; a man who voluntarily nailed himself to a cross; and one who, as Dadu put it, stuck his finger in a hornets' nest.

'When is there going to be a proper battle?' Chaitan asked, pouting. 'It's been nothing but patrols and skirmishes and minor ambushes. You promised there'd be a big battle.'

Faisl laughed indulgently. 'That depends on many things; on the level of the river, on the information brought to Ghulam Khan by his spies; on when his astrologers, and Ramananda in particular, pronounce the moment to be auspicious.'

We dallied near a fresh intake of elephants. In northern India the big elephant markets, or *melas*, happen about four times a year. This batch of ten-year-olds had travelled several hundred miles from the Harihar Chatra *mela*, which takes place at the first full moon in November.

'But why did Brother Peter do it, Thomas? Why would anyone do such a thing?'

Some of the new intake were being driven down a specially

constructed alleyway between high stakes. It was so narrow that they could not avoid stamping on the sheep and goats placed in their path. Unless greatly provoked or frightened, wild elephants will step over a fallen body. Man has to teach them to crush living things underfoot. Later they would progress to live prisoners. We left Chaitan watching the spectacle and walked on.

'Why, Thomas? Why?'

'Do you remember, at the Feast of Fools, Bamian made reference to a woman in the camp who might possibly be a Christian?'

'Yes. Brother Peter became quite excited at the prospect.'

'Well, Frog went to see her yesterday.'

'And?'

'The whole thing was one of Bamian's tricks. She was a camp whore.'

Dadu had told me about it. The girl had been well paid by Bamian. He had instructed her in the strange ways of the white foreigner. When such foreigners referred to their cocks, they used their own special words such as 'Christ' or 'Jesus'. If he said something like 'Let us worship Christ together', she would know what to do. And they were very partial to kneeling positions. Then Bamian, who had become a student of the Scriptures through constant exposure to Frog's preaching, had gone about chortling to himself. 'His seed will not fall on stony ground. His cock shall crow thrice before he denies her.'

We passed Zalzalah, whose trunk curled out in expectation of a titbit or two. I fed him without fear.

'You were right, Faisl. Celibacy is too great a burden.'

'Break the bone of guilt and therein lies the marrow of remorse.'

'I think it was more than remorse. He believes God directed him to the Chota Chua.'

'I see. And suddenly smallpox strikes them down.'

'Exactly.'

'It was a cruel thing Bamian did,' Faisl said, turning to look at Chaitan who was sitting astride the stockade. 'Take care, my beautiful peach. Take care!' Chaitan ignored him.

'But that was Bamian's point, Faisl. It's a cruel world, directed by cruel gods. Frog's preaching may have incensed him, but, in his peculiar way, Bamian presented us with just as many parables of his own . . . I'll miss the ugly little bastard.'

'Excellent stuff, this, for growing roses,' Faisl commented, prodding a large elephant's turd with his pointed toe. 'Ah, Thomas, you should see the Ram Bagh in Agra. A garden to arouse the jealousy of paradise!'

Agra. A knife-sharp sword. Faisl prattled on, quoting verses from Nizami's *Iqbalnama*, unaware that he had extinguished the sun, raised the dead and set the seas of the mind in turmoil.

'You know, Thomas, I have seen men crucified before. Some hung there for as much as two days before they died.'

I pushed Mary from my thoughts and replied, 'According to the Scriptures, Christ died after six hours.'

'Hm. Most unusual . . . but then, his anguish was more than bodily anguish, was it not?'

'Well, Frog is not going to die, anyway. It may take more than three days before he rises, but he'll be up and about before long.'

Dushman-Kush, the Enemy Treader, was being treated for a badly poisoned foot. We both stopped and watched with interest. It may be heresy to say so, but it seems to me that our bodies function in much the same manner as the other hot-blooded creatures of this earth. The shepherds who frequented the Black Bull Inn at Honiton could tell me, for the price of a mug of ale, more about the process of giving birth than any midwife ever could. And these mahouts have known, for hundreds of years, many things about the treatment of wounds.

'Arrogance is a blindfold,' said I.

'And we doctors are in a maze at the best of times,' added Faisl. Faisl turned, summoned by Chaitan's imperious call. He tugged his beard. 'Do you think, my friend, I would look younger if I dyed it yellow?'

'No. Merely more foolish.'

Chaitan called again, impatiently. Faisl shrugged helplessly and departed.

'*Hakim*-sahib, come! Come quickly!'

An elderly woman I had never seen before tugged at my sleeve.

'It is the dancer, Mohini. She had been taken ill. She calls for you.'

'What is it? What is wrong?'

'I do not know, *hakim*-sahib, but she is very weak. Come, follow me.'

'Where is she?'

'She was dancing for my lord, the General Ghulam Khan, when she suddenly fainted away.'

'Can't you walk faster?'

'I am old.'

'Faster, woman! Faster!'

She led me through the royal enclosure to a back entrance in the several acres of tents belonging to Ghulam Khan. Could it be poison? The woman was panting, despite the slow pace.

'Hurry!'

'She was carried to . . . to an . . . inner apartment . . . in here . . .'

She stood aside at the entrance to a small canopied bower. Mohini lay on a couch with her back to me. I recognized the sari as one I had given her. I ran forward. Gently I turned her over. Damayanti's mutilated face grinned up at me and hissed and spluttered incoherent words. A cage door clanged shut. I had walked into a trap. I kicked the door; I shook the stout bars of the cage and shouted. Damayanti cackled loudly.

Something moved behind a carved ivory screen just beyond the bars. Razziya's laugh had lost its warmth. It was a hard, cruel laugh. 'Surely you did not think that I, a princess, would overlook an insult.'

I thought of the rejected gifts, the unkept assignation, of how I had vomited up her love-potion.

'You foolish, conceited man! You dared to think you might be my lover! Phah! You misconstrued my patronage for a man of learning, my kindness to a stranger in a foreign land.'

So this was to be her version of events. She probably even believed it by now. No doubt I had abused my privileges as a doctor and made indecent advances to her. Damayanti cackled again. Seeing her diseased, leprous body in Mohini's clothes only increased my loathing.

Razziya's words cracked like a whip. 'Fool! Ingrate! Instead of a princess for a lover, you can have her!'

Damayanti advanced upon me with outstretched arms. I pushed her away and backed into a corner of the cage, trembling uncontrollably, shouting hysterically. 'Keep away! I'll kill you if you come near me!'

The first day passed with me huddled in a corner, kicking out at Damayanti whenever she came near. The cage was twelve feet wide and twenty feet long. Even when we were at opposite corners, her presence made my flesh crawl, and something inside my brain to scream and keep on screaming.

Food was brought. One platter for the two of us. I punched her away and ate first, keeping an eye on her all the time. I slid the platter across to her. She fell upon the food, burying her face in it like a dog.

Several times Damayanti addressed me. With no roof to her mouth, a collapsed and rotting nose, half her gums missing, lips that were welts of thick warty skin, her speech was meaningless to me, mere babblings, sprayings of spit and volumes of foul breath. It grew dark. She gestured to me, with hands so different from Mohini's, to take the couch. She would sleep on the floor. I shook my head, reluctant to abandon the comparative safety of my corner.

In the blackness of my prison, every hiss of breath, every beat of a beetle's wing, became translated into Damayanti slowly sliding across the floor towards me. Then I would lash out, expecting to contact raw, pulpy flesh. Later she began to snore, an inhuman, animal noise, but, like ships' bells in a fog off Chesil Bank, it indicated her whereabouts in the dark.

I woke with a start and struck out with hands and feet. The snoring had stopped. It resumed. I felt for the bucket which had been placed in the cage for purposes of urination and defecation. I squatted above it, trying not to touch it with any part of myself. And now fears, other than my immediate and overwhelming terror of lepers and leprosy, assailed me. Nobody knew where I was. How long would I be incarcerated here? Till the dreadful affliction claimed me? And what of Mohini? Was it all fabrication about her being taken ill? Razziya's jealousy would surely focus on her sooner or later.

With the dawn arrived the first ray of hope to lighten the darkness of my despair. Faisl would work it out. Faisl, Mohini and Dadu between them would conclude that Razziya was bound to be behind any sudden disappearance on my part. But would they discover where I was? And, if they did, what could they do? I concentrated hard on believing that they would not give up, that someone out there loved me who would save me.

The second day passed. I found that I understood the odd word, even a whole sentence here and there, of Damayanti's strange speech. I gave much thought to Frog's fear of leeches, to my fear of elephants. These had been conquered by understanding and knowledge; by replacing imagination with fact. That night I slept on the couch. She was, she assured me through signs and the occasional comprehensible phrase, well used to sleeping on the ground – in fact, she slept better on the ground.

By the seventh day, Damayanti and I were holding conversations. She was not the old crone I had taken her for. Only the ravages of leprosy made her seem thus. She was of an age with Mary. From Damayanti, the first leper I had ever talked to at length, I learned many things. She told me that she had been a leper for twenty years. For all but the last five of these years, she had lived on an island in the river Ganges, which was inhabited solely by lepers. It was her opinion that the disease was not fatal. There were many on the island who had lived longer than she. Her suffering and pain had seemed to ease after a number of years, or at least to reach some kind of plateau. She still continued to lose parts of her limbs, however, joint by joint, and it was the disabling effect of this which she found one of the hardest things to bear.

And on the eighth day I learned from her gurglings and gutturals that, in her opinion, the disease was not as contagious as we, the outsiders, the rest of the world believed. I, as part of the rest of mankind, believed her not. She was only saying that to comfort me, or so that I would let her come nearer to me. Or perhaps it was some kind of self-deception. She told me of Buddhist priests who lived on the island among the lepers. Only in rare cases did they contract the disease, and some had lived there for five years or more. She spoke of several instances of husband or wife who, themselves untainted, lived on the island with their spouse, apparently without ill effect.

'Lies! Lies!' I shouted. I swore at her. I abused her. She insisted it was true. Furthermore, it was not unknown for a perfect baby to be born of two infected parents. I screamed at her to be silent. I covered my ears with my hands and banged my head against the bars.

She came close and snuffled in her hoarse, palateless way, 'You are not interested in me, only in my disease.'

'It is Mary of whom I think.'

'Maaaaa.'

'Mary! Mary!' I roared, trying to exorcize the guilt that haunted the cage.

Why was I not in Agra? How could I have let myself be so distracted? I wept with grief, vexation, remorse. If ever I got out of this cage, I would break off all ties with that silly superstitious girl, Mohini. Henceforth I would not stray from the purpose for which I had come to India. If. If was a big word, and help was a long time coming.

The ninth day found me in calmer mood; resigned. I thought of Apu, the mahout. 'Zalzalah will not harm you,' he had said. Fear had made me believe otherwise. And I remembered the shikaree I had met at Muttra. A successful hunter studied the animals closely and learnt their ways, he had told me. Observe, test, record: that was the path to follow. More than any other disease, leprosy, or the fear of leprosy, banished reason, was subject to belief without evidence, assertion without fact.

I questioned Damayanti on many things pertaining to her condition. I observed her closely. I noted the lobes of the ears enlarged and thickened, the large and prominent rugae over the eyes, the absence of hair on the eyebrows. I examined, in detail, the way the tubercles on the skin became cracked and divided by fissures, and how these were the seat of ulceration or dry, sordid scabs. I studied carefully the nature of her amputated joints and was puzzled. In my opinion, ulceration alone would not account for so severe a damage to and loss of the extremities.

On the tenth day I touched her.

Then, on the twelfth, or was it the thirteenth, night, I woke to see a rat gnawing at her foot. She slept on, feeling nothing. I had not realized, till then, the degree to which sensitivity in the limbs was lost. Pain is the lookout that cries 'Beware'. Without that warning, there would be occasions such as now, when she would not be aware of the damage being done and therefore would do nothing to remove either the endangered part or the source of the danger. More than likely, this was the cause of the slow erosion of her extremities. As a child I had thought that heaven, at least, must be free of pain. If that were so, then all the angels would be sans fingers, sans toes, and sans other things besides. I must remember to tell Frog that when . . . when . . . and Coryat the detached, impartial man of science was suddenly Coryat the lonely, whimpering prisoner, uncertain and afraid. And Damayanti, the woman sore afflicted, comforted me and bade me be of good cheer.

Three days later, the guard opened the door and left it open. Nothing was said. I took Damayanti by the hand and walked out of the cage. Faisl was waiting for me in the passageway. He was holding my medical bag. He embraced me, gave a handful of gold to Damayanti, then led me towards – yes, he embraced me, embraced me – towards the private chambers of General Ghulam Khan. While I shaved and bathed, I learned from Faisl that it was Mohini's idea which had secured my release.

Ghulam Khan was in the habit of demanding from Faisl various antidotes for the effects of his drinking bouts. Under this guise, Faisl mixed up a brew which reproduced in his patient symptoms very similar to those caused by a largish and immovable stone in the urinary tract – the chief such symptom being a pain so excruciating that a man will do almost anything to escape it. What Ghulam Khan did was to stop pretending he did not know my whereabouts or how his senior wife was amusing herself. The termination of his pain was more urgent than the commencement of mine. My skill in treating for the stone, particularly in the operation called lithotomy, was required. Razziya had been ordered to release me.

Faisl had prepared Ghulam Khan for the operation. He was drowsy with *quunubus*, lying face down. For a brief moment I held the great general's testicles in my left hand and a scalpel in my right. It was not Ali Pasha of whom I thought, but of Razziya. How long since she had held them, I wondered. For the benefit of his mullah, who was present, the servants who were assisting and the guard at the door, I explored his rectum. By an elementary sleight of hand, I produced a stone which I had extracted from another patient and, luckily, had kept, hoping to make certain tests upon it. I avoided Faisl's eye. I was breaking my Hippocratic oath. They say that violence spawns violence; and now I, who had suffered the abuses of power and privilege, was countering in like vein.

One hour later, Ghulam Khan was sitting up, greatly pleased to be free of pain. He praised my skill, delighted that the operation was causing him almost no discomfort. He would return the stone to me, he said, after he had set it in a silver ring and clustered it with diamonds. It seemed I was back in favour.

The taste of freedom, the feel of fresh air and sunlight on my face. I walked slowly. Beside me, Faisl talked eagerly of this and that. I wasn't listening. How was I to tell Mohini that our love was at an end? She was there, waiting for me, outside the royal enclosure. Faisl slipped away discreetly. Her joy at our reunion was unbridled. We walked, entwined together, she laughing, crying, babbling like a brook in flood; I silent, rehearsing the words I must use.

Inside our tent, she let her sari fall from her, unloosed her bodice and stood naked before me. 'Oh, Thomas-jun, it has been a long time.'

'Mohini, I . . . I have been confined with a leper for these two weeks past. I may be infected, I . . .'

'My love, what do I care?' She held out her arms to me.

I stepped back. 'It is not safe. I would not like to be responsible for . . .'

'Thomas, you are my lord, my life. You are my sun, my moon and stars. My fate is your fate. Do not send me away.'

'Mohini . . . Mohini . . .'

'Please do not send me away. To die of a broken heart would be the crueller fate, for it would be alone, without you.'

Only now, when I was resolved that we should part, did I recognize her true worth and match her love with the same intensity. We were both crying, then embracing, then kissing. Perhaps one last time; perhaps the parting would be easier this way; a final act of love, a memory to hold.

I awoke. Trumpets sounded in the artillery lines. The same message rang out in the elephant lines. The call to arms was sounding through the entire camp. Ghulam Khan and Shershan were about to engage in a major battle. Temporarily, Mohini was forgotten.

To prepare an army of two hundred thousand men for battle takes many hours. All that day and far into the night, the camp swarmed with activity, like a disturbed ants' nest. The elephants were dressed in their thick string armour, the protective padding slung from their flanks, the spiked bracelets attached to their forelegs, the fortified howdahs lifted on to their backs. Some were painted with tiger stripes, the more to terrify the enemy. Just before battle commenced, the huge beasts would be fed on cat meat, for it is believed that this makes them aggressive; and they would have chilli-juice squirted in their eyes to enrage them to a murderous pitch.

At midnight Dadu came to me and begged to be released from my service for the duration of the battle. Outside the tent, orders rang out, bugles sounded, marching feet trampled by. Dadu's eyes gleamed in the candlelight.

'I beg you, Khoratji. Those are my comrades-in-arms out there. To fight side by side with men creates bonds stronger even than making love.'

'What about that leg, Dadu?'

'I'll manage, never fear. This sword has a long reach.' He whirled it about his head, accidently decapitating Hamza. 'Hah! That shall be the fate of the enemy!'

I laughed. 'All right, Dadu. Good luck!'

Faisl, who was with me, checking the supplies we would need for the next day, said, 'By the snorting chargers, and those who strike fire with their hooves, and those who make incursions in the morning and raise the dust therein, take care, old soldier!'

I think he was quoting from the Koran.

At first light on the next day, Ghulam Khan's army crossed the Yamuna. The artillery, the horses and the men were poled across on huge rafts. The elephants and camels swam. First to land were the cavalry. They patrolled the far bank and its approaches against surprise attack. Next were the cannon. They were dragged by elephants to the areas of high ground which commanded a field of fire across the plain and which were already held and fortified. Faisl and I and the other men under our command accompanied them, for one of these rises was to be the location of a dressing-station for the wounded.

We watched two elephants labouring up the slope with a heavy artillery piece. The master elephant of the battery charged forward with a thick chain in its trunk and thrashed them to renewed effort. Massive war elephants, grey moving hills in the half-light, advanced across the plain. Huge drums, slung either side of camels, beat time, the pulse of tens of thousands of helmeted men who marched to their battle positions.

Ghulam Khan arrayed his forces in the shape of a great bird. A mile across the plain, Shershan's rebel army was counter-arrayed in the form of a half-moon. Forests of spears glinted red against the rising sun. Banners fluttered in the wind. Then the entire rebel army faced the direction of Mecca and prostrated themselves on the ground.

'Now would be the time to attack,' I said.

Faisl smiled. 'Look!'

The Muhammadans of our own army, which was about half of the entire host, were doing the same. Faisl did not follow suit. We watched both armies praying to the same god for victory.

'That should put Allah in a dilemma,' I said, knowing that Faisl, like Akbar himself, did not follow a narrow, fanatical path regarding the teachings of Muhammad.

Faisl regarded me with his gentle brown eyes. 'See those men standing at the river bank?'

'Yes.'

'All they see is a straight stretch of water, flowing northwards. From where we stand, we can see that the river bends and twists, but has a general trend towards the east. So it is with this battle. Whatever twist or turn events take today, none of us here can say whether, ultimately, it is for the better or for the worse. Only Allah, who sees the rivers of our lives flowing into the vast ocean of time, knows that.'

Ghulam Khan, his standard flying from the howdah of his elephant, caused the horns and trumpets to be blown. Two hundred thousand men gave a great shout. For miles around, birds rose into the air. Then the artillery opened fire.

The two wings and the sharp beak of the bird-like formation were armoured elephants, which now charged upon the enemy. Shershan held back his own elephants. Instead, he sent out horsemen. Some dismounted and drove sharp stakes into the ground in front of the advancing wall of tusks. Others scattered spiked caltrops in their path. The wily rebel then released rhinoceros at the oncoming beasts, followed by camels soaked in oil and set alight. These shrieking, blazing animals, like fireships amongst a fleet, caused utter panic in the ranks of the elephants. They trampled and mauled each other in their efforts to escape, or ran headlong into those still advancing from behind. Though the archers, rocketeers and musketmen on their backs still poured death into the enemy, the charge was broken. The cavalry swept past them, driving deep wedges into the rebel formation. The foot-soldiers closed with their adversary. The din was deafening. A thick dust arose and hid most of the action from our sight.

The first casualties arrived; crushed, burned, ripped and bleeding bodies. Pain and fear unmask us, strip away our actors' robes, leave us naked and shivering. One hour as a field-surgeon would teach our philosophers and theologians more about the nature of man than all their books.

Faisl had charge of the Muslim wounded, I of the Hindus. Even so, a young soldier in my care died refusing a cup of water because it had been touched by a member of a lower caste. He entered death's dark womb in the same fashion that he was born, covered in blood, eyes unseeing and after much travail.

During the morning, the artillery battery next to us came under bombardment. Luckily, the enemy cannon were out of range. The cannon-balls bounced and rolled up the hill as if someone was playing bowls. Among them rolled a bearded head, teeth bared in a grimace. As in a storm, there were lulls, sudden squalls and periods of sustained fury. Again and again the two armies disengaged, re-formed and hurled themselves at each other anew, breaking into a thousand combats, swirling and mingling fiercely, like the currents of the Yamuna and the Ganges meeting. Briefly, I caught sight of Dadu leading an assault on rebel artillery emplacements. A cannon-ball carried away his left leg. Unabashed, he advanced on the foe at a hop. Overawed, they fled before him.

Neither Ghulam Khan nor Shershan was willing to break off the engagement. Both obviously believed that victory could be theirs, that Allah had heard their prayers. The sun set and still the battle raged. Then Ghulam Khan drew up his forces in a formation called the Thunderbolt. Each foot-soldier held a blazing brand; every horse carried two such burning lamps and on each elephant six were placed. The army, radiant, flames reflecting from armour, helmets and swords, advanced across the darkened plain like a cloud of fireflies and fell upon Shershan's men. The flaming brands burned low and went out. The night was filled with shouts, cannon- and musket-fire, the neighing of horses, the screams of the wounded. How many men, in the confusion and the darkness, were slain by their own side, will never be known. Gradually the noise faded. Men toppled from their saddles in exhaustion and slept where they fell. Others slept on their feet or sprawled within a few yards of their slumbering enemies. Elephants knelt, their trunks resting on the ground. All was motionless and silent, like a forest unstirred by the wind.

The moon floated up from the east and the two hosts rose up as the ocean rises at spring tide. Tired though they were, they fought again. It was Akbar's superior artillery power which, as Dadu predicted it would, gave victory over the rebel. Just before dawn, the rebel army broke and fled, and were pursued and hunted down.

From our vantage point we saw the plain strewn with bodies, discarded weapons, helmets, shields, swords, dead horses, elephants and camels, smashed howdahs, upturned cannon.

'Like the earth in spring when it first flowers,' said Faisl.

'Like the drinking garden of Death himself, as if he had been revelling here and just departed,' said I.

Packs of jackals gorged themselves, packs of Chota Chua darted hither and thither, searching the dead for valuables. We descended our hill and wandered through the scene of carnage. A platoon of soldiers were building a victory tower of heads; a prisoner was being held by a nose-ring while being blinded with a red-hot spear; we passed a heap of slaughtered females, camp-followers of the rebel army.

'It is inevitable,' Faisl remarked, sadly. 'Since women wear all their wealth in the form of rings, bracelets and other trinkets which cannot be removed without mutilation, and since a soldier's pay is insufficient unless supplemented by loot and booty . . .' He shrugged.

Amidst this chaos, a man was ploughing in his ruined wheat crop, weaving his ox and plough between the wreckage that lay about his field. Unless he could plant another crop he would starve.

'He'll starve anyway,' said Faisl. 'He won't have enough grain set by both to feed his family and to re-seed his field.'

The plough made a detour round a group cutting up a dead elephant. The parts were laid out in order of value. First among these was the penis and the nerve pulp inside the tusks, for from these are made aphrodisiacs of great value; then the tusks themselves, the vital organs and the best cuts of meat. I bargained for and purchased the heart. Perhaps it would reveal to me things which the eye cannot see in the smaller human heart. I stood inside the caverns of the bare rib-cage, holding this massive heart wrapped in a discarded cloak, and marvelled. No cathedral built to the glory of God ever impressed me so much.

On returning to the south bank of the Yamuna, I was met by Frog, astride a donkey. Though his hands and feet were still bandaged, his face showed no trace of the suffering he had borne. Quite the contrary. His eyes sparkled and he beamed at me.

'Frog, my instructions were that you should stay in bed.'

'It's happened! It's happened!' he burbled. He began laughing, then weeping. I wondered if he was delirious.

'I have saved a soul for Christ! A young girl of the Chota Chua!' I had never seen Frog look so jubilant. 'I baptize her tomorrow. Others will follow – I know it!'

'I am glad for you, Brother Peter.'

He rode off, shouting hallelujahs and praising God.

'*Shabash*! *Shabash*!' Dadu hobbled up on a crutch, minus his false leg, dragging a sack full of what I supposed was loot. '*Shabash*!' he cried. Obviously he had enjoyed the battle. 'You see! No injuries to speak of, other than the odd leg missing!' He grinned broadly. 'And what spoils of war have you collected?' he asked, pointing with his crutch at my bundle. 'A silver chalice, perhaps? A golden standard?'

'An elephant's heart.'

He roared with laughter, then nearly choked, when I showed him.

'And what's in your sack, Dadu?'

'Aha!' he said, tapping his nose. He winked and jerked his thumb over his shoulder. Trailing behind him were a score or more of men, covering bloody faces with their hands. 'This sack contains Ghulam Khan's revenge.'

Reaching the river edge, he emptied its contents down the bank. A sackful of bloody, severed noses. The wretched victims fell upon them, snatching them from one another, each trying to find his own in some wild hope that, while still fresh, they could fit them on and they would grow again. I turned away. Dadu followed me, recounting with relish his version of the battle.

'Dadu, do you not mourn your comrades? Did you not fear death for yourself?'

Dadu rolled his eyes and coughed, unsure whether to give some bluff, soldierly reply or answer me seriously. After a mumbled consultation with his tapeworm, he said, 'I am a soldier, not a guru, but . . . but it seems to me that we should neither mourn the dead nor fear death. Rebirth is certain for one who dies, just as death is sure for one that's born. At no time did I not exist, nor shall cease to exist in any future happening. There is a part of me which is never cut by weapons, is never . . .' He broke off with a laugh. 'But I duck the arrows, all the same, and run when it is expedient.'

Dadu sighed heavily and paused on his crutch to mop his brow. I have noticed that, since he lost his leg, he sweats more profusely.

'I was hoping to capture a nice fat wench for a prize,' he said. 'No such luck, though. Most of them were so thin you could smell the shit through them. It's always the same after a good battle – my thoughts turn to touch-holes of a kind not found on cannon.'

And so did mine. After the sight of so much killing, injury and pain, I longed for the oblivion I would find in Mohini's young body. Our parting could be postponed until tomorrow. I would tell her tomorrow.

Mohini's young body was what enthralled and engrossed a thousand men. Inside the red canauts, Ghulam Khan's officers, the grandees of the Mogul court, celebrated their victory. I was proud, jealous, sad, all at once. Proud that Mohini, of all the dancers in the camp, should be the one chosen to dance solo at the victory feast; proud that this girl, whose body I knew as no one else knew it, could make a thousand pulses beat as one and, through such mastery of pose and rhythm, mould time as though it were a piece of clay. I was jealous of the lascivious gaze of Ghulam Khan. And I was sad. Suddenly every moment with her was precious. Like a miser with his hoard of gold, I begrudged every second she was not with me. Our time together was running out. Now that Shershan was defeated, the camp would be breaking up; the soldiers going their different ways; I to Agra, she . . . well, there was no lack of opportunity for a dancer of her talent. It had been merely a casual affair along the road, no more than that. I had to think of it like that, or my resolve would weaken. One last night together, just one. Tomorrow I would tell her. Tomorrow we would go our separate ways.

It was during this dance that Faisl was summoned from the audience.

'It is the general's favourite wife,' he whispered in my ear. 'She has been taken ill.'

Mohini's dance ended. The drums tapped, the flutes took wing, the audience stirred and murmured. She was going to dance the duet with the Demon King, from the story of the *Ramayana*, the dance for which she and Bamian had been famous throughout the camp. To dance it on her own could only be interpreted as a reproach to Ghulam Khan for the dwarf's death.

Mohini began the introductory solo passage. Ghulam Khan half rose from his pile of cushions. She arrived at the point where the Demon King makes entrance. There was a flash, a puff of smoke – and there stood Bamian. He was not dressed as the Demon King but in the singed clothes in which he had been immolated. There was a stunned silence. Bamian stepped forward, bowing deeply to Ghulam Khan.

'O Tiger Among Men, I have had a most interesting time with your ancestors in heaven. I have done my best to entertain them. Now they send me back to say that what they really want is an astrologer.'

Ramananda leapt to his feet with a yell and ran from the pavilion. We never saw him again.

Making love in a howdah, on the back of a gently swaying elephant, with the moon glinting on the Yamuna, must be a foretaste of paradise. I had arranged it with Apu, the mahout. To be exact, Apu had suggested the idea, probably knowing that I would pay him well. After the victory feast, Zalzalah and Apu were waiting for Mohini and me in a quiet corner of the camp. Mohini was happy. I had not told her this was to be our last time together.

We drank more wine and laughed anew at Bamian's dramatic

entrance and Ramananda's hasty exit. It was Frog who saved
Bamian's life. All the time the Chota Chua had been rendering the
vicinity well-nigh uninhabitable with their psalms, they had been
covering the noise of digging. Directed by Frog, they had dug a tunnel
from his tent to the spot chosen for the pyre. After the bales of hay
had been piled on top of the dwarf, a cleverly constructed trap-door
had let him into the tunnel. That Frog should do this for someone
who had missed no opportunity to humiliate him was no surprise to
me.

Mohini, of course, had a more colourful explanation for these
events. Having already convinced herself that Frog had brought
Dadu back from the dead, she had no difficulty in believing that he
had simply repeated the miracle for Bamian. She smiled tolerantly at
my need for mundane, worldly explanations and fed inwardly upon
her knowledge, like a woman who has discovered she is with
child.

'I see Bamian as an instrument of God,' Frog had said to me.

'God certainly does work in mysterious ways.'

'Through him I have been privileged to know some infinitesimal
part of the agony of the cross and to bear, for the rest of my life, the
most blessed stigmata. And if Bamian had not tormented me I would
not have needed to exercise forgiveness and try to save him from the
burning. And that led to the digging and the psalms . . .'

'Those psalms! More than an infinitesimal taste of hell!'

'They succeeded in bringing the Chota Chua to me like nothing
else had done. Without them a little girl would not have renounced
the Devil and all his works, would not, tomorrow, be letting the
waters of the Yamuna flow over her head to mark her baptism into
the Faith.'

Learning that he was an instrument of Frog's god had quite spoilt
the descent from heaven for Bamian. He had stamped about in a
temper for the rest of the day. He took comfort, though, from the fact
that Frog's god had a jester. A man called Jesus, who dealt in the
absurd and the impossible as any good jester should and took the
knocks for everybody, as was the custom in the trade. Frog had
actually laughed out loud at this idea and invited Bamian to the
baptism. I was invited too, of course.

'Tomorrow is the most important day of my life, Thomas. To have saved a soul from the Darkness; to have led a child to the Light – this one thing alone means that I have not lived in vain!'

Mohini was asleep in my arms. My own eyelids felt very heavy. Zalzalah crossed the Yamuna, swimming, so that all but the howdah was submerged and a moonlit island that was his head, upon which Apu sat. This should not be happening. We had agreed to keep to the south bank, in case there were still bends of rebel soldiers abroad. I tried to call out to Apu. My tongue wouldn't function properly. Mumbled words dribbled out in a jumble. Bodies floated by. Very small bodies. Whole clusters of them like rafts. Surely Frog was only baptizing one child?

Zalzalah touched bottom, gained dry ground and, urged by Apu, broke into a run. Desperately, I tried to shout. No words came. I fell into a heavy, drugged sleep.

Nine

The sun filtered through a canopy of leaves. Zalzalah swayed along a narrow jungle path, parting tall bamboo.

Mohini smiled down at me. 'I thought you would never wake.' She handed me a cup of water. 'Apu says the wine was drugged.'

I struggled into a sitting position. 'That treacherous dog! To think I trusted him!'

Mohini put a hand on my arm. 'I have spoken to Apu, Thomas-jun. It is not what you think. This is not Razziya's doing.'

I noticed that we had an escort. A dozen small, wiry men – Gonds, like Apu – walked beside Zalzalah. They were naked except for the leather pouch which held their genitals. Blowpipes were slung across their shoulders.

'Do you remember telling me, Thomas-jun, how General Ghulam Khan took revenge on the captive rebel leaders?'

'Yes. Those noses lying in the mud. I shall never forget them.'

'One of those men, my beloved, was the chief of the Gonds.'

'The Gonds?'

'Yes. Shershan enticed them out of the forests, to fight for him, with promises of gold . . . Apu was mistaken . . . he thought it was you, not Faisl, who grafted a new nose for Ghulam Khan. The Gonds have carried their chief back into the forest and we . . . you . . . you are being taken to him to . . .' She began to weep. 'Oh, Thomas-jun, if you refuse to do the operation, they will deface me in the same way and . . . and if you are not successful . . . Apu says . . . he says the Gonds will kill you.'

'But I have never done a rhinoplasty! I've only watched what Faisl did.'

'I know! I have told Apu, I have told him a hundred times! He thinks I am lying in the hope that we will be released. He says that Dadu impressed upon him, many times, how you yourself tended the general; how important you were.'

'The lying, boastful fool!'

Zalzalah carried us further and further into the forest. Through swamps, across rivers, past huge trees called teak, into areas of grass taller than a man and back into dense jungle. The elephant seemed to know when a branch was too low for our howdah. He would stop and break off the obstruction before proceeding. The sounds of unseen wild animals crashing through the undergrowth, the unidentified howls, the poisoned darts of the Gonds — there was no thought of escape in my mind.

I had several conversations with Apu. It was obvious that he meant us no harm, being cheerfully optimistic of my success. My instruments, books and medicines, he revealed, were in a wooden chest behind the howdah. But I worried. Faisl had admitted that there was an element of luck in whether one area of skin would grow on another. Not all grafts were successful, by any means. With these thoughts on my mind, it was some time before I recollected what I had seen, or thought I had seen in my drugged state, as we had crossed the Yamuna.

'Apu, those bodies floating down the Yamuna . . . were they the Chota Chua?'

'Yes, *hakim*-sahib. Our great general not only mutilates those who have surrendered to him, he murders children too.'

'Murder?'

'Yes, *hakim*-sahib. He ordered a massacre of all the Chota Chua in the camp.'

'Oh my God! Why?'

'His favourite wife died of the Red Flower. He holds the Chota Chua responsible. It was they, he says, who carried the disease through the camp.'

'All of them? Were they all killed?'

'All the children died. But you cannot kill the Chota Chua. As long as there are wars and famines and plagues, there will be Chota Chua. The general himself is the creator of that which he destroys.'

Frog would take no comfort from such a thought. His mission in life wiped out; the cup of success dashed from his lips. To what sin within himself would he attribute this disaster? What terrible self-retribution would follow? I feared for my friend.

Over the next few weeks, Mohini and I learned the ways of the Gonds. They were not the ways of other Indians I had met. The Gonds were hunters; they spoke a language of their own, so that we had to rely on Apu to interpret. They worshipped their ancestors and the spirits of the trees, the rocks and the rivers. They moved around the forest, making temporary villages which they then abandoned after two or three weeks. This way of life Mohini and I shared with them. We were treated as guests rather than prisoners. There was no need of bars: the jungle and the wild animals were sufficient.

The Gond chief, Rammu, resembled an undersized, elderly gnome. He was round-shouldered and walked with a limp caused by the bite of a wild sow, on whose litter he had, as a boy, inadvertently stumbled. Rammu bore the discomfort of the skin graft and rhino-plasty with great fortitude and cheerfulness. Although he was the cause of our abduction, it was impossible not to like him. I was thankful that I had taken detailed notes of Ghulam Khan's case. Nothing seemed to have gone wrong in the early stages. It was too soon, though, to say whether the final outcome would be successful or not. At least three or four months must elapse before the little Gond chief could be satisfied that he did, indeed, have a new nose.

'The month of Phalaguna is when I must have it,' he would say, through Apu, our interpreter.

Phalaguna, the month of February, was when he led his people out of the forest to harvest the wheat. Men, women and children would migrate over the dusty passes to the wheatlands on the plains to cut the crop for the farmers. One sheaf in twenty was their hire and, usually, the farmer made no objection if the wage sheaf was a little heavier than the others.

As I treated Rammu, my thoughts would turn to Damayanti. Perhaps I could try building a new nose for her. Would a graft work on diseased flesh? Could similar techniques be applied to hands? Anything I learned by working with Damayanti could be used to help Mary. But the time was passing. I should be at Agra; I should be questioning and observing Damayanti.

There were days when I walked valleys of impatience and despair; and there were days when I climbed peaks of happiness. I had steeled myself to part from Mohini and had been granted a reprieve. The matter had been taken out of my hands; I had no need to feel guilty. It was as if it were intended that we should be together.

It was Christmas Eve. Mohini and I could hear the women ahead of us shaking the foliage as they picked wild guavas and gossiped about the rock-python they had seen yesterday.

'But it must be true!' Mohini exclaimed. 'Everybody knows that it is so.'

Pythons, she claimed, were crocodiles which, when they attained a certain age, crawl up from the rivers into caves. Then their limbs drop off, and their hide, by much rubbing against stones, becomes thin and they turn into pythons. I tried to reason with her but, to Mohini, beliefs held since childhood were much the same as eternal truths. If superstition is a form of godless religion, she is certainly devout in her impiety.

'Thomas, I can't hear them any more! Where are they?'

We must have taken a wrong fork in the forest track while we were arguing. The fantastic twilight hour of India was upon us. The leaves and branches of the high canopy glowed red and pink, but in the canyons below it was dark. Monkeys ceased their chatter, birds fell silent. A hush crept over the forest, broken only by humming insects, sounds of stealth, or a distant cry of pain. Mohini pressed close to me.

'Thomas-jun, there are evil spirits abroad at night!'

'I have the charm you gave me, my love. Look, we will both hold it.'

It was not so much the spiteful forest spirits which worried me as the deleterious miasmata which rise from the ground at night. I have it on good authority, namely Faisl's, that such vapours can cause the sweating sickness and other fevers.

'Thomas! Thomas! Look, a red eye! And . . . it's winking at me!'

'No, my love. It's only a fire seen through the trees. Perhaps whoever tends it will share it with us for the night.'

We stumbled over fallen tree-trunks and rotten logs till we came to a clearing. A man with long, matted hair sat cross-legged by the fire upright and very still. The fire light flickered on his features. His expression was remote, but soft, almost feminine.

Mohini whispered, 'He is a sadhu, a holy man. Such as he come to the forest to meditate.'

We stood on the outer fringes of the dancing circle of light, wanting to escape the dark, not wanting to disturb his meditation. His eyelids flickered.

'As a person casts off worn-out garments and puts on others that are new, even so does the embodied soul cast off worn-out bodies and take on others that are new . . . Draw near, my children.' He smiled and motioned us to sit. 'The sixteen days of the waning moon are the most favourable to meditation.'

I leant forward, feeling the heat of the fire on my face.

'On what do you meditate, holy man?'

'On the transience of things, for life is but the shadow of a bird in flight. Know and believe, my children, that in this world we are but frogs in a waterless well.'

'What else is there, then?'

'There is *moksha*, my children. There is release from unreality, release from the wheel of rebirth.'

Somewhere in the jungle a tiger roared. Mohini shivered.

The sadhu's gaze was gentle, but utterly compelling. 'There is fear in the jungle, my children. There is fear all around. I feel the fear of the animals. I feel your fear. This fire will protect you from tigers, but where can you hide from the tiger that gnaws inside you?' His eyes captured mine. 'I think you have yet to meet Humbaba.'

'Humbaba?'

'At the centre of the labyrinth we call the mind dwells Humbaba. He is that which we fear most. For each of us he assumes a different form. Until you have come face to face with Humbaba, you will know no peace.' He seemed to be falling back into a trance. His voice was like bees droning. 'And I see chasms. Everywhere I look I see chasms. Leap, you deer of the forest! Leap, you people of this world! Leap . . . leap . . .'

The stars were bright, the night was cold. I lay with Mohini in my arms, her breath fanning my cheek, the sadhu's fire hot on my back. I studied her long, dark lashes which fluttered in her dream. I kissed her and thought of Christmas Days spent with Mary; of the piping and the dancing, the wassailing of the trees, of St George in the mummers' play. I thought of the beautiful Church of Sant' Antonio in Padua, where I had once attended midnight mass. And I wondered how things fared with Frog.

Zalzalah's trunk, snuffling in my ear, woke me. It was morning, and the sadhu was gone.

'You were lost, weren't you?' laughed Apu.

It amused him that a learned doctor was so unversed in the ways of the forest; that a literate man could not read the jungle spoor; that one so dextrous with the surgeon's knife could be so noisy and clumsy as to scare away the game for miles around; that a man who prided himself on his powers of observation could hardly tell one kind of deer from another. On many occasions I could not even see the animals to which Apu pointed. Only after staring hard for a long while and after much patient commentary by Apu would a shape materialize amidst the dappled tree-trunks. Doubtless that is how it is when I examine the leper-woman, Damayanti. I look, but do not see what is there to be seen. My eyes are untutored. I do not know what it is I am trying to see. Of all the different things I see, I do not know which are relevant and which are not.

As we rode back to the village on Zalzalah's back, Apu told us of a strange thing. Usually, after two or three weeks of hunting, the forest animals were alert to the presence of man and moved out of the area, or lay low. Then it was time for the Gonds to abandon their temporary huts and try another part of the forest. Instead of becoming scarcer, the game grew more abundant as the weeks went by. Meat was plentiful, the hunting never so easy.

'Apu! You are covered in bee stings!' Mohini exclaimed.

'Ah!' said Apu, smacking his lips and rubbing his belly. 'Meat is good, but honey is best of all.'

He described how, in the darkest hour of the night – for bees are dangerous even in moonlight – he and other men were lowered over the jungle cliffs to strip the rocks of their fat, dripping cones.

'Yes, we are always stung,' said Apu. 'Neither smoke nor wild garlic protects entirely . . . Ah, but nothing relieves the pain like the taste of honey!'

*

174

Epiphany and Serravati Puja were past, the cool season at an end. The goddess of spring wandered through the forest and, at her touch, the trees bloomed. Mohini and I explored the narrow, fragrant, flowering paths, discovering, not the jungle, but each other. We lingered by pools of water-hyacinth, embraced beneath the bright blossoms of the *jagadumar* tree, while golden orioles and rose-winged parakeets flashed through the branches overhead.

'All across India, we Hindus are celebrating the festival of Kamadeva, the god of love,' Mohini said. 'Kamadeva wields a bow of sugar-cane, and his five flower-tipped arrows are the five senses.'

Mohini, the ripple of your laughter, my skin upon your skin, the light in your eyes, the taste of you, the exciting smell of you.

A part of me wanted this time never to end; a part of me was impatient to be out of the forest. The decision was not mine – not ours. Although Rammu's nose was progressing well, he would not release us. Perhaps next month, he said. Daily, more and more animals filled the forest. The woods teemed with deer of all kinds, blackbuck, sambur deer, gazelle, chitral, antelope. Tigers, leopards, bears and Asian lions were sighted regularly. If Rammu, Apu and the other Gonds knew what was happening, they did not tell us.

One morning, Mohini and I woke to find the village deserted. The Gonds had disappeared. We searched every hut. Not a sign of life. Elephants trumpeted nearby. A herd of gaur were crashing in the undergrowth. Deer, in large numbers, ran this way and that in a state of bewilderment.

By the door of our hut I found my sword, which had been taken from me on arrival. Beside it lay a small packet, made of a plantain leaf, tied with grass. Mohini unwrapped it.

'A *malika*!' In her palm was something like a large black pearl. 'Thomas, in all India there cannot be more than a score of such jewels!'

Occasionally, very occasionally, there forms inside an elephant's tusk a black stone-like growth called a *malika*. It is a jewel much prized, very rare and of immense value. If Rammu chose to show his gratitude so handsomely, why had he left us to fend for ourselves among the wild animals? He had promised that, once my task was done, we would be conducted to the edge of the forest. Why had Rammu not kept his word?

I strengthened the bamboo door of our hut and dragged thorn bushes around the flimsy walls. That night we heard a tiger make its kill only yards from our hut. The tearing of flesh, the crunching of bone, set the imagination bounding, like a frightened deer, through its own dark jungles. Later, when the moon rose, packs of jackals howled and scratched and snuffled at the door. In the hour before dawn, a steady throbbing sound came from the east.

'Drums!' cried Mohini.

'The Qamarghah!' I shouted. 'That's what's happening – it's the Qamarghah!'

Fifty thousand beaters, week by week, had been tightening a circle, trapping thousands, even tens of thousands, of animals in an area of a few square miles.

'That will be why the Gonds left us behind,' Mohini said. 'They have the skill and the knowledge to slip through the cordon undetected, but if we were with them they would soon be discovered.'

'Apu always said that a whole herd of elephants could move more silently than I.'

'The Gonds are right to be fearful. It will not have been forgotten that they allied themselves with Shershan.'

What the Gonds probably did not know, which I now remembered, was that the hunting was the exclusive right of Akbar and his lords. Anyone found inside the enclosed area was liable to be considered as part of the sport and hunted as an animal.

Mohini received the news calmly. 'As long as we die together, Thomas-jun, it is a small matter.'

'I'm sure it won't come to that,' I said. 'After all, we were forcibly abducted here. It is not our fault.'

Mohini gave me a sad little smile. 'I think I would rather trust to the wild forest than to the cruel and capricious whims of those who find us here.'

But I, who believe in reason and therefore must must trust in the ultimate reasonableness of man, decided that we would stay in the hut and wait.

*

The drums were louder, nearer. The heat inside the hut was stifling. It was like a cage.

'Mohini, I . . . I have changed my mind. I have seen too much, of late, of what those with unbridled power can do. We must endeavour to hide until the Qamarghah is over.'

It was midday, probably the safest hour for us to travel through the forest, for most of the predators were asleep or resting in the shade. We headed for the cliffs where the Gonds harvested the honeycombs. I found one of the basket-cradles, attached to a rope of knotted creepers. We covered the outside of it with branches and grass so that, when suspended over the edge, it would look like just another vegetated ledge. While I tested the rope and the knot which secured it to a tree, Mohini gathered wild garlic. Provisions, water-skins, my sword, were loaded into the cradle. Mohini clambered in. Slowly I lowered the swaying basket down the cliff face for about a hundred feet. Then, tying a second knot, I climbed down the creeper to join Mohini.

Two hundred feet directly below us were piles of boulders and the tops of trees. Because of the rocky nature of the ground, the trees and undergrowth were relatively sparse, affording us a view of the multitude of animals which thronged the area. Wolf, panther, antelope, deer – predators and prey – moved to and fro within yards of each other. It was as if, faced by an even greater danger, a truce reigned among the denizens of the forest.

Through the trees, below us, trotted a score of richly dressed men. They rode down their quarry, wheeling and turning with practised skill, using lances to dispatch their victims. Only now did I see my mistake. I had expected that the line of beaters in our sector would pass us by, putting us outside the ever-tightening circle. But the sport had begun. The beaters had stopped advancing. We were inside the chosen area for the Qamarghah.

The slaughter continued for several hours. At some command, as in a military exercise, they downed their lances and slew with sword and later with bow and arrow. Many a wound was inflicted in return by tooth, claw, hoof and antler. We saw one man killed when a wounded panther sprang upon him from a branch and dragged him from his saddle.

'I think these are the high-ranking, the princes and the nobles,' I whispered to Mohini. 'The shikaree said that they were always given first blood, that the hunting was always done in strict order of rank and precedence.'

Finally they rode off, laughing and joking, leaving behind a scene of carnage and a sky black with circling vultures, kites and jungle crows. Later that evening, men arrived on foot and carried away the dead beasts slung on poles, or skinned them on the spot.

'Our turn won't come for at least three weeks,' I heard one of the men grumble. 'By which time there will be nothing left except squirrels, rats and the like.'

'And maybe a few Gonds,' joked his companion.

Mohini stirred in the basket. 'Three weeks! We can't stay here for three weeks.'

'What else can we do?'

Under cover of darkness, we climbed up the creeper to the top of the cliff – a feat that Mohini managed with a deal more agility than I. We stretched our limbs, refilled the water-skins from a stream, performed the natural bodily functions and then, frightened by the proximity of howling wolves, the rustlings and stirrings in the undergrowth, descended once more to our hide.

The fires of the army of beaters flickered in the dark, forming a semicircle in front of us. It seemed we were near the south-western edge of a circle whose area must be about ten square miles. Throughout the night, first one part of the circle, then another, would erupt in a blaze of rockets and clanging gongs. I remembered the shikaree had told me that the beaters erected wattle fences and nets to keep the game penned in. However, special measures, he said, had to be taken to repel a panic-stricken stampede by a whole herd of animals; and these fear-crazed assaults became more frequent as the smell of slaughter pervaded everything.

Next morning, a different group of nobles rode into view. They made their way along the base of the horseshoe-shaped cliff to the mouth of a gorge. They reined in their horses and waited. Suspended on the cliff, level with the gorge, Mohini and I looked across the natural amphitheatre – and waited, too.

Drumming hooves echoed around the cliffs. The rock vibrated against my back. On the plateau opposite us, stampeding deer by the thousand careered towards the lip of the gorge. Mohini gripped my arm. Two stags bounded straight for the chasm and sailed over it. After that, the deer came in waves, whole herds at a time; thundering hooves and heaving flanks approaching the climactic leap. Those that hesitated or tried to turn back were driven over the edge by the oncoming rush. Running among the gazelle, blackbuck and antelope were wild boar, jackal, red-dog and hyena. These, along with the old or ailing deer and those that would not commit themselves to the leap, fell to their deaths. Dust, noise, gracefully airborne creatures, twisting, falling bodies . . . then it ended as abruptly as it had begun. The beaters, bringing up the rear, gathered on the edge of the gorge, their gongs, cymbals, and other instruments of noise, silent. The nobles, in good humour after this diverting spectacle which had been laid on for their benefit, trotted towards a glade. Here, a host of lackeys had spent the morning unloading two elephants, erecting screens, laying out carpets, putting up awnings and fans and preparing food against the arrival of their lords.

'That's Faisl!' whispered Mohini.

Sure enough, the man tending a wounded beater was none other than he.

'Then that must be Ghulam Khan,' I said. It was not his features I recognized, for my eyes are not as sharp as Mohini's. It was his roaring laugh, the deference of those around him and the way he tilted his goblet.

The sun was pitiless, the cliff face scorching to the touch. Despite the leafy hide, the heat was overpowering. The sound of a spring bubbling from the boulders at the base of the cliff mocked and tormented us. We sweltered, and listened drowsily to the reverberating bees.

I sat up. The laughter and commotion was caused by an ape. It was cavorting before the courtiers, performing lewd deeds with a banana. The creature seized a musket and put it to its shoulder. From the reaction of all around, there could be no doubt that the musket was loaded and primed. The ape staggered about under the weight of the weapon, which was longer than itself, pointing it first one way, then another. The shot thudded into a bees' nest, twenty feet below us. An angry swarm rose up the cliff. I threw myself on top of Mohini, trying to cover her, trying to hide my own eyes and face. Mohini was screaming. Fingers, knuckles, scalp, ears, mouth . . . everywhere, stinging, stinging . . .

I emerged from a black, buzzing swoon. My eyes would not open properly. The ape was looking down at me. To be exact, its detached head, which it was carrying underneath its arm, was looking down at me. Faisl and Mohini knelt beside me, rubbing soothing herbs and ointments into my tortured skin. I tried to smile at her. My lips were two fat serpents of fire.

'The pain will pass,' Faisl said.

Mohini raised my hand to her lips and sucked out poisoned barbs.

'I would gladly be stung all over for such attention as that,' said the ape. It was, of course, Bamian.

'She escaped the worst, thanks to you, Thomas,' Faisl said, holding a cup to my lips. I drank, wincing at each encounter with the rim.

Creak, thump! Creak, thump! Dadu towered over me, leaning on his sword. 'I've seen prettier faces, I must admit. You see, Ali, what did I tell you? We can't let the *hakim*-sahib out of our sight for one moment without some mishap befalling him.' He straightened and stood as if on parade. 'Khoratji, I . . . I am sent to tell you . . . that is, you are commanded to present yourself to General Ghulam Khan. You must account for your presence in this forbidden area . . . You too, Mohini.'

In a once-quiet glade, which now looked like a charnel house, lounged Ghulam Khan. A canopy shaded him from the sun. A dozen servants stirred the air with peacock-feathered fans. I wondered whether a black *malika* of great value would appease him. Only then did I discover my loss. My purse, with the *malika* in it, was gone.

A soldier pushed me forward. Ghulam Khan did not look at me. Reclining on silk cushions, he fitted an arrow to a bow and took aim at the circling vultures.

'A hit! A hit!' chorused the men around him, although not so much as one feather was to be seen in evidence. Still without meeting my eye, he said, 'When this quiver is empty, you will be let loose in the forest to be hunted down . . . unless you can . . .'

'A hit! Another hit!'

'. . . unless you can persuade me otherwise.'

Nine arrows left. I mumbled my way through all that had happened, while Ghulam Khan called for wine and fired off arrows in increasingly erratic manner and the cries of admiration from his henchmen became more desperate, more fervent, with each miss.

'Liars! Flatterers! Sycophants!' roared Ghulum Khan, flinging down the bow and snapping the last arrow across his knee. 'You, Thomas Coryat, trespasser in the domain of the royal Qamarghah, what do you think of my marksmanship?'

Faisl was close behind me. I repeated the words he breathed in my ear. 'O Tiger Among Men . . . you . . . you shoot divinely. But Allah, in his wisdom, is merciful to the birds.'

Ghulam Khan stared at me open-mouthed. From that wine-smelling cavity emitted a trickle of sound, growing into a roaring cataract. He advanced upon me. Only when he hugged and punched my bee-stung body, jovially slapped my tender back, did I know that I . . . we . . . were forgiven.

'Phah!' he yelled. 'You stink of wild garlic!'

Graciously he embraced me a second time. The pain I did not notice. Over his shoulder I saw, approaching through the trees, the golden howdah of his senior wife, the Princess Razziya. I stepped back, bowing low. Most amiably, he squeezed my arm and forced upon my swollen finger a ring, a kidney-stone set in diamonds. I stepped back, bowing low. The ground came up to meet me. Like a river in full torrent, Ghulam Khan's laughter closed over my head.

I knew Mohini's soothing touch without opening my eyes, I knew it was her tears which anointed my hot flesh.

'Mohini, my love, being near you is enough to sooth my pain; do not cry, my love.'

Mohini's nails dug into my wrist and fresh tears flowed. I sat up. Around us were portable cages, in which sat trained hunting leopards. Faisl, Dadu and Bamian were standing over me as if it were a wake. It was Dadu who broke it to me in his own delicate way.

'It seems that the princess's beloved leopards have lost interest in the deer. They are bored, sated. So you have been prescribed as the ideal appetizer for the jaded appetites of her darlings.'

'When you say "you", you do mean just me, don't you?'

'He means both you and Mohini,' Bamian bawled, clearly agitated. 'She could have saved her own life, but . . .'

'Bamian, don't say anything, please, I beg you!' Mohini pleaded.

But Bamian could not stop himself pouring it out. I heard what had transpired in the hour that I had lain, for a second time, in a swoon. Razziya had invoked the law of the Qamarghah and claimed the lives of Mohini and myself to provide a little amusement for her hunting leopards. Ghulam Khan had decreed that her demand should apply only to me. As for Mohini, she should dance for him and, if she pleased him, there would be a bright future for her under his patronage.

Bamian's voice was sad, bitter, accusing. 'But you who are perfection of movement, danced like a novice, you . . .'

'Bamian, please do not . . .'

'You tripped, you stumbled, you deliberately displeased the general.'

A two-edged knife twisted deep inside me. Joy and pain, pain and joy. Mohini had chosen to die with me. Until that moment I did not know the real meaning of love.

'Well, Ali says your fortunes are just like my prick – down, then up, then down again!' Dadu's gaze followed the plump figure of one of Razziya's handmaidens. 'And with any luck they'll be up again soon!' He sat down and began unstrapping his leg to reach a hidden wine-skin.

'But he had already pardoned us!' Mohini cried out. 'How can we now be condemned? It is not an honourable thing he does!'

Bamian picked his nose and shook his head. Faisl said: 'The protocol of dishonour is more complex, even, than the question of who should have precedence over whom in matters of honour. Is the dishonour of retracting a pardon greater than that of publicly denying a request from your senior wife? The general's advisers debated the matter for a full hour.'

'I think you and I, Dadu, might play a little dice,' said Bamian.

'I didn't know apes could play dice – not even ones cleverly disguised as dwarfs . . . yes, quite realistic till you get a close look!'

Bamian seized Dadu's unstrapped leg and ran off with it. 'Either you win this back with the dice, or I'll chop it up and burn it.'

Dadu hopped after him, bellowing abuse.

'Here, Dadu here. It's cooler here.'

Bamian squatted in the dust close to the golden howdah. Dadu sat down with a thump. A eunuch advanced, cracking a whip.

'Keep your distance, filth!'

They shuffled out of range, sliding on their bottoms. Bamian rattled the dice.

'Best of five throws. Your leg against these three *shahrukis*.'

With each throw he edged a bit closer to the howdah.

'I win!' called Dadu, snatching back his leg, and scooping up the three coins.

'Let me, at least, try to win back my money,' Bamian pleaded. 'Here's another three *shahrukis* to match them.'

Dadu won again. He yawned. 'The dice pass the time, I suppose, but the first game man ever played is still the best and I must get some sleep if I'm to be fresh for the luscious Aqiqua tonight.'

'No! We must play on!' Bamian started stripping off his clothes. 'I stake these!'

'Huh! What good are those to me?'

'Well, this then!' Bamian produced a purse; my purse. The *malika* rolled to the ground. 'A pretty stone — it must be worth a little . . . the six *shahrukis*, perhaps?'

Dadu laughed good-naturedly. 'All right! Perhaps it will amuse Aqiqua for a moment or two.'

Dadu lost. He lost first the money, then his leg, then the sword with which he tried to redeem his leg. He offered his shoes. Bamian shook his head.

'I have no need of a boat.'

Dadu offered his coat. Again Bamian found the stake unacceptable.

'Tents are unnecessary in the forest.'

Dadu offered Aqiqua, his lady-love, saying, 'She will agree to spend a night with you, if I ask her.'

'What! Would you have me crushed to death?'

'But I must have my leg! I cannot do without it!'

Bamian yawned. 'That was a good idea about getting some sleep.'

'Bamian, my friend, please . . .'

Razziya's voice rang out from the golden howdah. 'I stake a

thousand gold mohurs against all that the dwarf has won! . . . And you, good soldier, throw well for me and you shall have your leg and a great deal more.'

Quicker than a forest fire, the word spread through the glade. A circle of onlookers formed round the two players. Ali Pasha placed a bag of coins on the ground. Razziya's voice vibrated with passion.

'Everything on the one throw!'

Bamian licked his lips and rolled the dice. The news rippled through the crowd. 'A nine! A four and a five; he's thrown nine. The dwarf has thrown nine.'

Dadu rattled the dice above his head, blew on them and cast.

'Seven! The dwarf wins!'

Bamian lifted the bag of coins and stood up.

'Wait!' cried Razziya. 'Another chance! Give me another chance – I pledge my twelve hunting leopards.'

Bamian inclined his head in aquiescence. 'The best of ten throws, then.'

For a full hour the gambling match continued. Razziya lost her hunting leopards, a casket of rubies, a handmaiden of Bamian's choice and a valuable five-headed emerald ring. Its value far exceeded that of the emeralds, Razziya explained, for under each jewel lay an antidote to the poisoner's arts. Was I imagining it, or was Bamian using what, in London, was called a High Fulham? In London I once treated a man who made his living through the dice. The fickle Lady Luck, he explained, had temporarily shifted her allegiance. He paid me by telling me some of the tricks of his trade. A High Fulham was two dice loaded so that they were biased towards the four and the five. Thrown in a certain way, the chance of landing these numbers was high. Was I imagining it? Or was it luck that always kept Bamian just a narrow margin ahead of the princess?

'Another chance! I beg of you, another chance.'

One side of Bamian's face was screwed up, holding the *malika* in his eye. The other eye gleamed mockingly.

'My needs are simple, princess. You have nothing more I want.'

'Name anything . . . anything.'

'In that case, I ask for the dancer Mohini and the Englestani doctor.'

Mohini and I were led into the centre of the circle of faces. We

LORD OF THE DANCE

stood behind Dadu, balancing the pile of wealth beside Bamian.
Dadu held the dice. He looked at Ghulam Khan. The general gave no
sign of dissent. Dadu turned to me.

'Khoratji, I would as soon cut off my hand as be the means by
which your two lives are forfeit.'

'It is in other hands than yours, Dadu. Play and be done with
it!'

'Double fives shall decide it,' called Bamian. There was sweat on
his brow. He did not acknowledge our presence, but stared at the
ground where the dice would fall, panting like a man running for his
life.

'Now!' screamed Razziya.

Throw followed throw. Encircling faces, moving mouths that
hummed and buzzed like the bees on the cliff, staring eyes which
stung with their excitement, curiosity, cruelty, lust. But the double
five eluded both players.

'Oh, Dwapara, spirit of the dice, I invoke you!' moaned Razziya.

I turned my face from the play, enfolding Mohini's trembling body
in my arms. A huge roar. A cry of anguish from Razziya. Bamian had
won.

'Best of five is a better way to win,' I heard Bamian say. My head
jerked round. His expression was fixed, intense. He had used the
passion which he understood so well to bring Razziya, throw by
throw, to this point. Now, that same passion had overwhelmed him.
He did not want the gambling match to end.

'Come, we will change the dice. We shall use your dice.'

Razziya did not deny she possessed dice. I had thought I knew the
woman, yet I had not suspected that this was the ruling force in her
life. Bamian, the fellow gambler, had understood her better than I.
We stood behind him, one of his winnings. One of his forgotten
winnings. He was oblivious to everything except those fascinating
cubes of bone, those beautiful numbers. Ali Pasha placed the new
dice in Dadu's hand.

'Best of five for a double five!' Dadu called.

'Agreed,' said Razziya.

'Agreed,' said Bamian.

Immediately, Dadu threw a double five. On his next turn, he did it
again.

'Help! Help! The young prince is drowning! Come quickly, he's drowning!'

The gambling match broke up. Ghulam Khan's retinue raced through the trees towards the shouts. Listlessly, Bamian returned my purse and my *malika* to me.

'You put it to very clever use, Bamian, for which I thank you most heartily; but how did it come into your possession?'

'When the bees attacked . . . the beaters at the top of the gorge lowered the cradle to the ground. I took it before some thieving soldier's hands got to it . . . I was going to return it . . . until . . .' He shrugged.

I was going to go to Agra until . . . I was going to give up Mohini until . . .

Bamian put the five-headed emerald ring into my hand. 'Here, take this, too. I think you will have greater need of it than I.'

I reached the river bank in time to see the shiny bald head of Bag Lal, the untouchable, bobbing up and down in the water. Clutched tightly in his arms was the young prince. An eddy swirled them into the bank. Helping hands pulled them from the river.

'Untouchable!' gasped Bag Lal.

The Hindus drew back, but many, who were Muslims, crowded round the prone figure of Prince Salim.

'Stand back!' I shouted, pushing my way forward.

Salim, whom I judged to be about seven years old, lay pale and limp. I recalled the corpse of the drowned soldier upon which I had experimented. Plucking a hollow reed from the river bank, I tried inserting it down the boy's windpipe. The reed broke.

'Begging your pardon, Khoratji . . .' It was Bag Lal, dripping water all over me. For some reason, two sealed water-jars were strapped to his waist.

'Keep away, man! Give me room to work!'

I tried again. Faisl joined me. Still no success.

'Begging your pardon, sahib.'

'Go away, Bag Lal! Not now!'

'I've seen sword-swallowers, Khoratji-sahib. They do it by putting their heads back. It makes a straight line, you see.'

I looked at Faisl. 'He's right!'

The reed slipped down Salim's trachea. I blew gently, filling

Salim's lungs with air, while Faisl, taking his time from me, pressed on his diaphragm to expel it again.

'He's starting to breathe on his own!' Faisl cried. 'Blow with it, not against it.'

Salim's eyelids fluttered. He sat up, retching river water.

'He saved the prince!'

'Well done!'

I was pleased that the spectators recognized my skill. But it was Bag Lal they praised. The moment demanded a hero and the chosen one was he.

'Stand back!' I shouted. 'Let the prince have space around him!' I shook Bag Lal by the hand. 'It seems that you, who cannot swim, saved the prince from drowning.'

'I did?'

'Here are a hundred witnesses who will testify that they saw you do it.'

'I thought he had saved me.'

Salim was shivering and whimpering. I put my cloak around him, and Faisl spoke reassuringly to him in Persian.

'So, what really happened, Bag Lal?'

Bag Lal stopped bowing to the crowd. He lowered his voice. 'I got to thinking of Petagurusahib's story of that man who walked on the water. All you need is faith, he said. Well, I thought it might be easier than learning to swim, so . . . well, it didn't work and . . . and then I saw this boy in the water coming to save me, so I grabbed hold of him.'

'What are those jars tied to you for?'

'Ah. That was just in case this faith stuff wasn't all it was cracked up to be.'

The crowd parted, bowing low, as a man on a white horse rode through their midst. He leapt from the richly jewelled saddle and gathered Salim in his arms, oblivious to all else.

'Sheikhu Baba, firstling of life's rose-bowl, you breathe! Allah is merciful!'

I was in no doubt that I was looking at the great Mogul emperor, Akbar.

'Shekhu Baba, my first-born son, jewel of the imperial mine!'

Faisl was on his knees. He tugged at me, indicating that I should do the same. I could not have been more than 5 or 6 feet away from Akbar. He was of middling height, broad of chest, of wheat-coloured complexion. On his left nostril was a fleshy mole the size of a split pea. He trembled, his eyes rolled upwards and he cried out in a loud voice:

'This world is a bridge. Pass over it, but build no house here. Who hopes for an hour hopes for eternity. The rest is unseen . . .'

There was a long silence. The company remained bowed or kneeling, except for his scribe, a young man who wrote down his every word and action.

'Only the dust of the petal remains for those who sell perfume. Only the dust remains.'

Another long silence. Feeling like a naughty child peeping through his fingers at church, I raised my bowed head. His turban was of gold cloth, his tunic of white silk, delicately embroidered. Ropes of immense pearls festooned his broad chest. What held my attention was the high forehead, the determined but sensitive mouth, the bearing which emanated command and authority.

'God has spared my son. In humble gratitude, I spare God's creatures, the animals of the forest. Break the barriers! Lift the nets! Beaters, princes, nobles, huntsmen, cheetahs, hounds – all withdraw! Let the animals run free, the Qamarghah is over!'

The trembling in his limbs ceased. He set Salim gently on the ground. The boy was led away. Then, Jalal-ud-din Muhammad Akbar, Ocean of Intelligence, Full Moon of Religion, Refuge of the World, raised Bag Lal, the untouchable, to his feet and embraced him.

'I am Bag Lal, O *Jahanpanah*, Refuge of the World. I carry the slain deer to your camp and cut the meat from them.'

'And what do you desire most in all the world, Bag Lal?'

'In all the world, *Jahanpanah*, Refuge of the World?'

'Name it, faithful subject, who saved my son from the river.'

'If it is not asking too much, I need a new set of knives and skinning tools.'

'More than that! Ask for more than that!'

'Well, *Jahanpanah*, this loin cloth is old and torn and . . .'

'Ask for more! Much more!'

'Er . . .'

'You shall rule my empire for a day. You have but to command and you shall be obeyed.'

Bag Lal shook with terror. 'I beg of you, do not place this great burden on me. Only you are strong enough to carry such a weight.'

Akbar laughed. 'So be it. You carry the deer on your shoulders and I'll carry the cares of the Mogul Empire. You dispense meat to the hungry and I'll dispense justice to my people.' He unwound his pearl necklace and gave it to Bag Lal.

'Great lord, it is too much, too much.'

Like the moon going behind a cloud, Akbar's mood changed. 'Shershan's rebels charged me with thinking I am greater than God. What say you? Am I greater than God?'

Bag Lal was silent. Akbar turned to Faisl.

'Do you think I am greater than God?'

'Why, *Jahanpanah*, beyond doubt you are.'

Akbar eyed him coldly.

'Certainly you are, *Jahanpanah*, for there is one thing you can do which God cannot.'

'And what is that?'

'If you want to banish a man, all you have to do is send him from your kingdom, but if the Lord of the Universe wants to banish a man, where can he send him?'

'You have answered well, Faisl Abu al-Qashandi.'

'You know my name!'

'You are one of the court physicians, are you not? I never forget a face or a name . . . nor a service rendered. And now I appoint you the new tutor to my son, Salim.'

Faisl bowed.

'And you, Thomas Coryat, apart from honey, what do you desire most in all the world? . . . Yes, you too I know, for your companion, Brother Peter, is in my camp even now.'

'Brother Peter!'

Akbar's eyes twinkled. 'I could hardly fail to notice him, for, when the assembled multitude knelt, there was he, standing upright, saying that he was an ambassador of One who was greater than any earthly king and that he would never kneel to any man.'

There was about that sensuous mouth, which now twitched at the corners, a reminder that his grandfather was Babur, descendant of Genghis Khan and Timur the Lame.

'I am glad he found refuge with you, O Refuge of the World. Is he well?'

'If the ability to preach at me day and night is a sign of health, then he is very well. We have much discourse on religion. He tells me many interesting things concerning the Christian faith.' He laid a heavily jewelled hand on my shoulder. 'No reward can repay what I owe you, but tell me what you desire, *Hakim-Nadir*, Physician Unparalleled, *Jalenus-uz-Zamanah*, Galen of the Century.'

Faisl winked at me, knowing my opinion of Galen.

'*Jahanpanah*, I desire knowledge. I desire the riches which are locked in the great library at Agra.'

My request clearly pleased him. He assured me that the services of his clerks, librarians, scribes, scholars and translators would be at my disposal. I barely heard what he was saying. I realized what I had done. I had walked away from Mohini, leaving her in the crowd. For the past hour I had not given her a single thought. Mohini who, this morning, had chosen death at my side, rather than life without me.

'And I appoint you Court Physician, seventh grade, with a salary commensurate with that position . . . Are you feeling all right?'

'Yes . . . thank you, Majesty . . . I am overwhelmed.'

Akbar raised his voice and announced: 'On our return to Agra, there shall be a feast. One thousand children, born in the same month as Salim, shall be gathered and dressed in cloth-of-gold. One thousand men of the Karaga caste shall . . .'

A man was dragged in front of him.

'O Majesty of the Fortunate Conjunction, O Jewel Ornament of the World, have mercy on me!'

Akbar struck the man across the mouth. 'You, his tutor, were responsible for the safety of my son, the heir to the throne. He nearly drowned. For that, you shall drown.'

'Have mercy, great lord!'

'As I was saying, one thousand Karagas shall be honoured . . .'

Splash!

'One thousand physicians shall . . . Scribe, are you writing all this down?'

'Every word, Majesty.'

The news swept through the assembly like wind through grass.
'Shershan is captured! Shershan is taken!'
'Along with twelve of his amirs,' said Ghulam Khan.
'Bring their twelve heads to me!'
Revenge is indeed a fever cured by letting blood.
'And Shershan – sew him into the skin of a freshly killed ass and bring him to me facing backwards on a donkey.'

Akbar read the expression on my face. He sighed. His eyes were sad. 'I was a beardless boy of thirteen when I defeated my father's enemies and became emperor. I have learned in the years since then the truth of the saying that dictators ride upon tigers from which they dare not dismount.' He addressed the assembled men:

'The Qamarghah is at an end. Tomorrow we break camp and journey to Agra. As for that rebel dog, Shershan, have him waiting for me when we join the great highway.'

The last twenty miles of the highway were lined with stalls and markets. Their owners lay prostrate at the passing of their emperor, the Light of the World, Lord of Hindustan. By invitation, Frog and I rode at Akbar's left hand. On his right, in the place of honour, was his conquering general, Ghulam Khan. If Akbar noticed that his general was drunk and half asleep in his saddle, he said nothing.

Behind us, in a cloud of dust, wound the thousands of men who had made up the great Qamarghah: the mounted officers, the elephants and howdahs carrying the harems of Akbar and Ghulam Khan, the foot-soldiers who had acted as beaters, the camels, bullocks and other baggage animals. Somewhere amidst them all was Mohini. At the very rear, choking on everyone's dust, was the prisoner, the rebel Shershan. The ass's skin into which he was sown, drying and tightening in the sun, would gradually squeeze and suffocate him to death.

With us rode Salim and Faisl, his new tutor. The latter, distinctly nervous after witnessing the fate of his predecessor, was trying to question the young prince on his knowledge of books. The boy, however, would talk of nothing but hunting, warfare and animal fights.

A few paces behind us was Akbar's Captain of the Guard, Bahadur

Singh. This swarthy man of immense strength carried the emperor's personal standard, from which dangled the twelve heads of Shershan's allies. At least Rammu's head was not there. Could this ruthless, avenging Akbar be the same man under whose patronage and interest the art of the dance, poetry, the translation of manuscripts and miniature-painting flourished as never before? I thought of the skulls of the thirty noblemen which I had seen stuck upon poles on London Bridge. Perhaps our Sovereign Queen Elizabeth also rode a tiger she dared not dismount.

An hour since, at Sikri, we had passed the site of a vast new palace which had been begun seven years ago at Akbar's command. He discoursed enthusiastically about his plans: the raised audience chamber, reached only by aerial walkways, the libraries, the Panj Mahal with its five pillared floors, the Ibadat Khana or House of Worship which would be used to discuss the views of all the world's religions, the water-tanks and roof gardens – and all to be executed in pink sandstone, sawn and tailored as if it were wood.

'It is to commemorate the birth of my first son, Salim,' Akbar told us, 'and to honour the holy man, Sheikh Salim Chishti of Sikri, whose prayers and prophecies brought me an heir.' He turned and looked with some intense emotion upon his son. Then he groaned and rocked to and fro in his saddle, smiting his brow. 'Allah saved him from the river. There was a man once saved me from a river. Why do I not let him go free?'

Akbar questioned me about the countries of Ferengistan, their strengths, their ways of fighting, their customs, religions, governments, their rise, progress and decay, and where, how and by what accidents and errors these great revolutions of empires and kingdoms happened. His grasp of these matters and of their underlying principles was astonishing. The breadth and authority of his vision, which in no way diminished the warmth of his manner, captivated me.

Every now and then, he would stand up in his saddle and look back. 'Captain of the Guard, what of Shershan?'

'There is no report from the rear of the column, great lord.'

'He says nothing?'

'Nothing, my lord.'

'Does he not beg for mercy?'

'No, my lord.'

Akbar put a question to Frog. 'Supposing several children were reared without hearing anyone speak, except themselves, in what language would they converse?'

'Beyond doubt, it would be Hebrew,' Frog replied, 'for that is the language in which the Holy Scriptures were revealed and in which the Ten Commandments were written.'

Akbar laughed. 'For the same reason, could it not be Sanskrit, for is that not the language of the other holy books?'

'Hebrew,' said Frog.

Frog's torn brown cassock made contrast with Akbar's blue turban with peacock plumes and uncut ruby as big as a walnut, his coat of fine Patiala cloth embroidered in gold. But, were they to exchange garb, there would be no mistaking who was the ruler of millions and who the servant of God. Frog was thinner than I had ever seen him. His face was gaunt. Lines of suffering ran from his mouth – lines put there by the massacre of the Chota Chua, the doubts, the questioning of the Lord's will. Like a bone which knits at the break to become its strongest part, he had emerged from the crisis with a renewed sense of purpose, with new fire in his belly.

'Suddenly I saw it all so clearly,' Frog had told me. 'The Chota Chua were a test, a stepping stone. Without them, I would neither have encountered nor have been ready for Akbar. He is my true mission. It was to convert the ruler of all Hindustan that I was sent!' And Frog's eyes had burned with a frightening zeal.

Mary was my mission in India. Faisl had informed me that he had made arrangements for Damayanti, the leper-woman, to be escorted to Agra, where I could continue my observations of her case. My mission was Mary. My mission was Mary. I, too, stood up in my saddle and looked back – searching for a glimpse of Mohini.

Family after family who knelt by the roadside at the passing of their emperor were near to starvation.

'Once the wheat harvest is in, things will be better,' said the vizier, who was of the company.

'Not with grain prices as high as they are,' Akbar commented. 'If the rains are late again, I fear a terrible famine.'

The vizier, a Hindu, shrugged. 'It is their karma.'

Frog exclaimed: 'The Bible tells us that we are our brother's keeper. The wretchedness of the poor is not a sign of sin in some previous life, it is a sign of the sins of the privileged in this life for allowing it!'

There was a gasp of horror at this impertinence. The Captain of the Guard drew his sword and looked enquiringly at Akbar.

Akbar merely laughed. 'If that is what his Bible says, then I am interested in hearing it. As long as I am on the throne, holy men of any persuasion shall speak their minds without fear of persecution.'

Frog, ever the thick-skinned one, blundered on unperturbed. 'I have heard that you have in your possession a diamond, the value of which would feed half the population of the world for a day.'

'Ah! A magnificent jewel!' Akbar's eyes were aglow. 'A rose-tinted diamond beyond compare; like a mountain of light! It came into my father's hands when Babur, my grandfather, defeated the Raja of Gwalior at Panipat.' He regarded me shrewdly. 'And you, I hear, have a black *malika*, fit for an emperor.'

There could be no mistaking the intended hint. I presented it to him with as good a grace as I could muster, consoling myself with the thought that it was an investment for the safety and protection of Mohini and myself. If Razziya coveted the jewel as she had coveted me, I was well rid of it.

'Vizier, pay these mothers to part with their infants.'

Akbar gave instructions that any starvelings along the roadside, under the age of three months, should be conveyed to the palace, given the best of care, but isolated from all human speech except each others' until they reached the age of twelve. A passing whim, which soon left his mind, for when he addressed Frog it was on another matter.

'Would it not be ludicrous if, on leaving the splendour of my palace, I decided to tour my kingdom in the shape of a worm?'

Frog grasped the point. 'Not if it was to the worms that you wished to reveal yourself. How else could you bridge so great a gap? And if such a change in condition defies the imagination, think then on God's love for us, his extreme condescension in entering the abasement of this world, for the difference in state between God and us is far, far greater than between you and a worm.'

The vizier gave an outraged cry. Akbar shook his head. 'It seems like poor planning to me, that your god should send his spirit into one person, in one corner of the earth. He ought to have breathed his spirit into many bodies and sent them all over the world.'

Frog breathed in a conveniently passing fly. Akbar smiled and continued.

'I have often asked myself why a universal god did not reveal one religion only, to all the world . . . Captain of the Guard, what of Shershan now?'

'Great lord, the skin squeezes him near unto death, but he bears it bravely.'

'He does not ask for mercy?'

'No, my lord.'

Frog bounced in his saddle. 'What possible motive can one so powerful as yourself have for revenge?'

I was sure I had heard that before somewhere.

Faisl hissed at him, 'You approach a powder keg with a naked flame; you tread on forbidden territory.'

The foolish trespasser heeded him not. 'Judges, fourteen, fourteen . . . now that would be a fitting text for the day . . . Out of the strong came forth sweetness.'

I directed a sideways kick at Frog's horse, sending it prancing and rearing.

'Speaking for myself,' I said, fingering my lumpy bee-stung face, 'I find that out of sweetness hath come strong pain.'

The storm, gathering on Akbar's face, cleared. He laughed. His gaze moved past Frog, over the heads of the prostrate figures at the side of the highway, to a piece of bare ground outside the walls of a small town. A polo match was in progress.

'*Chawgan!*' he cried. Spurring his horse, he cleared a stall, charged through a field of wheat, seized a spare polo stick from an onlooker, galloped on to the field of play and, taking the ball the length of the ground, scored a goal.

'A thousand gold mohurs for the side that wins!' he yelled, and recklessly launched into the game, always in the thick of the fray amidst the jostling ponies and clashing sticks. With the scores level, he called a halt to the game, laughing and congratulating the players, presenting prize-money to both sides.

While the column waited on the highway, Akbar rested and refreshed himself beside a river which ran near the polo field. His vizier had anticipated his every wish. A canopy had been erected, potted roses laid out, rich carpets set down. Ghulam Khan, Faisl, Frog and I shared this 'simple repast' with the emperor – merely several dozen silver dishes of long rice flavoured with chicken, curds, saffron and fragrant black cinnamon seeds, plates of meat-balls stuffed with apricots, loaves of royal bread made from the finest flour, trays of sugared figs, roasted sesame seeds and almonds.

Akbar took a long, hard look at Ghulam Khan, who had been drinking steadily throughout the polo game and now lay stretched out, snoring.

'There is one battle he has still to fight; one victory still to come. My grandfather, Babur, grappled with the same enemy for many a year, an enemy which can bring death in life. Then, before the battle of Khanua, he ordered all his silver goblets to be broken and vowed to be done with wine. The fragments he gave to the holy men and the poor; the wine was poured into the ground or salted to make vinegar. It was a vow he kept until his death . . . Of what were we discoursing, Brother Peter?'

'You were posing the question, Your Highness, that, if God was universal, why did he not reveal one religion to all men?'

'Ah, yes. Well, it seems to me that different minds require the truth in different ways. As fire, which is one, becomes varied in shape according to the object it burns, so the One Self within all beings becomes varied according to whichever it enters. God is a candle inside a multi-coloured lantern. Only by looking at all the faces of the lanterns can we arrive at the true nature of the flame within that lantern . . . which is why I am interested in what you have to say, Brother Peter.'

Frog was striding up and down at the edge of the river. 'I say that all the faces of the lantern but one are false. They do not reveal the true nature of the flame; they obscure it, they present it in false colours. But there is one face of clear glass called Christianity which . . .'

Akbar's domed forehead wrinkled. 'I am suspicious of any religion which renders its followers intolerant and disdainful. Religions are at their most perilous when certain of the truth; at their most productive when they only think they have that truth and are searching for the certainty.'

'Sire, I disagree. Principles have no modesty. They insist on ruling.'

196

'Scribe, are you writing all this down?'

'Yes, great lord, every word.'

'Well, add to your text that our victory over the rebel Shershan was a victory over bigotry, over those who would war against all who have not received the same revelations as themselves, over those who would seek to convert others to their beliefs by force, over . . .'

Salim rode up, a polo stick in his hand. 'Father, I scored a goal!'

'Oh, see his gold-scattering, heart-expanding presence!' cried Akbar. He fell to his knees and rent his clothes, groaned aloud and hammered the ground with his fists. 'Captain of the Guard, Bahadur Singh!'

'You called, Light of the World?'

'Shershan, how is he now?'

'He groans and cries out. He is near his end.'

'And I groan and cry out! Was it not Shershan, then a young officer in the Kashmir campaign, who saved my life in a mountain torrent? Did he not risk his life for mine?'

'So I have heard, O *Jahanpanah*, Refuge of the World.'

'Cut him loose! Dress him in a robe of honour. Have him escorted with due dignity to this place. No, I shall meet him halfway. Take this ring, place it upon his finger, assure him of my forgiveness. Go! Quickly!'

I thought of Dadu's prick. If a man's rise from disgrace could be so sudden, how much swifter might not be a man's fall from grace?

Ten

Several hundred officials of the Mogul court filled the outer chamber of the Diwan-i-Am, the Hall of Public Audience. Every morning, when Akbar held audience, I, as a court physician and some kind of unofficial ambassador from the West, was required to be present.

Faisl was conversing with Abdus Samad, the leading court painter. The Prophet Muhammad proclaims that any man who tries to imitate Allah by making an image of a living thing will be required, on the Day of Judgement, to give that image life and, if he fails to do so, to surrender his own. However, Akbar's love of the Persian miniaturists was not to be denied. Circumstances alter the interpretations of such passages.

Around me were court astronomers, poets, chamberlains, the Chief Huntsman, the Grand Master of the Horse, the Keeper of the Emperor's Roses. Others were there who had been waiting day after day for an audience. Some were seeking advancement for a relative, some redress for an injustice, others to be allowed to present a wife as a wet-nurse to one of the children of the royal harem.

On arrival at Agra, three weeks ago, Akbar had sent me a set of robes more fitting to my position in court. I was dressed in a light cotton surcoat of yellow silk, close-fitting white cotton trousers and, upon my feet, pointed babouches – all so much cooler and more comfortable than my former clothes. Faisl was dressed in blue. Even his beard was dyed blue.

'Do you like it, Thomas? Do you think it suits me?'

'No. Chaitan does, though; and pleasing him is the object, is it not?'

Faisl smiled in his self-deprecating way. 'I have but to think of him and my pulse is like scattered leaves of trees, like fire-grass, like a taut thread, like a bubbling spring.'

Through an archway we could see the inner audience chamber. Here waited princes, emirs and ambassadors from foreign lands. Here, also, stood Akbar's Master Hangman, his Chief Executioner, with a hatchet on his shoulder, and others with whips, for punishment was frequently carried out on the spot. Halfway down this carpeted hall was a railing, beyond which no one trod until summoned. On the far side of the railing was a raised platform, then a second red railing and then, raised higher still, the golden throne. Sitting cross-legged upon his throne was the Emperor Akbar. Beside him stood Birbal, his Chief Minister, Raja Todar Mal, his Financial Adviser, Sheikh Mubarak, the tolerant and free-thinking leading palace divine, and a fourth person – his new Commanding General, Shershan. Smilingly, Akbar turned to his young scribe.

'And what have been the main excitements of my reign today?'

'Nothing much has happened so far, *Jahanpanah*.'

Akbar seized a spear and hurled it at the scribe. 'Now it has! Write that down!'

The youth bent his head to his task, trembling even more than the spear which quivered beside his shoulder.

A set of jewelled daggers were carried forward and presented to the Mogul emperor. A sumptuously costumed raja made obeisance at the first rail, then again at the second rail. The raja begged to be allowed to present a daughter to the imperial harem, or, as he put it, 'to let the occupant of the howdah of chastity be brought within the screens of purity'.

Gifts, petitions, favours, more gifts, dispatches from provincial governors, reports from various departments . . . my mind wandered.

Lord Shiva danced and the wheel of the seasons turned. February had moved into March, the wheat harvest was gathered in, the festival of Holi celebrated. A laughing, playful Mohini had inveigled me into the streets of Agra, where we mingled with garlanded revellers and threw red powder over each other and anybody in sight, regardless of rank. And so the cranes flew north again to the mountains of Tartary and Kashmir, and spring gave way to the hot, dry season.

The splendours of Agra, I had to admit, more than matched those of Padua, Venice or Florence. There was the huge fortress of red sandstone, begun eleven years ago by Akbar; there were the magnificent palaces of the ministers and grandees of the court; the Persian gardens laid out by Babur; but surpassing all was the imperial palace itself. The vizier had assigned quarters to both Frog and myself inside the palace. It had been assumed that, as my concubine, Mohini would share my quarters with me. The fine mosaics, the panels inlaid with lapis lazuli, jade and onyx, the ceilings encased in silver and gold leaf; the numerous towers and gilded domes, the terraces, galleries and castellated walls; the delightful courts planted with flowers and intersected by small canals; the pavilions, archways and columns, exquisitely carved – and I, the sophisticated doctor from Padua and London, had been utterly amazed. As for Mohini, for once she had been struck dumb.

Frog, of course, stubbornly refused to be impressed. He would insist on referring to the palace in monastic terms. The Diwan-i-Am became the chapter-house, the arched galleries and the avenues of cypress trees were the cloisters, the banquet hall he must call the refectory, and what he named the dorter were the beautifully marbled and tiled bath-houses. To Frog's great joy, Akbar had granted him permission to set up a small chapel within the palace. Frog saw this as a sign of interest, a first step in the conversion to Christianity of one of the most powerful and influential rulers in the world.

And it was the voice of this man, raised in anger, which brought a hush to the two chambers of the Diwan-i-Am. Before him, in chains, stood Jaimal, Rajput Prince of Chambal.

Faisl whispered in my ear, 'They say he was captured while leading a sortie from the gates of Chambal.'

'Chambal?'

'The citadel in Rajasthan which Akbar has besieged these last two years.'

'You have dared to defy me!' Akbar thundered. 'No man defies me with impunity!'

Jaimal held himself proud and erect. 'Padmati, my wife, shall never enter your harem. She will never surrender herself to you.'

Akbar's face was dark, and his voice shook with passion. 'If, by tomorrow, you have not sent for Padmati to be brought to me, you shall be thrown from the walls of the fortress and trampled by elephants.'

'Two years you have besieged my city in vain. Padmati shall never be yours!'

'Jaimal, hear me well, Jaimal. I make a solemn vow. Not one stone of Chambal shall remain standing, not one person shall be spared, unless Padmati is surrendered to me!'

He strode from the hall. The public audience was at an end.

'There'll be animal fights staged tonight, mark my words,' said Faisl. 'It always seems to appease him when he's aroused.'

Two elephants grappled with each other, rearing upon their hind legs, their trunks intertwined. According to custom, a third elephant was present, whose duty was to come to the aid of either of the contestants if it was being too badly mauled.

Mohini and I, Faisl and Chaitan watched from a balcony in the palace, which overlooked the flat ground between the red wall and the river.

'Of all the thirty-six tribes of the Rajputs, Jaimal is the ornament!' Mohini was weeping as if it were her own flesh and blood that had been condemned to die. She was a Rajput herself.

Faisl tried to comfort her. 'I have been at court a good number of years and more than once I have seen the ladies of the emperor's harem change the course of history.'

The two elephants struck their heads together with such violence that the forefeet of one gave way. The stronger of the two trampled on it and gored its flanks with lethal tusks. The third elephant moved in; men set off fireworks to drive them apart.

'Oh, yes, more than once,' said Faisl. 'Their opinions count for more than you might think. And Jodh Bhai is a Rajput.'

Jodh Bhai, daughter of the Raja of Amber, was the mother of Salim, and Akbar's favourite wife. She was one of his three hundred *muta* wives. The Koran limits the number of wives a man may have to four. However, there is a second and less permanent form of marriage called a *muta* marriage, upon which there is no limit. Perhaps Faisl had a point. Most of Akbar's *muta* wives were the result of political alliances with Hindu princes, many of them

Rajputs. These women were certainly able to influence him. Why else would he allow the strict sanctity of so Muslim an institution to be broken, and agree to a Hindu temple and Hindu worship within the zenana itself?

'Where's the sugar-cane you promised me?' demanded Chaitan. He grew fatter by the week.

Faisl conjured some from his sleeve. 'Ah, see how his face brightens, as the lotus brightens at the promise of spring!'

The wounded elephant struggled to its feet and charged, maddened, into the river, where it drowned.

'I could not bear it!' Mohini sobbed. 'So noble, so chivalrous a man!'

Next, for the emperor's entertainment, a snarling black panther faced a wild boar, whose huge mane bristled over his shoulders. Within seconds, the boar had ripped open the panther's belly.

'Kill! Kill!' yelled Chaitan, biting viciously on his sugar-cane.

'Do . . . do you think there might be some truth in the rumour, then?' Mohini asked. 'I . . . I hardly dared believe it.'

Faisl frowned. He liked to keep abreast of all the palace gossip. 'What rumour?'

'Well, the Hindu dancing-girls are saying that Akbar has relented. They say he has promised Jodh Bhai that he will treat Jaimal as if he were his favourite songbird. I hardly dared believe it, but . . .'

'Look! Look!' shouted Chaitan. 'This will be the best yet!'

A lion had been released. Facing it, with sword and shield, was the Captain of the Guard, Bahadur Singh. I began running down the curving stairway. If he survived at all, he would have wounds enough for the healing.

There could be no doubting the depth of Akbar's remorse at ordering his Captain of the Guard to fight a lion. And there could be no doubting the severity of the wounds inflicted on Bahadur Singh before he slew the beast . . . wounds which I had been made responsible for healing. In order to have this brave young man, son of a Rajput chief, constantly under my care, I had him moved to my own quarters. In fact, Mohini, rather than I, tended to his needs and changed his dressings. I had been seduced by the Great Library.

Hour after hour I delved in this mine of knowledge. Day after day, with the help of Akbar's scholars, scribes and translators, and assisted by my good friend Faisl, I worked the rich seams of Ali-Tabari's *Paradise of Wisdom*, Shanak's *Book of Poisons*, the *Herbiary* of Kia-Yen. I learned many things. I learned that in China they protect against the smallpox by sniffing the powdered crusts of the pustule into their nostrils — the left nostril for a boy, the right nostril for a girl. I learned much about the anatomy of the eye from the works of the Arab, Hainan. Of the cure for leprosy, I learned nothing.

Not from books and scrolls and obscure manuscripts, at any rate. But from Damayanti I continued to learn. Observe, test, record. As a special concession, Akbar had permitted Damayanti to be housed in a pavilion in one of the palace's more remote and secluded gardens. I embarked on the first stages of the rhinoplasty to restore her nose. I visited her daily, sometimes twice daily, always learning something new about the disease.

'Why do you spend more time with a foul leper than with me?' Mohini demanded to know. She knew the answer. None the less, she would ask the question, day after day.

'You're never here, Thomas-jun!'

'I'm sure Bahadur Singh doesn't complain about that!'

'What do you mean?'

'I know you hardly leave his side. I've seen the look in his eyes.'

She flew at me, claws out. I threw her to the ground, silenced her mouth with mine, made love to her violently.

The Yamuna had shrunk to half its width; the fields on either bank were dried and cracked, the mud forming hard plates which curled at the edges. The cows which scavenged in the streets of Agra were hide stretched over bone. Their fast was involuntary, unlike that of the Muslim population. For, on this day, the month of Ramadan began. Between sunrise and sunset no food or water would pass the lips of the devout. By coincidence of two movable calendars, Lent and Ramadan overlapped. Frog was vexed and, consumed by zeal to outfast the heathen, ate even less than the starving cows.

Amidst this drought, the walled gardens of the palace were like oases of coolness and shade. I sat beneath a *nimbu* tree, listening to running water. Through archways were vistas of cypress trees and lawns lined with mango, *asoka*, lemon and pomegranate trees. Damayanti's pavilion was hidden by groves of orange trees. I had left her sleeping. The rhinoplasty was going well. I had begun to make detailed drawings of what remained of her hands. The way the tendons tightened, causing a clenched fist, presented an interesting problem.

Old Mirza, one of the two hundred palace gardeners, was watering his favourite herb beds. If it had been me, I would have sprinkled them with a watering-can. This was India, and Mirza was scratching little irrigation runnels up and down the beds. Mirza was only a backdrop to my thoughts. This morning I had witnessed the blinding of Jaimal. True to his word, Akbar had spared Jaimal's life. True to his word, he had treated Jaimal as if he were his favourite songbird. Akbar's favourite songbird was blind. Red-hot tongs had been put to Jaimal's eyes. Then he had been stripped and forced into a little cage and suspended, for public view, in one of the halls. His only diet was to be raw seed. How could such cruelty stem from the fabled beauty of Padmati? How could it be the product of a passionate love?

By one of those strange coincidences which make one wonder whether we are all part of some vast preordained pattern, Mirza reached up to pick a trellised rose and lacerated his hand on the thorns. He caught my eye as he sucked his wounds.

'In the garden of life, pain is the companion of beauty, and the sweetest of fruits decay into bitterness.'

'Mercifully, beauty can come out of ugliness too.' I was thinking of the perfect baby, born of two leper parents.

'Possibly,' said Mirza. 'The last time I took a good look between a woman's legs — and it was a long time ago — I thought to myself, "How is it possible for that slimy, hairy thing to give so much pleasure?" . . . I mean, if you saw it crawling down this path, you'd squash it underfoot without a second thought . . . Allah preserve us! The tamarind has turned into a *waqwaq* tree!'

He referred to a mythical tree which is said to bear living heads. A closer look revealed that it was Bamian among the branches with a minah bird under his arm.

'What are you doing, Bamian?'

'Ah, Khoratji, I am persuading this minah bird to nest in this tree.'

'And why are you doing that?'

'See how these branches come close to the window of this tower?'

'Yes.'

'Inside that room are the children which our glorious emperor ordered should be raised without ever hearing human speech.'

'So?'

'So, a minah bird is not human, is it? It just so happens I have trained it in a few well-chosen phrases . . . most of them uncomplimentary to our glorious emperor!'

When I had stopped laughing, Bamian said, 'I saw Bag Lal today.'

'What did he have to say for himself?'

'Nothing much; he was polluting a sewer with his exhausted body. Every whore in Agra must be richer by a pearl or two.'

'I wouldn't have thought he had it in him.'

'He hasn't now, I can tell you that! He resembles nothing so much as the empty husk of a mantis, sucked dry by its mate.'

'I see. While I have been diving for pearls of knowledge in the Great Library, the whores of Agra . . .'

'For every pearl he has paid out he now produces a whole string of his own through his magic wand. Or, to tell you in correct medical terminology, he has the galloping knob-rot. In fact, he asked me if I could make a wicker one for him, along the same lines as Dadu's leg.'

'That big?'

'No; that stiff.'

'How is the old rogue? Have you seen him of late?'

The palace had its own army of specially trained servants. There had been no possibility of retaining Dadu's services. Anyway, he had wanted to resume the military life.

'He does guard duty on the fortress gates. He is hoping to be sent to join the siege of Chambal. A siege, he says, is like wooing a woman – the longer they hold out, the sweeter the triumphant entry.'

Bamian slid down the trunk and gave the tree a shake.

'Akbar caught syphilis from a monkey's bum!' called the minah bird.

Bamian grinned, turned a somersault and swaggered from the garden. Those recurring patterns.

'What would you say, Mirza, if I said that life was like a richly patterned carpet?'

'I would say, *huzoor*, that you would be happier as a moth.'

I returned to the shade of the *nimbu* tree. My skin was unduly sensitive to the sun. My face and hands were taking an inordinate time to recover from the bee stings. The lumps would not disappear. And, once more, I was experiencing strange and disturbing dreams filled with faceless figures and nameless obscenities just beyond the perimeters of recall.

A fountain played near by, the water gushing out in spurts. That goat I had seen sacrificed at the army camp . . . when its throat had been slit, its blood had spurted out and been collected in a grail. I had thought about that a great deal. The blood had issued from the artery in time to the animal's heartbeat. Subsequent experiments had shown me that, in less than an hour, the volume of blood spurted forth would exceed the total amount contained within the goat. How could this be? How did this fit with what we had been taught at Padua? The fountain continued to play, the water flowing into a canal and eventually returning to Yamuna. I could hear the men singing as they worked the huge pump which brought the water back to the tanks above the fountains. The rhythm of their song stressed each downbeat of the pump's wooden beam. I wonder if . . .

Faisl ran through the archway. 'Thomas! I have it! Listen to what I have discovered!'

Breathlessly, he recounted how he had been searching through the *Great Herbal* of Li-Shi-Chen, when he had read about *chaulmoorgal* oil.

'In the twenty-fifth volume, it says that oil expressed from the seed of the *chaulmoorgal* plant eases and arrests the afflictions of leprosy!'

Faisl and I cavorted around the garden, embracing each other, whooping and laughing.

'A great discovery!' I shouted.

'Think of all the men of medicine you have asked and none have read of this!' Faisl crowed.

'But, Faisl, how shall we obtain these seeds?'

'Li-Shi-Chen writes that the plant grows in Burma . . . Let's ask Mirza what he knows about the plant.'

'Yes,' said Mirza, when we approached him. 'I have cuttings of the plant in this garden. An interesting plant, that. They say the oil from the seeds will cure leprosy . . . you doctors, of course, will know all about that.'

'Akbar caught syphilis from a monkey's bum!' called the minah bird from the tamarind tree.

I ran, skipping like a schoolboy, to tell the good news to Mohini. My steps faltered. Oh, you blind fool! So eager to share with her the news that our parting was one step nearer. I would say nothing. Yes, Bamian, the gods, if there are any gods, must be laughing at this one! A good joke! Do you hear me up there? I'm applauding, I'm laughing so much the tears are running down my cheeks.

I entered our quarters silently, pensively. Mohini and Bahadur were sitting with their heads very close together. I turned and walked out. And yes, Mirza, the sweetest fruits decay into bitterness.

Nightmares. But the waking, worrying hours were worse. My doubts about Mohini a hard lump inside me, a leaden weight on my spirits. And something else . . . the burning in my skin – was it the bee stings, a heat rash, or . . . or . . .?

Bahadur's wounds were healed. I had discharged him from my care, yet twice I observed them walking together in the palace gardens. I was frightened to ask her, frightened of what the answer might be. Yet part of me wanted it to be true, wanted to be free of the guilt I felt at the hurt I would cause, wanted anything that would make it easier when the time came to part.

The inevitability of that parting was never far from my mind, for the efficacy of the *chaulmoorgal* oil was plain to see. I administered it both orally and externally to Damayanti. Already some of the permanent sores had begun to heal, the flesh to become firmer. My quest was nearing its end.

On the day of the Annunciation of the Blessed Virgin Mary, Damayanti announced that she had made up her mind to return to the leper island in the Ganges.

'By my disease I am untouchable. By birth and caste I am a harridan, an untouchable. I am doubly estranged from mankind. But, when I am on the island, leprosy unites me with people. On the island there are no divisions, no castes; I am no longer untouchable.' She took a knife and severed the grafting skin between hand and nose. 'I shall always be a leper. Begging is the only way I can ever make a living. Do you want me to earn less because I'm not as hideous as the others?'

'Damayanti, I . . .'

'Khoratji, my heart does not have leprosy . . . but . . . but you will never return the love which I have for you . . . I know that. That is where the pain is worst. *Chaulmoorgal* oil cannot cure that.'

I should have realized! How long since a man had taken any notice of her? Shown her any tenderness? Spent so much time with her?

Matins, Lauds, Prime, Tierce, Sext, Nones, Vespers and Compline, Frog tinkled bells and celebrated services throughout the day, singing his psalms and delivering his sermons to an empty chapel. On this occasion, though, I had not the heart to refuse his invitation. His sermon had been going a mere hour and a half and was just warming up – with a little help from hell's fires – when Akbar honoured the chapel with a visit. He bent his knee before the cross, then gazed intently at the framed picture of the Virgin Mary.

'See how he adores the Blessed Virgin!' breathed Frog.

Akbar clapped his hands. A servant carried in several loaves of bread.

'Made with the first flour to be milled from this year's harvest,' Akbar said. 'I have heard of your Christian Harvest Festival. Please accept this small offering.'

Frog thanked him. I could see, though, that he was perturbed. Smiling, Akbar withdrew.

'We cannot have a Harvest Festival in Lent!' Frog exclaimed.

'My dear Frog, surely you must hold the Harvest Festival whenever the harvest is.'

'But the Church's calendar is fixed and most particular on these points.'

'So are the seasons of India. Perhaps upon the conversion of the emperor, they will see the error of their ways and rearrange themselves.'

Frog threw me a pained look. 'I shall give the loaves to the poor. Charity has no seasons, recognizes no boundaries.'

'I'll wager you'll have no more success giving them away than Akbar had in trying to give them to you. I'll wager you cannot give them away within the hour.'

A sacred cow followed us through the streets, snuffling at the loaves.

'Go away!' Frog shouted at it.

'Please don't hit it with your staff, Frog, I don't want to be stoned to death.'

A bent and tattered man hobbled in our direction. Frog offered him a loaf.

'What? During Ramadan? I don't expect to be insulted in my own city by strangers!' He hobbled off, glaring over his shoulder at us, muttering angrily to himself. A naked baby chuckled in the dust. Frog advanced upon it with outstretched loaf. A woman rushed out of a doorway, scooped up the baby and disappeared.

'It would help if you smiled, Frog. And you would look less like some harbinger of death if you put your cowl down.'

'How much?' said the next person we met, a pimply youth.

'It's free,' said Frog. 'It's a gift.'

'What's the catch?'

'There is no catch.'

'What do you take me for? I'm no country simpleton, I'm a city boy. I know a trickster when I see one!'

A gaunt figure crouched in a doorway, hunger in his eyes. Again, Frog offered bread.

The man shook his head. 'I am paid to starve and thirst.' His voice was weak. 'You see, unless the owner of this house grants my client's just demands, I shall die on his doorstep with dire consequences for him in the next incarnation.'

'And I am the retaliatory Brahmin, paid by the other disputant,' croaked a voice from the shadows on the other side of the street. 'My client shall win, I'm nearer death than you!'

'Oh no you're not!'

'Oh yes I am!'

We left them arguing. Angrily, Frog thrust the loaves into my hands and stalked off. Damayanti would like the soft, white bread. It would be easy on her rotting gums and missing palate. She wasn't there. She had gathered her few possessions and departed. I threw the loaves over the wall, where I knew the insatiable cow was waiting to gobble them up.

'Thomas! Thomas!' Frog returned, joy radiating from him, the miracle of the five thousand loaves that fed nobody obviously forgotten. 'Thomas, the Emperor Akbar came a second time to the chapel. He requested that I instruct his two younger sons in the Christian faith!'

'Murad and Daniyal?'

'Yes! I praise and thank the Lord for his goodness in granting me this opportunity!'

'He did say "instruct" and not "baptize", didn't he?'

'One step at a time, Thomas! Oh, praise the Lord!'

The festival celebrating the birthday of the Lord Rama fell on Palm Sunday. To mark the occasion, the Raja of Ambala, himself a renowned poet, had announced a poetry contest. The raja had sent his state barge down river to Agra to convey those from the imperial palace who were attending the great event.

For reasons I was not quite sure of, I had received a most flattering and pressing invitation. Perhaps it was rumoured I had the ear of Akbar himself; maybe it was because it had become fashionable at the palace to be treated by the Ferangistani doctor; or it might simply have been that I lent a foreign, exotic air to the proceedings.

'I think it's because the Princess Razziya has praised your poetry and your renderings so highly to the raja. I believe they know each other well,' Faisl said.

I groaned at the very thought of it, although I knew he was only teasing me. The darkness caressed like velvet; fireflies danced on the surface of the water. Mohini's hand slipped into mine. She and Bamian were aboard, for their fame as dancers had been quick to spread and they were in much demand.

'What is wrong, Thomas-jun? Tell me what is wrong?'

'Nothing. I do not feel well, that is all.'

An open accusation would be too painful – and, certainly, I had been out of sorts lately.

'It is more than that. What is it, Thomas-jun?'

'Nothing, I tell you! Don't keep asking!'

Her hand withdrew.

Faisl's eyes reminded me of a dog's when it hopes to be taken for a walk.

'Do you like it, Thomas?'

'What?'

'The poem I have just read to you. I think, from your melancholy expression, it has touched you, has it not? Ah, but you were right to say "What?" . . . Oh, yes, a very deep comment. A poem cannot exist as a poem until heard several times; it must mature in the mind like a wine, it must . . .'

Did Mohini hold Bahadur's hand like she had just held mine? Did she kiss him like she kissed me? Did she . . .

> ' . . . cheeks like pomegranate blossom.
> His eyes twin narcissi in a garden.

. . . There! What do you think on a second hearing, Thomas? Will he like it, do you think?'

'The raja?'

'No, I mean Chaitan.'

'He'll like anything that makes him the centre of attention. Where is he, by the way . . . He hasn't fallen overboard, has he?' I tried not to sound too hopeful.

'There he is, under the golden canopy, talking to Ibqal. See how the old goat eyes him! See how Chaitan returns his smiles!'

I gripped the arm of a fellow sufferer. Faisl looked at me dolefully.

'Do you think he will really like my poem? Do you want to hear it again?'

'A rendering from *De Fabrica* would be more to my liking, dear Faisl.'

He tugged his blue-dyed beard. 'Of course, of course. Forgive me.'

I told him about Frog's high hopes of turning the great Mogul dynasty to Christ. Faisl laughed softly and shook his head as one might over a sick patient.

'Brother Peter is deluded. Abdus Samad, the painter, was telling me only the other day that Akbar greatly admires the Western style of painting. He is particularly fascinated by the use of the nimbus, the halo. He is contemplating having this device employed in the next portrait of himself. . . That is why he studies the Virgin Mary so intently.'

'Oh dear! Poor Frog!'

'As for the instruction of Akbar's sons, Daniyal and Murad . . . well, your friend may be a godly man, but he is not a worldly one.'

'More delusions?'

'The fact is that Salim is Akbar's favourite son. Salim is the one he has chosen to succeed him. He wants no rivals. For Daniyal and Murad to receive instruction in alien, infidel ways would certainly discredit them as contenders for the throne. Other rulers would have poisoned all rivals. Instead, Akbar has . . .'

'But Faisl, I cannot believe that Akbar's interest in what Frog has to say is not genuine.'

'It is. But he is interested in all religions, not just Christianity. He rules a restless empire. He will use whatever means he can to hold this country together, to retain unity.'

'I see . . . Do you think I should tell Frog of this?'

'Would he believe you? Would he even listen to you?'

'No, probably not.'

The domed palace of the Raja of Ambala glinted in the moonlight. The state barge glided alongside flights of white marble steps. A troupe of girls sprinkled rose-petals in our path and hung garlands round our necks. The raja received us on his terrace of chequered black and white marble squares. As well as being a poet, he was a keen player of *chaturanga*, or chess, as we call it. He presented each of us with a robe of fine brocade. Mine was of a deep blue colour. Faisl sought me out.

'Thomas, I think this emerald green will be much more flattering to you. I will gladly exchange robes with you.'

'How thoughtful of you, Faisl. And how lucky mine is blue, when you have a blue beard and blue is Chaitan's favourite colour. Yes, by all means let us exchange; I might as well be miserable in green as in blue.'

I wandered through gardens, where water softly splashed and insects hummed around coloured lanterns strung from oleander trees. I found Faisl slumped beneath a statue of Kamadeva. He was dead. His face bore the expression of one who has been asphyxiated. His wrists and arms were inflamed where his robe had chafed bare skin. It was obvious he had been poisoned, his garment smeared with some deadly concoction which had been absorbed through the skin.

If only I had found him sooner. Perhaps the antidotes in my emerald ring could have saved his life. Kind, gentle, witty Faisl, who could possibly wish you harm? Who . . . no . . . the blue robes had been intended for me!

I was seized from behind, dragged up a flight of steps and forced to my knees in front of the raja.

'You are accused of murdering the doctor, the poet Faisl Abu al-Qashandi.' He looked down at me with eyes which said he would have no more compunction about putting me to death than he would have about squashing a fly. I was too stunned to reply.

Then a succession of witnesses came forward. One swore that there had been much rivalry between Faisl and myself as court physicians. His removal would advance my prospects of wealth and position. Another testified that I dabbled with corpses and brought them back to life and held long conversations with them concerning the black arts and necromancy. A third gave witness that I had spent hours in the Great Library poring over Shanak's *Book of Poisons*. My clothes were produced. In a pocket was found a half-empty phial. The remaining contents were daubed on a dog which died within five minutes. My mind was too numb to counter these absurd accusations. Oh, Faisl, you would have argued my case so eloquently!

I watched, as if it were happening to someone else, while I was condemned to be flung from the terrace on to the rocks a hundred feet below. I stared at the marble steps and saw the apple orchards at home.

'By the power invested in me as the ruler of this province, I pronounce that the sentence shall be carried out immediately.'

I was lifted and carried towards the edge of the terrace.

'Wait!'

It was Bamian, the Demon King, towering above the assembled people in his stilts.

'Is it not Mogul law, applicable in this province, as in every other, that the owner of goods and chattels bears the responsibility for them? If a cow tramples another man's crop, is it the cow who pays that man? If a slave commits a crime, who is held responsible? It is the owner of that slave.'

'All this is true,' said the raja. 'But of what relevance is it in this case?'

'I am the owner of this man, Thomas Coryat.'

There was a babble of excitement. A murder, a trial, an impending execution – it was almost as exciting as a poetry contest. The raja glanced sideways at his vizier.

Bamian continued. 'There are those here who can confirm that, as a captive in the forbidden area of the Qamargah, Coryat became the rightful property of General Ghulam Khan and that I won that property in a dicing match.'

There was a long, whispered consultation between the raja and his vizier. The raja gave a signal. The four men who held me rushed me towards the edge of the terrace, swung right, down flights of stairs, along a dark passage, and flung me into a black dungeon.

'Why?' My question echoed in the darkness.

The answer boomed round the cell. 'Ghulam Khan.'

'But, Bamian, I thought I was back in favour with the general.'

The dwarf's bitter laughter bounced from wall to wall. 'There are poisons more deadly than the one that killed Faisl. Hate, envy, jealousy. Razziya has not forgotten you. What poisonous words do you think she has been pouring into her husband's ear? Who do you think Ghulam Khan blames for his fall from favour with Akbar? Were you not with Akbar when he pardoned Shershan? Is it not said that the emperor seeks your opinion?'

I groaned. 'And what of Mohini? Is she safe?'

'She should be back in Agra by now.'

'Safe in the arms of Bahadur Singh, I suppose.'

'More poison!' bellowed the dwarf, and his foot smashed into my groin.

I swore and hit out. His head butted me in the face. I was on my feet, fists flailing, connecting with nothing in the dark.

'You ugly little pander. You've been arranging their meetings, haven't you?'

His teeth sank into my calf. I kicked out, stubbing my toe against the wall.

Bamian hissed, 'Your suspicions are more off target, even, than your blows.'

His voice gave me the range and the direction.

Thud!

I knelt beside his gasping form. 'Bamian, there's blood all over you! Are you all right?'

'It's not all blood. Mostly the Demon King's grease-paint, in fact.'
We sat back to back.

'Khoratji?' I could feel his deep voice vibrating through my spine.
'Yes?'

'When you presented Akbar with the *malika*, did he throw it away, did he trample it in the dust?'

'No.'

'Mohini's love for you is more precious than any *malika*. Her love is the greatest gift life will ever bestow upon you. Don't throw it away. Don't trample it in the dust.'

'You . . . you would know, wouldn't you, Bamian . . . if she was unfaithful to me, I mean?'

'Yes, I'd know.'

'I want to believe you. I long to believe you.'

'Believe it then, you doubting fool. Nothing is more certain in this world than her love for you.'

'The evidence, Bamian.'

Bamian grunted with impatience. 'Observe, record, test, you say. What have you observed of her true feelings for you? What have you recorded save jealousies of your own making? As for her devotion to you, you test it every day without knowing it.'

'Is that really how it is?'

'I know it, Khoratji.'

I could feel the antidote beginning to work, the dark suspicions to ebb.

'Khoratji.'

'Yes?'

'In this dark womb, I can say what I have not been able to say before . . . I love her. I have always loved her.'

'I know.'

'It's a relief to say it out aloud, to someone.'

'Do you really think she and Bahadur are not lovers, then?'

'I am certain of it, Khoratji.'

'Why do they meet?'

'Do you have no faith in her at all?'

'Yes, yes, I have! But we are disbelievers by nature, both of us.'

Bamian laughed. 'Faith is a form of speculation, a gamble; it appeals to me.'

'But why do they meet, she and Bahadur?'

I could feel Bamian sigh. 'I can only say, have faith in the one you love.'

No sun or stars marked the passage of time. Things rustled and stirred in the darkness.

'Bamian.'

'Yes?'

'Have you ever heard of bee stings taking so long to go away?'

'Courage, my friend. Who knows what the effect of so many at once might be?'

The cell thundered with the sound of heavy bolts being drawn. Light flooded into the cell.

I blinked. 'Is that you, Mohini?'

'It is I, Achmed, your gaoler. The Emperor Akbar himself is here. It seems he has a mind to play *chaturanga* on the terrace board.'

Bamian and I were escorted to one end of the chequered terrace, where a dozen or so people were assembled. A balcony ran round three sides of the huge marble chess-board. On the fourth side was the stone balustrade and the steep drop to the rocks below. The balcony was lined with archers and musketeers, their weapons directed at us. I scanned the faces around me, hoping, yet hoping not, to see Mohini. The raja, Ghulam Khan . . . Mohini! I pushed my way to her side and drew her to me.

'Mohini, my love, what are you doing here? What's happening?'

Her eyes were shining despite the seriousness of the words she spoke. She told me of the red bell-rope at the gates of the Diwan-i-Am in Agra. It sounded a bell inside the inner chamber. By this means, even the humblest of Akbar's subjects could attract the attention of their emperor and gain redress for wrongs. Those who pulled the rope had to be either very sure of their case or desperate, because, if the plea was dismissed, the penalty for misuse of the privilege was death. Mohini had tugged at the red bell-rope, gained an audience with Akbar and told how she suspected the Raja of Ambala of taking a bribe from Ghulam Khan to murder me.

Akbar appeared on the balcony above us. 'All of you standing before me took part in a game of deceit which ended in the death of an honourable man. Some plotted or poisoned; some have made accusations or borne witness to those accusations, others have been accused. Now all of you shall take part in a game of *chaturanga* . . . you shall be the live pieces on this chequered terrace.' He pointed to a screen which had been erected on the balcony. 'Two players shall shortly enter and sit behind this screen. They will not be able to see you. Indeed, they will be unaware that a live game will follow exactly each move that they make. When one of them loses a piece, one of you loses your life.'

Mohini was trembling. 'Thomas, supposing we are on different sides and . . . and it is me that causes you to . . . to . . .'

'Hush, my love.'

What was it Faisl had said? Akbar appeased his frustrations by staging animal fights. For him, this was merely an interesting variation. Jaimal, in his cage, must still be defying him, Padmati still safe behind the walls of Chambal. The Light of the World, looking down from on high, told us how we would be allotted our station, importance and part in the game. The pawns, the *piyada*, as they were termed, the most likely to die, would be common criminals from the palace dungeons, men already condemned to death. We below would draw from a black bag the pieces we were to represent.

One by one we were called forward to where Akbar's chamberlain held out the bag.

'The dancer, Mohini!'

She squeezed my hand. 'I love you, Thomas.' Then she stepped forward. I saw black in her hand.

'The *rukh*!' cried the spectators around the terrace, using the Persian word for a castle. She mounted a baby elephant which bore a small fortified tower and was led to the corner square.

'The doctor, Thomas Coryat!'

My hand was in the bag. The ivory piece felt heavy, knobbly. Pray God it was black.

'The white *diwan*! The tax collector!'

A drum was slung from my neck as I took up position on the bishop's square. My accuser and would-be executioner, the Raja of Ambala, was my opposite piece. Bamian drew the white shah. He stepped into a white howdah and was carried to the white king's black square. He waved mockingly to his subjects, his face, still smeared with the Demon King's grease-paint, giving him a grotesque appearance.

'An astrologer once predicted I would be a king,' he said. 'My mother was so pleased, she paid him double.'

Ghulam Khan drew black.

'The bag is empty!' called the chamberlain.

One square of the first rank remained unfilled. Akbar held in his hand the black *wazir*, the piece which, in Europe, we call the queen. He walked round the balcony to a point above the audience where rested the palanquin of Princess Razziya. Akbar hurled the chess piece against the palanquin. Razziya was dragged forth. A gasp went round the courtyard. She was not veiled. For the first time since she was a girl, she was exposed to public view. Of her famed beauty there was no trace. Only a wrinkled, toothless, pockmarked face. She cursed and railed at all who looked upon her and wept bitter tears.

The *piyada* marched out, arrayed as foot-soldiers. Akbar moved behind the screen. I was positioned directly underneath it. The two chess players must have entered from a room behind the screen, for I heard one of them say:

'It is games of chance, like backgammon, which I hold to be sinful. But chess is a game of skill and therefore is not gambling.' It was Frog. 'The black bag is a lesson to us all!' he exclaimed. 'From the darkness we emerge, to the darkness we return. We have our tasks for the duration of the game and, when it ends, the black bag of death renders us all equal, all of no value.'

'I see it this way,' replied his opponent. 'The black and white board symbolizes the joys and sorrows of our chequered existence.'

Frog was not one to be outmatched in drawing a moral. 'This piece, for instance; in Christendom we call it the bishop. It never leaves the colour of the square it starts from, exemplifying the firm faith and steadfastness of purpose of the true believer.'

'Very interesting,' said Akbar. 'Now tell me, do you, Nazarene sage, and you, learned mullah of the Muslim faith, do you both believe that God guides our actions?'

'Most assuredly, if we pray for guidance,' said Frog.

'Without a doubt,' said the mullah.

'Then, if you were both to pray to God to guide your moves, I would know that whoever can cry out '*Shah mat*!' The king is dead!' is the one who is the true servant of God.'

'But I'm no good at chess!' wailed Frog.

'I'm even worse,' lamented the mullah.

Akbar dangled the bait. 'The position of tutor to my son, Salim has . . . er . . . been vacated once again. I have not, as yet, decided who shall fill the post.'

There was a scrabbling noise behind the screen, followed by a duet of mutterings, gabblings and invocations.

'White to play. Your move, learned mullah, and may this game of *chaturanga* be an instrument of just rewards.'

'It's nice to get out into the fresh air,' said the pawn in front of me, a common thief. He smiled and hummed to himself. He had no idea of the rules of chess. He thought he was taking part in some play or pageant. Three moves later, he was captured by the black knight. Before he had comprehended the truth, he had been cast on to the rocks at the base of the cliff.

The knight, or *ashwa*, was Ghulam Khan. His hands were shaking. There was pleading in his eyes. 'Coryat?'

I thought he was about to beg my forgiveness.

'Do you have some brandy . . . just to stop the shaking?'

'No.'

'Please . . . they will think I shake with fear, please . . .'

A sharp order came from the balcony and he moved away again. Razziya, the black queen, stalked the board, wreaking carnage. One pawn, who fell to her, tried to flee the board and was shot down by the archers in the balcony. Sacrifice and counter-sacrifice. In the quick exchange of pieces, the black bishop, the tax collector, was forfeited. The Raja of Ambala was dragged, screaming, from his own chequered terrace and flung into the abyss.

The mullah exclaimed peevishly: 'How can I concentrate with all that noise going on below? The younger generation have no consideration these days!'

The sun climbed in the sky. Our shadows across the board grew shorter. Despite the shaded aspect of the court, the heat was intense. There were long pauses between each move. I tried to think ahead, to see what strategies were developing, always calculating the risk to Mohini.

'Check!' Frog shouted. 'I mean, *shah mat*!' Razziya, his queen or *wazir*, was prodded forward.

'Ah, but not mate,' purred the mullah. 'My tax collector takes your *wazir*.'

I walked down an avenue of white squares to Razziya. Briefly she and I stood on the same square. What passion did I read in her eyes? Was it hate, love, fear? I could not tell. And, at that moment, I could not have said where one ended and the other began.

She went to her death proudly, walking to the edge of her own accord and throwing herself off.

This development placed me in a position which directly threatened Mohini. There was a long wait while Frog thought about his next move.

'Aha! Thought you were going to capture my *rukh*, did you?' I heard Frog say. 'That will put paid to your plans! . . . No, wait! I see a better move. There! *Shah mat*!'

'Your hand left the piece. You cannot retract your first move!'

'It did not! Look, my finger was touching it all the time!'

'It was not!'

Akbar turned towards the screen. 'The first move must stand!'

I relaxed as a pawn stepped into the clear path between me and Mohini. The man was breathing with difficulty and sweating profusely. He looked exceedingly ill to me.

Despite the disallowed move, black was in a strong position and pressing home the attack. Four moves later, Frog manoeuvred his knight, Ghulam Khan, into a position where, if he took me, he would have Bamian, the shah, in checkmate. Akbar gave a signal. Two servants pulled on ropes, raising the screens. Frog and the mullah stared in amazement at the live game below them.

'I am interested to see', said Akbar, 'whether you, Brother Peter, will knowingly sacrifice your friend, Coryat, in order to win the game. Yes, a very interesting little problem.'

Frog said nothing. His eyes bulged. I knew that, the longer he thought about it, the louder would become the voice that told him to lay aside his personal feelings and seize this God-given opportunity to become tutor to the heir to the Mogul throne. Akbar pointed at the sand-glass which stood between the players.

'Time is running out!'

The pawn, who had saved Mohini, collapsed at my feet. His flesh was puffed and swollen. There were lumps as big as apples on his body. A messenger hurried on to the terrace and mounted the balcony stairs.

'Great lord, the plague is raging through Agra and is likely to spread to Delhi and beyond.'

I straightened. 'It is here already!' As I spoke, another pawn from the dungeons of Agra fell to the ground.

Akbar's raised hand quelled the commotion. 'The game is abandoned. God has guided the hands of these two players. I am satisfied that those who met their deaths deserved to do so. The rest are pardoned.'

Eleven

We, the court physicians, sat in council in the imperial palace inside the Red Fort in Agra. We debated the causes of the plague and the best action to take. Mir Amad, an elderly Arab physician, held forth. 'As Saturn doth cause the black plague, so Mars doth cause the red plague.'

By virtue of knowing the entire Koran by heart, he had earned the title of *Rafiz* and was much respected. Even though some of us believed the plague to have causes other than astronomical conjunctions, the swooping passage of comets or balls of fire, it would not be respectful to challenge openly the opinion of a *hafiz*. If only Faisl were here.

'Those of Saturn, long in rising, seldom break,' said Mir Amad. 'Those of Mars come to a head quickly, often break of themselves and give off much matter.'

Ibn Hassan spoke. He had twice been on pilgrimage to Mecca and might be permitted a mild difference in interpretation without causing offence. 'If such conjunctions are what brings the hot season and what causes putrid emanations, then I agree with the learned doctor.'

He discoursed on the possible causes of putrid emanations – putrefaction of dead bodies, miasmata arising from decomposition of noxious matter, deleterious vapours exuded from the ground and particularly dangerous after earthquakes. I spoke of what I had seen at the seaports of Venice and Genoa. There, the civic authorities combated plague by means of the *quarantena*, the forty-day sequestration. If any ship was suspected of carrying the plague, all crew and passengers were isolated for forty days and all cargo and merchandise impounded for the same period. There were nods of agreement.

In fact, Akbar had already surrounded Agra with his soldiers. Nobody was to leave the city until forty days after the death of the last plague victim.

Commercial, political and social forces nearly always range themselves against the first announcement of a plague. They fear panic. Rapid flight spreads the disease, and, among those who stay, animosities, like the plague boils themselves, come to a head and burst. Deaths are followed by accusations of poisoning; dark plots are discovered by one section of the community against another; riots break out.

Thus, officially, there was no plague. The carts, which collected the dead to be burned or buried outside the city walls, moved only at night. His own edict notwithstanding, Akbar had ordered his entire court and harem to move to Ajmer until the plague was over. The palace was bustling with preparations for the move. A man coughed apologetically and scurried across our council chamber with a rolled carpet on his shoulder. My gaze, following his receding figure down vistas of exquisite blue-tiled archways, found Bahadur Singh. Coryat, the professional man of medicine, took in his limp and judged that he would never walk normally. Thomas, the jealous lover, registered that he was younger and more handsome than I. The doubts were still there, quelled, battened down, held at bay, but there.

Bahadur leant against a pillar. Mohini approached from the far end of the vista and stopped on the other side of the same pillar. Only from where I sat could it be observed that they were conversing. The doubts escaped and ran riot.

Someone was saying, 'The symptoms, are we agreed on the symptoms? Headache, dizziness, blurring of the vision, a staggering gait, a . . .'

I strode down the avenue of tiled archways. I would confront them with it! I would force it into the open once and for all. They saw me. They hurried to meet me. Mohini put her hand on my arm.

'We need your help,' said Bahadur.

Together, they explained to me that they, and several others within the palace, had been planning the escape of Jaimal.

'We are Rajputs first and foremost,' Bahadur said. 'The allegiance I owed to my emperor perished on the claws and teeth of that lion.'

Mohini was speaking to me. Her lips were more enticing than I could remember for a long time. 'We must seize our chance . . .' Her hand was still upon my arm. How different her touch felt now! '. . . and use the confusion caused by the plague and the move to Ajmer to . . . Thomas, are you listening?'

Bahadur said, 'It is an excellent opportunity, except for one thing . . . Only on Akbar's personal word can Jaimal's cage be opened . . .' He paused while somebody walked past. 'Unless, perhaps, Jaimal was pronounced dead, stricken by the plague . . .'

'And you, dear one, have the authority to do that,' said Mohini. 'Will you help us, Thomas-jun?'

The answer jumped straight from my guilty, misjudging, wildly happy heart to my lips.

'Yes.'

Mohini had been steeling herself to leave me, in order to save Jaimal. She, too, had been torn asunder by conflicting loyalties, by different kinds of love. We had walked the same dark tunnel, and the daylight at the end was more lonely, more frightening, than the dark. We lay in each other's arms with new understanding and tenderness, with a deeper kind of love. Our union had never been so sweet. We tried to make time stand still; we tried to shut out the future; we knew this must last us for ever.

Mohini planned to escort the blind Jaimal, in secret, all the way to Chambal. Messages had been smuggled between Chambal and the palace. The Princess Padmati knew of the planned attempt and had laid her own plans by which her husband could gain entry to the beleaguered city. Once Jaimal was restored to his place beside his wife, it would be no secret that he was, in fact, alive. I would be under immediate suspicion as the one who had pronounced him dead. If I did what Mohini and Bahadur asked of me, I would have no choice but to flee Agra. I would have committed a treasonable act, for which the penalty was execution under the trampling feet of elephants. For all that, I could think of it only as a stay of execution. It delayed the dread moment of parting with Mohini.

Mohini was insistent on one point. 'You must not tell Petaguru-sahib. It is for his protection as well as ours.'

Frog, I knew, would not leave the Mogul court until his divine mission was accomplished. Probably I would not see him again.

The evening before the plan was due to be carried out, I visited Frog in his chapel. I had not seen him since the chess game at Ambala. From the way that he avoided my eye, I knew which move he would have chosen. When I was old, centuries ago, before I met Mohini, I would not have understood.

We talked of trivialities. Faisl had said . . . Faisl with the gentle, self-deprecating smile and the mask of asphyxiation . . . From what he had told me, I doubted whether Akbar would have let Frog become Salim's tutor. However, Frog did not know that. He knew only that, as with the Chota Chua, the cup and the sweet wine therein had been dashed from his lips.

Frog stretched forward to light a candle for St Roch. 'All who are stricken with the plague and pray for aid through the intercession of St Roch shall be healed.'

Below the chapel was a wing of the royal kitchens. Women were singing to a steady rhythm as they churned buffalo milk to make ghee.

'Frog, I may not see you for a while.'

'Ah, the plague. It keeps you busy, no doubt. Too busy, I expect. You look tired.' He lit another candle. 'St Roch, he nursed plague victims till he caught it himself. He was so disfigured that at Montpellier, his own town, he was not recognized and was imprisoned for five years as a spy.'

I took a taper to light a candle. It fell from my fingers. My fumbling attempt to retrieve it was watched closely by Frog. The song slowed as the cream thickened and, with the stiffening of the curd, changed to a long-drawn chant. I dropped a second taper. Frog looked at me keenly.

'What are you staring at? There's nothing wrong with me!'

The singing stopped; the curd was being sliced. The candles spluttered and smoked. Frog talked of how eagerly Murad and Daniyal received their instruction in the Christian faith.

'Frog, why can't you see the truth? Why can't you see that . . .'

'That what, Thomas?'

'Nothing . . . Look after yourself, Frog.'

I touched his shoulder and walked from the chapel. The song

began again, a strong beat, as the curds were thumped on the boards to expel the whey.

I stood in the ornately pillared public chamber of the palace in which hung Jaimal's gilded cage. The air was heavy with incense, burned as a precaution against the plague. It so happened that I was talking to the Captain of the Guard when the Rajput prince was seen to slump to the bottom of his cage. I ran forward. Two sentries blocked my way.

'I must examine him!' I protested. 'If it is the plague, he must be isolated at once.'

They hesitated. 'Only on the word of the emperor himself can . . .'

I took a step foward. 'Do you want to be responsible for the plague spreading throughout the palace? Do you wish the emperor's favourite songbird to die because of you?'

They looked to Bahadur to tell them what to do. He nodded. 'I will take responsibility. Open the cage.'

'Yes, captain.'

'Stand back!' I cried. 'I can see this is a highly contagious case.'

Bahadur said, 'I suggest, *hakim*-sahib, that we place the prisoner in that empty palanquin and convey him to some less public place.'

Jaimal was covered in a piece of sacking. We lifted him out, still covered in his sacking, and placed him on the box-seat of the palanquin.

'Draw the curtains,' I instructed. 'It will help confine any malevolent effluxions.'

The sentries carried the palanquin towards the carved doorway at the end of the public chamber.

'Plague! Plague!' called Bahadur.

The words ricocheted off tiled columns and walls inlaid with semi-precious stones, scattering courtiers and servants more effectively than any fusillade of bullets could.

'Halt!' The young officer at the doorway saluted Bahadur. 'Captain, the prisoner cannot leave this chamber, except I see his condition for myself and am satisfied that he does indeed have the plague.'

'Meshed Khan, is it not?'

'Yes, captain.'

'Well done, Meshed! You are a good officer. I picked you for the Palace Guard because of the very qualities you now display.'

'Thank you, captain.'

'However, since the prisoner is now in my charge, you may stand aside.'

'With respect, captain, I cannot disobey an order given directly by the emperor . . . You taught me that yourself.' So saying, he wrenched apart the curtains. 'By the Archangel Jibrael!' Meshed's eyes were wide with horror.

Jaimal was a mass of ugly, purplish-black swellings. Several had burst and were dribbling evil greenish slime. His breathing was fast and harsh. The stench emanating from his body turned even my hardened stomach. Jaimal's breathing stopped.

I lifted his wrist. 'He is dead.'

I turned to Meshed Khan. 'You may confirm that fact by placing your finger . . . here . . . between these two buboes.'

With a violent movement, Meshed closed the curtains. He nodded to us to proceed.

'Plague! Plague!' called Bahadur.

The palanquin was hurried along vaulted naves pierced by shafts of dusty sunlight, across a secluded garden to a door in the wall. I gave the two soldiers baksheesh for their services. They salaamed and departed with obvious relief.

'They are good men,' said Bahadur.

'Can I come out?' Bamian's voice sounded muffled.

'Yes; we cannot be seen here,' answered Bahadur, pulling aside the curtains.

Jamail stood up, peeling boils and buboes from himself. The lid of the box-seat opened. Bamian's grinning face appeared.

'Am I, or am I not, a giant among men when it comes to grease-paint and disguise?'

Bahadur helped Jaimal to step from the palanquin. Despite his near-nakedness, his blindness, his half-starved body, there was dignity in his bearing.

'Come with us, Bahadur, I beseech you.'

'Sire, I can do more good here. I can lull suspicion and gain you time.'

Jaimal clasped his arm. 'You are a brave man, Bahadur Singh. If you are found out, you know what to expect at the hands of the torturer.'

'I will never betray those who helped my prince!'

I, who have seen brave men scream and sob and beg to be put out of their pain, was not so sure.

'We Rajputs understand honour,' said Jaimal. 'I am sensible of the sacrifice you have made. You, Captain of the Guard, did not lightly betray the trust of the men under your command. I know that, Bahadur, and I thank you.' Prince Jaimal of Chambal lifted his sightless eyes to the sky. There was still bird-seed in his hair. 'The name of Bahadur Singh shall always be honoured in Rajputana.'

Bahadur knelt and kissed the hand of Jaimal. He turned and limped towards the palace.

Bamian knocked on the door in the wall. 'Mohini, are you there?'

'Yes. The cart is here and the street is empty.'

The door opened. Mohini had discarded her usual bodice and flowing skirts for the all-enveloping black *burqah* of the Muslim woman in purdah. She took Jaimal's hand and helped him make his first blind steps outside his cage. We were still within the walls of the Red Fort. Mohini led the buffalo across a quiet square behind the palace. Inside the covered cart, Bamian transformed me into a red-bearded Afghan.

'A horse-dealer travelling with his two wives,' said Bamian, handing Jaimal a *burqah* similar to Mohini's.

'Those slim wrists and ankles should win you a few admirers.'

'I will submit even to this indignity if it will return me to the side of my beloved Padmati.'

'What about you, Bamian?' I asked. 'I don't fancy you as my third wife!'

'I'm not coming, Khoratji. A dwarf is too conspicuous. You'll be safer without me.'

'But Bamian . . .'

'No, I've made up my mind . . . besides, I want to teach that minah bird a few more phrases.'

'Let the dice decide, Bamian. Even numbers you come with us.'

228

He licked his lips. 'No. Not this time. I will do nothing to endanger Mohini . . . Say goodbye to her for me.'

He toppled backwards off the cart, rolled over several times and sprang to his feet. Then the cart turned a corner.

The sound of the wheels changed. White glare blinked into welcome gloom, cool as a melon. We were passing through the Red Fort's huge North Gate. Only the traffic entering the fort was checked by the soldiers. We were leaving it.

'*Shabash*!' There was no mistaking the perpetrator of that great sound. If Dadu recognized me or Mohini, he might give us away before he knew what he was saying.

Two peasant women, carrying baskets of fruit, walked past the guard-house.

'Ho there!' Dadu called. 'I have a friend who would like to meet you. A bald-headed, one-eyed man who is simply longing to be introduced!'

The women screamed with delight.

'One eye, you say? He's sure to lose his way!'

'Bald-headed? Why, he's probably too old to stand up!'

Dadu shook his fist at them good-humouredly. Our cart drew level with him. He gave Mohini a slap on the rump. 'The eyes tell everything! This one's all of a flutter . . . Fancy me, do you, my darling?' He peered into the rear of the cart as it lumbered past. 'Too skinny!' he pronounced. 'Fatten them up a bit, man! Feed them on butter and sheep's tails.'

I acknowledged his advice with a face-concealing wave of the hand.

From the guard-house a voice bellowed, 'Get back on duty, you cock-brained, jug-bitten layabout!'

The cart rumbled into the teeming streets on the other side of the red walls. Though the plague stalked the city, it was bound to be somebody else it called upon; meanwhile, there was a bargain to be struck, a profit to be made.

I sent Mohini into the back to join Jaimal. I, the Afghan trader, with my two wives demurely out of sight, led the cart out of Agra. Beyond the waste ground and the deep lime pits for the dead was the cordon of soldiers whose duty it was to prevent egress from the city till the plague had run its course.

'That was your stupid idea,' said Mohini.

'It was not! I merely confirmed that it was a suitable procedure.'
Soldiers surrounded the cart. '*Ist!*'

Plain, honest bribery, we had been advised, was our best tactic. It is
well known that the plague passes by the gates of the rich, knocking
instead on the doors of the poor. Thus, in a most satisfactory
demonstration of the correct order of things, only those least likely to
spread the plague could afford to buy their way out of the city. The
more virile the contagion, the higher the price. Even so, it was higher
than I had expected.

'It is *dustoor*, you see,' said one soldier, apologetically.

A soldier had been executed yesterday. Not, of course, for actually
taking a bribe, but for not giving his officer a big enough cut from the
deal. After all, the officer, too, had to pay *dustoor* to his captain.

Bahadur had counselled against asking the Rajput women of the
imperial harem for their jewels. There were no secrets in the harem.
The gold in my purse had come from the sale of the ring that Ghulam
Khan had given me and various other tokens of appreciation that
my wealthy palace patrons had bestowed upon me. I counted
out the money with clumsy fingers. A coin fell to the hard, baked
earth.

'Drink our health with that one,' I said. 'And wish us a safe journey
north.'

Dawn, and the cart creaked westwards towards Chambal, wheels
jolting in the sun-hardened ruts. We passed through a sleeping
village, rumbling in and out of people's dreams and the verses of a
woman's song:

> 'Once my hands were smooth and soft, and bright with
>   jewels of gold.
> Now in old age they twist like roots.
> Not otherwise is the word of the truthful.
>
> My hair, clustered with flowers, was like a bowl of sweet
>   perfume.
> Now in old age it stinks like a rabbit's pelt.
> Not otherwise is the word of the truthful.'

In another hour or so the parched landscape would be shimmering in the heat. Ascension and Whitsuntide had rolled by, uncelebrated, one hot day much like another. We crossed a dry river-bed. A few months ago it would have been a powerful river. The whole country-side yearned for rain.

'I wish to hear a story!'

Even here, Jaimal expected his wishes to be treated as commands. And another thing – heroic qualities are all very well at a distance, but when you are confined in a small cart with them they are exceedingly tedious. Every revolution of the wheels, every jolt and bump, took us nearer to Chambal, nearer to the moment of separation from Mohini. She and Jaimal would enter Chambal without me. I had resolved to find some means of slipping away at the last moment. I had not told her.

' . . . and the Chara woman said, "I have come to claim the boon, O king. My husband is a leper and can be cured only if he bathes in the blood of a man who possesses twenty-five virtues." "Who can that be?" said the king. "Your son," was the reply. "But I have only one son. How can I kill him to cure your husband?" '

'He is a Rajput king!' interjected Jaimal. 'A Rajput's given word is more precious than life itself. He will put death before dishonour. I am certain of it!'

'Only because you know the story!' I snarled.

The son was duly sacrificed by the father, and the story ended with the refrain as old as story-telling itself.

> 'Thus the story endeth, thus the tree doth wither.'
> 'Why O tree dost thou wither?'
> 'Thy cow on me browseth.'
> 'Why O cow dost thou browse?'
> 'My child doth cry.'
> 'O child, why dost thou cry?'
> 'The ant doth me sting.'
> 'Why O ant dost thou sting?'

If only our last precious days together could have been alone. If only I could satiate my eyes with her beauty, instead of being forced to look upon a black shrouded figure. If only . . . O ant, why dost thou sting?

Another village; another well with buffalo plodding round and round. The low thunder of a grindstone, old men with anxious eyes cast skyward.

'The rains will be late this year, mark my words.'

'This time last year the first clouds had appeared.'

'You only have to sniff the air to know . . . It should smell softer, sweeter than it does.'

'Yes, and the soldiers who were here yesterday said they'd heard that the monsoon wasn't moving north like it should.'

'What soldiers?' My voice was sharper than it should have been.

'Oh, they were looking for four people . . . fugitives of some kind . . . . they wanted to know if we'd seen a blind man and a dwarf.'

I purchased *churma* cakes made from wheat and thickened sweet milk, called *kheer*, before moving on. So Bamian had been right.

'We are safe in our disguises,' said Jaimal. 'Bahadur would never betray us.' He delivered a diatribe on the Rajput warrior's code of chivalry, the gist of which was that you should never insult a Rajput's honour, his sword, his horse, or his wife . . . in that order.

We passed an emaciated peasant, harnessed to a heavy plough.

'You're late with things this season!' I shouted from the cart.

'My ox died and there's nobody but me to pull the plough,' he panted.

'Of what did it die?'

'There was nothing for it to eat . . . no straw . . . not even any husks.'

'Why was that?'

The man struggled with the heavy implement, barely moving it through the hard soil. 'Because last season I was weak from lack of food and was late with the ploughing and my field was not ready for the rains and . . .' He shrugged hopelessly. Pointing to a roadside shrine, he said. 'Perhaps I shall make sacrifice to this new deity.'

'There is but one god and that is Allah,' I said, remembering my disguise.

'The Chota Chua erect shrines to this god wherever they go, and they make sacrifice to him.'

I climbed from the cart and walked up to the shrine. 'What do they sacrifice?'

'They steal babies, for this god commands them to bring little children to him.'

'And you . . . what will you sacrifice to this god?'

The man shrugged again. 'Our baby will die anyway. Better it die to save its brothers and sisters. It is a powerful deity. They say he drinks the blood of Vishnu and eats his flesh to draw strength therefrom. They say he walks about in human form, raising men from the dead. They say he sleeps every night nailed to a tree.'

I examined the crudely carved figure in the shrine. It was a man with bulging eyes, wearing a long robe with a knotted rope round the waist. The effigy was smeared with blood. The skulls of human babies lay at its feet. I felt sick. I smashed the image against a stone.

'A false god!' I screamed.

Wearily, the peasant pulled on his harness and resumed his ploughing.

The protesting wheels of the cart had a new refrain. 'Thou shalt not make unto thyself any graven image . . . thou shalt not make unto thyself any graven image.' Mile after mile, 'Though shalt not make unto thyself any graven image.' Suddenly I was more afraid for Frog than I had ever been.

'Look!' exclaimed Mohini. 'Look, straight ahead! The hills of Rajputana!'

They floated above the horizon, bare, red hills.

She clapped her hands. 'Nearly there now! Won't be long now!'

The hills disappeared.

'It is *depasur*,' said Jaimal. 'The mirage, the illusion.'

He began to sing, and Mohini joined in with him. They sang of the warrior Arjuna, third prince of the legendry Pandava brothers, and of his charioteer, the god Krishna in disguise. Arjuna pleaded to see Krishna in his godly form and was given a divine eye for the vision. Overwhelmed by the vision, Arjuna begged Krishna to assume once more a form that mortal mind could comprehend. In mid-song, Mohini leapt from the cart, dragged the head of the buffalo round, turning it off the road. We plunged down an embankment, crashing through bushes.

'You crazy fool, Mohini!'

'There's horsemen coming, Thomas!'

'Well, what of it?'

'I . . . I don't know . . . I'm frightened.'

A bullock cart hove into view, on which sat a merchant and his two wives.

'Horsemen!'

'No, Thomas, I heard them, I know I did!'

'We'll wait two minutes and then . . .'

They swept down the road, hooves drumming on the brick-like surface. They surrounded the merchant and his wives; made him dismount; stripped him of his clothing; forced his wives to submit to the indignity of lifting their *burqahs*. They were not robbers, they were soldiers.

'That's not them! Perhaps they're further on.' They mounted and rode off.

Mohini was moaning softly, 'Oh, Bahadur, what have they done to you to make you tell? What have they done?'

'He held out a long time,' I said. 'Long enough to let us get this far. Do you see the red hills in the distance? This time they are no illusion.'

We lay among the red hills, looking over the besieging army to the walls of Chambal. Ten days ago, we had abandoned the cart and our disguises and, eschewing all roads, had made our way to this point.

'Why do we delay?' Jaimal demanded, yet again. 'Two days we have lain here and Padmati waits for me.'

'My lord, we await the army of Rama,' Arjay replied. Arjay had come to us when Mohini had flashed the prearranged signal on her mirror.

'The army of Rama, the greatest army in the world, will appear against the setting sun,' Arjay said. 'Then we will make our move.'

He was a Sesondia, tall with a long beard divided into two pointed whiskers. He carried a shield of rhinoceros skin, transparent as amber and embossed with gold. From his side hung a *catar*, the heavy Rajput broadsword. He had brought a similar weapon for his prince.

Jaimal knelt upright and slashed blindly at the air, narrowly missing Arjay. 'Yes, this is the way to enter my city. Not hiding under women's clothes, but with a sword in my hand.'

'We must wait for the Teeth of the Wind,' said Arjay.

Jaimal sighed. 'Fair is Padmati's face as the moon's soft image

amidst the waters. Tell me, Arjay, is her beauty as great as when I had
eyes to see it? Are her eyes like those of a gazelle in spring?'

'My lord . . . I . . . have you not heard? She . . . the day she received
the news that you were blinded . . .'

'Yes?'

'She ordered her handmaiden to blindfold her and to seal the knot
with your own royal seal. She took an oath that, as long as her prince,
her beloved husband, was sightless, the seal would remain un-
broken.'

'Oh, Padmati! I shall defend Chambal a thousand years for such as
you!'

'Ay, my lord, she has made us all feel like that. It is she who has
rallied us in your absence, who strengthens our resolve to resist the
Mogul oppressor.'

I recognized the layout of the besieging encampment. The elephant
lines, the cavalry lines, the royal enclosure.

'They say', growled Arjay, 'that Akbar has left all his carpets
spread in his tent, as a sign that he will return to witness the fall of our
city.'

'That day will never come!' cried Jaimal in a voice that must have
been heard by every patrol for miles around.

In the centre of the encampment, towering above all else, was a
pyramidal column of marble, the Chiraghdan, a mighty beacon
which lit the camp at night. From where we lay, we could see two of
Chambal's seven gates – the Gate of the Sun and the Elephant Gate.
The latter was framed by two life-size elephants, carved from solid
rock. Zigzagging across the open ground towards the city walls were
the *sabats* of the besieging army. These were covered approach-ways
which protected the artillery, musketmen and archers. They were
broad enough, Arjay informed me, for eight men to march abreast.
Each day, workers extended the *sabats* with embankments of mud
and rubble, covered by timber and boiled hides, bringing them ever
closer to the walled city. Arjay reckoned that at least two hundred
of Akbar's men were killed daily in this work.

The sun was setting. From a balcony below the flaming lamp of the
Chiraghdan the muezzin's cry rang out:

'*La-ilaha-illa-l-lah, Muhammadur-Rasulh-ilali* . . . No God but
One God and Muhammad the Ambassador of God.'

A pink flush spread over the hills. Arjay drew his *catar*. 'Here they come!'

It was locusts. Millions and millions of locusts.

'The army of Rama,' whispered Mohini. 'They breed somewhere in the desert, then march eastwards. They're still young – see how pink they are.'

'The Teeth of the Wind,' said Jaimal. 'I hear them rustling.'

A pink tide crept over the plain, overrunning the army and its encampment. Horses reared and neighed, elephants stamped and trumpeted, men ran to and fro, beating, squashing, pulping the encroaching horde.

Arjay led us down a ravine. In the last rays of the sun, Mohini flashed another signal. Cannon on top of the city walls opened fire on the troops not yet engaged by the locusts. Instead of taking cover, men leapt from their emplacements, ran out from the *sabats* to wherever a cannon-ball might land and began to struggle with each other.

Arjay was chuckling. 'Sire, so great is the love the Princess Padmati bears for you that she has melted down her throne and all her personal wealth. Each golden cannon-ball has inscribed upon it words which say that it belongs to whoever shall find it.'

Next came grapeshot and chainshot of jewels. The Gate of the Sun opened. An armed host sallied forth.

'*Jai*! *Jai*! *Ka* Jaimal! Victory for Jaimal!'

Nobody paid any attention to them.

'Now!' shouted Arjay, breaking cover and running towards the Rajput host. And now was the moment I had dreaded. Mohini, my love, one last look before I leave you.

Jaimal cried out, 'By all the Hindu gods, let the enemy come close, then, blind as I am, I shall be as a flame in a dry forest!'

He swung his sword. I failed to duck. Blackness exploded inside my skull.

Twelve

I paced the battlements of Chambal, raging against Mohini, continuing our quarrel inside my head, inventing all manner of cruel and cutting things to say. A cannon-ball thumped into the wall below me, causing the flagstones underfoot to jump. I peered over the battlements. Akbar's army had worked hard, digging ditches, erecting wattle fences, lighting fires to divert the locusts. Now they flowed along the base of the city's north-west wall. Not even Akbar's mighty army would take three days to march past a city, yet, in the three days since I had been dragged unconscious through the Gate of the Sun, the advance of the locusts had never ceased. In those three days they had turned from pink to a russet red.

Crump! The walls shuddered under the impact of another heavy cannon-ball. Each morning, for three days, the *nakkaras*, the giant kettledrums ten feet in diameter, had proclaimed that Prince Jaimal had returned and sat once more upon his throne in the Durikhana. For three days Akbar's artillery had been silenced by the locusts, but this morning, on the first stroke of the kettledrums, the bombardment had resumed.

I ducked as the edge of a turret disintegrated into flying stone chips. In only three days I was quarrelling with Mohini. The sweetness of regaining consciousness and finding Mohini beside me had turned sour.

Crump! The battlements shook. Men were lowering thick matting squares to protect the area upon which the siege guns were concentrating.

Lying in the red hills, I had prepared myself for the emptiness inside me; I had planned, as any surgeon does, how best to draw together the edges of the wound after the amputation.

'You seem so distant,' Mohini had said, and had started to cry. She had picked the wrong moment. In delving into a pocket, my hand had closed on a chess piece – the white bishop, which I had drawn at the palace of Ambala. Frog's voice had come to me. 'This piece never leaves the colour of the square it starts from, exemplifying firm faith and steadfastness of purpose.' What steadfastness of purpose had I shown? Mohini had dragged me on to a square of a different colour. Yes, it was her fault! And, if Chambal had defied Akbar for two years, for how many more years might I be incarcerated in this besieged city? And all the time, leprosy would be eating into Mary. So much anger, guilt and remorse had suddenly exploded. The bitter accusations I had made! I hurled the chess piece over the battlements. How could I have said those things?

Crump! I started running back to the palace on the hill, where Mohini and I were living. I would tell her I loved her. I would beg her forgiveness. Down steep, worn steps, past the Jain temple, through a tiny courtyard where a shrine was piled high with roses and hibiscus. A child pressed herself against a wall, staring at my face. Up lanes which wound round the Durikhana, the great hall of the Rajput princes, into the palace's honeycomb of narrow corridors and galleries, frescoed in turquoise, aquamarine and peacock blue. But Mohini was not there. Only the stray cat she had adopted greeted me; a cat she spent hours cuddling and talking nonsense to. My impatience with her returned. The moment of contrition passed.

I looked in the mirror. The image was obviously distorted. For all its gilded frame, the Indian craftsman was no match for the Venetians. I smashed the mirror on the marble floor.

Rama's army, the Teeth of the Wind, marched eastwards towards the fertile plains. Within a week or two they would be able to fly. I thought of the peasants who had anxiously scanned the skies for the rain-clouds. Perhaps dark clouds of a different kind would bring, not assurance of full granaries, but famine. And famine would beget more plague and together they would swell the ranks of the Chota Chua who, like the locusts, would soon be gathering in swarms again.

Day by day the rain-clouds grew bigger. Day by day the *sabats* crept closer. Gradually the advantage shifted to the attackers. As the range shortened, the destructive powers of Akbar's artillery increased, while that of the defenders decreased for, beyond a certain angle, the cannon-ball rolls out of the barrel before it can be fired. The *sabats* were close enough for the miners to start digging their tunnels towards the walls. Once under the foundations, they would pack a chamber with gunpowder and attempt to breach the defences. The men of Chambal, in their turn, dug listening-posts out from their own walls. Guided by the vibrations, they would undermine the approaching tunnels.

Within the walls of Chambal there were fields and orchards and terraced slopes, which could produce almost enough to feed the defenders . . . provided there was rain. Without rain the city was doomed.

'Tomorrow the monsoon will break!' was the greeting in the streets, on the battlements. But the tomorrows withered into yesterdays and still there was no rain. The heat was unbearable. Stones became too hot to touch. The cracked earth split open into deeper, wider fissures. Each day the buckets dropped deeper into the wells.

There came a day when, despite the terrible toll on those below, one *sabat*, then another snaked up to the wall, latched on to it and began to gnaw. Time and time again, sorties charged from the gates in an effort to disrupt or destroy the *sabats*. Each time they were driven back with heavy losses and many prisoners taken. After over two years of siege, the first breach in the walls was made. Desperate hand-to-hand fighting ensued before the men of Chambal threw back the intruders and blocked the hole with rubble and piles of dead from both sides.

My bad temper was not helped by the increasing dampness of the air. The dry heat had been hard enough to bear, but this sticky, oppressive heat was infinitely worse. It caused my skin to break out in a red rash which, when I scratched it, turned to running sores. Mould grew everywhere . . . on the *sogra* bread, in my *chupli* sandals, on my precious *chaulmoorgal* seeds and phials of *chaulmoorgal* oil. I opened a phial, smelt it, swallowed some and rubbed some on the worst of my sores. I caught Mohini looking at me.

'God Almighty! Trust you to jump to some panic-ridden conclusion! I'm merely checking its condition. Understand? Merely . . .' I stopped, panting hard.

Crump!

The rash would clear, I told myself, when the monsoon broke, and the temperature dropped. Often I had discussed with Faisl how, once the mind has seized on a particular diagnosis, all symptoms and evidence seem to bend to fit it. Mary and I had once been lost in a mist on the Blackdown Hills, and descended into a strange valley because I had convinced myself I was seeing landmarks which were not there.

Crump! Crump! The stones trembled.

Endeavouring to return the packet of *chaulmoorgal* seeds to the jar of rice in which I kept it, I spilled the seeds over the floor. I crawled about on hands and knees, trying to retrieve them. The two chains round my neck swung free, bumping against each other. Mohini's lucky charm, Mary's locket. My fingers felt as they used to after holding a snowball too long. Mary and I used to throw snowballs at Frog.

'These blasted seeds! They're so small!'

'Let me help you, my love.'

I pushed Mohini away. 'I can do it!'

Crump! Crump! Crump!

More clouds. Unlike the rain-clouds advancing from the south, these approached from the east. Clouds of dust, flaming scarlet in the dawn. Akbar was returning. Gaunt, battle-tired men watched from the ramparts. If Chambal fell, the absorption of Rajputana into the Mogul Empire would be complete. In claiming Padmati for himself, Akbar was striking at the honour, the pride and the last vestiges of the freedom of Rajputana. They knew that, this time, Akbar would not leave until the issue was settled.

Another breach in the wall. Another quarrel with Mohini. How could I have let that foolish girl ensnare me? Thunder in the distance and flickering light. Surely it must rain. In a lull in the bombardment I heard a familiar ringing of bells. I listened carefully for them after that. Matins, Lauds, Prime, Tierce . . . Frog was with Akbar in the camp.

The rising sun, magnified in the shimmering air, was a vast orange ball. Jaimal and I walked the eastern ramparts.

'*Hakim-Nadir*, she will listen to you, who risked his life to help me escape.'

I shrugged, then remembered that he could not see me. 'Raja-sahib, she will not swerve from her vow. She will not break the royal seal and remove the blindfold.'

'Try once more to persuade her, *hakim*-sahib ... for my sake.'

'I will try again, but her answer is always the same: "Except I share the darkness with my lord and become as he is, how can I be truly one with my prince as a wife should be?" That is what she will say, raja-sahib.'

Jaimal grunted, then sighed in ecstasy. At least, I thought he did. But when I turned my gaze from the sunrise, he was lying on the ground. A musket-ball had entered his armpit and, travelling up-wards, exited through his neck.

He knew he was dying. He raised himself on one elbow. 'My soul revolts at perishing ingloriously by a distant blow ... my sword ... let me die holding my sword.' His breathing was laboured. 'Padmati! Already I see your face more clearly!' He choked and bubbled and the breath rattled in his throat. 'I depart this body as a friend bids farewell to a friend.'

Jaimal departed this world with dignity, leaving his body to its own undignified, inglorious end. In the period before rigor mortis sets in, the muscles relax, the contents of intestine and bowel come pouring out. A dark stain spread down his leg. I covered him with my cotton surcoat. The rites of death are for the benefit of the living, and those who can do best to keep their illusions about the manner in which most of us die.

On Chambal's highest tower the funeral pyre was lit. The bombardment had ceased. A stillness lay on besieging and besieged alike. Forty thousand upturned faces watched the flames consume Jaimal. Only the beat of the giant kettledrums broke the silence, proclaiming that the Prince of Chambal was about to leave his city and go forth on a journey. Padmati stood close to the burning pyre, her dress fluttering in the same wind that fanned the flames. In a clear voice she cried out:

'I shared his blindness and the darkness shone upon our love. Now I share his death that our love may have eternal life.' She smiled. 'But my lord will chide my dallying.' And she sprang eagerly into the flames.

On the balcony of the Chiraghdan, Akbar watched Padmati, the woman he desired above all others, burn. He fell to the floor, limbs thrashing, then was hid from view as his ministers and generals gathered round him.

The cannon pounded the walls as never before. Two massive subterranean explosions reduced the Elephant Gate to rubble. Akbar's troops poured through the gap. The defenders knew every twist and turn of their city. Akbar's men were lured into the labyrinth, split up and slaughtered in dark alleys and narrow stairways, or ambushed from the roof-tops. Very few of those who forced entry on that day survived the close-quarter fighting. Chambal was still in Rajput hands.

One prisoner only was taken. He was carried, bleeding and unconscious, to the cool, shaded courtyard within the inner fort, where I had set up my surgery. The man was General Ghulam Khan. What did it signify that, this time, we were on opposite sides? A musket-ball smashes bone impartially; the blood flowing in the gutters knows no creed, caste, rank or clan. What did it signify? The entire siege was a mere bubble in the ever-flowing river of pain and suffering. In a thousand years, who would remember why we had fought? Or care? But in a thousand years bone would still smash and flesh still tear. I began to clean his wounds with wine. His eyes opened. They followed the movements of my hand . . . not the one which touched his wounds, the one which held the wine-skin.

'Put it from my sight, Khoratji.'

I did what he asked.

'At . . . at the chess game, when . . . when the first among my wives . . . when she jumped . . . do you know what I thought?'

'Do not tire yourself, general. You must rest now.'

'I thought about how much I wanted a drink of good red wine.'

'Rest now.'

When next I came to tend him, he said, 'Do not blame her, Khoratji. As this land yearns for rain, she yearned for my love. If I had looked upon her as longingly as I looked upon the *mowrah* brandy; if I had craved her lips as much as I craved the red wine . . . but I loved my regiment more, and then I loved the wine even more than that.' He laughed bitterly. 'Of all the enemies I have faced, this is the most cunning, the most relentless. Khoratji, I am engaged in the most important battle of my life.'

He drifted into sleep. A wounded soldier near by said, 'He is mistaken. It is not a battle, it is siege. He, the besieger, is under siege. And it is a siege which will never be raised; a siege in which the defender must be constantly vigilant.'

'You speak with feeling. Do you know the same enemy?'

The soldier nodded. 'A lifelong enemy. This man beside me . . . he is a Muslim, I a Hindu; he follows Akbar, I the Rajput banner; he is a general and a nobleman, I belong to the Vaisya caste and am of farming stock. Yet I have more in common with him than with any other man here. This one thing makes him my brother.'

A fresh batch of wounded were carried into the courtyard.

'They've breached the south wall!' a stretcher-bearer panted as he carried his mutilated burden past me.

'And the Gate of the Sun has been battered down!' cried out a bloodstained youth. He could not have been older than fifteen or sixteen. 'Our men withdraw to the inner fort. Half the city is taken!'

He struggled to rise and rejoin the fray. An old soldier pushed him down.

'Youth was ever spendthrift, even with its own lifeblood,' he growled.

'Akbar means to keep his oath,' said Ghulam Khan. 'Make no mistake about that. I may not be privy to his counsel, as once I was, but there can be no doubting his intention. He will take his revenge to the full on the city which chose to let Padmati burn instead of surrendering her to him.'

Was this the same Akbar who had captivated me with his charm and wit, who had impressed me with his tolerance and wide-ranging views? All his reign he had sought unity among diversity, yet now he created a gulf of bitter memories which would outlive his reign many times over.

Women, when they cry, are far from attractive. The blotchy, crumpled, tear-swollen face; the snivelling nose, quivering lips and staccato respiration which renders whatever recriminations they are uttering unintelligible. I stalked the streets, preoccupied, scowling. Immature, that was the trouble with Mohini. An explosion breached my stony thoughts. So far, the inner fort, which contained the palace on the hill, the Durikhana, the main wells, the arsenal, had held out.

Smoke rose from the central square, rising above the city. The bustle in the street ceased. People paused in mid-action, eyes fixed upon the rising column, faces shocked.

'The *jauhar*! The *jauhar*!'

The cry spread from one street to another. There arose a sound like the moaning of a wind, a collective wail of despair. People were running from all directions, a swelling river of people sweeping towards the central square.

'What's happening? Will somebody tell me, what is the *jauhar*?'

But they kept running, staring straight ahead, grim-faced. I joined them.

Drawn up in ranks around an enormous bonfire, white-hot at the centre, were some eight thousand Rajput warriors.

'Your forgiveness, *hakim*-sahib,' said the man who stood next to me on the terrace above the square. He wore an evil-smelling sheepskin jacket.

'What?'

'Your toes, *hakim*-sahib, I am standing on them, but I cannot move for the crowd around us.'

'What is happening down there?'

'It is the *amal la kharna*, the eating of opium. Taken from the hollow of a fellow warrior's hand, it is an inviolable pledge.'

'To what do they pledge themselves?'

'They pledge themselves to become the living dead; to enter battle knowing they have already forfeited their lives and have nothing to gain but glory.'

Jaimal their prince was dead; Padmati, the jewel of Rajputana, was dead. In a matter of days Akbar would batter his way into the inner fort. Rather than wait for an inglorious end, Jaimal's brother had commanded the *jauhar*.

First the great vassals of the Crown, then the *thakurs*, the feudal lords, then the Kshatriya or warrior caste put on the saffron robes in which the dead are dressed. From a dark tunnel slowly advanced the wives of the Rajput warriors. As they entered the square, they broke their marriage bracelets, casting them to the ground, announcing their widowhood. The line never faltered. They walked into the fire, committing the act of suttee in front of their husbands, the living dead.

That day, with lightning flickering in the sky and thunder rolling in the distance, five thousand women immolated themselves. The next day, at an hour appointed by the astrologers, the saffron-robed warriors would unlock the gates of the inner fort and charge out to fight their last battle.

The dawn thunder was nearer, louder. Smoke from yesterday's pyre still hung over the city. Before the day was out, Akbar would be in complete possession of Chambal. I made love to Mohini. This might be the last time.

I knew she was only pretending to enjoy it. I smoothed her tears away with thickened fingers.

'What is it, my love? Why do you weep?'

'I weep for you, Thomas-jun.'

'Why?'

'Do you not know why?'

My voice was rising. 'No. Should I?'

'Thomas . . . Today, eight thousand men will face death bravely . . . and you must face the truth. I ask you again . . . Do you really not know? . . . Thomas, please answer me.'

'Yes . . . I know.'

'Say it, then.'

'No!'

'Say it! Say it!'

'Damn you! I have leprosy! Thomas Coryat is a leper!' I snatched up my sandals, beating them together like a clapper. 'Unclean! Unclean!'

Mohini put her arms around me and held me tightly.

'Mohini, you knew and yet you let me make love to you. You did not flinch from me. I have not deserved such love.'

'You will need me now, Thomas-jun.'

'Listen!'

It was the morning hour for the muezzin's call. From the balcony of the Chiraghdan a voice, which I knew so well, cried out:

'*La-ilaha-illa-l-lah, Zarat, Isa Ibn Allah* . . . No God but One God and Christ the Son of God!'

I rushed to the window.

'No God but One God and Christ the Son of God.'

Men appeared behind Frog and dragged him from the balcony. Frog, what made you do it? You always did crave martyrdom. Perhaps you recognized the new deity of the Chota Chua; perhaps the truth about Murad and Daniyal has reached you at last. I have a truth to face as well, dear Frog; but I have Mohini to share it with. Whom do you have? Oh yes, I forgot.

And this was the fatal moment for the final rite of the *jauhar*. The gates were flung wide.

'*Jai*! *Jai*! Jaimal!' chanted the eight thousand, clashing their swords against their shields and running, almost joyfully, to meet their deaths. I turned away. Mohini lay on the floor in a faint. Beside her was a half-empty cup of dark, malodorous fluid. Poison! Had she chosen to join her Rajput sisters in death? Had I, the leper, driven her to it? The five-headed ring! I levered back each emerald and poured the contents down her throat.

Her eyes opened. She smiled at me.

'Mohini, why did you take poison? Why did you do it?'

'Poison?'

I held out the cup. She giggled. 'It is not poison. I would never leave you, dear heart. And besides . . . I am carrying your baby, Thomas-jun.'

I embraced her.

'Are you pleased, Thomas-jun?'

I nodded. 'But what, then, is this evil-looking stuff in the cup?'

Mohini's blush turned honeyed skin to ripe peach. 'You'll be cross if I tell you.'

'Not today, my love.'

'An astrologer sold me this medicine. It is a remedy for the morning sickness, you see . . . made only when Venus is in the –'

I closed her mouth with a kiss.

Outside, the sounds of slaughter continued.

Mohini said, 'I shall dance the Dance of Shiva, the Destroyer, the Creator. Amidst all this death a new life burgeons.'

Her body so lithe; her feet so precise; her movements so graceful; her eyes so mobile. She was writhing on the floor, limbs jerking, eyes staring. Her body went rigid. She was dead.

I don't know how long I sat holding her hand. One hour, several hours, I don't know. Despite the heat, I was shivering. I was numb. The chill, awful certainty of what I had done crept over me. I rinsed the ring in a saucer of milk. I watched the cat lap up the milk. It staggered a few steps, whirled round and round and fell dead. Deception, the invisible sixth head to the ring. Each of the five jewels contained, not the antidote, but the poison itself. Razziya, you are well revenged!

A madness, a blind rage seized me. Sword in hand, I ran screaming, shouting, cursing out of the fort to join the living dead in their last battle. The sky cracked open. The monsoon burst. Water fell in solid sheets, splashing and bouncing on the hard ground. A giant of a man stepped in front of me and clubbed me down. My last thought was 'It's over! Thank God it's over. No more pain!'

'What's that you say, Ali? You think I hit him too hard? Nonsense! All foreigners have thick skulls, everyone knows that!'

The rain was falling on my face.

'You are in bad shape, my friend,' Dadu said.

'I am a leper, Dadu.' It was easier to say the second time.

Dadu nodded. 'Ali thought as much.'

'You can sit further away, if you want. I shall not be offended.'

Dadu ignored that. 'You will be safe here. I carried you to this far corner of the camp. Everyone is in the city, fully occupied with looting and massacre.'

'Massacre?'

'By nightfall, not one inhabitant of the city will be alive.'

'There are thirty thousand men, women and children in Chambal! Thirty thousand!'

Dadu hung his head. 'None dared try to dissuade the distraught, crazed emperor from this course, except Petaguru sahib. He alone spoke out against this intention.'

The earth soaked in the rain and gave out a wonderful sweet smell, tinged with a bitter odour of bruised plants and long-dried dung rewetted. In this life-giving rain, people were dying. Shiva the Creator, the Destroyer. Something numb inside me was beginning to throb and hurt.

'What happened to Frog?' I asked. 'Did he die a martyr's death after he was dragged from the Chiraghdan?' What did I care? What did I care about anything when Mohini was dead?

'They let him go. They believed him to be mad. I saw him just after they released him. He was heading northwards into the hills, with a wild gleam in his eyes. When he noticed me, he cried out: "My true mission! At last I have found my true mission!"'

'Did he say what it was?'

'No.'

A tower crumbled, followed by the sound of explosion.

'And Mohini?' Dadu asked.

'I killed her.' My throat rebelled against the words.

Dadu said gently, 'Better by your hand, than at the hands of Akbar's men.' He stood up. 'Well, I must be about my duties. What will you do now, Khoratji?'

'I shall make my way to the port of Surat and await a trading ship to England.'

Dadu's massive hand gripped my shoulder. 'Farewell, my friend. When first we met, you told me you were both a seeker and a fugitive. I hope you find both that which you seek and a place of rest where you need flee no more.' He lurched down the puddle-strewn track, muttering to Ali.

The rain fell with renewed vigour. Like the monsoon itself, my grief burst. Rivulets ran down my face. The rain was soothing to my skin, the tears soothing to my heart. As the ground softened and swelled, the cracks and fissures closed. The air was heavy with lush, intoxicating odours. In a few days the land would be fresh and green and the birds would sing again. I was a leper like Mary; my flesh was now as her flesh. A ravine no longer stood between us. Out of my pain and ugliness love would be reborn. I had made the leap.

Afterword

Where it has suited my purposes, I have telescoped or invented events. For instance, there was no siege of Chambal, although much of what I describe occurred at one or other of the three sieges of Chitor. These, however, were several centuries apart. Although Akbar did indeed order a massacre at Chitor, everything I have read about him suggests that he was a wiser and greater man than his brief appearance in this book would indicate. In 'departing from the plain of veracity and dropping the reins of accuracy' as Faisl would say, I have tried to reach truths which are more important, perhaps, than the dates of battles. I think Akbar would have forgiven me. I hope the reader will.

'One of our most gifted and poetic young writers'
JOHN FOWLES

THE AFFIRMATION
Christopher Priest

When Peter Sinclair loses his father, his lover and his job, he withdraws to a country cottage in an effort to rebuild his life. But the autobiography he begins to write turns into the story of another man in another, imagined, world whose insidious attraction draws him forever further in.

Christopher Priest was selected as a 'Best of Young British Novelist' for THE AFFIRMATION, his finest work to date.

'The atmosphere of solitude and mental disequilibrium ... is beautifully conveyed, suggesting too the void that underlies all our reality'
D.M. THOMAS

'Priest opposes madness and sanity, life and art, the elaborate narrative and the empty page – and then makes them interchangeable ... an original thriller, a study of schizophrenia set against questions of persona and plot'   *New Statesman*

'Original and haunting'
The Times

'Rich and provocative'
Times Literary Supplement

ARENA

'Wickedly amusing ... a new and original woman writer who could be the best bitter-sweet comedian since Beryl Bainbridge'
ROBERT NYE, *The Guardian*

THE NATURAL ORDER
Ursula Bentley

'The adolescent male is the nearest thing to primordial slime still to be found in its natural state' concludes Carlo at the end of her first day's teaching. Brought up with her friends, Damaris and Anne, in an unshakeable belief in a Brontë-esque destiny, little has prepared any of them for the eccentric, brutish masters and sweaty pupils of the Blessed Ambrose Carstairs Grammar School for Boys.

Only Shackleton, the Adonis of the Sixth, transcends that world of aggressive, adolescent yearnings and clumsy rebellion, but even he, the perfect golden boy, is more – and less – than he seems.

THE NATURAL ORDER has not only received wide critical acclaim but has also won Miss Bentley a place among the 'Best of Young British Novelists' for 1983.

'Excellent ... a novel of style, originality and wit'
Daily Telegraph

'Vivaciously misanthropic, cheerfully lascivious'
Sunday Telegraph

'A romping dorm-feast of a novel'
Observer

ARENA

TEN YEARS IN AN OPEN NECKED SHIRT
John Cooper Clarke

'In a vain attempt at bourgeois credibility, Lenny changed his name to John Cooper Clarke and under this title embarked on a polysyllabic excursion through Thrillsville, UK. Yes, it was be there or be square as, clad in the slum chic of the hipster, he issued the slang anthems of the zip age in the desperate esperanto of the bop. John Cooper Clarke: the name behind the hairstyle, the words walk in the grooves hacking through the hi-fi paradise of true luxury…'

This is the collected poetry of John Cooper Clarke – rock poet, story-teller and humorist – and publication is planned to tie in with the Channel 4 series of the same name. The book is brilliantly illustrated by Steve Maguire.

COMING SOON!

'**Magnificent ... Miss Tremain has fashioned the totality of one life – and conveyed the evanescence of all human existence**'
Sunday Telegraph

THE CUPBOARD
Rose Tremain

At the age of eighty-seven, Erica March died in a cupboard. She wrapped her body in a chenille tablecloth, laid it out neatly under the few skirts and dresses that still hung on the clothes rail and put it to death very quietly, pill by pill. She left a note, but the note made no mention of her suicide, nor of the cupboard in which she had chosen to commit it. And she had known, of course, that it would be Ralph who would discover her body – and that when he found her he would do everything she had asked, exactly as she had asked it.

The Cupboard is an evocative, complex and imaginatively perceptive novel about freedom and the will to live by one of Britain's most highly acclaimed young writers. For another of her novels, *Letter to Sister Benedicta* (published by Arrow), Rose Tremain won a place among the 'Best of Young British Novelists' for 1983.

'Strongly constructed . . . highly relevant . . . thoroughly fascinating'
Sunday Times

'Deeply evocative . . . a book brimming with life . . . remarkable'
The Times

'A fascinating *danse macabre*'
Scotsman

To be published on 8th September 1983

ARENA

ARENA NON-FICTION

BACK TO THE ROOTS
Richard Mabey and Francesca Greenoak

Have you resigned yourself to a world where all herbs look pretty much the same and come in glass bottles – or do you sometimes think that it would be nice to have your own herbal garden, if only you knew how to go about it?

Richard Mabey, author of FOOD FOR FREE, and Francesca Greenoak have written a unique guide to every type of domestic plant – from herbs and vegetables to flowers and trees – which will initiate even the most city-bred among us in the traditional skills, methods and benefits of British plantcraft.

SACRED SUMMITS
Peter Boardman

This is the story of a year in the life of a climber: three expeditions, each very different from one another in mood and style, to sacred mountains around the world. Tragically, the last book that the brilliant young mountaineer Peter Boardman was to write, *Sacred Summits* is a dramatic and moving testament to one man's will not to conquer but to understand.

'Much more than a climbing book ... as much an adventure of romantic discovery as one of physical challenge'

CHRIS BONINGTON

FOR FURTHER INFORMATION
ABOUT ARENA BOOKS,
PLEASE WRITE TO
Arena Books
17 Conway Street
London W1P 6JD